MISSING

ALSO BY D. E. BECKLER

Writing as David Beckler

Antonia Conti Thriller series

A Long Shadow
A Stolen Memory
A Nuclear Reaction

Mason & Sterling series

Brotherhood
The Profit Motive
Forged in Flames
The Money Trap

Anthology

The Road More Travelled: Tales of those seeking refuge

A CITY STREETS MYSTERY

MISSING

D. E. BECKLER

Published by Thomas & Mercer, Seattle

www.apub.com

EU Product Safety contact:
Amazon Publishing, Amazon Media EU S.à r.l.
38, avenue John F. Kennedy, L-1855 Luxembourg
amazonpublishing-gpsr@amazon.com

ISBN-13: 9781662528279
eISBN: 9781662528286

Cover design by Dominic Forbes
Cover image: © Abigail Miles / ArcAngel Images

Printed in the United States of America

To my wife, Tricia, who gives me brutal but fair feedback and never demands I get a real job with a salary.

CHAPTER 1

Alina followed the guard with the snake tattoo, her trepidation increasing. It wasn't unusual for the girls to be booked out to clients, but she felt an unaccustomed sense of dread. At the bottom of the stairs, the doorman opened the pink door and gave a mock bow. He was one of the nicer ones, so she forced a smile.

Outside, in the icy drizzle, the black SUV waited, engine running and lights cutting through the darkness. Alina pulled her thin coat tighter, teetered across the pavement and climbed in the back. She settled into the seat, enjoying the warmth engulfing her. The tang of the driver's aftershave almost overpowered the aroma of leather and freshly shampooed carpet. As she secured her seatbelt, the passenger door slammed.

What the heck was going on? The heavies never escorted her on a job, unless they went on a special job. But the women never did those alone. Checking neither man was looking at her, she tried the door handle. Locked. Hell!

The car pulled away, its wheels squealing on the wet tarmac. They passed the far end of the square, and she watched one of the homeless men who lived there follow the vehicle with his gaze, his dog huddled against him under the blue plastic tarpaulin.

Why in such a rich country do they have people like him? Why wasn't he living in a house and doing a useful job?

Her sympathy for him faded as she considered her own predicament. Why was the guard coming with them? She had done nothing wrong. Had one of her family back home transgressed? She couldn't believe any of them would risk her suffering the retribution, even her careless little brother. Maybe it was a new client, and they were worried about her safety. It was almost laughable, but she was an asset.

Alina told herself not to worry and peered out of the window. The usual route on these jobs took them south of the city, past the glass skyscrapers and towards the wealthy suburbs, or even further afield to the small towns housing businessmen and celebrities. They were going the other way now, north, in the direction of the scruffy flat she shared with three other women.

But then she recognised where they were going, and it wasn't home. The realisation made her sick.

Her unease grew when the car slowed and took a left. They drove past darkened industrial units, taking another turn, until they stopped outside a pair of gates held together with a padlocked chain. Behind it a warehouse with shafts of light spilling out of the gaps round the openings. Snake Tattoo got out and ran to the gates, unlocking the padlock and pulling them open. She stared at the building. The last time she came here, she'd been with Jehona. Her insides lurched at the memory, but the big bonus they'd received made it bearable. It would only be a few hours.

The car shot forward and stopped opposite the entrance, which swung open. Light flooded out, making her squint. Snake Tattoo opened the door, water sliding down his shaved skull and dripping off his nose. Alina stared at him.

'Come on, get out.' He pulled at her arm.

She stumbled, and he pushed her ahead of him through the doorway. A familiar scent surprised her. Was there another girl here already?

Her eyes grew accustomed to the harsh lighting. The bare walls of the corridor reflected the light. Snake Tattoo pushed her towards the stairs. Her footsteps clanged on the metal treads as she climbed. She'd never been upstairs, and unease settled in her stomach like a heavy weight. She reached the top and Snake Tattoo pushed her to the right, along a narrow corridor. They passed a big blue rubbish bin, incongruous in the carpeted hallway. The stench of bleach seeped from it.

A door opened ahead, releasing a red glow from the room beyond. Alina inhaled a deep breath to prepare herself. Snake Tattoo stopped and directed her through the doorway. She took two steps and stopped. The crimson lights illuminated a bare room covered in acoustic tiles.

The door closed behind her and a lock clicked.

Only one person waited in the room. The figure facing her wore a mask, white coveralls and blue rubber gloves. And, cradled in the gloves, was a hammer.

Alina's stomach turned to water, and she screamed.

CHAPTER 2

As I shivered in my sleep, I welcomed the heat which spread across my back. Then a laugh seeped into my fogged brain, waking me and shattering the dream of enjoying a hot shower back home in Bristol. The stench of garbage attacked my nostrils.

Groggy with sleep, I rolled over. Then liquid splashed on my cardboard mattress. The warmth at my back faded as icy air hit the wetted fabric of my many, layered tops. I looked up. A laughing figure loomed over me in the dark alley, zipping up his fly. I scrambled to my feet and a second voice joined in the laughter.

'What the hell you think you're doing?'

'I'm pissing on a pile of rubbish,' the figure slurred. 'What are *you* doing?'

The second man, a silhouette against the light at the mouth of the alley, said to me, 'Sorry, he didn't realise you were there.'

Anger rising, I stepped towards the first man. 'You did that on purpose.'

'What you going to do about it?' He stood a good six inches taller than me, with a large black beard and the well-fed bulk of a rugger bugger. His beery breath carried over the stench surrounding us. The night air penetrated the now soaked layers of fabric on my back, and I shivered.

Beery Breath grinned in triumph. 'I thought so.'

He tucked the university scarf draped across his shoulders into his coat and turned away. For a second, I stood, shame scorching my face, until a surge of frustration and rage propelled me forward.

I drew back my fist, and his sidekick shouted, 'WATCH OUT, MILES!'

My fist caught Miles a glancing blow on his head. He spun round and, with a roar of rage, he charged. The impact emptied my lungs and drove me backwards into a nearby door. My skull smashed into the timber, and I fell. A shocking pain filled my head. I wanted to lie there, but a voice inside told me to get up. Before I could, a boot struck my shoulder. I smashed into the door again. The metallic taste of blood filled my mouth.

Another blow crashed into my arm. Trapped between the ground and the door, I couldn't escape. Instinct took over, and I curled up into a ball. Blows streamed into me. Another smacked into my head. My grip on consciousness faded. At least whatever happened now, I wouldn't know about it. Then, without warning, the attack ended.

A voice came from a distance. 'I TOLD YOU, MILES, NOT ROUND HERE!'

I lay still, not daring to hope he'd gone. Car doors slammed, and the thrum of a diesel engine faded as it left. After a few moments, I lifted my head. A figure walked back to the entrance of the casino. From the size and shape, it was one of the bouncers. Had he intervened to save me, and if so, why?

I tried to rise. Intense pain seized my body, and I lay there panting, acid burning my throat. Then, a centimetre at a time, I pushed myself upwards until I sat up. My soaked clothes stank and cold penetrated my bones. I needed to get changed, but the thought exhausted me. I pulled the damp sleeping bag over me, and despite the cold, I dozed.

A wet tongue on my face woke me with a start and I pushed against Oscar's warm, furry body. 'You've come back, now the action's over.'

Did you see how big he was?

'Now you're here, warm me up.'

He sniffed me. ***Have you smelt yourself?***

'Come on, I'm freezing here.' Despite his obvious distaste, he let me snuggle up against his warm body. Terrified my attackers would return, I stayed awake but was too tired to react when Oscar slipped away. The cold seeped into me and I called him, but he didn't respond. I checked the dark corner where he slept in a packing case when he deigned to accompany me at night, but he'd disappeared. Without his body to keep me warm, I needed to get up.

My bed lay in a soaked tangle. I resisted the impulse to throw it all into the dumpster a few paces away. Even a damp, stinking sleeping bag was better than nothing in this weather. Shivering, I sorted through the remains of bedding I'd spent weeks collecting.

I binned the worst of it, recovered my stash of spare clothing and, cursing Miles, struggled into a dry top. As it did in the early hours, my mind took me to dark places. How the hell had I got here, sleeping behind a bin, and getting pissed on by a drunk?

I packed up my bed and wandered out onto the square.

To my relief, I was alone. It must have been well past the time for the clubbers to go home. Then I saw movement and tensed, but recognised the guy I'd seen hanging about for a couple of days. Despite a moustache and glasses, which looked like he'd got them in a joke shop, he seemed harmless. Probably another victim of 'care in the community', although he had a car. I ignored him and, favouring my right knee, I set off. That bastard Miles must have kicked it.

Lost in my thoughts, I didn't notice where I'd wandered until I heard running water. I'd ended up on one of the bridges crossing the river. I rested my elbows on the stone balustrade. What the hell was I doing here?

I'd almost lost count of how long I'd lived like this. It must have been almost a year, but it seemed forever. At first, I'd counted the days, then weeks and months, determined I'd get back on my feet, but each time I saw *normal* people, I seemed further away from them.

Moonlight illuminated the dark waters below and I stared into them. How deep was it here?

The surface rippled as it flowed downstream. It would soon carry me to the weir. I doubt I'd survive if I didn't struggle, but what about my girls?

Yeah, but imagine if they saw me now, filthy, and stinking. They were better off without me, and Oscar would welcome my demise. He only hung around with me out of habit.

I gripped the parapet to climb up. Something dark swirled in the water near the bank. It looked like a polythene bag. Then I heard the high-pitched barking from that direction. I fished out my glasses, thankfully undamaged, and peered at the object. It hadn't moved. Was it stuck on something? I couldn't tell because it was still too dark.

I heard the plaintive yap again.

My own worries forgotten, I rushed to the far end of the bridge and scrambled down to the bank. I could now see the dog, standing on something in the water and whining in fear. Less than three metres of water separated us.

I held out a hand. 'Come on, boy.'

The dog whined and looked at the water between us.

I searched in the gloom for something to bridge the distance to it. I saw nothing nearby. The dog barked again. Then it was in the water, its front legs splashing as it fought to stay afloat. The current swept it past me, and its head disappeared.

I stuffed my glasses in my pocket and jumped in. The cold stole my breath, but my feet hit the riverbed before I went under. I couldn't see the dog. Teeth chattering, I searched. Four metres away, a dark object bobbed up. I half swam, half waded to it and swept it up. The current tugged at my water-sodden clothing as I scrambled for the bank.

A concrete wall lined the river, its top a half-metre above me. The dog had stopped struggling, and when I placed the limp creature on the wall, it remained still. I reached up to pull myself out, my ribs screaming in pain. The river was deeper here, and I didn't have the strength to pull myself up. Panic gripped me. Downstream lay the bridge and, beyond it, the weir.

There was nothing for it. I pushed against the current and headed back upstream.

My feet just reached the bottom, then without warning, they didn't. My head went under. A powerful determination to live refuted my recent wish to die. My foot hit the bottom, and I pushed with all my strength. I broke the surface, and, coughing and spluttering, I gulped air. My bruised arms thrashed the water and slowly, I made progress.

When my feet at last found the riverbed again, I pushed towards the bank and threw myself out. I lay panting and shivering, then made myself get up. I staggered back to the little dog and looked her over. She lay on her side, not moving. Unable to accept I'd failed, I racked my brain. My rudimentary first aid training didn't cover dogs. But what about babies?

I picked her up, laying her on my left forearm, and gently pushed against her diaphragm. Would I have to do mouth-to-mouth? Then, with a pitiful cough, she vomited over my hand and started breathing. My relief didn't last long. Her body trembled in my arms like a leaf in a gale. It wasn't freezing, but wasn't far off. Such a small creature wouldn't survive long.

As I rinsed my hand in the river, I became aware of *my* body. My teeth chattered and I couldn't feel my extremities. I needed to get dry, or I wouldn't be long for this world. I slid the dog inside my top and, leaving a trail of water, hurried back to my lair. Within a hundred paces, I was staggering, my mind fuddled, and I could barely see my way. I focussed on putting one foot before another. Even if I made it back, would I have the energy to get changed into the last of my dry clothes? And if I did, would it be in time for me and my tiny charge?

After an interminable journey, I arrived at Sackville Square, I don't know how. I set the little dog down and, with the last of my energy, fought out of my soaking clothes, dried myself and got dressed before drying the dog and tucking her back inside my top.

I lay shivering, hoping for oblivion, and then shouts woke me from fitful sleep. Heart thudding, I listened and realised the shouts came from further away. I sat up and took a few moments to get my bearings. It was still dark, so I couldn't have slept long. Oscar wasn't anywhere about, and neither was the little dog. Oh God, after all that, had I lost her on the way here?

Then I remembered placing her in my top. But where was she now? My body hurt like hell, and it took me an age to get up. The shouting had stopped, but I checked where it came from.

The casino cum lap dancing club I slept behind stood in darkness, except for light spilling out from an open doorway at the side of the building, fifty metres from where I lay. The pink door led to the upper floors and three figures clustered outside it, engaged in a struggle. I found my glasses and peered through the scratched lenses. Two leather-jacketed men held a third figure between them. A woman. One had her by her hair while the other pointed into her face, then slapped her.

I'd seen a fair amount of violence in my time on the street, often disputes that flared out of hand, but this man's cold, naked aggression shook me. My fists clenched, and I wanted to help. But even a fully fit me couldn't have taken on either of those thugs, let alone both. I'd seen them, or their ilk, hanging about there. Huge and menacing, they looked like they'd rather use fists than talk. He slapped her again. I'd failed to find something I could use to distract them when a figure to their right moved. The thug saw it.

'Oi, what the fuck you doing?'

The figure ran. The thug who'd hit the woman chased him, leaving his mate to hold on to her. The newcomer veered towards me, running awkwardly, clutching something in one hand. I recognised the moustachioed man I'd seen earlier. The much bigger thug closed on him, and me. I cowered into the alcove, urging the quarry on.

As they neared, I noticed the pursued man's camera, its long lens hindering him. As he passed the open dumpster, he threw it in before thrashing away up the alley.

I watched until they both disappeared round the corner. I looked back at the other thug in time to see him drag the woman into the open doorway, then close the pink door behind her with a bang. It sounded final, like a lid going on a coffin.

I watched the door, but what could I do?

A sense of hopelessness washed over me, and tears stung my eyes. But I *could* do something. The moustachioed man must have taken a picture of the men attacking the girl. After checking nobody was looking, I hobbled to the dumpster. There, on my ruined clothes, lay a camera. I picked it up, pulled it into the alley's diffuse light and recognised a Canon EOS 100D with a 180 mm lens. A slew of memories hit me. I'd bought this same model with my first month's pay after graduating. If the owner escaped and returned for it, I'd get a reward. If he didn't, I'd send the memory card to the police with a note and sell the camera. I'd get more than enough to buy some new clothes.

I returned to my bedding and hid the camera at the bottom of the carrier bag where I kept my few belongings. Bag for life, they called them. *Bag of my life.*

Lying there trying to sleep, my mind raced. What if the thug saw him throw it in the bin? He'd come searching for it and then he'd find me.

I lay rigidly awake, a combination of the cold, still infused in my body, and fear banishing sleep. Every sound made me jump, most made by my imagination.

Then footsteps – real footsteps – sounded on the pavement. I sat up so fast I gasped in pain. The footsteps halted. I froze and tried to blend into the darkness.

CHAPTER 3

I lay staring at the concrete underside of the floor of the offices above me, reliving the sense of relief when the thug walked on past me on his return from pursuing the photographer. Had the moustachioed man got away?

Daylight had woken me a while ago and I should have got up, but the cold kept me under the pile of fabric that offered me some protection. The plaintive hoot of a tram told me it was rush hour.

The fact Oscar hadn't come to wake me didn't concern me. He often didn't. But the disappearance of the small dog I'd rescued did. Had I dreamed the entire episode?

A loud clang from nearby roused me from my reverie. A man with his back to me stood at the nearest dumpster, rummaging through its contents. I must have made a noise because he spun to face me. The moustachioed man from last night. He'd got away, then, and unhurt, from the look of him. He approached wearing a worried frown.

'You been here all night?'

'No, I was in my suite at the Midland Hotel and decided to take in the sights.' I waved a hand at the surrounding buildings.

His frown deepened. 'I lost my camera. It's worth— I'll give you a fiver if you find it.'

I laughed. 'A *fiver*?'

'Okay, a tenner then.'

Tight get. 'Lens is worth a hundred times that.'

'You've got it, then.' He stepped forward threateningly.

He was about the same size as me, five-ten or so, although less emaciated and at least ten years younger, but he didn't convince as a tough guy.

'Too late.' I gestured towards the doorway through which the man had dragged the woman. 'The lads from in there gave me fifty for it.'

His belligerent manner deflated like a burst balloon, and he gazed disconsolately at the pink door. 'When did you see them?'

'The one who chased you came back, and I offered it to him.' As if the thug would've done anything other than batter me and take it. This guy was pretty gullible.

He seemed to deflate even more and, turning, trudged away. Despite his belligerence, I felt sorry for him. 'How much for the memory card?' I called after him.

He rushed back. 'You kept it?'

I produced it from my pocket, having put it there in case someone took my stuff.

He took out a wallet and opened it, then hesitated. 'How do I know it's the right one?'

'You're right, it could be one of the many I keep on my person.'

His look soured. 'You're a bit of a smartarse, aren't you?'

I grinned. I never held the upper hand when talking to people these days, and I was enjoying it. 'Do you want it or not?'

He took out three notes. 'Fifty. But I'll come back if it's not the right card.'

'What's on it?'

He waved the notes. 'Do you want the fifty?'

Not only would I be able to buy clean clothes, I could also save some of it. I passed the card with one hand and snatched the notes with the other. Although tempted to keep the camera, I wasn't yet reduced to stealing. Though I'd wait until he'd got to the corner and then call him back for it.

He wasn't hurrying away. 'What the hell happened to you?' He indicated my face and wrinkled his nose.

'Some dickhead thought it would be funny to give me a good kicking. He pissed on me while I slept, first.' After my river dunking, I'd put my piss-soaked top back on over my only cleanish sweatshirt.

'Shit! I'm sorry.' His expression softened. 'Does that happen often?'

'How infrequently would it need to happen for it to be acceptable?'

'That's not what I meant.' He checked his watch. 'I've not eaten breakfast yet. Do you want a shower and a bite at my place? I'm sure I've got some clothes to fit you.' He held out a hand. 'Kasper.'

'Victor, Victor Mitchum.' My new name still sounded alien.

Although suspicious of his changed manner, the thought of a hot shower and food overcame my objections. I packed my bedding in a second bag. As I put it away, claws scratched on tarmac as Oscar trotted back. He must have heard our talk of food.

Kasper saw him. 'Oi, get lost, you mongrel.'

Oscar turned a disdainful glare on him. ***I don't know how any*** **human** ***can call any dog a mongrel. Your kind is nothing but.***

'He's a pedigree Schnauzer, I'll have you know.'

Kasper studied Oscar anew. 'He's a bloody big one.'

'You're thinking of miniatures. They're the ones who appear perpetually pissed off. He's a standard.'

Standard, not average.

Kasper studied him. '*He* looks pretty pissed off.' Keeping a wary distance, he set off.

Oscar stared after him. ***Interacting with idiots will have that effect.***

'Where's your car?'

At the sound of 'car' Oscar's ears pricked up. He loved riding in cars, but I'd assumed after so long, he'd have forgotten.

'Not far.'

'Come on, Oscar.' I followed, and he trotted beside me.

'Whoa.' Kasper halted. 'I'm not taking your dog.'

'I'm not leaving him.' The reply came unbidden.

Kasper studied him and Oscar's stump of a tail wagged as he gave his impression of a smile.

'You're shameless.'

Yeah, and?

'Hmm . . . He doesn't seem too dirty.'

Yet, I'm a piss-soaked tramp and you're taking me. 'He's a very clean dog.'

'Okay, he can come.'

Oscar couldn't help giving me a smug look. ***See? It works.***

Kasper grinned. 'Oscar, as in Wilde?'

Embarrassed, I confirmed. 'His Kennel Club name is Oscar Wilde III.'

'He's registered with the Kennel Club?'

'Have you got a problem with your short-term memory? I just told you he's a pedigree.'

'Yeah, but I didn't realise you meant . . .' He studied Oscar again. 'You sure he's yours?'

'No, I'm an expert on dogs and know all their names.'

We reached the car, a battered-looking red Dacia Duster. Oscar studied it. ***You want me to get in* that*?***

Kasper said, 'Are you sure he won't make a mess in my car?'

'Schnauzers don't shed.'

Kasper looked at him before, with a sigh, opening the back door to reveal what closely resembled the inside of a bin. I exchanged a look with Oscar before ushering him in.

He stuck his snout in, sniffed, then backed out. ***Forget it.*** He trotted off.

'Oscar. Come back here.'

He gave me a disgusted glance over his shoulder. ***No chance.***

'He's highly strung,' I offered Kasper in way of apology. I'd bloody kill him if he messed up my chance of a meal and shower.

'Yeah, whatever.' Kasper opened the front passenger door and scooped up a pile of papers and food wrappers from the seat before shoving them into the back.

The sweet, sickly odour of overripe bananas infused the air. As we drove away, I checked back on Oscar, who sat watching us from the pavement. Had I made a mistake getting in the car? Images of a headline announcing the death of yet another homeless man swam before me. Kasper appeared harmless, but if psychos looked the part, they'd be far less successful.

'So,' Kasper said, as though just making conversation, 'why didn't you do anything when you saw him chase me?'

I laughed. 'Like what? Beat him up?'

'Hmmm.' He glanced towards the club. 'What happened to the girl?'

'The other guy dragged her back inside.' The feeling of helplessness returned. 'Who is she?'

'Dunno.'

'You not bothered about what happened to her?'

'What can I do about it? Anyway, I'm searching for another girl.' He leant across and rummaged in an untidy glove compartment before finding a business card. 'Kasper Dąbrowski, private investigator.' He passed me the card.

The dark blue card had the name KZD Investigations across the front in a cursive font and his name and details filled the back.

'So, what you investigating? Or would you have to kill me if you told me?'

He winked and returned his attention to the road. We passed Old Trafford then he turned off the main road into a warren of streets lined with mid-century semi-detached houses and finally arrived at a nondescript pebble-dashed semi which looked like an ex-council house. The variety of doors on the identical neighbouring houses confirmed it. I smiled at the idea of me being sniffy about someone's house.

'What's funny?' he demanded.

'A random whimsical thought.'

I followed him into a cramped hallway with two doors off it. A staircase on the left led to the upper floor and a door on my right to a tidy but traditional living room. Flowers in a large vase in the middle of a marble-topped coffee table on wrought-iron legs scented the room.

'This way.' He led me to the other door, towards the back of the house. It opened into an extended living-room, dining-kitchen with a glass back wall.

'Food or shower first?'

My stomach rumbled, but I could tell from his expression that he'd prefer it if I first dealt with my stink. 'Shower, if you don't mind.'

He didn't hide his relief and set off up the stairs.

I looked at my bags. 'Is there somewhere I can leave these?'

'Through there, in the kitchen.'

I dismissed my unease at being separated from my *life* bag. He wasn't going to rummage through my stinking belongings. I dumped them under the table and followed him up to a narrow landing with four doors off it. He backed out from one, carrying a pile of clothes which he handed me.

'I'll get breakfast on. There's towels in the cupboard and we've got a combi, so use as much water as you need.'

The presence of women's toiletries surprised me. He didn't strike me as a married man. The powerful jets washed away the filth and massaged my bruised body. I stayed under until the water ran clear and the skin on my fingertips wrinkled. For the first time in days, I no longer felt cold.

I realised my conversation with Kasper was the longest I'd had since coming onto the streets. Of course, I didn't count my exchanges with Oscar. I'd spent my first six months avoiding my fellow street dwellers after two nasty experiences early on. In that time, the only soul I spoke to, apart from exchanging a few words with the people who gave me money, was Oscar. He began answering back after a few months and, although I'd never tell him, he saved my sanity.

I've never made friends easily, even at school. Most of my relationships since then were with colleagues who I could discuss work with, but I'd always needed someone to talk to. For most of my adult life, that had been Carol, my wife. Now it was Oscar, and we were running out of conversation. He never told me what he got up to when he wandered off.

Without work to talk about, I couldn't imagine making another friend. I'd got to know some people on the streets in the last few months, but I wouldn't class any as a friend.

Dismissing such cheerless thoughts, I turned the shower off and got out. Steam filled the small bathroom, and condensation flowed down the mirror and wall tiles. At least for the moment, life had undeniably taken a turn for the better.

The soft towel smelled of lavender, and I applied some of Kasper's deodorant before putting on his clothes. The jeans were a bit short, but his shirt and jumper fitted. I folded my clothes, aware of their stench, and took them downstairs. Kasper sat at a pine table in the dining area with several items in front of him, including his camera.

'You said you'd sold this,' he said, nodding at the camera.

I swallowed. 'You only offered me a fiver.'

'What about these?' He gestured at the other items on the table. A bank card and iPhone.

'They're mine.' I stepped forward.

'Oh yeah?' He picked the card up. 'This isn't your name.'

'Give it here.' I snatched at it, but he pulled it out of reach. Anger set my face aflame. 'You can have your bloody camera, but give me my stuff back.'

'Oh, I can keep *my own* camera? Very generous of you.'

'You threw it in the bin.' Although I'd intended giving it back, his snooping through my stuff pissed me off. 'I'm entitled to keep it—'

'No, you're not. If anyone's entitled to it, it's the company which empties the bin for the council.'

I wasn't sure of my ground. 'Just give me my stuff back.'

He hesitated for a few moments, then put the card on the table. 'Why didn't you phone the police last night? If that bloke had caught me . . . And you saw them hit the woman . . .'

'Why didn't *you*? Instead of taking photos.'

'Shit!' He jumped to his feet and ran to the cooker. Flames flickered under a pan on a gas ring. The stench of burning meat and oil filled the room, and a shrill alarm sounded from the open doorway.

'Blast!' He switched off the gas and picked up a tea towel before rushing into the hall. The smoke alarm fell silent, but instead of returning, Kasper stayed there and made a phone call. *Is he calling the police?* He'd closed the door so I couldn't hear his words.

I picked up the bank card and phone and he returned, red-faced.

'Help yourself to coffee.' He gestured at a chrome cafetiere. 'Hope you don't mind burnt sausages.'

'Who were you speaking to?'

'Just work, nobody important. Now do you want breakfast?'

The thought of hot food overcame my concerns, and I'd started my second coffee when he placed a plate piled high with blackened sausage, eggs, bacon, beans and toast in front of me. Saliva squirted into my mouth as I picked up the cutlery and attacked the food. Halfway through the meal, someone opened the front door. I froze, then looked at Kasper.

'Won't be long.' He rose and walked out into the hallway, again closing the door behind him.

I wolfed down half of what remained on my plate, grabbed my bags and tried the back door. Locked and bolted. I searched two drawers before I found the key under the tea towels. Where I used to keep mine. I pulled the bolts, turned the key and waited. My insides tensed up. Through the closed door I heard a murmur of voices, Kasper's, and a higher voice. A woman's? At one time, it would have reassured me, but my experiences when I lost my job had forever changed my view.

Whatever they were talking about took an age and I contemplated running, but I'd left a sausage and half an egg. The front door slammed, and I waited, hand on the door handle.

'Sorry about that, took longer than I . . .' He studied the bags. 'You going somewhere?'

'I wasn't sure . . .' I inclined my head towards the door and, feeling foolish, returned to my seat.

He eyed the mixture of congealed beans, egg yolk and bacon fat. 'I'll bin these. Do you want more coffee?' He reached for the plates.

'I'm going to finish mine.' I'd eaten far worse, and at least I knew the bite marks in the toast came from my own teeth. 'Can I have yours if you don't want it?'

He made a face and took his mug. 'Suit yourself. More coffee?'

'Not for me.' Although tempted, I didn't want to spend all day dying for a piss, and each time I left my pitch meant someone else might take it. I shoved the remains of my breakfast in my mouth and reached for his plate.

I checked the time on the clock on his fancy oven. Gone nine. I'd missed the morning office rush, but a shower and a hot-ish meal were worth it. I finished chewing and plunged the fork into the last piece of sausage.

'Sorry about giving you a scare.' Kasper placed a steaming mug on the table and sat opposite me. 'I should have gone into the office. I needed to give my . . . PA some documents, but as you're here . . .'

'My fault for jumping to conclusions. You'd said it was work.'

After a few awkward moments of silence, Kasper said, 'Do you want a backpack?'

'What? Err, yeah, sure.'

He returned in a few minutes with a small backpack. 'It's worn but serviceable and waterproof.'

'Thanks.' I put it on my bags. I could keep my few valuables in it.

He sat back down. 'So how did you get . . . End up . . . You know?'

There's no way I'm telling you. 'So, you're working for the girl's parents?'

'What? Yes, sort of . . .'

'Your problem is, you stand out.'

'Oh yeah?'

'I saw you straight away, and you were there a couple of days ago, weren't you? You wore a baseball cap and resembled someone's dad trying to be "cool". And those glasses and moustache . . .' I shook my head.

His cheeks reddened, and he took the glasses off. 'So, you're some sort of expert on covert surveillance, are you? I'll have you know I've done a course. And I got a distinction.'

'Can you get a refund?' I swallowed a piece of solidified egg yolk.

'Fuu . . .' He swigged some coffee. 'You *are* a bit of a smartarse, aren't you?'

'You stuck out because you looked like someone who wanted to be elsewhere.' I gestured with my fork. 'You didn't see me, did you?'

He thought for a few seconds, then a slow grin lifted the tips of his moustache. 'Is that what you did, then? Before? Snoop on people claiming benefits?'

'No chance. Try sleeping on the streets. You become invisible.'

He finished his coffee and stared into the bottom of the mug as he swirled the dregs around. 'Do you want a job?'

We just looked at each other for a long moment.

'Oh yeah?' I said finally. 'What sort of work?'

'That place is a brothel and sex club. I need to keep it under surveillance.'

That explained some of what I'd seen. 'What's that got to do with me?'

'I can't go back there. The guys have clocked me now, but you can monitor them.'

'And do what? Take some photos?'

Kasper laughed. 'Like I'm going to let you use my camera. How long before it ends up with a dodgy pawnbroker?'

Heat flashed into my cheeks, and I jabbed the fork at him. 'I'm not a thief.' A globule of tomato sauce dripped off the prongs onto the table.

'You tried to nick my camera.'

'I intended to give it back. Anyway, you went through my things.'

He raised a hand. 'Sorry.' He cleared the now empty plates away.

Time I went. I rose and gathered my bags.

'I was being serious,' he said from the sink. 'We'll pay you.'

I'd spent months dreaming of getting a paid job. 'How much?'

'Fifteen quid.'

Fifteen an hour? That was more than I expected. I could save enough for a flat, and then . . . *Don't get ahead of yourself.* 'How many hours?'

'Well, you're already there most of the day, aren't you?'

'So you'll pay me . . .' I wouldn't expect to get paid while I slept, but at least twelve hours a day. 'Hundred and eighty a day.'

'You what? No. Fifteen a *day*.'

I snorted and lifted my bags. 'You're taking the piss.'

'Twenty then. You're there anyway, so what's the big deal?'

'Big deal? You're trying to exploit me because you think I'm desperate, and somehow, *I'm* the one in the wrong?'

'Okay, how much?' An edge of exasperation in his voice now.

I paused by the door. 'Minimum wage, you pay me for eight hours a day—'

'Whoa, that's nearly a ton a day. I'm not made of money, as you might have noticed.' He waved a hand round the room. 'Thirty, that's my final offer.'

'You do it yourself, then,' I said, 'and next time, shave the moustache off, it might take them a day or two to spot you.' Disappointment weighed me down as I collected my bags. After almost a year on the street, I'd had the chance to improve my lot and I'd blown it.

CHAPTER 4

Still annoyed by Kasper's attempt to rip me off, I hurried to my hideaway, hefting my two bags and new backpack. I walked along Portland Street, where monstrosities from the end of the last century dominated the surviving Victorian and Edwardian buildings. A delicious aroma wafted from the direction of Chinatown. As I'd expected, the morning rush of office workers had ended by the time I neared my pitch. A woman I hadn't seen before occupied the spot by the cash machines just off the square. Young and obviously new to the streets, she appeared too well dressed to garner much pity yet. Experienced beggars used these spots only as a last resort. Nobody's going to give you a note from the machine.

She shook a coffee cup with a few coins in it as I approached and I smiled in sympathy until she responded with a 'Sod you, tight bastard!' when I walked on.

My flash of irritation passed in an instant. Did I appear that 'normal' in Kasper's castoffs? No point in taking a chance. I'd better put one of the older tops from my stash over the new outfit. Oscar waited at my usual pitch, his manner accusing.

'Don't try to guilt-trip me,' I told him. 'You chose to run off. You could have come with me.'

In that rust bucket? I'm amazed you survived.

I ignored him, removed my valuables from my life bag and put them in my new backpack.

Where'd you get that from? He poked his snout in the opening.

'Oi, keep your nose out. If you'd come with me, you'd know.' I hid the bags, keeping a grungy top to wear later for when it grew cold.

Oscar, as I knew he would, sneered. ***Please, don't wear that rag. It's bad enough begging, but looking like a scarecrow . . .***

'It's alright for you. All you need is to wag your stump of a tail and look hopeful. People don't give me anything unless I appear desperate.'

The pink door on the side of the casino opened, and I went cold. I was pretty sure the thugs from last night hadn't seen me, but I didn't want to be anywhere near them. I hid the bags. My hiding place, at the top of a narrow archway in the wall behind the bins, was secure enough, but it imparted a strong smell of mould on my belongings, so I only used it when necessary.

I patted my pockets, checking my glasses, phone and bank card. The phone lit up when I touched it. Shit! Kasper must have switched it on. The panic that he'd accessed it passed as I checked the screen. There was no way he'd have got through the password I used in the time he had. All he'd have seen was the screensaver, the picture of my girls.

But that wasn't true. They weren't mine anymore.

I stared at the image, remembering the holiday in Lesvos we'd taken it on, but shook myself out of my nostalgic melancholy before I could go fully under. No point in it. The phone's battery showed 20 per cent. I left it off so it would last. I'd have to see if the guy at the greasy spoon I sometimes used when I'd amassed a few quid would let me charge it. He did if I spent money, but with what I'd had at Kasper's, I couldn't justify eating there today. Still, my phone did need charging.

I checked Oscar. 'Are you coming?'

Not if you're wearing that. Oscar studied the old top in my hand before trotting back to his packing crate.

'Suit yourself.' *Get a dog*, they said. *It'll be good for your self-esteem.*

I made my way to Deansgate, but someone had already taken my favoured spot outside the convenience store. A large bloke with a matted beard and long hair. I'd seen him a few times but avoided him. He always seemed angry and had a reputation for using his fists to settle disagreements. He'd acquired a dog, I noted. A small Yorkshire terrier with a red ribbon in her hair. Recognition hit me, reinforced when the dog yapped and ran to me, wagging her tail. We got reacquainted as she licked my hands, and I stroked her head.

Her owner scowled at me. 'Come on, Trixie, leave him.'

I left, relieved she was okay. I hurried on, hoping to get to the café near the cathedral before the early morning rush ended, but I was out of luck again. Brother John, short and rotund with a halo of hair clinging to the side of his skull like a tonsure, sat cross-legged on a piece of cardboard placed on the pavement outside the café.

'Hello, Brother,' he greeted me like he did everyone, male or female.

''Right, John.'

A customer came out jingling his change, which he funnelled into the flat cap between John's knees. Behind him, a woman held a sandwich, which she gave to John with a smile and a brief exchange. The glare she gave me confirmed I wasn't welcome. Nothing for it but to return to my usual spot. I sometimes got a few quid at lunchtime, but I did best there in the morning.

I'd cooled down by this time and I welcomed the scuzzy top I carried with me. The stench hit me as I slid it over my head, something I'd have not noticed before my luxurious shower at Kasper's. Oscar watched me from his crate. His presence at my side would increase my takings, and I waved him over, but he pretended not to see me.

My mind worried over the decisions I'd made that morning as I sat collecting a few scraps of change from passers-by. The bright pink door through which I'd seen the woman disappear kept snagging my attention. What lay behind it? Over breakfast, Kasper had claimed it led to a brothel run by the Novak family, who owned the casino.

The door swung open as I stared at it and one of the gorillas stepped out, his long black leather coat swinging as he swaggered towards a large black SUV with tinted windows. *Why do these guys have to be such a cliché?* A bright yellow parking ticket sat in the centre of the windscreen, and he ripped it off before dropping it in the gutter.

Even though he didn't turn my way, I tensed, not relaxing until he fired up the engine and roared past me. Seconds later, a familiar old banger coughed to life and pulled out in front of a bus, earning a loud blast of its horn as it limped off behind the gangster's car. I caught sight of the driver as it passed me. Kasper. Even shaved and wearing sunglasses, I recognised him. *Idiot.*

The afternoon wore on, and I found myself worrying about him. Had the gangster he followed noticed him and confronted him? Had the thug set off as a decoy and led Kasper into an ambush? My musings ended when Kasper's car returned, and he reversed into a space close to where he'd been before. It would only be a matter of time before they spotted him.

The fact my income today had amounted to seven pounds and a bag of crisps helped make my decision easier. As did the fact that the sky had darkened, and rain threatened.

I packed up my paraphernalia and strolled to his car. I tapped on the window, making him jump and dislodge his sunglasses. After hitting the down button twice, he pushed the door open.

'What you doing?' he hissed up at me. 'I'm on a job.'

'You don't say. Look around. Who else do you see wearing sunglasses?'

He snatched them off. 'What do you want?'

I glanced across at the pink door. 'How long do you think before they spot you here?'

'With you standing here, about two minutes.' He gave an exasperated sigh. 'Get in.'

I walked round the car and, removing a chocolate wrapper, took the passenger seat. Neither of us spoke for a few minutes. I guessed we'd both seen the same video about leveraging silence in negotiations. He cracked first, beating me by seconds.

'You only spotted me because you recognised the car.'

'And they wouldn't spot it?' I waved a hand towards the front of the vehicle. 'If you drove something without the distinctive rusty scratch on the wing, you might stand a chance. But you need a new car.'

'New car! You think I'm made of money?'

'No, but I'm sure you could come to an arrangement with a car-hire company and get the client to pay for it on expenses.'

He cocked his head. 'Okay, that's not a bad idea.' He glanced at the pink door. Still closed. He looked back at me. 'I'm assuming you didn't come over to give me advice on how to blend in?'

'Even without your moustache and a new car, those guys are going to spot you before long. Whereas I'm almost invisible.'

'We've been through this. I can't bloody pay you what you want.'

'How much will it cost you to hire a car?'

He shrugged. 'Fifty a day? Why?'

'Right, you pay me that, and I'll watch them. No need for you to hire a car.'

Kasper pondered this for a moment and opened his mouth to speak.

I cut him off with a gesture. 'Before you say anything, that's my final offer. Take it or leave it.'

I watched thoughts chase across his features. Amazing how much better I could read people since I'd ended up on the streets. I knew he'd decided to accept my offer before he even looked my way again.

'Okay, fifty a day.'

Unable to control the huge grin which made my face ache, I shook his hand. 'When do you want me to start?' Had I known what the future held, I'd have said goodbye and never returned.

CHAPTER 5

Kasper pulled into the car park behind a row of nondescript shops on Cheetham Hill Road. I let Oscar out of the back, the dog having overcome his fastidiousness. I held the rope lead I'd brought with me when we left home. Kasper made it clear he wanted it on the dog before letting him in the car. We followed Kasper, dodging potholes, then onto the pavement and towards a door with 'KZD Investigations' etched in a brass plate next to it. A fried-chicken takeaway and a solicitor's specialising in immigration law flanked the entrance. Oscar paused at the food shop, but a tug on his lead dissuaded him from going in. A camera in a cage observed us as Kasper unlocked the door.

'Zofia, it's only me.'

We made our way up narrow stairs covered in a ginger patterned carpet. Embossed wallpaper coated in pale blue paint lined the walls. The smell of fried food seemed to permeate everything. A small landing at the top led to a door with 'KZD' stencilled on the glass panel in the upper half. A woman in a smart skirt suit opened the door and smiled at Oscar.

'Hello, who are you?' She stroked his ears.

Oscar gave his film star smile and wagged his stump.

'That's Oscar. Can I let him off?'

She nodded, and I unclipped his lead.

Behind me, Kasper sighed. The dog gave him a look of triumph and trotted through the door.

'Hello, I'm Zofia.' She pointed to the Z in the name. 'I'm his big sister.'

You couldn't doubt their relationship. They shared the same round face, pale blue eyes and blond hair, although she styled hers into a smart bob.

'I'm P— Victor.' I took her hand, rattled I'd almost given my real name away. There was no reason to hide it, other than my conceit that Peter Timothy didn't live on the streets. I'd use it once I had a home again.

'Victor's the guy I told you about. He's agreed to work for us.' Kasper gestured for me to go through the door.

I thought his sister wanted to say something, but she kept it to herself. I went through the door into a small, windowless reception area with two beige chairs, separated by a small coffee table and a large Kentia palm in a blue pot. Two doors led off this, one a toilet. We passed through the other into a large office with three desks arranged in the centre of the room and filing cabinets, bookcases and more plants around the walls. Oscar had already completed half a circuit of the room, and paused at one of the plants, sniffing the pot. I hoped he wouldn't embarrass me by marking his territory.

Oscar! I mouthed. 'No.'

He looked at me. ***We're inside. Do you think I'm an idiot?***

'I won't answer that.'

Kasper frowned at me. I needed to watch it if I didn't want them to think I was unstable and decide they didn't want me to work for them. I could imagine Kasper telling her, *He doesn't just talk to his dog. He listens to him.*

But seriously, who doesn't talk to their dog?

A large map of Greater Manchester covered the left-hand wall. Ahead, windows overlooked the car park. Opposite the map, two more doors, one leading to a small kitchen and the other to a room set up for meetings and containing an Ikea dining table surrounded by six chairs.

Zofia offered me a drink. She brought Oscar a bowl of water, then left to make my coffee, while Kasper led me to the tidiest of the desks. He switched on the computer, slid the chair to one side and offered it to me while he wheeled another across from the nearest desk. Several plug-in air fresheners scattered around the room couldn't mask the fried food stench. Oscar, having finished his inspection, settled down under a desk and lay on his side.

'I'll show you what we've got so far.' Kasper angled the screen towards himself and punched a series of keys.

'Coffee, milk and four sugars.' Zofia placed the drink on a coaster and stood behind her brother.

I lifted the mug and inhaled. It wasn't instant.

Kasper moved the screen so I could see it. 'That's Catriona Robertson.' He tapped the screen.

The intense brown eyes of a striking young woman stared out at me. Late teens or early twenties, she had an oval face with plumped-up lips and a not quite straight nose. The tips of her ears peeked through black hair which hung down to her shoulders.

'Is this who we're searching for?' *We.* How easily I fell into the language of belonging.

'She's been missing for five weeks.'

'You've been looking for her for over a month?' I couldn't believe I'd not spotted Kasper for that long.

'Her family contacted us last week.' Like her brother, Zofia sounded full Manc. Better than my effort, although I'd attempted to blend in since I'd arrived, hiding my West Country roots. 'They told us the police in Aberdeen weren't interested because she's over eighteen.'

'Why do they think she's in Manchester?'

Kasper and his sister exchanged a look I couldn't decipher. 'Her family heard through one of their contacts that she's down here.'

'And who's she with? I'm assuming the lad who chased you wasn't a boyfriend.'

'They're, err . . . business rivals of Mr Robertson.'

'What the hell business is he involved in?'

The siblings again conducted an indecipherable, silent exchange before Zofia gestured at the cooling mug before me. 'What's the coffee like?'

I recognised when someone was fobbing me off, but I let it go. 'Very nice, thanks.' I drained the warm liquid. 'So, you want me to keep an eye on the casino?'

'It's also a lap dancing club,' Kasper said, 'but as I mentioned, we want you to check who goes upstairs, which is where they have their offices and the sex club.'

'Sex club? You said it was a brothel?'

'It's a combination of a swingers' club and brothel, where people go to have sex with strangers *and* paid prostitutes.'

'You think she's being forced to work there? That should definitely be a police matter.'

'No.' Kasper consulted his sister again. 'Don't worry about the police. They're not interested.'

What did he mean by that? I pondered while Kasper tapped keys and pictures of the building he'd been watching replaced the young woman's image.

'Apart from this pink door, there's an emergency exit round the back, but I've seen no one use it.'

A series of images scrolled, all showing the same building, and taken from every angle until one I didn't recognise appeared. A modern warehouse with breeze-block lower walls and blue corrugated sheeting above. 'Where's that?'

'That's where I followed that guy this afternoon. It's an industrial estate, Vale Park, off Hazelbottom Road.'

I'd heard the name and knew it lay north of the city centre. 'You want me to watch that as well?'

He shook his head. 'I've placed a motion-activated camera on a wall opposite. Though I might need you to replace the batteries. It's a grey plastic box wedged in the eaves. Have you got email on your phone?'

I had, but I'd only given the address to my daughters and the various institutions I needed to log into. 'Why do you need it?'

'I'm going to email you the information. And I'll need your phone number in case we need to speak.'

With my number, a private investigator could trace my real name, and my family. 'I'll ring you if I need to get in touch.'

'Look, Victor,' Zofia said in a soothing tone. 'It's normal for an employer to have their employee's details.'

'Shall I give you my landline?'

Zofia got her phone and looked at me expectantly.

'He's taking the piss,' her brother said.

Her obvious disappointment made me wish I'd kept quiet. An all too familiar feeling.

Kasper opened a drawer in his desk and produced an old iPhone with a cracked screen. 'Here, it's been wiped but there's a sim card in it and it's linked to an email address.' He slid it across and told me the PIN. From another drawer, he pulled out a charger. 'I've charged the battery. Can you top it up?'

'Yes.' With the money he'd pay me, I could afford to eat in the caff every day.

I powered the phone up while he sent the details. I saved the attachments to a file and scrolled through the images until I got to the photo of Catriona. 'What should I do if I see her?'

'Take a picture and let us know.'

'You don't need me to contact her?'

'NO!' they both said.

'And whatever you do, don't call the police.' Kasper emphasised his words with a cutting gesture.

Kasper took me and Oscar back ten minutes later, me with my new phone, complete with contact numbers for my new employers, payment for today and an advance for tomorrow, and Oscar with a new adoring fan back at the office. The thought of being able to get a hot meal should have buoyed me, but a sense of unease had burrowed into my insides. What had I got myself into?

As I watched the pink door, a convoy of vehicles arrived, disgorging heavies who entered the building, their bearing devoid of the usual swagger. If I had to guess, I'd say they'd been summoned for an admonishment. I told myself it wouldn't be anything to do with what I was here for. The last one went in and slammed the door behind him.

'Where the hell is Alina?' Milan Novak jabbed a finger at the security staff gathered in his office above the casino.

Like everyone else, Tomaz avoided his gaze and shuffled his feet.

'Nobody seen her? Is that what you're saying?'

Nobody replied, and he slammed a fist onto his desktop. 'She can't have disappeared. What about the girls she lives with?'

One of the others finally spoke. 'Jehona's upstairs with a client. Shall I get her?'

'While she's with a client? Are you retarded?' Milan's forehead had turned bright red. Always a bad sign. His victim's reaction confirmed he wished he'd kept his mouth shut. Like everyone else in the room, Tomaz remained on edge until Milan controlled himself.

He took a deep breath. 'Has anyone seen her since Monday?'

Tomaz weighed up the risks of saying nothing or provoking Milan further. While he pondered, the driver who'd taken them spoke up.

'Boss, we took her to Vale Park on Monday night.'

'We? Who's we?'

'Me and Tomaz.'

Milan walked out from behind his desk. 'You two stay here. The rest of you, get back to work.'

The rest of the security guys, hard men all, scurried away, their sense of relief palpable. Sweat popped out on the back of Tomaz's neck, and he swallowed. Or tried to, past the dust-dry obstruction in his throat.

Milan stopped in front of him. 'When were you planning to tell me?'

'Erm, Boss, I assumed someone had seen her since Monday.'

Milan turned to the driver. 'What time did you bring her back?'

'We didn't, Boss.'

'You didn't.' Milan's voice had grown quiet, another bad sign. 'Okay, why didn't you bring her back? Tell me you took her home afterwards?'

The driver dried up, so Tomaz spoke up. 'We didn't, Boss.'

'Why the fuck not?' Spittle sprayed Tomaz's face, but he dared not wipe it away.

'Marko said—'

'He was there?'

'Yes, Boss.' He could smell Milan's breakfast.

A low growl sounded in Milan's chest, and he marched to the desk, scooping his phone off the surface and punching a button. 'Where are you?' He listened. 'Get up here, now.'

The next five minutes passed at a glacial pace for Tomaz, and he resisted wiping the sweat from his neck. His right calf was cramping up when the door opened.

'Alright, bro, what's the panic?' Despite his bluster, Marko radiated nervousness.

'Alina?'

'Ah. Right.' He glanced at the two men, still at attention. 'We don't need them.'

Tomaz gave a silent thanks and prepared to escape, but Milan stayed them with a gesture. 'They can stay. You involved them in your business.'

Marko looked ready to argue with his brother but reconsidered. 'She was becoming stroppy. Some clients complained—'

'Who?'

'What do you mean, who?'

'Which clients complained?'

Marko threw up his arms. 'I can't remember.'

'So, you took it upon yourself to get rid of her? Which flight did you put her on?'

The silence thickened.

'Let me guess, you personally got rid of her.'

Now Marko reddened.

'It's going to cost us to replace her. That's coming out of your money. And each time you do this, we have to get rid of the evidence. You're paying for that as well. Now get out of my sight. All of you.'

Tomaz reached the door first and pulled it open. Behind him, he heard Milan's parting shot at his brother: 'If you carry on doing this, it's going to cause us big problems. And don't expect me to pull you out of the shit.'

CHAPTER 6

After dropping off Victor – or whatever his real name was – and his dog, Kasper drove back to the office. He checked the rear seat but couldn't see any dog hairs. Though now that he looked at it, even he had to admit the interior needed a clean. He locked the car, returned to the office and let himself in. The stench of stale cooking fat hit the back of his throat. Even Victor, no stranger to the stink of the gutter, wrinkled his nose.

Zofia sat at her desk, headset on, and seeming oblivious to the odour. 'No problems?'

'Nah. I'm having a coffee. Do you want one?' He walked towards the kitchen.

'No, thanks.' She gestured at a half-empty mug on her desk.

'Doesn't the stink bother you?'

'You get used to it.'

'Yeah, but our clients don't.'

'What clients?'

'Exactly.' Kasper filled the kettle and spooned coffee into the cafetiere as it boiled. 'We need to find somewhere else.'

'We've paid the rent on this place for another three months. And how much did we spend doing it up?' She punched keys. 'Our current account stands at fourteen hundred and twenty-three pounds. That includes the advance we got from Mr Robertson.'

The kettle boiled and Kasper poured the water over the coffee. He didn't need his sister telling him how precarious their situation was. At least they owned the house, courtesy of their frugal mother, who'd left it to them following a lifetime of working round the clock. Otherwise, he could all too easily imagine himself joining Victor.

He took his coffee to his desk. 'I could take the job at Acorn Kitchens.'

'No! You'd bloody hate it. Selling overpriced kitchens to people desperate to get one over on their neighbours.'

'Yes, but it's part time and I could do it in the evenings, especially now Victor is doing legwork on the Robertson job.'

'No!' Zofia used the voice she'd used when left to take care of him while their mother worked. 'If anyone is going to take another job, it's me.'

The fact his sister possessed a first in chemistry, while he'd studied maths for three years and left without even an ordinary degree, filled him with shame. The detective agency had been his chance to redeem himself, and as usual, Zofia supported him. And even more typically, he was making a mess of it.

He sat and logged in to the system. 'We've got those enquiries from the ads we put on Facebook. Let's follow them up and see how we get on before we panic.' He'd gone way past panicking, but wouldn't let Zofia see that.

'I've started, it should have updated on your database. I'll carry on going down. Do you want to start from the bottom?'

He opened the database and saw the mass of red lines through the ones his sister had contacted. The only respite, two yellows for 'possible' and an orange for 'unlikely, but don't give up yet'. He scrolled down until he got to a pale green line. His excitement faded as he read the details. An old man wanted to trace a childhood sweetheart to apologise for his behaviour and leave her a bequest in his will. That wouldn't save the business.

With a sigh, he scrolled to the bottom, realising his sister had already cleared almost half. With little hope of finding anything, he read the details on the last line. The murmur of Zofia's voice as she spoke to another prospect reminded him to put on his headset. Three calls later, his sense of despondency had increased. Each was just a tyre-kicker.

Zofia finished chatting to someone and ended the call. 'That's promising. A technology company recruiting a senior member of staff wants someone to do background checks on the candidates.'

'They're not coming here, are they?'

'They're based in Leeds, so I offered to meet them at their head office. I told them I'd be going there on a job.'

'Great.' He felt both buoyed by the bite and even more of a failure.

'Why don't you take the rest of the day off? I'll finish the list.'

'It's okay. I need to pull my weight.'

'You worked late last night. Take the afternoon off and I'll finish the list. Then, in the morning, we can get out there and get some new clients. I've got a good feeling about this one in Leeds. He said they're expanding fast so would need to recruit for several senior positions.'

'Could be a con man bulling up his credentials.'

'I've done this before, you know. I'll do a background check on them before I even agree to meet them. You go get some rest. We'll order a takeaway tonight.'

The urge to sleep won over his need to show his sister he wasn't a complete liability. 'Okay, I'll close my workstation down.'

Zofia glanced at her screen. 'I did a background check on our new member of staff, Victor Mitchum. He doesn't exist.'

'I'm not surprised.'

'There are four in this country, but none could be our chap.'

'Does it matter?'

'He's obviously hiding from something or someone. We don't want it to come back and bite us.'

Kasper wasn't sure if the man was hiding, or just keeping his past life separate from his current situation. It's what Kasper would have done. He had other concerns about Victor. 'Should we have told him about Mr Robertson?'

'Why? The chances of Victor meeting him are almost zero.'

'Yes, but what if something goes wrong? It was you who found out that stuff about Robertson.' Kasper still felt ashamed that he'd pretended to be surprised when his sister told him what she'd dug out about Robertson and his activities. He'd decided to ignore the information when he'd discovered it. Aberdeen was a long way away from them, and they were desperate for the work.

Zofia took a deep breath. 'He just needs to keep out of the way of those thugs until he sees the girl, then leave it to us.'

Kasper wasn't too sure. *He* wouldn't be happy if he'd been doing this job without knowing who and what Robertson was.

CHAPTER 7

I spent the next two days keeping a watch on the pink door, Oscar by my side. My initial nervousness about being near the thugs who'd chased Kasper faded. I was truly beneath their notice. My bruises from the encounter with Miles were fading, but my ribs still hurt and my desire for revenge hadn't abated.

Although I'd not been actively watching the door over the weeks I'd occupied this patch, I'd noticed the patterns of arrivals and speculated about what happened behind it. Some young women arrived mid-morning and a larger cohort arrived early evening. My observations yesterday and this morning confirmed that. Their customers arrived from lunchtime on, but as I'd been tasked with searching for a young woman, I focussed on the workers.

Many arrived by car, either in the back of large SUVs with tinted windows or in one of three black minibuses, but some arrived on foot. A few of this last group left at mid-afternoon to return in the evening. If I could find out where they went, I could follow and look for opportunities to ask them about Catriona. Kasper forbade me from speaking to her, but he'd not said I mustn't ask about her.

At three, I stood to put my mat and collection bag away in readiness. Oscar watched me, his tail twitching in anticipation. When I returned to my spot, he looked puzzled.

Aren't we going for a walk?

'Don't worry, we'll be going soon.'

Why don't we go anywhere nowadays? It's not as if you get much money from the tight gets who come here.

'I'm searching for a woman.'

You're going to have to smarten yourself up for that. And have a wash. I'm only a dog, but even I can tell.

'Ha, ha. Not like that. I'm being paid to keep a lookout for a particular woman.'

Paid? Does that mean you can afford to give me a trim?

'That's not a priority.'

Maybe not to you, but you're not the only one looking for romance. Have you seen the state of my pelt?

I ignored him.

What does she look like?

'Who?'

This woman we're looking for. You'll probably miss her – especially if you forget to put your glasses on – whereas I won't. We're renowned for our observational skills, you know.

'So you keep saying.'

Go on, then.

I tutted. I knew he'd keep on until I showed him. 'Here.' I found the picture on my phone, and he studied it.

What does she smell like?

'How do I know? And how the hell would I describe it to you if I did?'

How am I supposed to do a good job without all the information?

I put the phone away and went back to ignoring him. He sat a few paces away, his back to me.

The door opened and three young women came out, long coats covering the flimsy outfits I'd seen most of them wearing. They strode off towards Portland Street and Chinatown beyond.

I stood. 'Come on, boy.'

Oscar looked at me. ***Even I can see she's not one of those three.***

'Get a move on. Do you want a walk or not?'

I stepped towards him and clipped his lead on. A tug on it and his reluctance to join me evaporated. The three women turned left onto Portland Street, and I hurried to catch up. More recent concrete tower blocks dwarfed the handsome brick buildings lining the road. There were few people on the expansive pavements, so I hung back.

Oscar didn't look impressed. ***You know I don't like coming this way.***

'It's not all about you.'

We crossed Oxford Street, lined with buildings reflecting the history of the city built by cotton. On my right I could see the neo-classical pillars of the Central Library. We entered the curve of Chepstow Street. As we passed the ornate art nouveau brickwork of Canada House, Oscar attempted to examine the greenery bordering the small car park at the front of the building.

'Come on, we haven't time for that.' I tugged on his lead, and he reluctantly followed me.

The three women entered a café and sat at a table by the window. Once here, my resolve to speak to them faltered. I examined my clothing. My jeans, a pair I'd got from Kasper, looked okay, but my top wouldn't pass muster. Would the people let me into the café? The humiliation if they refused would be bad enough, but I didn't want to draw attention to myself.

If I was honest, I also had to admit to a bout of nerves. I'd got out of the habit of engaging strangers in conversation. Most people shoved coins into your hand and rushed away without even making eye contact, which I had to admit was my preferred mode of exchange.

I retrieved Kasper's phone. What would he say if I told him what I was doing? I suspected his sister would be far more sympathetic.

'Hi, Victor, has anything happened?'

'Erm . . . I'm just outside a café.' I gave her the address. 'Three of the women are in there. I thought we could speak to them . . .'

'And what?'

'We could ask if they've seen Catriona.'

Zofia didn't speak for a few seconds. 'I don't think that's a good idea.'

'It could save you a lot of time.' It would suit me if this job lasted forever, but I'd never been good at stringing jobs out.

'Okay, I'll join you,' she said. 'Wait there, but don't approach them.'

'Okay . . . and, Zofia, could you bring a decent jacket for me?'

'Sure, Kasper has a couple here he doesn't need.'

With a silent 'thank you' for fielding my request with such grace, I switched the phone off to preserve the battery. A feeling of lightness infused me. Zofia was easy to talk to.

Oscar gave an impatient growl. ***What are we waiting for?***

'Sorry, boy, we're working. You'll have to wait.'

Can I go over there, check those trees out? He indicated the few shrubs and stumpy trees we'd passed.

'Just wait, will you? I won't be long.'

He gave me the side-eye and sat with his back to me. I ignored him and pretended to study the blank screen of my phone while I waited. Before Zofia arrived, two of the women stood and took their leave of the third. She stayed at the table, engrossed in her phone.

Should I follow the others or wait here? Before I could decide, a blue Nissan Micra pulled into the car park opposite and reversed into a space. Zofia got out holding a dark hooded jacket. We crossed over the road and waited while she bought a ticket.

'Hello, Oscar.' He trotted to her and let her ruffle his ears.

'Two of them have just left.' I pointed towards Deansgate. 'Do you want me to follow them?'

She peered towards the café. 'Is that the other one?'

'Yeah.'

'Shall we talk to her, then? It's better than speaking to three. If there's more than one, it can inhibit people. They worry what they say might get back to their . . . employers.'

'Oh, right. I hadn't thought of that.'

She held the jacket out to me. 'It needs a wash anyway—' Her cheeks flushed. 'I meant . . .'

'Don't worry, thanks.' I slipped it over my top. Although tight over my layers, it would do the job.

Zofia led the way across the road. Oscar and I followed. 'Sorry, boy, you'll have to wait outside.'

After making me hang about.

Zofia studied him with concern. 'Will he be alright?'

'He's used to it. Most places serving food won't let dogs in.'

She looked at me as if to say, 'How would you know?'

I smiled and attached his lead to the rail outside the café. A bowl of discoloured water sat on the pavement nearby and Oscar studied it with disdain.

You think I'm going to drink that?

'Okay, I'll get you some fresh.'

The aroma of coffee and baking enveloped me as we entered. Warm air blew down from a heater above the door. A short queue waited at a counter which ran along the right-hand wall.

'What do you want?' Zofia gestured at the array of cakes under the glass counter.

I checked the prices. 'Just a coffee, please.'

'I'll be putting it on expenses.'

'Oh, okay, can I have a piece of walnut cake?'

'I'll have the same.' She handed me a credit card in her name and crossed the room to where the woman sat on her own.

Although alarmed, the woman gestured to the seats opposite. Zofia asked her something, and she shook her head, gesturing at her mug.

'Can I help you?' The barista's words didn't go with his scowl.

'Two medium Americanos, two walnut cakes and a jug of milk, please. Oh, and can I have clean water for the dog bowl?'

After inspecting me, he filled a jug with cold water and prepared my order. I replenished the dog bowl, returned, paying with Zofia's card, and carried the tray to the table.

'Hello, I'm Victor.'

Petite with fine features, pale blue eyes and shoulder-length brown hair, the young woman looked terrified for a moment, then offered a tight smile. 'Jehona.'

I distributed the refreshments and sat. Zofia had obviously gained the young woman's trust, and I let her lead the conversation while I attacked my cake.

'You work at the casino?'

Jehona looked puzzled.

'In Sackville Square.' Zofia indicated the direction I'd come from.

'Oh, yes. Casino.' She gave a small laugh.

'How long have you worked there?'

'Hmm, maybe six month.' To my inexpert ear, Jehona's accent sounded central European.

'We're searching for a friend's daughter-in-law. We think she might be working at the place you work.'

'Could be. Lots of girls work there.'

'Her name is—'

'You must go.' Jehona gestured behind us.

Her two colleagues were returning. If we left, they'd notice us. I picked up our plates and cups and, placing them on the tray, took it to an empty table across the room. I sat with my back to Jehona's table, so they'd not see me. Zofia gave Jehona a card and rushed to the seat opposite me.

'Good thinking,' she whispered.

We waited a few minutes, finishing our drinks before leaving. I collected Oscar, and we accompanied Zofia to her car.

'Good idea of yours, Victor. I think she'll get in touch.'

I watched her drive off, buoyed up by her praise, but the memory of the woman being slapped by those thugs made me worry about Jehona and her friends.

Jehona had avoided looking at the woman who'd spoken to her and tuned in to what Katya was saying. After a few moments, her attention wandered across the café. Who was that man with her? He seemed familiar. They left, and she followed their progress through the window. He collected the dog, and she recognised him. Was he watching *them*, or their employer?

'Are you in the room with us?' Katya's gaze followed Jehona's, then returned to her.

'Sorry, yes,' Jehona said. 'I was thinking about Alina.' What did she say that for? Too late now, the mood had become sombre.

They sat in silent contemplation for a few moments, then Katya gave a signal and the two of them stood. 'We need to buy a few things. See you back at the club.' She patted Jehona's hand and left.

On her own, she contemplated her position. She'd resigned herself to staying here for two years, as she'd agreed, but suspected they'd extended it to three, which would be bearable. What she hadn't considered was that something might happen to her. They were far safer working for the Novaks than many other women in a similar position, but Alina's disappearance, following so soon after the other girl's, made her reconsider.

She'd barely known the other girl, and they'd assumed she'd escaped with the help of a client who'd grown fond of her. It happened, although she suspected far less often than they liked to imagine. Like all the others, she'd seen *Pretty Woman* more than once, imagining herself in the Julia Roberts role. But Alina was like a sister to her. Even if she'd kept her impending escape to herself, there's no way Jehona wouldn't have spotted the signs.

Something must have happened to her, as Katya had suggested. Jehona and the others had dismissed her claims, and the notes she kept, as paranoia, but maybe she was right, someone was preying on them. And in that case, none of them were safe. Maybe this woman could help her escape. She'd have to think very hard about how to arrange it. One slip and she *would* disappear. Or, worse, her family would suffer.

CHAPTER 8

The next morning, I saw the image of the pink door set in its brick wall as though it had been seared onto my retina. I'd watched it until midnight, reckoning I owed Kasper a few hours to make up for my time in the café with Zofia.

I thought of our client – *our*. Again, I was making myself a part of Kasper's organisation, although I wasn't sure he wouldn't want to see the back of me once we finished this job. How must the client have felt to know his daughter was with people like this? What would I have done if someone like the men who ran this place took either Helen or Em? I'm not a violent man, I'm not built for it, but I can imagine taking revenge on someone who did that to either of my daughters.

The injuries from my attack had faded, and my main sleeping bag had dried. But getting up still caused me pain, and I felt like an old crock. As I put my bedding away, Oscar trotted up, his erect ears and energetic stride mocking my decrepit state. At least with the money Kasper gave me, I could get a coffee and breakfast. I glanced across at the pink door. I'd seen no one go in this early and reckoned I could abandon my post for an hour or so.

Oscar decided he didn't want me to attach the lead.

'Come on, be reasonable.' I held his gaze. 'You're still sulking about yesterday's walk, aren't you?'

I'm not sulking.

'Look, I'll give you a sausage and we can go to Piccadilly Gardens afterwards.'

Two.

'Okay.'

And a piece of bacon.

I'd given in too easily again. 'Whatever.'

He let me clip the lead on him. I took a longer route to Tib Street. We walked along Nicholas Street, entering the heart of Chinatown. Workmen swarmed around the ornamental arch over Faulkner Street putting up the decorations for the upcoming New Year celebrations. Chinese restaurants occupied the basements and lower floors of the nineteenth-century stone and brick buildings. The smell of food from these made my stomach rumble. We passed the art gallery, a two-century-old columned structure, evidence of its citizens' desire to make sure the world's first industrial city had a rich cultural life. I'd always wanted to visit but didn't dare for fear of being refused entry. We crossed the tramlines and at the top of the street, entered the financial district.

Expensive cars filled the parking bays, and a mixture of old and new office blocks lined the streets. The journey to Tib Street took an age as I walked the stiffness out of my legs. Oscar let out a low whine of sympathy when he saw me struggling, but I ruffled his ears and gave him what I hoped was a reassuring smile.

By the time I reached the café, I felt like I'd run up Bridge Valley Road. Although the locals decried the gentrification of this area, where many of the businesses lining its narrow streets had been replaced with expensive bars and eateries, it still reminded me of the scruffy but trendy Cotham back in Bristol, a place where I'd loved living before the responsibilities of parenthood weighed me down.

'Sorry, Oscar. You know you can't come in.' The café had a 'dog-zone' covered by CCTV by the entrance. They'd provided bowls of water and rings set into the wall to attach your lead to. A yappy Scottie was already attached to one. Oscar resisted when I tried to clip him alongside.

I'm not spending the morning clipped to that thing.

'Come on, don't be difficult.'

I won't run away.

I recognised his determined expression. 'You'd better not.' I tucked the lead into his collar.

He trotted to the furthest corner, lay down, giving the Scottie a disdainful look, and closed his eyes. Confident he wouldn't run off, I stepped inside. The aroma of frying bacon and fresh roasted coffee made me salivate.

Trev looked up as the bell above the door pinged and scowled at me. With a heavy, dark beard and shaved scalp, he resembled so many trendy young men. He possessed the bulky upper torso of a bodybuilder, let down by a spreading gut and skinny legs which he screened behind the counter.

Unsure why I warranted a scowl – my visible bruises had almost faded – I smiled and made my way to the counter. 'Hi, Trev, could I have a full breakfast and a large mug of tea?'

He didn't move until I produced a fiver and a pile of coins from my pocket. I'd hidden the rest of the money Kasper gave me in my socks. A bit obvious, but at least anyone nicking it would suffer before getting the money.

Trev finished counting the money and signalled to his assistant, who made the tea. 'Sit through there.'

He indicated a small room at the back, through an archway and on the way to the toilets. Half the tables in the far brighter main room remained unoccupied, but I didn't argue.

'Okay to charge my phone?'

He grunted an affirmative and his assistant placed the steaming mug in front of me. I took it through the arch. As the only one banished to the back room, I had my choice of tables and took the one nearest the plug in the corner, leaving my charging phone on the chair next to it.

A copy of *The Big Issue* a previous customer must have bought from a homeless person lay on one table and, conscious of the irony, I read it while I waited. My breakfast arrived and as I laid into it, I heard voices which brought back unpleasant memories. It took me a few moments to place them and when I did, I dropped my fork so it bounced on the table. Sweat broke out across my shoulders as the voices neared.

Miles and his companion from the other night came through the arch and stopped.

A shadow fell across my plate. I kept my head down, concentrating on the stain of beans and egg yolk left by the fork I'd dropped. My hand gripped the knife tighter, although I wasn't sure why. Barely sharper than a spoon, it wasn't much of a weapon.

I glanced up, expecting Miles to be glaring at me, but he and his companion weren't even aware of my presence. His friend finished his anecdote, and both laughed before continuing past me to the toilets.

I wiped my mouth with the see-through napkin and took a sip of tea. He'd left the room, but he might as well have remained standing before me. My heart still thumped in my chest. I could see every hair on his head, the sour look on his face even as he laughed, the electronic ID tag bouncing against his jacket from the rainbow lanyard around his neck.

A body I knew well pushed against my leg.

'Oscar! What the hell you doing in here?'

It's* him, *isn't it? He focussed on the door through which my attacker had gone.

'Get under here.' I put the knife down and pushed him under the chair I'd put my phone on.

He gave me a hurt look, like I was punishing him for being good.

I checked through the arch. Neither Trev nor his assistant paid me attention. They couldn't have seen Oscar, but how would I get him out? That was assuming nobody saw him before I finished. My heart racing, I picked up my knife and fork. The fear of being thrown out almost trumped the fear of Miles recognising me. I wolfed the food down. Focussed on my plate, I didn't notice Miles returning until Oscar emitted a low growl and shot out from under the chair.

His lead must have got tangled in the leg and it went flying, taking the table and the remains of my breakfast with it. As the not-yet-empty plate slid out of my reach and the mug followed it, Miles let out a yell. Oscar had sunk his teeth into the man's calf. Miles, yelling obscenities, took a swing at Oscar.

'Hey, leave him alone!' I jumped up and grabbed his fist.

'Get your mad dog off me!' He shoved me hard and, windmilling my arms, I hurtled backwards atop the overturned table.

Miles's companion came out of the toilet and made a grab for Oscar, who released his prey and snarled at the new threat.

Trev rushed into the room. 'What the hell's going on?'

'This rabid dog attacked me.' Miles rolled his bloody trouser leg up as his companion swung a boot at Oscar.

'Get off my dog.' I struggled to my feet.

Trev's huge hand grabbed my shoulder, almost crushing it. 'Right, you, out. And your bloody dog.'

'He attacked me.' I nodded at Miles and pointed to my fading bruises.

'You had those when you came in.'

'He did it Tuesday night.'

'I don't care. Now out.' He propelled me towards the door.

'Hang on, my phone.' I pointed to the tangle of wires on the floor next to the upturned table.

He let me collect my phone and charger. 'Come on.' I gestured at Oscar, who glared at Miles and his companion before trotting to me.

'I'm reporting you and the dog to the police.' Miles jabbed a forefinger towards Oscar. 'It's a dangerous animal.'

'That's rich, coming from you. You going to tell them about you attacking me and giving me a good kicking for no reason?'

Miles reddened, then craned his neck round to check his wound.

'Right, come on, out.' Trev laid a heavy hand on my shoulder and escorted me through the front of the café, which had by now filled up.

Everyone in the room fell silent and stared at the strange procession – dog, tramp and skinny-legged bodybuilder. My face hot with humiliation, I concentrated on my feet. Oscar walked with a jaunty step, as if leading a victory parade.

Trev's 'And don't bother coming back' felt like an unnecessary kick up the backside.

Arsehole.

Once outside, I grabbed Oscar's lead and walked away. If Miles actually did report Oscar, we were in trouble.

'Come on.' I tugged on the lead and walked faster. 'Well done. You got me barred, *and* I didn't finish my breakfast.'

Oscar gazed at me, hurt and disappointed. ***Aren't you going to thank me for sorting him out?***

He looked so forlorn that I sighed and stroked his head. 'Yeah. Well done, boy. A bit late, coming to my rescue, but you got there.' Miles's leg would be sore for a few days. 'What's that in your mouth?'

A broken lanyard trailed from it. I took it from him and examined it. Miles's electronic pass from where he worked. I must have grabbed it when he pushed me. It bore his full name and the address of his employer. Ash and Caulk, accountants. So, he wasn't a student, as I'd assumed. How could I use it to get my revenge?

CHAPTER 9

As Zofia settled down to watch the United game with her brother, her phone rang. A lifelong Blue, she was still smarting about the loss in the derby last month, a feat Kasper, a Red, kept reminding her of. At least City remained above United in the league and held most of the recent bragging rights.

She didn't recognise the number, but it could be a much-needed job. She silenced the TV. 'Hello, Zofia Dąbrowski.'

The earpiece echoed for a few seconds before a small, hesitant voice said, 'Hello, is Jehona.'

'Jehona, how lovely to hear from you. How can I help you?' Zofia hadn't expected her to ring so soon.

'Yesterday, you say you help people. Can we talk?'

'Of course.' She waited for Jehona to respond. 'Do you want to meet?'

'Yes, please. We meet.'

They agreed on a venue and Zofia ended the call.

'Who was that?' Kasper juggled with the controls, eager to put the sound back on.

'Jehona, the young woman Victor and I spoke to.'

'Hmm . . . I still think it was a mistake to talk to her.'

'Only because Victor suggested it.'

Kasper didn't contradict her. 'What does she want?'

'To talk.'

'Has she got information about Catriona?'

'I hope so. I won't know until I see her.' Although she doubted it. They hadn't even got as far as mentioning Catriona to her yesterday, at least by name. But she'd got in touch, and they could build a relationship. She stood. 'See you later.'

Kasper's grumpiness irritated her, but he'd given up his season ticket in a belt-tightening exercise, so she could forgive him. United were at home, so traffic would be a nightmare everywhere, a penalty of living so close to the ground. The gloomy drizzle would add to the traffic as people avoided using public transport.

She cut across through Whalley Range, the potholed streets lined with bare trees and faded mansions, and then Moss Side to join Princess Road, traffic still a pain as others copied her. Expecting delays, she'd allowed an hour to get to her rendezvous, a pub just north of the city centre.

She found a parking spot on a side street, ten minutes before she was due to meet Jehona. The Marble Arch, an iconic Manchester pub renowned for its beers, sat on the corner of Rochdale Road, a main artery going north of the city. She'd only been there once, as a teenager ten years ago, taken there by a beer-loving boyfriend.

The post-industrial wasteland which once surrounded it was now replaced by blocks of apartments on the city side, with more towers going up behind it. She approached the marble-columned entrance with a sense of trepidation. She'd been one of very few women when she'd last gone in there and wondered why Jehona had picked it.

The hoppy aroma of spilled beer greeted her. She remembered the ornate tiled floor, illuminated by decorative chandeliers, even in the afternoon gloom. A leather banquette ran along the long right-hand wall, ending at the fireplace, which was unfortunately not lit. Beyond it stood the small bar. None of the half-dozen customers reacted to her entrance. The pub didn't have a TV, so would have few customers today. She walked the length of the narrow room to the bar, remembering the pronounced slope of the floor, and bought a sparkling mineral water.

She took it back to the entrance and sat at the top of the banquette, out of sight of anyone entering. She studied the tiled walls and vaulted ceiling as she sipped her drink, wishing she'd ordered something hot.

Jehona was late. Had she changed her mind?

Just as Zofia gave up hope, the door opened, letting in a blast of icy air and a slight figure enveloped in a parka.

'Jehona?'

She spun, wide-eyed with fright, then smiled. 'Zofia.'

Once they'd settled with their drinks, Zofia said, 'You asked if I could help you.'

'Yes. I . . .' She checked her surroundings; nobody sat in earshot. 'I come from Romania. My family must leave. My mother and brother are in Bucharest, but they are in bad situation.'

'I'm sorry to hear that. How can I help?'

'My brother needs treatment, but it very expensive. Is why I come here to work.'

'Okay, do you want help to get them out?' Zofia had family in Poland and knew how difficult it could be getting into the UK since it left the EU.

'I know is difficult,' Jehona said, 'but I have cousin in London. If I can get to him, he can take me to Paris and we get my family to France.'

Zofia wasn't sure where she came into this. 'What can I do?'

'If I leave work to go to London without permission, they will hurt my family. I need time to get them out of Bucharest. Just one or two days is okay. Then, when we're all in France, we will be safe.'

'That's awful. Can't you go to the police in Bucharest?'

She gave a grim smile. 'Is police there who make them suffer.'

And we can't trust the local police.

Zofia had heard of women in similar situations but had never met any. How would she feel if it happened to someone in her family? 'What do you need from me?'

'Sometimes, customer invite girls to party. We go for one night or two, and they pay my boss. Can you be customer—'

'I'm not sure about that.'

'Please. I can give you the money back. I have saved. You say you want me for weekend trip to Amsterdam. They give me my passport and then I have two days to get my family out before they realise.'

Jehona had obviously given it some thought. 'I'll have to ask my brother if he can be the customer.'

Jehona smiled. 'Sometimes we have women customer. I don't care.'

Zofia's face warmed. 'Okay, I'll have to think about it.'

'Thank you.'

The expression of hope on Jehona's face filled her with sadness. 'Another drink?'

'No, I have to go home, change for work.' She indicated the jeans and thick jumper, which almost swamped her.

'I'll take you.'

They drove out of the city in silence, along a tree-lined road crossing a railway line and passing blue-clad tower blocks. Zofia's thoughts raced, veering between the thoughts she mustn't get involved and she couldn't let Jehona down. After two kilometres, they turned off, following signs for North Manchester General Hospital. Two hundred metres later, they arrived at their destination, a dull grey tower block at the end of a narrow cul-de-sac. Zofia pulled into the small car park.

'You must have a good view from the top.'

'Yes.' Jehona smiled. 'From my bedroom, we can see mountains.'

'Jehona, can you do me a favour?'

'Of course.' Jehona frowned, puzzled.

Zofia produced her mobile and called up the photo of Catriona. 'Do you know her?'

Jehona's reaction made the question superfluous. 'Why you look for her?'

The venom surprised Zofia. 'Her family want to find her.'

'Not English.'

'No, she's Scottish.'

Jehona shook her head. 'Not Scottish, I think – *Cacat!*' She ducked down. 'Please go. NOW!'

Her tone infused Zofia with a sense of urgency and she reversed out of the bay. The black SUV, which had just arrived, loomed in her rearview mirror as it passed her car and pulled into the next space. She put the car into first and pulled away, resisting the urge to race out of the car park.

'What's wrong?'

Jehona twisted round in her seat, peering through the back windscreen. 'Those men in that car. They work for my boss. They must not see me with you. Leave me at bus stop. I walk.'

'If you're sure.'

She dropped Jehona off with a promise to think about what she had asked of Zofia. She checked her mirrors. Although she could no longer see the SUV, she couldn't shake off a sense of unease at their close escape.

By the time Jehona walked from the bus stop, the SUV was empty. They were probably up in the flat, or one of the other ones she knew they kept girls in. Her pulse racing, she rushed to the tower block, punched in the entry code and pushed the door open. As she stepped into the gloomy entrance, the stench of piss and skunk welcomed her.

Then she yelped and jumped. Tomaz had materialised before her, staring at her with hard, dark eyes. 'What's up with you?'

'You made me jump.'

'Where have you been?' He turned to peer out of the entrance and the snake tattoo poked above his collar.

Even though she knew Zofia had long gone, her insides clenched. She lifted her chin. 'Out. I needed some fresh air.'

Behind him, the other girls stood alongside the other goon, dressed for work. She had a moment's panic and checked the time, but she wasn't late.

Tomaz hadn't finished. 'Which way did you go?'

'What's this, an interrogation? Are we only allowed in certain places?'

'Which way?' He stepped into her, his body odour overpowering.

She'd learned to keep close to the truth, if possible. 'I visited the park along the main road.' She pointed in the direction of the city centre.

'We just drove from town along there. I didn't see you.'

Her heart pounded in her chest.

Katya said, 'You can go through the cemetery and come out behind the houses.'

'Show me.'

Katya stepped forward.

'Not you, her.'

Jehona hid her fear behind indignation. 'What's this? You don't believe me?'

He stood, impassive.

Rescue came from an unexpected source. 'Come on, Tomaz, don't be an arsehole all your life.' His partner winked at her, then nodded up the stairs. 'Go on, get changed, we'll wait for you.'

She rushed upstairs and got changed, returning to find the others waiting in the car, engine running with the heater on, but the atmosphere was still icy. She avoided Tomaz all evening and was relieved when one of the others drove her back in the early hours.

Sunday passed slowly, and she knew something was wrong when they cancelled her evening shift. No explanation. She went to bed early but couldn't sleep. At two thirty, just after the others returned, banging on the door shook the flat. She knew it was for her, but didn't move.

Katya came to her room. 'Jehona.'

Before she could get out of bed the hulking figure of Tomaz filled the doorway. 'Get packed, we're moving you.'

'Where to?' Katya demanded. 'And why this time?'

'You can join her if you want?'

Katya gave him a venomous look but stepped back.

He stayed where he was and watched Jehona dress. She packed in a trance, feeling hollow, not even aware of the cold. The two goons watched her throw her stuff into a case, knowing she'd need none of it. They left the apartment – she, flanked by the two men who towered over her, her heels clacking on the tiled floor.

In the lift, they avoided her gaze. To her surprise, she wasn't afraid. In fact, she felt nothing at all as the box squeaked and clanked to the ground floor. But as they crossed the car park, her legs gave way. Tomaz caught her by her bicep, making sure she stayed upright, the strength of his grip showing he didn't care if he left a bruise.

Of course he didn't.

Silent tears coursed down her cheeks as she thought of the people she loved.

CHAPTER 10

Two days after my humiliation at Trev's hands, I still hadn't found another place to charge my phones and despite my efforts to conserve the batteries, both needed topping up. I'd have to go to Kasper's office. I remembered how difficult it had been to find somewhere like Trev's café where they let me charge my phone. The fact I'd identified Miles and where he worked didn't make up for the loss. I hadn't figured out how I could use the information to get a measure of revenge for his assault and the latest indignity.

Oscar had spent the night away and hadn't returned yet. The fear of losing him to whoever fed him at night nagged at me. Apart from my affection for the animal, he represented my last link with my former life. I pictured getting him as a puppy and bringing him home for the first time, watching as Helen and Emily fought to be the one to hold him, he as determined not to be held. Even then, he'd known his own mind. I gave up waiting for him and set off for Kasper's office.

As my injuries gave me little trouble, the walk took me half an hour. While I waited for him to answer the door, I studied the queue outside the takeaway next door. Did people eat fried chicken for breakfast?

'Why are you here?' Kasper greeted me at the top of the stairs.

I ignored him and brushed past into the main office. Zofia, at her desk and speaking into a headset, waved before gesturing at the kitchen. Kasper followed me into it and closed the door behind us.

'Right, what's happened?'

'Nothing.'

'So, why the hell are you here? You're supposed to be watching those guys. That's what I'm paying you for.'

'Not twenty-four seven.' A mixture of defensiveness and irritation made my voice high. 'Anyway, nobody arrives before lunchtime.'

Zofia came in before Kasper could reply. 'Morning, Victor. Hasn't he offered you a drink?'

Kasper choked back the retort he'd prepared and filled the kettle. 'Tea or coffee?' It came out like a threat.

I remembered they drank decent coffee and placed my order.

'Why are you here, then?' Kasper busied himself making drinks.

'Can I charge these?' I took the phones and chargers out of my pocket and placed them on the counter.

'I thought you could get them charged.'

'Yeah, I could, but I ran into a bit of a problem . . .'

'Oh, yeah?' The kettle boiled, and the rich aroma of coffee filled the room.

I told them about my problem at Trev's café.

'I hope your dog's not preventing you doing your job,' Kasper said.

'Ignore him.' Zofia put the phones on charge.

We took our mugs and trooped out into the office.

'Do you think you'll find somewhere else to charge them?'

'I'm sure I will.'

Kasper took his mug over to his desk. Zofia rummaged in her handbag and produced a metallic pink object the size of a mobile.

'Use this. It's good for two charges.'

I weighed it in my hand.

'Hang on, I gave you that for Christmas,' Kasper said.

'I'm sure Victor will take care of it.' She turned to me. 'I'll get you another, same colour?'

'Er . . . could you—'

She gave a rich laugh. 'I'll get something grey or black.'

'Thanks.'

Kasper sat with his arms folded. 'Do you have *anything* to report?'

'Yes. I've identified twenty-seven young women who work in there.' I produced the battered notebook I'd been using. 'The first column is a brief description—'

'What's that number?' Zofia pointed at a figure.

'If I've got a decent photo, I've added them to a spreadsheet, and that's the row number. I've only got good pictures of twenty-two.'

'That's good work, Victor,' she said. 'Did you get a picture of Jehona?'

'Yes, I got a good one on Saturday. She normally walks, but that afternoon, she arrived with the other two in a car driven by one of the meatheads.'

'Was it a black SUV?'

I checked the back of my notebook and put it back down. 'Yes, why?'

Before she could reply, Kasper picked up my notebook. 'What are these columns?'

'I've arranged them by date, and I list when they arrive and leave, and how they get there. Most come in the minibuses or cars driven by the heavies who work there.'

Even Kasper seemed impressed, although he tried to hide it.

Zofia took the book off him and studied my notes. 'What does "SD" mean?'

'Ah, different cars pick some of them up, driven by people I assume are clients. I put SD for sugar daddy.'

'And how long are they gone for?'

'Usually just the evening, but three girls came back two days later.'

'Two days? Are you sure?'

'They may have come back after I'd gone to bed and gone out again. But the same three girls in the same car?'

Zofia seemed very interested. 'You get the car reg numbers?'

'I didn't know you wanted them, but I have. I search for patterns in number plates and like to check where the cars were registered.'

'That's great.' The two PIs exchanged a look. 'Can you write an account of what you've done so far? We'll include it in our report to the client.'

'Yeah, okay.'

'Use this desk.' Zofia crossed the room and powered up the desktop, entering a password and bringing up a blank Word document while I sipped my coffee.

My rusty keyboard skills meant the report took longer than I'd expected, but I finally finished. Zofia read it, seeming surprised I could string sentences together. I also realised by her reaction when she came close, although she tried to hide it, that the effects of the shower at Kasper's house had well and truly worn off. I'd have to use some of my money to get a shower or book into a hostel for the night.

'Would you be able to pay me for the days I've done?' Less than fifty of the hundred Kasper gave me remained.

'Of course. Shall I pay you until Wednesday, two fifty?' Zofia produced a money box from a drawer in her desk and, after rummaging in it, said, 'Sorry, will two hundred do? I need to go to the bank.'

'Sure.' I'd pay this straight into my account.

She counted out the notes and handed them to me. I asked if I could use the toilet, and placed my money in my socks, half in each. When I came out, Kasper swore.

'What's up?' Zofia said.

'The camera I planted at Hazelbottom Road isn't working.'

'Do you think someone's found it?'

'It's probably the battery. I'll change it later.'

With this reminder, I returned to the kitchen where my phones and chargers sat on the worktops. Both batteries showed full, and I put everything in my backpack.

'Which phone are the photos you took on?' Zofia said.

I held up Kasper's phone. 'This one. I'll email them.'

'Here, I'll download them.'

I gave her my cable, unlocked the phone and handed it to her. 'What about the photos you took, Kasper?'

'What photos?' He studied me with an annoyed expression.

'The ones you took when you almost got battered. The ones I recovered for you.'

'Oh.' He returned his attention to his screen. 'They weren't any use.'

Zofia returned my phone, and from her reaction, I guessed Kasper had just lied to me. But why?

CHAPTER 11

'You shouldn't have given him two hundred. You don't know what he'll do with so much cash.' Kasper's mood hadn't improved with Victor's departure. Victor seemed to be able to wind him up. He wasn't sure why. Maybe it was the fact he seemed better at this detective business than Kasper.

'I imagine much as he did with the hundred you gave him Wednesday. Anyway, it's none of our business. He's already earned most of it.'

'So he says.' Why did Zofia always take his side?

'I've got the photos he took, and his notes are comprehensive. Unless you think he made them up. We either trust him, or tell him to stop.' Zofia took the dirty mugs through to the kitchen and returned. 'Anyway, why did you lie about the photos you took?'

'It's none of his business.'

'Of course it is. If one of our operatives is on a job, we need to give them a full briefing.'

'He's not an operative, he's just a—' The shrill sound of the doorbell cut him off. 'I bet that's him now, complaining someone has mugged him.' Kasper ignored his sister's exasperated reaction and reached for the intercom. The image on the screen halted his next sarcastic comment.

'Oh, shit!'

'What?' Zofia joined him and recognised Detective Chief Inspector Grimes.

'Open up, Dabriski.'

'It's Dąbrowski,' Kasper corrected.

'I don't give a damn. Open up, or I'll be coming through this door.'

Kasper pressed the button, and a crash followed as Grimes shoved the door open. A young woman with shoulder-length black hair followed the bulky policeman through the doorway. The stairs shook as the shaven-headed detective clomped up.

'Stinks in here,' he complained to Kasper as they met on the landing. 'You been frying cabbage soup, or whatever it is you lot eat?' He pushed past Kasper into the office.

The policeman filled the doorway as he passed through it, his scalp brushing against the top of the frame and his shoulders, the sides. His assistant, an attractive mixed-race woman of about Kasper's age, wasn't much shorter, although a fraction of his width.

'Inspector,' Kasper heard Zofia say to Grimes, 'can I get you a drink?' She pasted on a smile.

'It's Chief Inspector.'

'No to a drink, then? And your colleague?' Zofia turned her smile on the young woman.

'Detective Sergeant Bowling.' She spoke with a Peak District accent.

'Would you care for a drink, Sergeant Bowling?'

With a pleasant-enough expression, the sergeant indicated she wouldn't require one.

Grimes removed his black leather gloves, and jabbed a sausage-like forefinger at Kasper. 'I told you to keep your nose out of my investigations. I hate amateurs at the best of times, and if they get under my feet, I trample all over them.'

Kasper kept his tone even. 'I'm not sure what you're talking about, *Chief Inspector*. Would you care to enlighten me?'

'I'll enlighten you with my boot up your arse.'

'Is that a threat?' Zofia said.

'No, a promise.'

'Just to let you know, Chief Inspector Grimes,' Zofia said, 'everything being said in this room is being recorded.'

He stepped close to her. 'You can bloody stop that.'

'It's automatic.'

'Turn. It. Off.' He emphasised each word with a jab of his finger on her right shoulder.

Kasper wanted to intervene, but didn't fancy angering Grimes further.

As usual, Zofia did what he should have: 'If you hit me again, I'll report you for assault.'

Grimes glared at her for long seconds, then said, without turning Bowling's way, 'Sergeant, find the device and switch it off.'

The sergeant's body language suggested she wouldn't obey.

Zofia saved her from defying her boss. 'We save it all to the cloud, so everything you've said, including your threats, is already preserved for eternity.'

'Sir?' Bowling waited, uncertain.

'Forget it, Sergeant.' Grimes returned his attention to Kasper. 'If we catch you interfering in our investigations . . .'

'I've no idea what you mean.' Kasper cursed the wobble in his voice.

'Why does that not surprise me?' Grimes heaved a sigh. 'I'll make it simple for you: Stay. Away. From. The Novaks.'

'I still don't know what—'

Grimes slapped the desk with his gloves, and it sounded like a shot. 'One of them chased you on Tuesday night. Ring any bells yet?'

Kasper swallowed, embarrassed he'd jumped. 'I've not been back since.'

'Keep it that way.'

'Why are you bringing this up now, Chief Inspector?' Zofia said.

'I only found out about it today.' He directed a nasty grin at Bowling. 'You can't always get the staff, can you?'

Kasper cleared his throat. 'Are you investigating the Novaks?'

'The hell I'm going to tell you who I'm investigating.'

'We might have information which could help you.'

'Oh yeah? I verymuchfuckingdoubt it, but if you've stumbled across anything which might help us in our enquiries, you're duty bound to share it. Or I'll arrest you.'

Kasper focussed on his shoes.

'Well? Have you got anything to tell me?'

'No.'

'I thought not. Just keep out of the way.' Grimes pulled his gloves on and strode to the exit, where he paused. 'And if you say anything to the Novaks, I'll do you both for interfering in an active investigation.' Then he let his sergeant go ahead of him so he could slam the door behind him.

Kasper waited until the crash of the outside door faded before speaking. 'Since when do we record everything in this office?'

Zofia held up her phone. 'Since I saw that pig at our door.' She punched keys and Grimes's voice played back. Not broadcast quality, but clear enough to identify him.

'And the cloud backup?'

Zofia smiled. 'That *was* bullshit.'

He returned to his chair. Unable to focus on the work he'd been doing before Victor's visit and the invasion, he mulled over Grimes's words.

Zofia interrupted his thoughts. 'Why do you think he came round here today?'

'Rather than last week? It sounds like the sergeant hadn't told him before now that they'd seen me there.'

'Hmmm.' She didn't sound convinced. 'What do you think he's investigating them for?'

Kasper snorted. 'Take your pick. Prostitution, people trafficking, drugs, money laundering.' He didn't want to articulate some of the other stories he'd heard about them. 'Anyway, I've heard a rumour the Novaks have a senior policeman on their payroll.'

'You think Grimes?'

'Would it surprise you if it was?'

Zofia shook her head. 'What about our client?'

'What about him?'

'Robertson said no police. If Grimes barges in there and finds Catriona, Robertson won't be pleased.'

'We can't do anything about that. What, should I ask Grimes to ease off his investigation until we've located Robertson's daughter-in-law for him?'

'Don't be childish, Kasper. I meant should we tell Robertson that Grimes is likely to get involved?'

'No way. You heard what Grimes said. If it gets back to the Novaks—'

'How will it get back to them?'

'I don't know, but let's not risk it.' He hated hiding things from Zofia, but thought it best for her not to know. He'd discovered Robertson and Novak knew each other, and their mutual hatred of the police would trump whatever dispute they had over this Catriona. He wouldn't put it past the Scotsman to warn Novak if he knew of a police investigation.

'We'll have to tell Victor.'

'Tell him what?'

'Warn him to look out for Grimes. In fact, we should call him off. If he falls foul of Grimes, I don't want to think about what would happen to him.'

'Grimes's people will never imagine a vagrant is watching the Novaks.'

'They spotted *you*. And they arrived just after Victor left. What if they saw him coming out of our office?'

'He'd have been long gone by the time they arrived. Anyway, they probably traced my car. They'll be using the camera network.' He still couldn't recall spotting anyone who might have been a cop. 'Victor blends in, and he hasn't got a car.'

Zofia sniffed. 'It wouldn't surprise me if Grimes had sent one of his own men there disguised as a homeless person. What if Victor talks about his new job?'

'What, and make his pals think he's got money, so they mug him in his sleep?'

'Of course not.' She rubbed the back of her neck. 'I'm worried about Victor. And what would happen if the police catch him and trace him back to us?'

That worried Kasper as well, but what was the alternative? 'I'm sure Victor will spot Catriona in the next few days, and once he does, our job for Robertson is over.'

'I still think we should tell Victor to stop now. Tell Robertson we can't do any more and—'

'Are you mad?'

'We can give him a refund. We've done a few days' work, so we can keep some of it. I'm pretty sure we'll get that new job in Leeds.'

'It's not that. We can't give up. What do you think that will do to our reputation?'

'Do we want to work for people like Robertson? What if he does trash us in his circle?'

She was right, but it was *Robertson's* reputation, and what he did to people who displeased him, which worried him much more.

CHAPTER 12

The hulking, angry-looking man I'd seen going into Kasper's office after I left concerned me. I'd seen him before but couldn't recall where. The fact he made me uneasy suggested it wasn't something positive. The mixed-race woman I'd never seen before. Were they customers or something else? I worried at the problem as I hurried away.

As I approached the fountains in Piccadilly Gardens, Brother John shouted and waved me over. He and another guy I didn't recognise sat on the steps under the statue of our second longest reigning monarch.

'Hello, Brother, how are you doing?'

'Hello, John.' I nodded a greeting at his companion, a young man with extensive bruising across his cheek, and sat on a nearby step.

'We don't often see you away from your usual haunts.'

Although I didn't know John well, I knew he dealt in information and I'd heard he sometimes shared people's secrets, so I wasn't keen on him knowing my business. I shrugged. 'I just fancied a bit of a change. Get some exercise and see how the other half live.'

'Not so well.' John gestured at his companion. 'Our brother here had a run-in with a couple of ne'er-do-wells. Tell him what happened, Toff.' He prodded the young man, who cringed at the contact.

'Someone gave me a twenty so I could pay for a hostel.' The young man's nasal Scouse accent made him sound as if someone had broken his nose. From his name, I'd expected a posh accent. 'Two guys jumped me and took all my money. Almost thirty quid.'

'Did you recognise them?'

'I didn't see them, but they sounded local and one of them brought a dog with him. I could hear the little shit barking and it bit my ankle.' He pointed to the shredded fabric on a leg of his jeans.

I exchanged a look with John. We both knew someone with a small dog and a propensity for violence. 'Sorry to hear that, mate. Did you say your name's Toff?'

'Yeah.' He held out a grubby hand and grinned at my puzzled expression, showing a mouthful of brown stumps. 'I'm an Evertonian. Toffees?'

'Of course.' I'd never been into football. I'd grown up in Gloucestershire before moving to Bristol and we paid little attention to the round-ball game. Now I was pretending to be a Manc, I needed to brush up on football lingo.

'I told him to be careful,' Brother John said. 'There are some disreputable people on our streets. They're not all good Christians like us, are they?'

'Err, no, they're not,' I agreed. And I'd better get rid of my money before I bump into one of them. 'Right, I'll get going. See yer, John, and nice meeting you, Toff.'

I started back to my patch, intending to throw John off the scent, then go straight to the bank. My stomach hadn't stopped grumbling, so I bought a meal-deal from a discount supermarket.

Feeling guilty, too, at neglecting Oscar, I'd bought him a pack of dog treats he liked. He'd returned during my absence and twitched an ear when I greeted him. I wasn't sure which I preferred, this indifference or his accusatory 'Where the hell have you been?' look.

'Look, I got your favourite treat.' I took the packet out and unwrapped one stick, releasing a meaty odour.

He raised his head and studied it suspiciously. ***You've been up to something, haven't you?***

'Do you want it or not?'

He roused himself and took it, his distrust fading as he sank his teeth into the chewy snack.

I'd just settled in my place and started eating my sandwich when a car pulled up outside the pink door. It opened and a shaven-headed thug with no neck and a tattoo disappearing under his collar strode to the car and pulled the back door open. Three young women spilled out as he scanned his surroundings. Jehona's friends and a new woman. I took a few pictures on my phone before the thug's gaze appeared to rest on me. He was fifty metres away so I wasn't sure how much he could see, but I let the phone drop into my lap and focussed on eating the remains of my sandwich. A piece fell onto the pavement, and I picked it up, just beating Oscar to it. It had landed dry side down, so I brushed it clean and ate it.

I caught the thug screwing up his face in disgust at this before closing the car door and following the three young women into the building. My pulse slowed, and I chewed the last of my sandwich, spitting out a piece of grit I'd missed. I'd check the photos once I got away from this place and send the best one of the new woman to the office. I was pretty sure she wasn't the woman we were looking for.

Oscar had finished his snack and lay beside me with his eyes shut.

'So much for your help.'

Okay, I'm going to keep my eyes shut and tell you who's nearby. Three workmen in overalls. Two elderly women with

shopping bags and a young mum with a buggy and dragging an older kid picking its nose.

This stopped me. 'Okay, how did you do that?'

Easy. The workmen are wearing boots and have been sweating. Old women smell different to young women. The mother smells of baby sick and the kid in the pram needs its nappy changing.

'What about the one picking its nose?'

It was scuffing its shoes. The nose-picking was a guess, but they almost always do.

I didn't tell him, but I was impressed. He'd make a better detective than either me or Kasper.

After another half hour, during which nobody arrived or left, I set off for the bank, worried about the cash in my shoes. The nearest branch of my bank wasn't far, but I didn't want the thugs who'd mugged Toff to see me.

We passed the plastic-shrouded town hall, undergoing an expensive refurbishment. I wondered how many homeless people they could house with the hundreds of millions earmarked for the project. We passed building sites every few hundred metres on our way to Salford Precinct. Thousands of apartments going up, but I'd have bet the numbers of homeless wouldn't decrease. The walk usually took me forty minutes, but Oscar appeared determined to mark every tree and lamppost we passed.

'How big is your bladder? That's the seventeenth piss you've had.'

I'm not 'having a piss', I'm leaving messages for other dogs.

'What messages?'

'Bugger off, this is mine.'

'But it isn't, is it?'

It is until someone else marks it.

Maybe I should try it. Mark my territory in a small semi. It seemed the only way I'd get somewhere to live.

'Come on, let's go.'

All this walking should have been good for me, but the more calories I burned, the more food I'd need. Near the bank, I found a secluded bench down the side of a small park, slipped Oscar's lead over the arm, and took my shoes off to get my cash. Oscar retreated from me to the full extent of his lead and sat facing away.

'What? You embarrassed to be seen with me?'

I don't want people to think I've got anything to do with you. Can't you smell them? I enjoy a stink as much as the next dog, but you're abusing the privilege.

I ignored him and retrieved my money. After straightening the notes, I put them in my pocket and led Oscar to the bank.

'Do you want to come in?'

Is there food in there?

I left him with his lead hooked over a rail, took out my bank card and went into the branch. The lunchtime rush had ended, so I marched to the cashier's desk and paid in my money. The three hundred and fifteen pounds in the account had taken me six months to accumulate.

With a strained smile, the cashier gave me a printout showing my account now contained over five hundred. I bet she'd be telling her mates how wealthy we street-dwellers were. Sod her. If I could make this job last a few weeks, I might get enough together to get somewhere to live. Lost in my fantasy, I didn't recognise the person stroking Oscar outside the bank until he greeted me.

'Hello, Brother.'

Brother John straightened.

I jumped and dropped my statement.

John moved quicker and picked it up. 'You're doing a lot of walking today?' He handed it to me, but couldn't have missed seeing how much money I had.

'John. Hello. Thanks,' I mumbled, and grabbing Oscar's lead, set off. 'Come on.'

You never let me make any friends. Scared I'll find them more interesting?

I ignored Oscar's protests and tugged on his lead. That's all I needed, for John to know I had money in the bank. How long before he shared what he'd found out? My stomach churning with half-digested sandwich, I hurried away.

CHAPTER 13

Kasper had avoided discussing Jehona's request all weekend by talking football, then claiming to be too busy at work yesterday. Zofia collared him at his desk, playing solitaire.

'Okay, let's talk Jehona, you're obviously not too busy.'

'I'm just having a break.' He killed the screen and shifted guiltily.

'You can talk during your break. I think we should help her.'

He took a deep breath. 'Okay, suppose we do ask to book her for the weekend. Do you think they'll let a random person take one of their valuable assets—'

'She's a person, not an asset.'

'To us, but these people don't think like we do. I'd imagine you'd have to book her at the club a few times before they let you take her off the premises. And even then, I doubt they'd let you take her for two nights straight away. How long would that take us, to gain their trust? And how much would it cost?'

Zofia exhaled in frustration. 'We could at least try.'

'And what happens if she disappears while she's off with us? They're not going to shrug their shoulders and say, "You lost one of our girls, never mind." They'll want revenge, or compensation.' He swallowed. 'Or both.'

'So, what do we do?'

'Nothing. We can't help everyone. And if we ask for her, they'll become suspicious.'

She knew he was right. 'There are organisations that help women like her. I'm going to contact them.'

'Okay, you do that, but don't get involved. It's too dangerous.'

His computer pinged, signalling a new email. A message from Victor with four attachments. He opened one to display an image of three women outside the pink door.

'Those are Jehona's two friends.' Zofia pointed at the screen. 'Why isn't she with them?' She checked the other photos and thought she recognised the shaven-headed driver with them.

'Maybe she's on another job.'

'I don't think so.' She told him about the men in the car park when she'd dropped Jehona off after their meeting on Saturday. She tapped the photo. 'He was one of them.' Had they seen Jehona in her car and become suspicious?

Kasper's eyes widened. 'Did they recognise you?'

'I don't know. I'm more worried about Jehona.'

'They're dangerous men. I don't know if I'd still be here if they'd caught me.'

Zofia retrieved her phone.

'What you doing?'

'I'm ringing Victor.' The dialling tone clicked off as it connected. 'Victor, when did you take those photos?'

'Yesterday around lunchtime. Why?'

'Have you seen Jehona since then?'

'No. But she might be with a client.'

Kasper nodded. At last, something Victor had said that he approved of. Zofia rolled her eyes.

'I don't think so. Can you meet me outside the café where we spoke to her?' She ended the call.

'You going somewhere?'

'To Jehona's flat to check she's okay.'

'Whoa, whoa, you can't barge in there. You could make things worse.'

'I'll be careful. It's only just nine. I'm sure the thugs working for the Novaks will still be in bed.'

Ignoring Kasper's further protests, she put her coat on and left, grabbing the jacket she'd lent Victor last time on the way out. A steady, icy rain fell, adding to her despondency. The thought she might have placed Jehona in danger squeezed her insides as she drove.

Victor wore a baseball cap, and she almost missed him, but recognised a drenched Oscar. She pulled up beside them.

Victor opened the passenger door. 'Okay if I bring Oscar?'

'Yes, jump in. There's a rug on the back seat.'

The stink of wet dog and damp clothing filled the car.

'Sorry,' he said. 'I didn't want to leave him. I've not fed him yet.'

'Don't worry.' Like Kasper's jacket, the car needed a clean.

'Where are we going?'

'I'm worried about Jehona. I want to see she's okay.'

'Do you know where she lives?'

'In a tower block in Harpurhey.' Embarrassed that she might have endangered her, she didn't say any more.

Victor looked across at her. 'How come you ended up being a private detective?'

It was a question she was asking herself more often these days. 'Long story, but I've always been nosey.' She gave a self-deprecating laugh.

'That sounds like you're avoiding the question.'

He was more perceptive than he looked. 'Okay, how about this: I studied chemistry because I'm fascinated by how everything is put together, but working as a research chemist wasn't the life I imagined. When Kasper decided to set up the agency, I jumped at the chance to join him.' Was she being honest? Part of her had feared Kasper would mess it up and she knew he couldn't face another failure. And the way things were going, it looked like her efforts to help avoid or even forestall that had been in vain.

'You enjoy it?'

She nodded, buying time to consider her reply. 'Most of the time. I *am* nosey and I like helping people.' She just hated the precariousness and working for the kind of scumbags employing them on this job. But if it gave her the opportunity to help someone like Jehona, some good would come out of it.

They arrived at the tower block, bringing a welcome end to Victor's questions. She pulled into the car park, seized by a sense of trepidation as she recalled her last visit here when she'd encountered the men who'd terrified Jehona. She checked it out, but none of the aged and rusted cars in it looked like they belonged to gangsters.

Victor craned his neck to examine the tower block. 'Which floor is she on?'

'I don't know. She didn't give me the full address, but she's on the upper floors. She mentioned the view.'

He looked worried. 'Okay. What are you planning?'

'We'll start at the top and knock on doors, show her picture until we find her. We'll tell them we're working for her family who are worried about her.'

Victor indicated his soaking clothes. 'Do you think anyone will answer the door to me?'

'Kasper's jacket's in the back. There should be a couple of business cards in the inside pocket. Just tell them you're a PI. Most people are intrigued.'

Victor seemed uncertain.

'I'm sure you'll be fine.'

On the kerb to the left of the car park stood a row of bins. She turned the car round and parked on the pavement behind them, out of sight, but ready for a quick getaway. Victor struggled into Kasper's jacket and found three of the promised business cards.

'Are you going to bring Oscar?'

On hearing his name, he wagged his tail.

'I suppose it doesn't appear too professional.' Victor studied the sky. 'It doesn't look like it's stopping soon. He'll be okay with the windows cracked open.'

They left the disappointed dog in the car and approached the tower block. A group of young lads wearing hoodies clustered near the entrance. She was glad she'd brought Victor with her, although most of the boys towered over him. They watched her approach. Two stood astride chopped-down bikes. She acknowledged them with a smile. The stench of skunk wafted off them and one lad exhaled a cloud of smoke.

'Want us to mind your car, mister?' a pale youth with a fuzzy moustache asked.

'It's alright, I've got a dog.' Victor gestured at the car.

'Can he put out fires?'

The lads laughed.

Victor smiled. 'Not only does he put out fires, but he'll bite the bollox off the arsonist.'

One of the lads snapped his fingers, and the others jeered at the pale youth. He reddened before stepping aside.

Zofia mouthed, 'Well done.'

A digital lock secured the main door with a keypad alongside it. She'd have to ring a few bells until someone let them in. The patchwork of stains on the buttons made her wish she'd worn gloves, but the security door swung open before she touched anything. A harassed-looking man scuttled out, and they eased themselves into the building before the door shut.

The stink of rotting rubbish joined the skunk as she studied the pair of lifts facing her. One waited at the ground floor, the one serving the odd floors was on the thirteenth. She punched the call button to open its door, but a pool of vomit in the far corner persuaded her not to use it.

She'd missed a few sessions at the gym, but should be okay if she paced herself. She wasn't sure about Victor. 'You alright using the stairs?'

'Did you see a defibrillator anywhere?' He put a pair of glasses on.

'I didn't know you wore glasses.'

'I can get by without them, but I thought it might make me appear more intelligent.' He did a rapid blink behind the lenses.

She laughed. 'I'll take the top floor, and you do the one below it. We'll work our way down.'

By the third floor, where someone's dog had used the landing as a toilet, she wondered if the lift might have been the better bet. She concentrated on avoiding obstacles in the gloom caused by broken and missing bulbs. Victor's laboured breathing told her she hadn't lost him. She'd grabbed the handrail for an instant until she remembered the horror story of an unwary firefighter encountering a needle taped to the underside of one in a similar block.

Three figures lurked on the half-landing between the fifth and sixth floors and watched her approach. She slowed, waiting for Victor to catch up.

Her pulse raced as she approached, and not just from exertion. She made sure she didn't falter.

'Excuse me.'

They moved at the last minute, and she brushed past, holding her breath. Victor followed, now panting. By the time she arrived at the thirteenth floor, warm and breathing hard, she felt she'd been through an assault course. She waited for Victor, who arrived a minute later and collapsed against the wall.

When his laboured breathing subsided, she said, 'You okay to take this one? We'll meet here once we've finished.'

After a frustrating circuit of the top floor, she found a downcast Victor. 'Only one person answered the door to me, and they swore at me because I didn't have their pizza delivery.'

By the time she'd worked her way down to the eighth floor, Victor seemed to have gained confidence, and was on the seventh. They must be close, as much lower, and the distant hills Jehona had mentioned – either Winter Hill to the north or the Derbyshire Dales to the east – would be out of sight. She rang the bell at the first flat on the eighth.

A thin Black woman with wild, frizzy hair opened the door. 'Yes?'

'Hello, my name is Zofia. I'm a private investigator trying to trace a young woman for her family.' She held up the phone with the image Victor had taken of Jehona on the screen.

'Can I see?' She took the phone off Zofia and studied the image. 'She's one of the girls in the flat across the landing.'

'Really?' Zofia tried to control her excitement.

'Four of them arrived a few weeks before Christmas. They seem nice girls. Two blokes brought them up here.'

'Have you seen the blokes around?'

'Yeah.' Her expression clouded. 'They don't come round often, but they're big and nasty-looking. Both looked like steroid-users, bit like my ex. Keep out of their way.'

'Don't worry, I will.'

'One of them's got a shaved head, and the other has one of those stupid little beards on his chin.' She giggled. 'My ex used to call them quim beards.'

Zofia smiled. One sounded like the man Victor photographed. 'Which flat did you say I could find Jehona?'

'It's eighty-three.' She gestured over her shoulder. 'The other side of the stairs.'

Zofia took her phone back, thanked her and left. She worried about the two heavies, but as she'd told Kasper, it was still early. Flat eighty-three didn't have a bell, and she knocked on the door. Nobody replied, but she heard someone moving about.

She tried again. On getting no answer, she knocked harder. 'Hello, is Jehona in?'

Urgent whispers came from behind the door and locks turned. The door yawned a few centimetres, a metal bar keeping it in position, and a pale face appeared in the gap. 'Yes?'

Zofia looked into the frightened blue eyes, recognising the woman from the café. 'Hello, my name is Zofia. I'm a friend of Jehona.'

Another figure out of sight spoke to the first woman in a language Zofia didn't understand. 'Jehona not here,' the woman in the opening said and pushed the door.

Zofia blocked it with her foot and showed the image. 'I just want to talk to her.'

The young woman didn't speak, but tears gathered at her eyes.

Zofia's stomach clenched. Something must have happened to Jehona. 'Is she okay?'

The woman didn't reply, and another woman took her place. The other one from the café. She seemed more composed. 'Please go away.'

'I just need to know where Jehona is.'

'Please go.' She pushed the door, but Zofia's foot blocked it.

'Can I talk to you?'

'They will come.'

'Who?' In her bag, Zofia's phone vibrated.

'Please go.' The woman pushed against Zofia's foot.

Behind her, the lift motor stopped, and the doors slid open with a screech. The doors to the corridor swished and footsteps thudded on the tiled floor.

The woman's eyes widened as she looked past the private detective.

Zofia spun round. Five paces away, and closing rapidly, were the two men the woman across the landing had described.

CHAPTER 14

Kasper gave up trying to contact Zofia and returned his phone to the desk. She'd always brought home injured waifs and strays and still had the same instinct, but she needed to learn she couldn't help everybody. And even if she could help this Jehona, to do so was too dangerous. If he knew where she'd gone, he'd fetch her back.

He realised he could easily discover where his sister had gone. They'd both included find-my-phone software when they'd upgraded their handsets. He woke his desktop and opened the app. Then hesitated. How would she react if he tracked her down? She'd be furious if she thought he'd been spying on her.

He closed the app and put the phone down. And why did she take Victor? *He* should have been the one to go with her. He was the detective, and they were a team. In the week since he'd come across Victor, he'd already come between him and Zofia. What made him trust the guy in the first place? He'd lied to Kasper about his camera, trying to steal it from him. And he'd had a stolen bank card . . .

But what if he hadn't stolen it? What if it belonged to Victor, but in his real name? Kasper closed his eyes and tried to picture the scene in his kitchen. The name on the card remained elusive, however hard he tried. It had been very English-sounding and almost a hairdresser's name, where both could be first names. They stayed at the edge of his memory, though, like a silver sprat flashing through a sunlit patch before disappearing into darkness.

With a groan of frustration, he opened his eyes, recognising the futility of continuing. He focussed on his screen and opened a database of missing people. After narrowing it down to men over forty, he scanned the names. He'd slept badly, worrying about Zofia's obsession with helping Jehona and other concerns, and his eyes drooped. He made another pot of coffee and came back to the database.

The list of missing people ran for pages, and realising he needed to refocus, he opened a database of traditional English names. He got to T and read Timothy. Recognition jolted him awake. He opened the missing persons screen and searched for people called Timothy. He found many, but none of the names triggered a memory.

What about surnames? Few Timothys and one grabbed his attention. Peter Timothy. He recognised the name and searched Google. Sure enough, he found a LinkedIn profile. Timothy presented himself as a data analyst for a private healthcare firm. Kasper studied the photo. An unremarkable-looking man of about forty with neat hair and wearing a suit. It could be Victor from a few years ago. He found a Facebook profile, but the private setting wouldn't let him access it.

On the off chance he'd filled out the electoral register before becoming homeless, Kasper checked it and found him, no attempt to hide his address. He wrote Victor's name and Peter's address on a pad, buoyed by his success. He remembered Victor's crack when Kasper had told him he'd done a course on surveillance. 'Ask for a refund', eh? The cheeky sod.

He checked the time. Almost eleven. Zofia must have found the girl by now. But what if she hadn't? He tried her phone again, but she didn't answer. She was probably still annoyed at him for trying to stop her. He returned to his desk and studied the email Robertson sent yesterday, demanding an update. Kasper had sent a revised bill, including the money to pay Victor, disguised as 'car hire'. A check of their account showed they'd spent all but a few hundred.

They could do with another interim payment but, as they still hadn't found Catriona, he needed to offer Robertson something to secure it. The pictures Victor had rescued from Kasper's memory card showed Marko Novak, the second Novak son. Robertson had asked them to check if Marko had returned to Manchester while they searched for his daughter, but he'd made it clear nobody must know of his interest. He was going to wait to send that information once they'd found Catriona, but that could be a long way away.

After mulling it over, Kasper decided he'd tell him and ask for a cash injection. He used WhatsApp to ring Robertson's burner, sweating as he waited for a response.

'Yes?' The smooth Scottish accent could have been a doctor's or lawyer's.

'Mr Robertson, it's Kasper Dąbrowski.'

'Ah, Mr Dąbrowski. How pleasing to hear from you. I presume you've some information for me.'

'Yes, we've discovered the whereabouts of Marko Novak. He's back in Manchester. I've got photos of him at the family business headquarters.'

'Verra good. And Catriona?'

Kasper hesitated. 'We haven't located her yet, but we've got someone on the inside of their organisation now. It shouldn't take long before we've located her.'

'Someone on the inside, you say. I presume you'll be paying them. How much is that costing me?'

'So far, nothing. But will it be a problem if we do have to pay them?'

'As I told you, Mr Dąbrowski. To find Catriona, money isn't an issue.'

'Great. I'll send the photo of Marko. Erm . . .' He swallowed. 'Would you be able to settle the invoice I sent yesterday?'

Robertson spoke to someone else, then came back on. 'You'll get it in Bitcoin, as before. And Mr Dąbrowski?'

'Yes?'

'If you're stiffing me, you'll regret it. Not for long, but you *will* regret it. Goodbye, Mr Dąbrowski.'

With trembling fingers, Kasper sent the images of Marko Novak. Sweat drenched his back and neck, and he took deep breaths.

Archie Robertson ended the call with the detective, shut down his burner phone and placed it on the leather-topped desk. The smell of the peat fire mingled with the odour of cigars which infused his study. He glanced at Hamish huddled in his wheelchair beside the granite fireplace, the orange flames reflecting off his glasses.

'You sure it's a good idea to trust this Kasper guy, Dad?'

Hamish's voice still sounded shaky, like an invalid's, which, Archie had to admit, is what he now was. 'He's just finding a missing person for me. My beloved daughter-in-law.'

'*We* should be looking for her. What if he talks?'

'First of all' – Archie counted off on stubby fingers – 'he's too scared of what could happen if he crosses me. Manchester's a long way from Aberdeen, but not far enough to escape my reach. And second – what's he going to say?'

'I still don't like it. We should use our own guys.'

Archie's anger at being defied passed in an instant. At least the boy's spirit remained unbroken, unlike his body. 'None of them know the city and their idea of investigating is to beat information out of people. How long before the locals, especially you-know-who, realise they're down there? It could get very messy.'

'I'm still not happy.'

'Well, we sometimes have to put up with what we don't like.'

He got up, walked to the mahogany sideboard and poured himself a generous measure of thirty-one-year-old Aberlour from the decanter. Hamish was probably right. This Kasper could be a loose end. He'd decide what to do with him once they'd done the job.

CHAPTER 15

After being collared by a Jehovah's Witness at one of the flats, I managed to extricate myself. But not before I'd taken a handful of her leaflets and two copies of *The Watchtower*.

In my eagerness to escape, I ignored the last flat on the seventh and rushed out onto the landing, expecting to find an impatient Zofia.

Five minutes later, guessing she'd been ensnared by a similar resident, I took the stairs up to the eighth floor to help free her. Voices came from the corridor. I was right – unless Zofia had found someone with information. Best not barge in. I listened, but it didn't sound like a civilised conversation. More like a dispute between neighbours. I pushed through the fire doors and saw the backs of two large men. Facing them, her back to a closed door, a terrified-looking Zofia.

My mind went blank, and I wanted to run. She saw me and hope flared in her eyes. The bald thug from the brothel turned to follow her gaze. Zofia's expression gave me courage and my brain worked at speed.

'There you are, my dear. It's the floor *below*.' I smiled and walked towards them, holding the leaflets in front of me, like a shield. 'She's always doing this, going to the wrong address.' I forced a laugh. 'It's not as if we get invited into many people's homes. You'd think she'd remember, wouldn't you?'

Both men now stared at me, suspicion and aggression wafting off them.

'Have *you* gentlemen found God?' I brandished the leaflets and held out the copies of *The Watchtower*. 'We're supposed to be delivering these to a lovely couple downstairs, but do you want a copy? I've got plenty down in the car.'

Expressions of horror had replaced the aggression. 'Err, no,' said the bald one. 'Thanks.'

'Are you sure?' I stepped towards them.

'Come on, Balthazar, don't bother these men.' Zofia stepped through the gap between them and took my arm.

'Okay, dear.' I resisted the urge to run, and even gave the men a wave as we passed through the fire door.

Zofia led me to the lift and hit the call button. The lights above the lift car showed it on this floor, and we waited for the doors to open. My senses stretched taut as I listened for sounds of the men following. We should have taken the stairs, but I doubt I'd have made more than a couple of floors before collapsing. The doors opened, and I staggered into the car and stood, trembling. Zofia released my arm and punched the button to close the door and another to take us to the ground floor.

We exchanged a glance as the lift began its descent, but didn't relax. What would happen if they followed us and pressed the button? The ammonia smell penetrated through my fear. We got out at ground floor, and strode out of the building, almost running. The youths outside had gone, probably scared off by the thugs, whose SUV blocked the entrance to the car park.

Zofia unlocked her car and got the engine running before I jumped in. Oscar barked and stuck his head between the front seats. I let him lick my hand as Zofia engaged gear. She left rubber on the pavement and took the first bend on two wheels. We hit the straight of the main road and exchanged a look.

Our laughter burst out simultaneously. Oscar let out an excited yap and stood on the back seat.

'Balthazar?' I snorted.

Zofia raised her eyebrows. 'At least I came up with a name.'

'Yeah, I didn't think I'd be able to speak.'

'Well, you did brilliantly. Well done.'

I basked in her praise and was still buzzing when we pulled into the car park behind their offices ten minutes later.

Kasper greeted us with a scowl. 'You seem pleased with yourselves.'

'We've just had a bit of a scare.' She told him of our encounter while I sorted out a bowl of water for Oscar.

'I told you it was a stupid idea. Anything could have happened.'

'Well, it didn't, thanks to Victor.'

Kasper gave me a grudging nod. 'What about the woman?'

'Jehona?' Zofia's defiance deflated. 'Her friends seemed terrified, and I think something's happened to her.'

She told us how the other women had reacted, and I felt someone walking on my grave.

'I warned you, Zofia. Why do you have to stick your nose—'

'It's not her fault,' I said. 'If anything's happened to Jehona, it's due to those thugs. We just met her for a coffee.'

Kasper looked at his sister accusingly. 'Didn't you tell him?'

Zofia gave an embarrassed smile. 'I met her on Saturday and took her home. That's how I knew where she lives.' Her head dropped. 'I think the bald guy saw her in my car.'

'Yes, but . . .' I fumbled for something to say to comfort her. 'You could have been anyone. A stranger giving her a lift . . .'

'A stranger who just so happened to be outside her flat a few days later?' Kasper seemed determined to upset his sister.

'But if he'd seen Zofia in the car, why didn't he say anything to her today?'

'Did he?'

We both looked at her.

'No, they just asked me what I was doing there. Before I could think of an answer, Victor arrived. Anyway, I don't think they saw me on Saturday. I was on the other side of the car.'

'They'd have seen the car again.'

'I parked behind some bins.'

I'd wondered why she'd done that. 'Does it matter?' I asked. 'If anything's happened to her, it's not because we went there today. And if they saw her in Zofia's car on Saturday, why would they assume there was anything untoward?'

'Maybe she found someone else to help her.' A note of hope entered Zofia's voice.

'You seriously believe that?' Kasper's voice dripped contempt.

'Believe what?' What was he talking about?

'She asked my sister to help her get away. But I doubt she'd have found anyone between Saturday and today.'

Zofia said nothing, but obviously agreed with him.

My mind worked fast. 'If she asked Zofia, she might have asked someone else a while ago and they finally decided to help. Either they helped her, or the fact she was asking got back to her employers. You can't blame your sister.'

'What about you? If the thugs saw you today, they'll recognise you. How can you do your job?'

'I wore a hat and glasses, and I was waving those leaflets in front of my face. I'm sure they won't recognise me.' Was I right? Maybe I should change my appearance.

Kasper's belligerence drained away, replaced by a worried frown. 'Yeah, well, what's happened to Jehona isn't *our* problem.'

'Kasper?' his sister asked sharply.

'I, um . . . I spoke to Mr Robertson, and he's agreed to pay an interim balance.' He kept his gaze on his busy hands.

'Okay,' she said. 'But there's something else. I know you too well.'

'Yeah.' He unlocked his phone and handed it to her. I peered over her shoulder at a message.

> I've paid your money. You have one more week and if you don't find her, we'll be wanting a refund. In full.

The colour drained from Zofia's face. They both looked terrified. Who the hell *was* this client of theirs?

CHAPTER 16

Zofia spent the next morning in the office, following up proposals they'd sent to potential clients. The message from Robertson had concentrated their minds. By lunchtime, she'd had enough and rang Kasper, who'd gone to meet a contact to find out who paid the council tax on the flat Jehona occupied. 'How did you get on?'

'Not great. It's under the name of Jehona Sorokin.'

'So, a dead end?' But she could tell from his tone there was something else.

'Not exactly. It's owned by a company, KND Holdings. They own eleven properties in the city. I'm going to check them. It's possible Catriona is in one of them.'

'Okay, do you want me to check some of them?' She could do with getting some fresh air, get away from the stench of burnt cooking oil.

'No need. They're close together, I should manage.'

She ended the call and sat at her desk, thinking about Jehona. They'd jumped to the conclusion something had happened to her, but maybe she'd been on a job. Neither of her flatmates had said anything about her. One seemed upset, but she could have just been frightened that Zofia's visit would get her in trouble. It wouldn't hurt to check again. She should discuss it with Kasper, but he'd talk her out of it.

She rang Victor. 'Have you seen the SUV from yesterday?' She recited the reg.

'It's here now, outside the club. They brought Jehona's flatmates and parked up. Why?'

'How did they seem?'

'Now you mention it, they looked quite upset.'

'Did they?' That decided it. She would go. 'Keep an eye on them and let me know if they move.'

'Sure. Do you want me to do anything else?'

She would have preferred him along, but he'd be better monitoring them. Her email pinged, and ending her call, she checked it. It came from one of the companies she'd contacted. Their CEO was in LA, but he wanted to speak to them at two, LA time. Zofia did a quick calculation. It would be 10 p.m. here. She accepted, texted Kasper and left the office.

She should go home and get a few hours' sleep, but she needed to know Jehona's fate. She parked behind the bins again, made her way to the main entrance, let herself in and called the lift for the even floors.

As it clanked down, she studied the dismal foyer. It looked like nobody had cleaned it for a decade. The lift arrived. A faint smell of bleach told of the attempt to remove yesterday's vomit. The juddering box stopped on the eighth floor and the doors slid open. She checked the landing before stepping out and striding to flat eighty-three. She banged on the door, and it swung open under her fist.

'Hello, Jehona?' She pushed the door open. 'Are you in?'

The silence echoed. On the floor above, a baby cried. She retrieved a pair of gloves from her handbag. Under it lay the canister of Mace Kasper gave her for Christmas. She put it in her jacket pocket and zipped up her bag. Dismissing her fears, she stepped into a narrow hall, her nerves stretched tight as she imagined meeting the thugs she'd encountered on her last visit.

The stench of bleach fought for supremacy with stale food and cheap perfume. She pushed open the first door, a cramped bathroom with an avocado suite. Next, a small room three metres square. Although empty apart from two wire coat hangers, she guessed it was a bedroom.

She finished checking the flat. Someone had stripped every room. Not one stick of furniture or piece of carpet remained. They'd even taken the lightbulbs.

The stink of bleach pervaded every room as if someone had poured it on the floors. She shuddered. This felt very wrong. What had happened in here? The only room not bare was the kitchen, where units with wonky doors sat below and above a scarred worktop. A stainless-steel sink, half misnamed, sat under the window, to the left of a cooker which wore the evidence of the most recent meals cooked on it.

She opened the nearest cupboard. Empty, but with the imprint of tin cans outlined in a sticky brown liquid on the shelf. She pulled the drawer above it out and placed it upside down on the work surface. She didn't know what she was searching for, but she'd seen it done in a film. The other drawer provided a surprise and exactly what she *was* looking for. A brown envelope taped to the base.

Zofia opened it and extracted a sheet of paper. She spread it out and studied it. A handwritten sentence, not in English, preceded a table with three columns, and the same person had written a shorter note alongside the table. The numbers in the first resembled dates, the centre one contained women's names. She recognised Jehona, but not the three others. They must have been the women she shared the flat with, but she'd only seen two.

The third column contained addresses, and two kept appearing. Vale Park Way and Dallimore Road. The first address sounded familiar, and a check on her phone confirmed it was where Kasper had placed his camera. A frisson of excitement surged through her.

She photographed the sheet and returned it to the envelope before replacing the two drawers.

After a last check around, she let herself out and pulled the door shut behind her until the lock engaged. If they'd left any other evidence for the police to find, she didn't want squatters or those lads she'd seen yesterday destroying it. She took the lift down and as she walked to the entrance, something she'd noticed earlier nagged at her.

The top corners of the walls of the lobby were, like the rest of it, filthy, except for one. She examined it and shone her torch into it. There, in the junction between the wall and ceiling, she noticed a dark object the size of a screwhead. She shone her light into it and a faint glint told her what it was.

A check of the cable on the far side of the wall told her it must come from the first floor. Energised by her discovery, she ran up the stairs to the flat immediately above the camera lens. The bell sounded in the flat, but nobody answered. She lifted the letter flap and listened. The odour of toast and the sound of a kettle boiling told her someone was home.

'Hello?'

No answer.

'I'm investigating a woman's disappearance, and I need your help.'

After a few seconds, steps approached, and she straightened.

'How do I know you're police?' The door muffled the man's voice.

'I'm not. I'm a private detective. Do you want to see my ID card?'

'I'm going to use the chain. You can show it in the opening.' Metalwork clanked behind the door, and it opened a fraction.

Zofia held her ID in front of her and stood in the gap.

A young man with long hair and a neat beard peered at her. He scrutinised both her and the photo before nodding and freeing the door of the chain. 'Who's gone missing?'

'A young woman called Jehona. She lives in one of the flats upstairs.'

'Come in.' He led her into a neat living room infused with the odour of incense. A pair of green settees faced each other across a dark-wood and glass coffee table. Zofia sat on one sofa, and he sat opposite. 'So, this Jehona, what does she look like?'

She opened her phone and passed it to him.

He leant forward, so his hair formed a curtain between them. 'Oh, yeah. I saw her a few times, with the others.'

'When did you last see her?'

He shrugged. 'Saturday or Sunday.'

'Do you record the stuff from your camera?'

He glanced at the sideboard, and the curtain of hair swept across his face. 'It's on my laptop.'

'Can I see the footage from the weekend?'

He swept his fringe away and got up, returning with a slimline laptop, which he placed on the coffee table. He powered it up and rotated it so they could both see the screen. 'From when?'

She'd dropped Jehona off before the match finished. 'Four thirty on the Saturday.'

He opened a folder with dozens of sub-folders, each with a date underneath. He opened the second one from the end, and he double clicked on one of the two files in it.

'It's motion-activated, so only records if there's someone there.'

The screen showed the gloomy entrance to the block and a woman with a pram and a toddler struggling to get in. The image flickered as he fast-forwarded, and a succession of figures appeared. Then he slowed it to normal speed.

'Stop it there.' Zofia leant forward. 'Can you freeze it?'

The still image of Jehona, her two friends and the two thugs she'd seen on her last visit flickered. She appeared to be arguing with the bald guy. He played it on. The heavies left with the two friends, then

Jehona rushed after them. They came back in the early hours of Sunday morning, but she didn't leave with them on the Sunday afternoon.

They found her at two fifty-eight on the Monday morning, escorted by the two heavies after they'd brought the other two home. One of them held her arm, as if scared she'd run, but she looked defeated.

Zofia studied the image. 'A shame we can't see their faces or their car.'

'I've got another one, covering the car park.' He opened the other file in the folder and found the footage of the thugs arriving in a dark SUV. It resembled the one she'd seen here the day Jehona got spooked. The image jumped to them leaving, one holding Jehona by the arm. They'd parked under a light, and before she got in, Jehona gazed back at the building wearing a sad expression.

Zofia took a deep breath and blinked. 'Could I have the footage?'

'I'll put them on a stick for you.'

'Great.' As she waited, she had an idea. 'Can you check today's footage?'

'Yeah, okay.' He plugged the memory stick in and checked it before saving the two files, then opened the latest.

The two heavies arrived around eleven and picked up the women, who each wheeled a case behind them. As they got to the car park, a removal van and three men arrived. They took keys off one of the heavies and came into the building. They emptied the flat within two hours and set off. Zofia made a note of the name on the side of the van and its registration number.

She thanked the young man and left, her mind in turmoil. The heavies had removed Jehona after she'd met Zofia. It didn't appear they were taking her to a luxury hotel. Had it been Zofia's fault?

CHAPTER 17

I spent the afternoon at my post, keeping a watch on the pink door. My thoughts returned to what I'd learned or surmised. Robertson, our employer, wasn't someone you dared disappoint. I assumed he knew nothing about me. I couldn't imagine Kasper trumpeting the fact they employed a homeless person at less than minimum wage, but Robertson could be bad news for the siblings. I felt a responsibility to make sure they didn't fall foul of him. Jehona's disappearance was another problem. I agreed with Kasper. It seemed unlikely she'd found someone to help her escape.

Oscar lay alongside me on my mat. 'What do you think, boy?' I talked over my concerns.

You seem to have wandered into a heap of trouble you don't need. Why don't you walk away?

'I can't. I don't want to let Kasper and Zofia down.'

I don't know why. Kasper barely tolerates you. I know he helped you out when you got beaten up, but you don't owe him anything.

'It's not just Kasper, is it?'

I know, she's nice, but is it worth this trouble?

I hated the thought of letting Zofia down. 'We need the money.'

What good has it done us? Look at the state of my pelt.

'I'm saving the money to get a place to live—'

He wagged his tail. ***We're getting a new home? When?***

'I need to save enough—'

My phone buzzed, ending the conversation. I checked the call.

'Helen?' My throat thickened. Although we exchanged messages every week, I'd only spoken to her once since I'd become homeless. Lying by text was much easier.

'Hello, Dad.'

The sound of her voice melted the months since we'd spoken. Oscar, sitting alongside me, stood and barked.

'Is that Oscar?'

'He's just here.' I stroked his ears as he nuzzled against me.

'Hello, Oscar.'

I held the handset to his ear, and he barked.

'Oh, Oscar, I've missed you. Has Daddy taken you to the park?'

I looked around, bins behind me and an expanse of rubbish-strewn concrete in front. 'Yeah, something like that. Anyway, how are you doing? Is everything okay?'

'No.' Her voice wavered. 'Dad, Mum's got . . .' She dissolved into a sob.

I could guess the rest, something I'd dreaded since I'd been forced to leave home. 'Helen, please talk to me, love.'

She sniffed and inhaled. 'Sorry, Dad. I swore I wouldn't do this.' She took a few more breaths to compose herself. 'Mum's got a boyfriend. We met him last night.'

Even though I'd already guessed, hearing Helen say it stunned me. I forced myself to speak. 'Is he nice?'

'He's okay, I suppose. A bit of a drip. He took us for a curry last night—'

'To Saleem's?' I pictured the restaurant, and my mouth watered.

'Yeah, Saleem asked about you, and Mum went bright red. It was quite funny. Anyway, the drip ordered a korma.'

'Well, not everyone likes hot food.'

'Yeah, I know, Mum ordered her usual lamb chops and chips, lame. But he started sweating when he ate his korma, using the napkin to mop his brow. It was so embarrassing, Dad. I'd have liked to see him eat one of your vindaloos.'

'Yeah, that would have been funny.' I stroked Oscar, feeling suddenly distant from my daughter. Would she and 'the drip' be laughing about this meal once he got to know her? 'So, how many times have they been out?'

'Not many, I don't think. Mum's pretending he's just someone she works with, but we've not been out with any of her other colleagues.'

He knew Carol wouldn't introduce the girls to anyone unless she was serious. The knowledge hit me like a punch.

'Daaad?'

'Yeah, darling?' She was going to ask me for a favour.

'Can I come and stay with you?'

My eyes stung. 'I'd love that, but I haven't got the room.'

'I can sleep on the sofa. Only for a few days.'

'What about school?'

'It's almost half term. Please, Dad. Mum's doing my head in, so's Em. I just need to get away.'

I fought to hold back my tears. 'Okay, I'll talk to your mum about it.'

Carol wouldn't let her come unless she'd inspected the accommodation, and that would never happen. Feeling cowardly for passing the buck, I ended the call. I dried my eyes, placed my phone on the floor and put my arm across Oscar's back, enjoying the comfort of his warm body against mine. I glanced across towards the pink door. A black SUV stood outside, and the driver got out to open the back door.

A woman exited, tall and confident, her body language unlike that of the others who worked there, and even I recognised she wore expensive designer clothes. She stared straight at me and Oscar. With a shock, I recognised her. I needed my phone. I found it but couldn't take a picture until she looked away.

Oscar got up and trotted toward her.

'Oscar, come back.'

He ignored me. When he got within a few paces, she bent down and beckoned him. He stopped, barked and sniffed the air. She beckoned again, and he trotted back to me. She straightened, spun on her heel and entered the pink door.

'Shit! What were you playing at?'

That's her, isn't it?

'Yes, but what were you doing?'

Did you take a picture?

'I couldn't. She was looking at me.'

You could have pretended to take a picture of me.

I hadn't thought of that, so I lied. It's embarrassing when your dog is a better detective than you. 'I would have, if you'd gone up to her. Why did you stop?'

Something about her I didn't like. He sat next to me.

The car drove off, and I wondered about her status. It wasn't just her manner and the expensive clothes. The driver deferred to her. Apart from the one I saw the night I met Kasper, I'd not seen them mistreat the women who worked there, but you could tell the men who delivered them were in charge. In this case, he seemed more like her chauffeur. I'd have to ask Kasper about why that might be. But first I had to get her photo.

I waited as darkness fell and the temperature dropped. Without taking my attention off the door, I retrieved another layer of clothes. Oscar grew impatient, eager for his evening walk, but I couldn't risk missing her again. Just past seven, the car returned. I noted the registration and took a couple of snaps. The pink door opened, and I prepared to take a picture. A man I recognised as

Marko Novak came out, Catriona Robertson behind him. I took a few pictures, but she stayed behind him until he helped her into the back of the car. He exchanged a few words with the driver and then returned inside.

I watched the car leave. 'Well, Oscar, that was a cock-up.'

I know, but don't worry, I know where she lives.

'What? Where?' Was he lying to make me feel better?

When I say I know where she lives, I mean you've taken me past it. Sometime, but I'm not sure when. I'll find it.

Did I believe him? 'Okay, boy.' I ruffled his ears and stood. 'Time for a walk.'

I stood, packed up my pitch, put it away and put a change of clothing in my backpack. Oscar grew excited when I clipped his lead on, and we walked up past the art gallery and the central library onto Deansgate. Once we'd crossed it, we wandered towards St John's Gardens, a forest of glass tower blocks and cranes in the distance ahead of us. I let Oscar wander round the deserted gardens, sat on one of the benches and rang Kasper to tell him I'd seen Catriona. The voicemail kicked in straight away, so I left him a message to call me. Although excited to tell him, I suspected he'd yell at me for not getting a clear picture.

Oscar finished and, bagging up his business, I binned it, and we walked down towards the bottom end of Deansgate. Light spilled out of the open doorway of the community centre, where I planned to get a hot meal and shower. A hubbub of voices greeted me as I walked into the main hall. The aroma of hotpot told me what was on the menu. After my conversation with Helen, I'd hoped it would be a delicious curry, courtesy of the local Sikh community, but as they say about beggars . . .

'Oscar, how are you doing, boy?' The shout came from Digger, a larger-than-life character helping to serve the food. He abandoned his ladle, ignoring the protests from the queue, and came round the counter to make a fuss of Oscar. 'What's the matter, boy? Isn't he feeding you?'

Oscar greeted him like a long-lost brother.

Digger returned behind the counter and fetched a bowl into which he ladled some hotpot. 'Let it cool down,' he instructed Oscar.

'Digger, don't—' Too late. He placed the bowl on the floor and Oscar yelped as he burnt his mouth.

He regarded me accusingly, as if I'd been responsible.

'You got a bowl of water?'

'Sorry, Victor. I warned him.' He gave a sheepish smile and fetched the water.

'He's a dog, Digger. They don't have self-control.'

Yes, we do. Oscar gulped another mouthful of food and spat it out.

A cry came from the growing queue. 'Come on, Digger, what about *our* food? Sod the dog.'

'An' wash yer 'ands, before you serve me, you dirty booger.' The complainant didn't look like he'd seen soap and water this year.

By the time I got my food, Oscar had recovered and emptied his bowl. I finished eating and got a key for the showers. I stepped under the stream of hot water and scrubbed myself clean before changing into my less dirty clothes. I urgently needed to visit the charity shop where I got my clothes washed.

After a last cup of sweet tea and biscuits, Oscar and I set off. I'd trained myself to only worry about the necessities. Food, where to sleep and keeping warm. Any thoughts of my future led to sleepless nights and depression. After that call, my mind strayed to thoughts of my family. I *would* get off the streets, and the money I earned now would be my route out.

That brought me back to my encounter with Brother John. If some people thought I had money, I would become a target. Should I ask John not to say anything? Or would he be insulted and even more likely to share what he'd discovered? The problem was, I didn't know him well enough to predict how he'd react. He'd probably want to know where I'd got the money from. The slip had stated how much I'd paid in.

The buzzing of the phone interrupted my reverie. Kasper. How had he got this number? Then I remembered I'd forgotten to screen my number when I'd called him earlier. He must have received my message. We'd returned to Sackville Square, so I unclipped Oscar and answered. 'Yeah?'

'What did you want?'

I checked for eavesdroppers. 'I saw Catriona Robertson.'

'You did? Brilliant. Send me the pictures.'

'Okay . . . but they're not great.' I explained what had happened.

'Why was she staring at you? You told me you're invisible.'

'Look, I've identified the car, and it's definitely her. It gives you something to tell her family.'

Kasper hesitated for a few seconds. 'Yeah, okay. Good work. I've got another job for you. Can you get over to Hazelbottom Road and—'

'I thought you'd sorted the battery out.'

'I did, but it's stopped transmitting again. Can you go down and check it?'

'Do you know what the time is? It's gone nine.'

'Yes, and we're still in the office. Did you have somewhere else you needed to be?'

'No, but . . .' *But you're not getting paid below minimum wage to be at someone's beck and call.*

'Do you want me to send the postcode?'

'No need.' This would have been a good time to take Oscar's advice and walk away.

CHAPTER 18

Kasper had returned to the office having visited and photographed each of the eleven addresses KND Holdings owned. Four had families living in them, toys and bikes strewn in their untidy gardens, and two seemed to contain students. The other five looked empty.

He unlocked the offices, wondering where Zofia was, but guessed she'd gone home before coming back for the late-night meeting. He should have done the same.

Why the hell did this guy in LA want to speak to them so late at night? Probably to show off his jet-set lifestyle. Kasper had carried out some background on the guy and wasn't impressed.

He opened his desktop and made notes on his visit to the KND properties while uploading the images. He wasn't sure he'd achieved much, but you could never tell in this job. He then checked the photos Victor had sent and, as he feared, they were useless. He was still annoyed at his reluctance to go and change the batteries.

The front door camera beeped, and he saw his sister. She didn't look happy. He waited for her to come upstairs.

'You okay, sis?'

'Not really.' She put her bag down and took her coat off, removing a canister of Mace from the pocket.

He pointed at the can. 'Did someone attack you?'

'Oh, this. No.' She retrieved a memory stick and plugged it into her machine. 'Something's happened to Jehona.'

'How do you know?' Even before he asked, he'd guessed where she'd been. 'You've been back, haven't you?'

Her cheeks reddened. 'They've moved out and stripped the flat.' She opened a file on the memory stick. 'Look, they took her at about three on Monday morning.'

Kasper watched the footage. 'They could have been taking her to a job.'

'Yeah, right. An execution, more like.'

'Where did you get this?'

'A guy in one of the flats.' The fingers of her left hand drummed on the desk. 'I think we should tell the police. The flat stinks of bleach—'

'You went inside?'

'They'd left the door open.'

'Of course they had.'

'Yes, they honestly had. And before you ask, yes, I wore gloves. I found this hidden under a drawer.'

'Of course you did.' Kasper studied the image on her phone. 'It looks Romanian.' He took it to his desk and opened a translation site, and punched in the first sentence. 'It says, "This is where they took us to see special clients." That's probably where Jehona is.'

'What does the second sentence say?'

He typed in the words. 'It says, "They did not come back."'

'Let's check the dates.' One of the women left three weeks ago, and didn't return. The second, someone called Alina, went a week ago and the third was Jehona. She left two days ago, on the Monday.

They stared at each other. The dread gripping Kasper reflected in his sister.

'We should go to the police.' All colour had leached out of Zofia's face.

'And say what? We'd have to explain how you came by this—'

'I found it in an unlocked, empty flat.'

'Taped under a drawer? You think they'll believe you?'

'That's the truth, Kasper. Anyway, I've left it there.'

'Second, remember Robertson's instruction. No police.'

'But if women have gone missing?'

'Nobody's reported them, so they've probably moved. The Novaks have lots of places.' Kasper wasn't sure whether he believed it.

They agreed to send the police an anonymous tip as soon as they found Catriona.

'Have we heard from Victor today?' Zofia said.

'Yeah, I forgot. He said he saw Catriona but couldn't get a photo because she was looking at him. He's bloody useless.'

'What was he supposed to do?' Predictably, Zofia defended him.

'He's *supposed* to be invisible, which is why we employed him. He must have done something to be noticed.'

'Shall we look at the pictures?'

Kasper brought the attachments up on the screen. Zofia leant across to see.

'Is that the younger Novak?'

'Marko, yeah. And Victor claims that's Catriona.' He pointed at the figure hidden by the man's bulk.

Zofia peered at the image. 'It could be. Did he send any more?'

'Yeah.' Kasper opened the others, but none showed a clear picture of the woman.

'I'll check on the car, see who it's registered to.' She made a note of the number. 'Do you know if Victor is still at Sackville Square?'

'He should be on his way to Vale Park. The camera died again. But he made a big fuss about it.'

'I'm not surprised. Have you seen the time?'

'*We're* still at work.'

'Only because we've got a conference call booked at ten. Why don't you ring and tell him to be careful? That's where they took Jehona.'

'We're not 100 per cent sure of that, and he's not going inside. He's just changing a battery.'

'Yes, okay.' She checked the time. 'We'd better get ready for our meeting.'

Despite their preparation, it became quickly obvious the potential customer wasn't seriously interested in hiring them. It took all of Kasper's self-control to continue the pretence that he was. They finished the call and sat in silence, a cloud of disappointment enveloping them.

'I should have told him where to get off and ended the call.' Kasper couldn't keep the bitterness out of his voice.

'I'm glad you didn't. That *would* have damaged our reputation.' Zofia moved across to her desk and punched some keys. 'I'm going to get off home.'

'I'll just check if Victor's sorted out the camera.' He logged into the app and brought up the view through the lens. Inky blackness. 'What the hell's he doing?'

'Maybe he's waiting until everyone's gone home.'

Kasper checked the time. 'It's gone eleven. There's no way they'd still be there.'

'If there's someone at the Novaks' unit, he might be waiting for them to go.'

'Or he's fallen asleep, or even not gone.'

Zofia closed her desktop. 'Right, I'm off. You coming?'

'I'm going to ring him.' He picked up his mobile.

'If he's trying to be inconspicuous, his phone going off won't help.'

He placed the handset on the desk.

Zofia put her coat on and waited by the door. 'Well?'

He doubted he'd be able to get to sleep for a while. 'I'll do a bit of paperwork. See you later.'

'Okay, and don't be harassing Victor. He'll ring when he's ready.'

Why is she so protective of him?

Zofia left, and after draining his coffee, he spent an hour composing a message to Robertson, starting it four times before deciding on the wording. He sent it and picked up the phone.

CHAPTER 19

As I ended the call where Kasper told me to check the camera, the phone beeped, warning me it was about to die. The battery on each phone lasted a day or so, and I'd still not sorted out a new place to charge them. I sent the pictures with the last of the juice and swopped phones over. The one Kasper gave me was also almost dead. I checked it. Eleven per cent, better than zero.

Oscar had retreated to his crate.

'We've got a job on the other side of town. You coming?'

He looked at me as if I'd made an indecent proposition, but a treat persuaded him to come with me.

We set off for Hazelbottom Road. I wasn't sure where it was, but had a rough idea. I visited a corner shop and used some of the money I'd collected today to buy batteries for the camera and asked the owner for directions. Eventually, we arrived at our destination. I recognised the unit from the images on Kasper's computer. Opposite stood the building where he'd attached the camera.

At this time, few buildings on the estate showed lights. I checked the buildings I passed, and none showed security cameras. Wasn't that odd? Although invisible in the city centre and around shops, round here I stood out, and felt very exposed. Right on cue, a van with black writing on the side and a logo of a shield on the door pulled up alongside. A uniformed figure with a bushy beard got out. 'This is private property. You're trespassing.'

Oscar growled at him.

He pointed at Oscar. 'Is that your dog?'

'No, it's my son transformed into a dog by an evil witch.'

'You what?'

A second figure came out of the van and lurked behind me. Thinner than Beardy, he wore his blond hair long and sported an ill-judged moustache. 'Looks like a pedigree,' he said. 'Have you nicked it?'

My pulse raced, but irritation overcame my nervousness. 'No, I haven't. Now bugger off and leave me alone.'

'You're on private property.' Beardy jabbed a finger at me.

Oscar growled again and bared his teeth. Beardy stepped back.

I checked for a sign denoting the status of the road. 'I'm on the road, which is public property.'

The other one shone a bright torch into my face.

I stepped away from him and lifted a hand to shield my eyes. 'Turn your bloody torch off.'

Ignoring Oscar's threat, he stepped closer. 'What have you got to hide?'

'Nothing. I just don't like pricks in uniform shining lights in my face.'

The two figures bristled. *Why the hell did I say that?*

'I asked what you're doing here?'

'None of your business.'

Two workmen in overalls and carrying backpacks strolled past on the opposite side of the road, looking our way.

'We're paid to make it our business. Now sling your hook.' The second security guard reached out and grabbed my upraised wrist.

'OI! Let go, that's assault.'

At the same moment, Oscar upped the ante and lunged at him, teeth snapping. The security guard released me and leapt back, producing an extendable cosh, which he raised.

'Leave my dog alone.' I tugged on the lead. Oscar didn't resist and let me pull him behind me.

The workmen had paused and were studying us. The moustachioed security guard lowered the cosh, his face thunderous.

'Come on, Ox, let's leave this stinking tramp.'

Beardy paused, then returned to the van.

'We see you round here again, Stinky,' his companion said in a low voice, 'and we'll show you and the smelly mutt what assault is.' He stepped away. 'Have a good evening, sir.' He gave an ironic salute with the cosh and got into the van, which roared away.

Show over, the workmen continued on their way.

Once my legs stopped trembling, I bent down and patted Oscar. 'Well done, boy.'

He looked pleased with himself and stared at the pocket where I stored his treats. I agreed he deserved another and unwrapped one while walking to the main road. I almost gave in to the temptation to return to the city centre and tell Kasper to do it himself, then reminded myself this was my opportunity to get myself off the streets and I couldn't afford to piss Kasper off.

We'd wandered around for some while when Oscar, fed up, sat on the pavement. ***Right, what are we doing?***

I checked the time. Surely, they'd have gone by now. 'We're going back.'

As we got closer, I kept an eye out for the van and even Oscar seemed nervous. The estate seemed deserted. As casually as I could, I strolled towards the units I wanted. The building housing the camera looked empty, no light escaping from any opening. The one opposite, Kasper's target, was the only one showing lights. Thin blades of it reached out at the bottom and sides of a large roller-shutter in the side wall. A flash sports car sat in the yard.

I approached the building where Kasper had hidden the camera. He said he'd wedged it under the eaves. A hedge a metre high screened the front half of the building. I shuffled forward in the gloom, not wanting to use the torch on my phone. Apart from saving the battery, I didn't want to attract attention. Something crunched underfoot, and I stepped back. Oscar picked it up.

He let me take it from his mouth. A chunk of plastic. I risked putting on the light. The camera lay in pieces on the flagged path which encircled the building. Someone had done a good job of mashing it underfoot.

I picked up the biggest piece and put it in my pocket. Vandals? Or had Kasper's targets found it and got rid of it? The hair on my neck prickled, casting its vote, and I scanned my surroundings. Were they watching me now? I didn't see anyone, but my unease didn't lessen. Oscar stood with tail and ears erect.

'What is it, boy?'

He kept his attention on the target building. A clattering made my pulse spike. The shutter lifted and light flooded out of the opening. I pulled Oscar with me and ducked behind the hedge. Peering through it, I watched two men wait for it to rise. Both wore black puffa jackets and gloves. One headed for the gate. He looked very much like the shaven-headed thug who'd confronted Zofia at the flat.

'Don't move, Oscar,' I whispered and placed a hand on his back.

His body trembled.

'Good boy.' I patted his head, then took several pictures through the greenery, but suspected they wouldn't show much.

As the thug opened the gate, an engine roared into life and a dark SUV rolled out of the building. It resembled the one I'd seen earlier. I took pictures, but the heavy tint on the windows made seeing the passengers difficult. I made out two figures, one large and the other smaller. As the car pulled out onto the road and roared off away from me, the two men stepped back into the building and returned, each dragging a heavy-looking blue wheelie bin.

They wheeled them to the corner of the building, put the lights out, locked up and eased the car out of the yard. Mindful of Kasper's admonishment, I took a picture, getting the number plate in focus. They closed the gates and secured them with a long chain before racing off, accompanied by loud, bass-heavy music from the car stereo. I waited until the throaty sound of the exhaust faded, then looked around.

Over the new few minutes, the odd car passed on the main road, but nothing nearer moved.

'You've got much better hearing. Can you hear anyone?'

Oscar glanced at me, and I took his silence as a negative. We edged out onto the strip of tarmac, illuminated by a streetlamp thirty paces away. Although they'd locked the gate, the chain enabled me and then Oscar to slip through. We ran into the shadows cast by the building. Without the illumination from the building, the yard surrounding the unit looked black.

Oscar stood and stared into the darkness.

'Come on, boy.' I shuffled towards where they'd abandoned the bins.

I grabbed the handle of the nearest one and tugged. Whatever it contained weighed a ton. Oscar whined. I lifted the lid and peered in. My phone's torch gave enough light to show the bundle of cardboard on the top. I lifted it off and exposed a green plastic sheet. My stomach lurched, and I wanted to go, but I pulled the sheet back. Oscar made a sound like a squeaky gate, stood on his hind legs, placed his snout on the edge of the bin and peered inside with me.

Dark red blotches marked the underside of the plastic. Oscar's agitation increased. I peeled more away, exposing dark hair matted with blood. Acid burnt my throat, but I held the vomit down. Heart hammering, I used a piece of the cardboard to lift the hair. A pale forehead, a bloody dent on one side, shone in the dim light, then a blue eye opened. With a cry, I dropped my phone.

CHAPTER 20

Once I'd recovered from the shock, I reached inside the bin for my phone, my head turned away to avoid looking at her. Pulse surging in my ears, I groped blindly and found it jammed halfway down, between her torso and the side of the bin. My shaking hand grabbed it and, with it, something soft and yielding. I dragged it and the phone out, trying to avoid touching the woman. I examined what I'd recovered. In the light from my phone, it looked like a plastic bag.

I shoved it in my pocket and looked again at the woman. The already feeble light from my phone had faded to almost nothing but I could see she'd closed her eye. Had I imagined it opening?

I should check the other bin. But before I could, Oscar barked a warning, and a vehicle approached. I switched the light off, pulled Oscar to me and crouched down behind the bin.

The vehicle appeared round the bend. The van containing the two uniformed thugs. I gulped and searched for somewhere better to hide.

A more intense darkness at the edge of the building suggested an alleyway. I stayed where we were, though, and watched the van pull up at the gates. A door opened and one thug got out, walked to the gate and fiddled with the chain.

They were coming here. Panic suffused me. They must have come back for the bins.

I couldn't leave the woman.

Hoping the darkness would be enough to conceal us, I grabbed the cardboard and threw it on top of her with a silent apology, then carefully closed the lid and dragged the wheelie bin with me to the side of the building. Oscar picked up on my fear and followed. The sound of the chain clanking onto concrete spurred me on, and I struggled to haul my cargo into the alley. The gates squeaked open, and the engine revved. Almost breathless with panic, I dragged the woman further down the alley.

Headlights swung across the car park and stopped, directed at the fence alongside me. The corner of the building stood out in stark relief against the harsh beams. The van engine died, and a door opened.

'*Ssshh.*' I patted Oscar and pushed him behind the bin.

'I thought they said two,' the thug called Ox said.

'Maybe they changed their minds.'

'We should ring and check.'

I let go of the bin and edged further away from it. I crouched beside Oscar deep in the alley, my heart pounding in my chest.

'Let's get out of here. Ring him later.'

'I don't know . . .' That sounded like Ox.

'Come on, let's get going. You know he told us not to use our phones anywhere near here. And if there'd been two, there'd be two. It couldn't have floated over the fence.'

Ox gave a resigned sigh. A grunt followed, then the sound of the other bin's wheels on the tarmac. Van doors opened and, with a count of three, the two thugs threw the bin into the van and slammed the doors. The engine started, moved off, then idled. The gates closed, and the chain rattled, then the van pulled away.

Drenched in sweat, I straightened and leant against the wall. I lifted the lid, removed the cardboard and threw it aside. I pulled the plastic away from the woman's face and held the back of my hand in front of her nose. Warm breath tickled the hairs. I hadn't imagined her eye opening. I should ring an ambulance, and the police. But what if they didn't arrive before those thugs rang their boss and returned? I needed to get her out.

After struggling to turn it round in the narrow space, I dragged the bin to the entrance. Even the faint streetlight had gone out and a sliver of moon provided the only illumination. I eased the two halves of the gate apart. *Bugger!* When they secured them again, they'd shortened the chain, and it barely allowed me through, let alone my wider cargo. I pushed the two halves of the gate apart, using my legs, while pulling on the handle of the bin, but nothing doing. I paused to get my breath, the bin solidly wedged into the opening.

Oscar, still in the compound, sat and studied me with a worried expression.

'Don't worry, I'll get it through.'

He didn't appear convinced.

After much effort, I somehow squeezed it through the gap, then jerked to a stop as the axle clanged against the gate and the wheels jammed.

'Shit!'

Exhausted and sweating afresh from a combination of exertion and fear, I paused and gulped air. After a minute, the fear the thugs would return galvanised me and, by wrestling the container through ninety degrees, I freed it. It fell on its side. I jerked backwards and sprawled onto the pavement. I lay there, gathering my strength. Oscar climbed over the bin, then waited beside me with a look of concern.

The sound of vehicles on the main road set me scrambling to my feet, pulling the bin upright. I needed to hide, so I pulled it across the road to the shadows of the building where I'd found the broken camera. Once out of sight, I reached for my phone. Where the hell was it? *Bugger!* It must have fallen out of my pocket. But where?

I started back across the road, but a low groan reached me from the container. Oscar's whine told me I hadn't imagined it. I had to get her to a doctor. I'd seen signs for the local hospital up the hill. It couldn't be far, but would I get her there at all, much less without being seen?

But I couldn't leave the phone.

Another groan made up my mind.

'Come on, Oscar.'

I dragged the bin behind me and headed up the hill. The phone was the burner Kasper gave me. In the worst case, if someone else found it, they wouldn't be able to trace it to Kasper or me. I focussed on pulling my cargo up to the main road. Oscar, recognising the seriousness of the situation, trotted alongside me.

Without my phone, I didn't know the time, but it must have been well past midnight. Even the main road was empty, the vehicles I'd heard having passed out of sight. I struggled with the load, dragging it behind me, the lid flapping against the back of my legs. My arm and legs burnt with the effort. Oscar studied me with concern.

Houses lined the left side of the road, and I contemplated leaving my cargo outside one and ringing the bell. But unless I tipped the woman out, or stayed to explain myself, they'd probably ignore it and go back to bed.

At last, ahead, a sign pointed to the left. Hospital, half a mile. I pressed on, alternating arms when each got tired. I knew from experience I'd pay for my exertions in the next few days. Houses lined both sides of the sloping road, and I panted as I ascended, hoping the rest of the way was downhill.

A park opened out to my left, and I turned onto a wider road. A vehicle came from behind me, and I tensed, slowing to a crawl. Oscar followed its progress, ears erect. *Please God, let it not be the van.* Then a taxi on a late-night errand shot past. What would the driver have made of us? Enough to place a call to the police? No, I decided. He'd been too hot on his mission.

Either way, there was nothing for it but to go on.

After two more changes of direction, each continuing uphill, I reached the outskirts of the hospital. The nearest buildings lay in darkness behind chain-link fencing. Much as I wanted to leave my load and scurry away, I couldn't simply abandon her. What if she wasn't noticed?

Ahead, a sign showed the way to the accident and emergency department. How much bloody further? But at least it was flat. With the sense of nearing my journey's end, I speeded up to almost a fast walk. Ahead, bright light spilled out of a wall of glazed doors and windows onto a stretch of reddish tarmac sheltered under a pitched roof.

I didn't see security cameras, but assumed there would be some. Although I could keep my head down to avoid being recognised, Oscar would be much easier to identify. I'd seen few standard Schnauzers in the city centre and none living on the streets.

'Stay here, boy.'

Despite his reluctance to leave me, he stayed in the shadows.

'Good boy.'

The thought of abandoning her, even outside a hospital emergency department, didn't sit right, but I could all too easily see myself getting dragged into a world of trouble. Before I reached the lit area, I wiped the handles and any other parts I might have touched while manoeuvring the container. I pushed it the last few metres, up against the pair of glazed doors at one end. Figures moved around behind the glass walls and, keeping my head down, I banged on the wall. A muffled shout told me they'd seen me, and I turned and ran.

The doors opened, and another shout followed me. Then the voice changed. They'd found her. As I passed Oscar, he joined me. We ran on, relief someone would now help the poor woman making me tremble. Once sure nobody was following us, I slowed to a walk, and we headed back to find my phone. A siren approached, and I ducked off the pavement into an alley, pulling Oscar with me. Blue lights flashed, and a police car raced past, heading the way I'd come. I waited a few moments, and we continued on our way.

By the time we reached the industrial estate, the sweat had cooled on my body, and I shivered. As we approached the unit where I'd lost my phone, Oscar's ears pricked up. I slowed and rounded the corner. The van sat in the car park and one of the uniformed thugs walked towards it from the far side of the building, a huge flashlight in his hand. We edged into the shadows.

A beam of light shone out of the gap where I'd hidden, moving as the person holding the torch stepped out. I crouched down, hiding behind a bush.

'Anything, Ox?' the first one said.

'Wheel marks in the soil and footprints, but nothing else.'

'Marks, like from a wheelie bin?'

'Yeah, exactly like.'

'Fuck! Someone moved it.'

'Moved it and took it away.' Ox shone his torch on the marks.

'What we going to tell him?' He sounded scared.

'Nothing to do with us. Someone took it before we arrived.'

'We didn't check down there, though. They might have been there when we picked the other one up.'

Ox said, 'He's not to know that.'

'If he ever finds out we lied . . . FUCK!'

'I told you we should have phoned.'

'Yeah, you did, Mr Smartarse. Thanks for—'

A feeble ringtone interrupted him. The two men looked at each other, then ran down the side of the building towards my phone. I reminded myself it was Kasper's burner. They couldn't trace it, but what if they hacked it? If they did get into it, they'd find my emails to Kasper.

CHAPTER 21

The blond-haired thug had answered my phone, but the device died almost immediately. Who the hell had rung? It could only have been Kasper or Zofia, but why call me now? I couldn't believe they had; it must have been a wrong number.

The blond spent a few moments trying to reanimate my phone before giving up and passing it to Ox, who did the same before pocketing it. My relief they'd failed lasted until I realised whoever employed them wouldn't give up as easily. All they needed was a charging lead, and a determined hacker.

I needed to warn Kasper, but first I had to recharge my own phone.

The men held a quick confab and then they locked up and left. Despite Oscar's obvious impatience to return to his crate, I waited until sure they'd not be returning, recycling regrets over losing the phone. A thin drizzle fell, adding to my discomfort and increasing Oscar's irritation.

'Come on, let's go, then.' I tugged on his lead and set off for the city centre.

That woman was there, you know.

'Which one?'

The one you're searching for.

'The one I took to hospital?' I'm sure she had blue, not brown eyes.

No. I couldn't smell her once we left the compound.

Had Catriona been in the other bin? I should have checked it, but I couldn't have saved both and she was probably dead, as the one I found should have been. I couldn't process this now. And I had to get back and warn Kasper. Did I have the energy to go to his house now? My head felt so muzzy, I doubted I'd find my way there.

We stuck to the shadows, even though there wasn't anyone around. A police car approached, blue lights flashing, and I tensed until it shot past, going north out of the city. Were they going to the hospital? I imagined anyone going to that incident would have done so long ago. I'd not got a good look at the woman, but the thought it was Jehona wouldn't leave me. Had they killed her because Zofia and I spoke to her? Why the hell had I followed her to the café?

Too exhausted to think straight, I let Oscar go ahead and concentrated on putting one foot in front of the other. My imagination played tricks on me, making me think the two uniformed thugs were following me. I hurried, moving as fast as my aching legs would carry me. My muscles screamed by the time I returned to my lair in the city centre. Oscar trotted off when I removed his lead. Too tired to check if he'd gone to his crate, I had enough strength to pull out my bedding before falling onto my makeshift mattress and pulling the covers over me.

The fear the two thugs would find me wouldn't let me rest, and I recovered my club, a short length of scaffolding I'd acquired following Miles's attack. Once I'd cooled down, I began shivering, but before long, exhaustion overcame me, and accompanied by a fantasy of taking my revenge on Miles, I fell into a heavy sleep.

I woke shivering, certain something other than the cold had woken me. The almost total darkness told me it wasn't daytime yet. I hadn't slept for long. A scraping noise made me stiffen, and I strained to hear. Was that Oscar? But what would he be doing moving about? Maybe someone else was nearby. Did they know I was here? If I kept still, they might not notice me and pass on by.

Another sound came from further away. Had they gone past? I needed to be ready to react if they hadn't, but, still exhausted from my earlier exertions, I doubted I'd be in a fit state to fight anyone off. Trying not to make a noise, I reached into my bedding until my hand brushed against cold steel. My fist closed round it, the icy metal numbing my palm. I'd almost convinced myself they'd gone when a yell came from behind me.

My heart jerked into overdrive. I threw my covers off and sat up. Then, another yell, but this from in front. Two of them. I had no chance. A shadow shifted in front of me. Without taking aim, I swung my club at it, catching it a glancing blow. The cry of pain gave me energy. Before I regained my balance, someone smashed into my back, knocking me forward. My wrist caught on the wall, ripping my club out of my hand.

A boot smashed into my ribs. I rolled away, but only into another boot. The figure I'd hit, and he wanted revenge. The air driven out of my lungs, I fought to breathe. A dog yapped. Too high-pitched for Oscar. Where the hell was he? The men who'd attacked Toff had a dog. Had John betrayed me? Then a fist grabbed my top and smashed my head into concrete. Consciousness faded.

After I don't know how long, the faint sounds of a struggle and high-pitched yapping seeped into my brain. A shocking pain split my skull and warm, sticky blood covered my forehead. The sound of running steps accompanied by shouts reminded me of my predicament. I peered through the darkness to see two figures, one supporting the other, making their escape. A third figure pursued them, then stopped and watched.

My left eye stung and closing both, I wiped at the blood covering it. The yapping dog came closer, and I let my hand drop and pretended to be unconscious. A wet nose pushed into my face.

'Come on, Trixie, leave him.'

I recognised the voice, and my insides roiled. Heavy boots shuffled closer, and I cringed. A hand grabbed my shoulder and shook me. The pain across my forehead made me gasp.

'Victor, it's me, Craig, Trixie's dad. Wake up.'

I tried to open my eyes. My left eyelid remained closed. Craig's bearded face loomed over me in the gloom. His foul breath made me gag.

'They've gone. You're okay.'

It took me a while to understand. 'You chased them off?'

'Fucking bastards. They've attacked a few of us, but they won't be back.' He grabbed my shoulder. 'You need to get up.'

With his help, and using the wall I'd smashed into for support, I got to my feet. The pain came in waves, and I fought the urge to vomit. I leant against the wall, panting like I'd run a 10K.

'You going to be okay?'

I gasped, 'Yeah,' and checked Oscar's crate. 'Have you seen Oscar?'

'Oscar?'

'My dog.'

'Sorry.'

Oscar must have wandered off to his secret benefactor. I waved a hand in the direction my attackers had run. 'Do you know who they are?'

'Some posh lads who think it's funny to attack homeless people.'

Was it Miles and his mate? Maybe he'd come for Oscar. Good thing he'd stayed away. I'd have to do something about Miles before he hurt my dog. An awful thought struck me. Had they hurt Oscar before attacking me?

'They attacked another lad a couple of days ago,' Craig said.

'Toff? Yeah, I saw him.' Craig seemed well informed. 'How do you know about them?'

'They attacked an old guy previous Saturday, took his dog.'

'You think they've taken Oscar?'

'Come on, let's get you inside and have summat to eat.'

Both would be welcome, but I couldn't. 'I need to find Oscar.'

'In that state? Let's get you sorted and then the three of us'll find him.' He gestured at Trixie, who now sported a blue ribbon and regarded me with affection.

I couldn't argue with his logic and pointed at my bedding, now scattered by my attackers. 'I need to put my stuff away.'

Bending over made my head swim so Craig collected my stuff, arranging it in a much neater bundle than I would have, and hid it in my cubbyhole when I showed it to him. He gave me a wry smile and added my scaffolding pole. As the adrenaline left my body, I shivered.

'Ready?' he said.

'Where are we going?' I hadn't forgotten I needed to warn Kasper.

'It's not far.'

'Can I charge my phone there?'

'You got it with you?'

I hefted my 'pillow', the backpack Kasper had given me. Craig walked on and I followed him, clutching my aching ribs. Trixie ran alongside us. Although still wary of Craig, my curiosity got the better of me.

'How come you know so much about the guys who attacked me?'

'I keep me ears to the ground. There's a few of us.'

I waited for him to continue, but he pressed on in silence. The grey dawn grew lighter, and the odd car drove past. We arrived at an eatery I'd always deemed too posh, and Craig knocked on the door. The poster on the inside of the window advertised 'Valentines Special'. The memory of last Valentine's Day filled me with sadness. A man in a chef's outfit opened the door and ushered us through to a small dining room at the back. Warm air bathed my chilled skin, and the rich aroma of curry and garlic made my mouth water. He produced a mat with two bowls on it, one of food and another of water, and placed them next to Trixie.

He saw my injuries and directed me to a toilet with a hand basin. I looked a mess. A cut above my left eye had deposited blood down the side of my face. I washed my hands in the welcome hot water. Then, without reopening the wound, I wiped off the dried blood, depositing a wad of reddened paper towels in the bin. Once I'd removed the worst of it, I checked my reflection. My skin looked like someone had taken a rough file to it and my nose seemed more bent than usual. I'd have two black eyes before long.

I took a few paper towels and placed them in my pocket. They were always useful and I was sure our host wouldn't mind. What the hell was this in my pocket? I took out the package I'd rescued from the bin last night. A plastic pouch with 'Medium Nitrile, Powder Free' printed on it. Inside, two blue rubber gloves. I removed them using a paper towel to hold the edges. Brown stains streaked them and, remembering the injured woman, I felt sick.

I held them up to the light. One had a cut across the knuckles. They looked like teeth marks. Blood stained the cut, and on closer inspection, I saw it was on the inside. It must have come from whoever wore the gloves. These would link the injured woman to her attackers. My head swam and I took a few deep breaths. Unsure what to do, I carefully repacked them, put them back in my pocket and returned to the dining room.

Large mugs of tea arrived, and I helped myself to one of them. The chef let me charge my phone and before long, we tucked into a steaming mound of rice, accompanied by a chicken curry with a thick sauce. Not as hot as those I enjoyed in Bristol. It was, nevertheless, delicious.

Melancholy overcame me as I remembered the family meals in Bristol. How were my girls doing? I needed to speak to Carol about Helen to let her know how upset our daughter was about what was happening with the new boyfriend. If she'd speak to me. I hated missing this precious time with the girls. Although I kept tabs on them via social media, it was no substitute to seeing them.

'You okay?' Craig's concern surprised me.

Tears splashed onto my plate, and I brushed at my eyes with the back of my hand. Craig, clearly embarrassed, focussed on his dog, still crouched over the bowl of food the owner had provided. I used a paper napkin to wipe my tears and continued eating.

A series of beeps warning of messages came from my phone attached to a plug in the corner. More people knew this number than the burner I'd lost, but not many more. I finished eating before checking the messages. Three from Kasper. Variations on Where the hell are you?

Our host removed the empty plates and brought more tea before tapping his wrist and holding up both hands to Craig. I checked the time, gone eight and it would be daylight outside.

'We need to leave in ten.' Craig slurped his tea.

Thankful of the chance to warm up and have a feed, I didn't object. We thanked our host and paused outside while I decided what to do. I should speak to Kasper. To send a text would be cowardly, so, despite my exhaustion, I decided I should walk up to his office and tell him in person. But first, I needed to find Oscar.

We returned to my pitch just in case he'd returned. Trixie grew excited and let out a high-pitched bark. A deeper one replied.

'Oscar?' I ran round the corner and almost tripped over him. 'There you are, boy.' Ignoring my injuries, I crouched down and hugged him.

What you doing? What's up with you? I've only been gone a few hours.

I released him and stood. 'Where have you been?'

We've been through this. Uh-oh. What are those marks on your face? Oscar studied my bruises and lowered his ears. ***Sorry!***

'Come on, we need to get going.' I took leave of Craig, thanking him again, feeling guilty I'd suspected him of attacking me.

After checking Kasper was at his office, I made my painful way there, Oscar accompanying me without complaint.

I said sorry.

'What?'

You look fed up with me about being beaten up.

'I'm thinking of what to say to Kasper. About losing his phone.'

You rescued that woman. I'm sure he won't mind losing a phone. It didn't look new.

'I'm more worried about it being traced.' Although he said it was wiped.

Can't help you there. That's outside my sphere of expertise.

'Mine too, boy. Mine too.'

The words to use to tell what happened whilst avoiding blame swirled around my aching head. What were the implications if the people who employed the uniformed thugs accessed the phone? I supposed I'd find out soon enough.

CHAPTER 22

Kasper didn't waste any time answering the door. He waited at the top of the stairs, looking even more knackered than I felt.

'What happened to you last night?'

'Let him get in, Kasper,' Zofia protested from behind him. 'Hello, Oscar.' He ran past Kasper to get his head scratched, then she saw me. 'Oh, God. What happened to you?'

'Did that happen at Vale Park?' Kasper grimaced. 'Did they catch you fixing the camera?'

'No, nothing to do with that. Just some hoorays jumped me while I slept.' I put my backpack down.

'Sit there and let's have a look at you.' Zofia led me to a chair and studied my injuries. The subtle scent of apple shampoo masked the stink of fried food. 'Kasper, make some drinks and give Oscar water while I get the first aid kit.'

With much huffing, he did it.

Zofia returned with a green box, which she opened on a nearby desk. 'Okay, this cut above your eye needs a stitch, but I'll at least butterfly it. And I'll need to clean up these grazes.'

She soaked cotton wool in medical alcohol and cleaned my wounds. I managed not to cry out and enjoyed being looked after. When was the last time a woman touched me? She finished cleaning my injuries, applied two butterfly stitches to my cut and stepped back.

'Not bad, if I say so myself.' She packed up the first aid kit and returned it.

She came back, opened her drawer and passed me a box. 'It's fully charged. They didn't have black, but will dark blue be okay?'

'Great, thanks.' I reached into my bag and returned her battery pack. 'I'm afraid it's dead.'

'Not to worry. Shall I charge your phones?'

'I charged it this morning, thanks.' I held up my phone.

'You've found somewhere else to charge them?'

Not sure how often I'd be able to use the place Craig took me to, I made a noncommittal noise.

'What about your other phone?' Kasper said. 'The one *I* gave you?'

Was it Kasper who'd rung me at the ridiculous hour? Should I challenge him or let it go? The uniformed thugs found the phone because he'd called it. But only because I'd dropped it in the first place.

Zofia broke the silence. 'How did you get on with fixing the camera?'

Kasper checked the app on his desktop. 'You've still not fixed it. What the hell were you doing?'

'Here.' I threw the piece of plastic I'd picked up onto his desk, retrieved the batteries I'd bought and added them. 'You owe me for those as well.'

He exchanged a glance with Zofia. 'Probably kids, otherwise why leave it there?'

The sensation of being watched I'd had last night returned. Had they had a camera on *me*? What if they recognised me?

'You okay?' Zofia said.

'Yes, thanks.' I sucked in air. 'I don't think kids broke it. The Novaks' people were up to something they didn't want anyone to see.'

'What?'

Despite thinking about what I intended to say to Kasper, I still hadn't decided what to tell them. 'Two men dragged wheelie bins out of the building and left. I waited and checked one of them . . .' Even now, the shock of what I'd found made my hands tremble.

'And what did you see?' Kasper didn't hide his impatience.

'A woman,' I whispered.

'What, dead?'

'Not quite.'

Zofia paled. 'You phoned the police?'

'No.'

'Why not?' Kasper said.

'My phone . . . I had no charge.'

'What did you do?'

'A van came back. To collect the bins—'

'And you just let them take them?' Kasper accused.

Zofia came to my defence: 'What did you expect him to do?'

'I hid one bin, and when they left, dragged it to the hospital.'

They both stared at me and finally Zofia said, 'You dragged her all the way to Crumpsall?'

'I think so. It said North Manchester.'

'I'm impressed. Well done, Victor. You say she was still alive?'

'Yes, although she had a nasty injury on her head, she was still breathing. I checked before I left her.'

'Did you recognise her?' Zofia exchanged a look with her brother.

I knew what I was about to say would upset Zofia, but I couldn't pretend otherwise. 'I . . . I thought it might be Jehona.'

Zofia gasped and covered her mouth. She took a deep breath and said to Kasper, 'I told you.'

'What?' I asked.

'She thinks they took Jehona there on Monday morning, early hours.' Kasper went to his sister and put his arm across her shoulder.

Good God. Had she been there three days before they dumped her? I couldn't imagine how the poor woman must have felt, knowing they intended to kill her. The urge to find who'd done it and make them pay made me quiver.

'Can you check how she is?' Zofia's voice came out a whisper.

Kasper squeezed her shoulder, returned to his desk and punched keys on his PC. 'Here it is: "Police are asking for anyone who might have seen a man dragging a blue wheelie bin through the streets near the hospital to get in touch." They give a number. Shit . . .'

'What?' Zofia said.

'Officer in charge: DCI Grimes.'

'It would be.'

I looked from one to another. 'Is he someone you know?'

'You could say that.' Kasper ran a hand through his hair.

'Is he the man who came here yesterday?'

'Did he see you?'

'I don't think so. Why?' I still hadn't remembered where I'd seen him before.

Kasper mumbled something I didn't hear and busied himself with his drink.

'Zofia?'

'He doesn't approve of PIs, but nothing to worry about.'

Her body language told me she was lying.

Kasper spoke before I challenged her. 'Did you get any photos?'

'A few of the guys who brought the bins out. I didn't get their faces, but I'm sure one of them was the guy who caught you at the flat.'

Zofia called up the images she'd downloaded. 'This one?' She pointed to the shaven-headed, tattooed man with no neck.

'Yes.'

She exchanged another look with her brother. What the hell was going on with these two?

'Does the article name Jehona?' she asked her brother.

He checked the story. 'No.'

'It might not be her.' She looked at me imploringly. 'You said you weren't sure?'

I wanted to reassure her, but couldn't.

'You said you photographed the car,' Kasper said. 'Did you get the van which picked up the other bin?'

'No, but I remember the logo on the side. A shield and some sort of animal and a name on the side. Great *something* Security.'

'Great Bear. Was it this?' Kasper punched keys and swung his screen so I could see it.

'Yes. And I'd recognise the two men.'

'Hmmm . . . Without a photo, it's not much use.'

Zofia said, 'The police might have them on their system.'

The wording of the report Kasper read out suggested the police regarded me as a suspect. Zofia and Kasper's attitude to the lead investigator further undermined what little trust I had in the police. Before I could object, Kasper spoke up.

'Let's wait a bit before we speak to the police.'

Zofia looked like she'd argue but said, 'Where's the picture of the car?'

I couldn't hold her gaze. 'It's on the other phone.'

'The one you've avoided telling me about.' Kasper fixed me with his gaze. 'Why's that, I wonder?'

'The two security guys took it—'

'You're not serious?' The colour drained from him.

I swallowed. 'I am. But it's backed up to the cloud, so I can retrieve the images.'

'How the hell did you lose the phone?'

I should have retrieved it before going to the hospital, so I constructed a small fiction. 'It fell out of my pocket when I moved the bin, and I didn't notice until I got to the hospital. When I went back for it, someone rang it, and the security guys found it.' It was almost the truth.

Kasper glared at me. 'How did you not know you'd dropped it?'

'I don't bloody know. I was in a hurry to move the bin, terrified they'd catch me.'

'Who rang you?' Zofia said, looking at her brother.

I grew even more certain it *had* been Kasper, but what I said was, 'Probably a wrong number, or a sales call. I got a few earlier.'

Nobody spoke for several seconds, but Kasper definitely appeared relieved.

'I'd upgraded the PIN to a password, so it should be secure,' I said. 'And it's a burner, so nobody can trace it to you.'

'Hmmm.'

'What is it, Kasper?' His sister studied him.

'It's my old phone. I've wiped all the data, but they could still trace it to me through the serial number.'

'Wouldn't they need a contact inside the manufacturer?'

'Or the distributor,' Kasper said.

I wasn't sure how likely that was. If they did have one, how long did we have?

◆ ◆ ◆

Tomaz had never seen Milan Novak so angry, and the fear he'd not get out of his office alive became a certainty.

Milan prodded his brother in the chest. 'What did I fucking tell you last time?'

Marko froze under his brother's glare, seeming unable to speak.

Tomaz felt he should defend him. 'You said—'

Milan turned on him, making him wish he'd kept his mouth shut. 'Who the fuck asked you? You too fucking stupid to recognise a rhetorical question?'

Tomaz's gaze remained on the floor as garlic-flavoured spittle sprayed his face. He then did what he should have done from the start. He kept his mouth shut.

Milan's casual slap staggered him. 'Stupid cunt.' He returned his attention to his brother. 'Talk me through it again.'

Marko jerked his thumb towards Tomaz. 'These guys put the bodies in a bin, plus any items with bloodstains on them. They're taken away to be incinerated.'

'What items we talking about?'

'Usually just the disposable coverall, mask and gloves.'

'And these were in the bin which went missing?'

'No, most of them were in the other bin. There was just one pair of gloves. The one with the hole in.'

'The one with our client's blood on them?'

Marko swallowed and nodded.

'Okay. I don't want to know who it is who botched this, but I want him offed. An accident.'

Marko shook his head. 'No. We can't.'

Milan's rage at being defied changed to incredulity. 'It's you, isn't it?'

Marko stared at the floor.

With a roar, Milan spun away and swept the nearest items off the top of his desk, scattering them across the room. Tomaz flinched as a mug half full of cold coffee smacked his leg, soaking his trousers.

Milan stood then with his back to them, panting, fists on the desktop like a silverback confronting a rival. When after some time his breathing quietened, he faced his brother.

'You sure the police haven't got them?'

'My contact says no.'

'What does that mean?' Milan used his dangerous voice.

'It means they haven't got them. Whoever took the bin must have them.'

'Yeah, so that could be anyone.'

'I don't think so. I'm pretty sure it's that little shit we caught taking photos outside the club.'

Milan sneered. 'Yeah, but you didn't catch him, did you?'

'I know who he is, though.'

Milan waited. 'You going to tell me?'

'He's a private eye called Dąbrowski.' Marko looked pleased at himself.

'And who's he working for?'

'That I couldn't find out. But he's got an office on Cheetham Hill Road.'

Milan walked back behind his desk and sat in his throne-like chair. After an oppressive silence which terrified everyone else, he spoke in a low voice. 'Sort this. Get those gloves back and make sure this Dąbrowski keeps his mouth shut.' He shooed them away. 'Now fuck off out of my sight.'

A surge of relief weakened Tomaz's knees. Despite his eagerness to escape, he waited for Marko to reach the door first.

Milan took his customary parting shot. 'And if you fuck this up, or do something similar again, brother or not, you and your men better dig your own graves.'

CHAPTER 23

I left Kasper's office worried I'd put him in harm's way by losing his phone. On top of that, the thought I should tell the police what I'd seen battled with the wariness of authority I'd imbibed during my time on the streets. Kasper and his sister's reaction to the officer running the investigation added to my caution. Neither told me *not* to contact the police, but they hadn't encouraged me either.

I also wasn't sure what to do with the gloves I'd found. Could they be used as evidence, or did the fact I'd removed them mean they'd be no use? I wished I'd left them in the bin.

Not wanting to go past the Arndale and through Market Street, I took a detour through Piccadilly Gardens. Oscar's reaction as we neared told me he sensed Trixie nearby, and with her would be Craig. Before we reached the gardens, I nipped into the supermarket and bought a couple of sandwiches, one for me and the second as a thank you to Craig.

We found them, along with Brother John and Toff, at the statue of Victoria. While Oscar and Trixie became reacquainted, I offered the food to the others, and we ended up with half a sandwich each.

John gestured at my new bruises. 'Craig tells me the men who attacked Toff had a go at you.'

'I'm not sure. A man' – I didn't want to share that Miles had pissed on me – 'attacked me last week, and we bumped into him in a café a few days later. Oscar bit him on the ankle.'

They all laughed, and Craig patted Oscar. 'Well done, boy.'

Oscar preened. ***At least your friends think I did good.***

'We got chucked out and he threatened to call the police.'

You always have to put a negative spin on things. I heroically defended you. Ask them.

'Be careful, Brother. The police are more likely to take the word of a guy with a home and job than one of us.'

With John's warning ringing in my ears, I took my leave and returned to Sackville Square.

As we neared my pitch, another thought struck me. What if the security guards at Hazelbottom Road had reported seeing me to their boss? They obviously feared him, so I should fear him too. Would they have mentioned Oscar in describing me?

Why are you looking at me like that?

'Oscar, you're going to have to be careful where you're seen. You can't be near me when I'm here, in case the men over there recognise you.'

You sending me away?

'It will just be temporary. Until this all blows over.'

He looked at me like I'd just kicked him. ***You don't want me anymore?***

'Come on, boy.' I recovered the last treat and unwrapped it.

You think you can bribe me?

I almost weakened, but he'd be safer away from me. 'It's for your own good. What if the guy you bit comes back to get you?'

He considered this for a moment. ***Okay, I'll find that woman you're searching for.***

'She was in the other bin, wasn't she?'

No, I think that's another woman.

How much could I trust Oscar's nose? I hoped he was right. 'Okay, I'd be grateful if you found her.'

I'll be in touch.

Oscar gripped the treat in his jaws and trotted off, disappearing round the corner without a backward glance. Despite telling myself it was only temporary, I felt more alone than since I'd lost my family.

I spent the afternoon watching the pink door, missing Oscar, and mulling over the events of the morning. Every time the door opened, I feared seeing the two thugs who'd disposed of the women. Even though they couldn't have seen me, I convinced myself they'd be able to recognise me.

A dark pickup with overblown wheels and tinted windows pulled up outside the door, leaking bass-heavy music. The sound swelled as the passenger door opened, then died with the engine. Two men came out. Although both resembled the type of thug who worked there, they weren't the ones I'd seen last night, but still I tensed, ready to run.

One of them paid me attention, something which didn't happen often. He came closer and my pulse spiked, but, as I prepared to flee, he rejoined his companion. They spoke for a few moments, and I held my breath. Then they went inside and slammed the door. Although relieved, I knew I wouldn't sleep here tonight. Not only did I fear a return visit from Miles and co., but I'd be a gibbering wreck each time the door opened, or a car arrived.

My logical brain told me they were unlikely to recognise me from a description, especially if I didn't have Oscar with me. The fact he spent many nights away from me should have reassured me he'd be okay, but what if his benefactor worked in the daytime?

Visions of the poor dog cowering in an alley while he waited for darkness to fall haunted me. I revisited the idea I should go to the police, but, still aching and exhausted from last night, I wasn't in a fit state to decide. I'd leave it until tomorrow, first getting a hot meal, shower and bed at the hostel.

The click of coins in my collection bag and a 'You alright, mate?' jerked me awake. Darkness had fallen, and the time showed past seven. *Shit!* With so many of us on the street and so few places, there was always a glut of people wanting to get into the hostel. The queue built up from five thirty, even though they didn't let anyone in until eight. After hiding my bags, I grabbed my backpack and rushed to the hostel.

I realised my fears before I reached the entrance. The line of people waiting stretched past the corner of the building and snaked into the piece of wasteland nearby. As I got closer, the stench of the unwashed penetrated even my desensitised nostrils. Although suspecting I was wasting my time, I rounded the corner to confirm the numbers waiting to get in. I estimated half of those queuing wouldn't get a bed for the night. They'd refuse anyone drunk or drugged up, but even if they refused a dozen, I wouldn't get in. Cursing, I resigned myself to a night in the open.

Two familiar figures stood nearer the front and one of them called me: 'Hey, Vic.'

I waved, but Brother John beckoned me.

As I passed those in the queue, some muttered, whilst others didn't even notice me.

'We saved your place, like we promised.' John gestured to a gap between him and Craig.

'Oi, don't fucking push in.' An aggressive young lad I'd seen around came towards me, jabbing a finger.

Craig stepped up to him. 'Are you deaf? We saved him a space.'

Although the same size as Craig, and much younger, the lad deflated and retreated, giving me a venomous scowl as he did so. I'd have to watch him. Yet another person to avoid.

A couple of muttered comments from others in the queue died under Craig's glare and he returned to my side. That was twice he'd saved me today. He dismissed my thanks with a wave, again embarrassed.

'Where's Trixie?' Did he know I'd rescued her? That could explain his changed attitude.

'Toff's got her for the night. Where's yours?'

'I . . . Someone takes care of him for me at night.' I couldn't hold his gaze.

Still conscious of the glares from those behind me, I waited. Two men came out, wrapped up against the cold, and one carried a clipboard. They inspected each person, examining their faces and asking them simple questions. They pulled one man out, and he stumbled away, his unfocussed eyes peering into the darkness.

When they got to me, a man behind accused me of pushing in. They ignored him, and the one with the clipboard peered at me and sniffed my breath.

He grunted. 'Name?'

'Victor.'

He wrote it down. 'Twenty-five.'

I got the money, a new twenty I'd recovered from my sock, and five coins, and handed it to his companion. They moved on, and I let out the breath I'd been holding in. Another five behind me got in, including the one who'd complained to them, but not the aggressive young lad. I avoided his glare and shuffled in through the doorway.

Damp heat infused with the aroma of food enveloped me and within minutes I sat at a table with John, Craig and the man who'd accused me of pushing in. Now we'd both got in, he wanted to be my best mate.

John made us wait while he said grace and we tucked in to a bland but filling corned beef hash. After mopping my plate with the two slices of white bread they gave me, I queued up for the pudding, apple crumble with custard and a top-up of tea.

'Did you hear about the poor young girl someone dumped in a bin?' John said.

I imagined everyone staring at me. 'Err . . . no, what happened?'

John gave a garbled account bearing almost no resemblance to the events. I made the appropriate noises, while my thoughts returned to what I should do with my knowledge.

After a welcome shower, I went to bed and fell asleep as my head hit the pillow. Confused voices and yells woke me. Someone had switched the light on. As I surfaced from a great depth, the words began to make sense. The police. How had they tracked me? Panic energised me and I rolled out of bed, only just remembering I'd taken an upper bunk in time to prevent myself from hurtling to the floor. The other occupants of the room remained where they were, some appearing still asleep.

Thankful we'd taken the room furthest from the entrance, I dragged the rest of my clothes off the bed and pulled them on before slipping into my shoes. Then rushed out into the corridor. Several people from the closer rooms spilled into it, protesting, and making a racket. A group of policemen gathered near them, telling them to go back to their rooms. My street sense told me to run, and I headed towards the fire exit I'd spotted earlier. A yell told me the police had seen me, and I forced my aching legs to run. I had to get away, then back to Sackville Square to get my bedding.

CHAPTER 24

The smell of toast and coffee filled the kitchen and streaks of water decorated the windows as gusts of wind splattered rain onto the glass. Zofia shivered, wishing she'd stayed in bed, even though she'd barely slept, thinking about Jehona, and wrestling with the decision they'd made to keep the information she'd discovered about her disappearance from Grimes. The door opened and Kasper walked in.

'Morning.' She reached for a clean mug. 'You're up early.'

'Not as early as you.'

'Couldn't sleep.'

'Snap.'

She didn't need to ask why and passed him a full mug. On the counter near the toaster, the radio burbled away, channelling the early morning news in the background. A phrase snagged her attention, and she reached for the volume control.

'. . . Chief Inspector Grimes said they were now dealing with a murder.'

Zofia cried out and covered her mouth. Guilt and sadness paralysed her.

'The police have released an image of the victim and have asked members of the public to contact them if they recognise—'

A gust of wind and spatter of rain filled the sudden silence as Kasper switched the radio off. Zofia opened a browser on her phone and found the image. *Oh, God.* It was Jehona. She felt sick. From Kasper's reaction he'd also found it. They looked at each other.

Zofia spoke first. 'We'll need to speak to Grimes.'

'Let's think about it.'

'What's there to think about?'

'Lots.'

'We need to tell him and show him the pictures Victor took outside their club, showing Jehona with those men.'

Kasper chewed his lower lip. 'We can't. Remember what he said about keeping away from the Novaks?'

'Yes, I remember, but a young woman is dead. Do you understand what will happen to us if it ever comes out that we sat on evidence?'

'What if we just sent the footage of them taking her from the flat?'

'We'd need to see how clear they are. I can't remember if they showed the men's faces.'

'What about the other photos Victor took?'

'They're on the phone he lost.'

'But he said he backed them—' Kasper retrieved his phone and opened it.

'What you doing?'

'The phone should still synch to my iCloud account.'

She waited while he scrolled through his phone.

'Yes!' He thrust the phone at her. 'Here they are.'

Taken in a darkened yard, the photos weren't great quality, but she could identify the shaven-headed thug she'd seen at the flat. 'We need to send these to Grimes.'

'Yeah . . . okay. We'll send them all together. I'll use a VPN so they can't track who sent them.'

Zofia didn't like hiding. 'What about Victor? We know he saw the man in the photos dumping the bin with the woman in it.'

Kasper shrugged. 'That's hearsay. All we know is what's in the pictures. He didn't take any pictures of them with the bins.' He made it sound like an accusation.

'I'm sure if he'd known they were dumping a body, and not taking out the rubbish, he'd have taken pictures.'

'But he didn't, did he?'

'No, he didn't.' Why did Kasper have such a downer on Victor? 'But he saw them and can give them more information.'

'That's up to him. We can't make him talk to the police.' He considered for a moment. 'Why don't we send the pictures and then ask Victor to speak to the chief inspector? Now the woman's dead, he may change his mind.'

'You could be right.' She drained her mug and rose. 'Let's go.'

'I've not eaten breakfast yet.'

Her glare stopped him, and taking a mouthful of coffee, he followed her. They drove to the office in silence, not wishing to share their thoughts. Neither listened to the radio murmuring in the background until the news mentioned a familiar address.

'. . . Police believe the dead man had been sleeping rough in Sackville Square and appealed to any witnesses who may have been in the area last night.'

Zofia punched the off button and exchanged a wide-eyed look with Kasper. 'Have you got his number?'

He already held his phone and punched the call button. He held it to his ear, waited, then said, 'Victor, if you get this . . . call me.' He didn't sound hopeful.

'It's him, isn't it?'

'We don't know that, Zofia.'

'How many people sleep rough in Sackville Square?'

He didn't answer, and she focussed on driving. That was two deaths caused by their carelessness. Tears gathered at her eyes, and she sniffed, determined not to cry. Neither spoke for the rest of the journey. Zofia eased the vehicle into the car park behind their office and they made their way past the empty chicken shop.

Even in her despair, she sensed something wrong when she opened the front door. 'I'm sure I put the alarm on.' She'd had a lot on her mind, but this wasn't something she'd forget to do. 'Oh, shit.' She studied the smashed alarm control panel with a mixture of relief she'd not forgotten and dread at what they'd find.

They entered the main office and paused. It looked as if every drawer had been pulled out and emptied onto the floor where it joined the contents of every cupboard. Fury gripped Zofia as she did a circuit of the main office. Despite the disorder, nothing seemed to have been deliberately damaged. Even the computer monitors looked intact, and, in the chaos, she couldn't see if anything was missing.

Kasper returned from checking the smaller rooms. 'They came in through the toilet.'

'Have they made a mess?' Zofia indicated the kitchen door.

'Not really. They'd searched all the cupboards, but they didn't break anything except a mug which fell on the floor.' He waved a hand round the chaos on the floor. 'What about here?'

'Same, I'd have to check after we've cleared up, but I don't think they've stolen anything.' The light on Kasper's monitor showed green, and she moved his mouse. 'Did you leave your computer on?'

'I'm sure I closed it down.' He cleared some papers off his chair, logged on and opened his files. 'Everything looks okay, but I'll run a scan while we tidy up.'

They spent the next hour putting everything back. While Zofia did so, she couldn't help remembering horror stories of 'messages' which had been left behind to be found by the victims of break-ins. She considered herself fortunate when she found none. The speed with which they were able to return all the files brought home to her how pitiful their customer base was. Fortunately, none of the files appeared tampered with.

So, if they weren't after their files, and hadn't stolen anything, who'd broken in, and why? The usual culprits, druggies after money, would have made a bigger mess and taken anything they could sell. Bored kids would have wrecked the place.

Kasper stood in the kitchen doorway. 'I think we've earned a coffee; you want one?'

'Why not.' Zofia sat at her computer and fired it up. The email icon flashed, and she opened it. The first new message came from Kasper's email.

It contained a brief note: return the gloves we know you took the bin. Under the words, the image Victor had taken showing Jehona the murder victim and the shaven-headed, tattooed man going into the pink door.

Had they left information which identified Victor in the office? His death *was* their fault.

'Kasper!'

He ran out into the office. 'What's happened?'

'It was the Novaks' people. They must have got Victor's details from us.'

'You can't know that.'

'They know Victor's been watching them.'

Kasper hesitated. 'Do they mention him?'

'No. But . . .'

'There you are. We don't even know it's him.'

'Get real. Who else would it be?'

He didn't answer.

She had to think. Even if Victor was dead, they weren't, and they had to make sure they stayed alive. 'Check your computer.'

He hesitated, then sat at his desk and hunched over his keyboard.

Zofia opened the next message, with the same subject but from a different address. It had an even shorter message.

were serious

Her mouse hovered over the attached image.

'Shit!' Kasper slapped his desk.

'What?'

'They've deleted every photo I've uploaded in the last three months.'

'Have you got backups?'

'Hmm . . . Should do, and Victor should have.'

Zofia swallowed. Did Victor have any family? They didn't even know his real name. She pulled herself together and reopened the first message for Kasper to read.

He joined her and leant over her shoulder. 'What gloves are they talking about?'

'I don't know. Maybe Victor picked something up.' Now, they'd never know. She opened the next message from the same sender and placed the mouse over the attachment.

'Whoa!' He grabbed her wrist. 'It could be a virus or Trojan.'

Zofia pulled her hand free. 'They would have infected both machines using a memory stick last night if they wanted to. We'd have never known about it.'

'You're right. Well, the deep scan should find anything.'

She opened the attachment, an image of her. It looked like her passport photo but someone had burnt out her mouth and eyes.

She felt sick. She still had a third email from the same source to open. This one had no attachment.

dont even think about running away we will find you

Like they'd found Victor?

CHAPTER 25

After my escape through the fire exit of the hostel, I'd first run towards Sackville Square to get my bedding, but teams of police swarmed around the area. I changed direction and made my way to Piccadilly, arriving exhausted and aching. I'd hidden under the arches below the station, terrified and unsure what to do. The police must have believed I'd caused the poor girl's injuries, but how did they know who I was?

Fear and cold kept me awake until exhaustion overcame me and I passed out. Sounds from outside woke me in a panic. After a few moments, my alarm stilled. It was just kids messing about. I'd found some cardboard to sleep on, but the cold seeped through from the ground. Without bedding, I was freezing, and my teeth snapped together as I shivered. At times like this, I most missed Oscar. What would happen if he returned to find all those police in our home?

My stomach growled. I'd anticipated a good night's sleep and a filling breakfast, but I'd had neither. My aching limbs complained as I struggled to my feet. I felt at least twenty years older than my forty-seven. The memory of a survey of homeless people my company did before they sacked me gave me pause. I was already six years older than the average life expectancy for men sleeping rough, although the fact I'd only joined their ranks in the last year made me an outlier. Would I ever see my girls grow up, see any grandchildren? Thoughts of my lost life made my eyes sting.

I dismissed these morbid musings and stretched my complaining muscles. Now I had some money, I should eat better, even start exercising. Although, how could I carry on working if the police wanted me? Why had I allowed Kasper to talk me out of going to them?

My stomach again reminded me I needed to eat, and I headed for a food van serving a nearby industrial estate behind Piccadilly station. The owner helped people on the street and often gave you extras. A steady drizzle made me wish I'd grabbed my waterproof before escaping from the hostel.

Apart from letting me have a double bacon barm and tea for two quid, the owner of the van gave me a tuna sandwich and an orange nobody wanted. Thanking her, I made my way to a sheltered spot between two buildings, wolfed the barm and washed it down. Although still tired and muscle-weary, at least I wasn't hungry.

Icy water seeped onto my shoulders. I needed dry clothes. My stash still contained some reasonable items, although nothing waterproof. Had the police found it? I hoped not and made my way across town, using side streets and sticking close to buildings to shelter from the wind and increasing rain. A sense of being hunted kept me alert.

I arrived at the bottom corner of Sackville Square and my heart sank. I counted six police officers wandering around the square, questioning passers-by. They'd stop me long before I reached my stash, even if it was still there. They appeared to be showing people a photo. How had they got one of me? I thought I'd hidden my face from the cameras at the hospital, but it must have been how they'd tracked me.

The sight of blue and white tape fluttering round the area where I hid my stuff increased my gloom. The cordon included

Oscar's crate. Where was he? He'd normally have returned by this time, although I'd warned him off. But he was a dog. What would my warning have meant to him? The thought they might have captured him deepened my despond. If they'd cordoned it off, they must have combed the area. Thankfully, I kept my important stuff in my pockets and backpack. *Shit.* I'd left it at the hostel when I ran. It contained Oscar's stuff and my papers.

I slunk away and found some shelter. What should I do now? Finding Oscar and getting dry clothes topped my list. I had a good idea where he went at night – not the location, but the general direction. He always left and returned from the other side of the canal. I circled round and headed for the small park across the bridge.

I came upon a couple on a bench in the far corner, a dog at their feet. The woman flicked chocolate buttons into the air and the dog snapped them in his jaws.

'Oscar, what are you doing? You know chocolate's bad for you.'

He gave a guilty look and closed his jaws, letting the button bounce off his muzzle.

'Are these the people you've been staying with?'

The young woman slid the packet of sweets into her handbag. 'Sorry, we just saw him here on his own. We weren't trying to steal him.'

'Nobody said you were, but you should never give dogs chocolate.'

I addressed Oscar. 'I've told you about this before, and you know it gives you the shits and that gets stuck in your fur. Come on.' I didn't have a lead, but he followed me.

Do you have to embarrass me like that?

'Well, it's true.'

It's true you stink like a mouldy rug, but you don't see me pointing it out to strangers.

Ignoring him, I retrieved my phone and switched it on. As it powered up, a pair of beeps warned me of my missed calls. The first came from Helen, and feeling bad I'd not spoken to her mother, I saved it for later. The other was from Kasper, and I listened.

'. . . If you get this message,' he said. Why wouldn't I get the message? He sounded panicked. The fact the police were spending so much effort to find me gave me a sense of unease. I opened my browser and checked the news.

Woman found in bin dies.

Oh no! Poor Jehona. With a deep sense of despondency, I read on. Something about the way she'd been killed triggered a memory. I'd recently read about someone who'd used a hammer to kill, but it couldn't be them. I finished reading the report, feeling hollow. She wasn't much older than Helen. Her family would be devastated. Losing either of my daughters didn't bear thinking about. Then it hit me: they must think I'd killed her. The combination of the bloodstained gloves and images I'd taken should convince them I had nothing to do with it. Although I'd not taken any photos of the shaven-headed guy with the bin, I'd taken one of him and Jehona outside the pink door. If I told them about the warehouse, they'd be able to find evidence inside. Surely Kasper would have given his copy of the photos to the police? Now it was a murder investigation, his fear of the policeman in charge shouldn't stop him. The photos alone would probably not be enough, but they should get the police interested.

I rang his mobile, but ended the call before it connected. What if they were monitoring his phone? I knew of a payphone which worked and made my way to it. A pile of disused fast-food wrappers and crushed cans littered the bottom of the kiosk, which stank of stale urine. I reconsidered my decision, but the handset didn't appear too mucky.

'Come on, Oscar.' I opened the door and ushered him towards the kiosk. Without a lead, I didn't trust him not to wander off, especially in his current mood.

You are joking.

'I'm not joking. Come on.'

He sat, wearing a belligerent expression. ***I'll just sit here in the rain, nice and relaxed.***

'You'd better not wander off.' I stepped into the kiosk, breathing through my mouth and, after memorising Kasper's number, I punched it into the keypad.

He answered with a wary, 'Yes?'

'It's me, Victor.' The phone hovered a few millimetres from my ear.

'Thank God, you're alive.'

'What? Why wouldn't I be?'

'Haven't you seen the news?'

'Of course, that's why I'm ringing. The police think I did it.'

'What?'

What was up with him? 'Jehona's dead, and the police think I killed her.'

'What do you mean?'

'They raided the shelter I slept in last night and they're crawling over Sackville Square—'

'So, you weren't at Sackville Square last night?'

How could he worry about that now? 'I told you I can't work twenty-four seven—'

'I didn't mean that.' He took a breath. 'Where are you?'

You expect me to tell you? 'Have you sent the pictures linking those men to Jehona?' I checked Oscar hadn't moved from where I'd left him.

'No.'

'Why the hell not? I know you're terrified of Grimes, but this is a murder, and I'm a suspect. Don't you care the police are hunting me?'

He didn't answer straight away. 'I need whatever it is you picked up outside the Novaks' place at Vale Park.'

'What?' I'd not told them, so how did he know?

'The Novaks know you picked some gloves up when you moved Jehona.'

'How did they even know I was there?' My mind raced in panic. Were they also looking for me? I checked around, but Oscar was still the only creature in view.

'They found the phone *you* lost.'

His accusing tone stung and I replied with one of my own. 'If you hadn't rung it, they wouldn't have found it.'

Kasper took a deep breath and released it. 'Does it matter? The fact is, they know you've got something they want.'

I felt bad I'd not already told them. 'I found bloodstained gloves in the bin. It looks like they've got blood on the inside *and* the outside.'

He didn't answer immediately. 'It's got the murderer's and victim's blood on it?'

'I can see why you're a detective.' I couldn't resist a dig.

Kasper just let it go. 'You need to give it back to them.'

I snorted. 'No way. They're my protection. If the police think I'm a killer, I need to give them the evidence linked to the real killer. Clear my name.'

'NO! No, please don't. The Novaks' lot threatened Zofia. I can't risk anything happening to her.'

The thought of Zofia coming to harm appalled me. I took a few seconds to absorb this information. 'Why doesn't she go away, out of their reach?'

'Just give them the gloves.'

'And let them get away with murder?' *And get me framed for it!*

'It won't be the first time.'

'That makes it alright, then?'

'She's a prostitute or—'

'So what? She's a young woman and both Zofia and I liked her. Are you saying her life doesn't matter?'

'No. But she's dead, and my sister isn't.'

'What does Zofia say?' I suspected his sister would want justice for the dead girl.

'Are you refusing?'

'I'm sorry. They killed a young woman. Imagine it was your daughter.' My money ran out, and I thumped the handset onto the cradle.

CHAPTER 26

Kasper slid his phone across the desk, full of frustration and anger at Victor's intransigence.

'Thank God, he's alive,' Zofia said. 'But then who did they kill?'

'Dunno.' Kasper shrugged. 'Some poor sod. But we've got our own problems, especially now he's refusing to give them the gloves.'

'I'm with him on that. We can't let Jehona's killer get away.'

Of course, she'd agree with Victor. 'What about the suggestion you go away until this blows over?'

'Another good point, except they would then target you.'

'Possibly. They need someone to hand over the gloves, and if they've grabbed me, who's going to do it?'

She exhaled in frustration. 'If we'd sent the photos to the police straight away, they might be investigating them now instead of looking for Victor, and the Novaks would have too much on their plates to worry about the gloves.'

'Well, they *are* looking for him. Which means he's not at Sackville Square doing what we pay him for.'

'God, you can be petty sometimes.'

'Don't you realise how much trouble we're in if we let Robertson down?'

'A woman is dead. *And* someone who was mistaken for Victor.'

'We can't know that. Homeless people are always being killed.'

'Yeah, and it's just a coincidence?' She stood and picked up her bag. 'I'm getting some fresh air. Do you want anything from the corner shop?'

'Do you think going out alone is a good idea?'

She grabbed her coat and left, slamming the door behind her.

Kasper kicked his desk. He understood she must feel guilty about Jehona's death, but it wasn't her fault. For the umpteenth time, he wished he'd never taken this job. He'd known it would cause trouble, but they'd been desperate, and he couldn't face another failure, and *this* one, he'd dragged Zofia into. He tried to focus on work. They needed to get more clients, but with what was going on, he couldn't concentrate. His email icon flashed. He checked it. It came from an unknown address, and he hesitated before opening it.

A simple message. YOUR RUNING OUT OF TIME

He clicked on Reply and typed out a few words. How to tell them about Victor's intransigence without sounding like he was stalling? He'd started the email three times when his phone rang. Unknown number. Had Victor reconsidered?

He snatched up the handset. 'Victor?'

A mechanical noise echoed in his ear, then an electronically distorted voice spoke. 'If we don't get the gloves by this time tomorrow, you can visit your sister in hospital.'

A lump prevented him from replying until he swallowed it. 'Please. I haven't got them.' Kasper held his breath and waited.

'Who's got them?'

'A . . . A man who works for me.'

'The guy who took those photos on your computer? Victor?'

Panic gripped him. What else had they discovered during the break-in? 'I can't get hold of him.'

The phone went silent and as Kasper was about to hang up, the voice returned. 'You've got an extra twelve hours to find him.'

The call ended. Sweat coated his neck and ran down his back. He checked the time. Nine thirty. A day and a half to persuade Victor. He sat, head slumped.

'Who was that?'

He jerked, dropping the phone onto the table. 'You made me jump.'

'Who rang?' Zofia placed his favourite bar of chocolate on his desk.

'Erm . . . wrong number.' His mind raced. He needed a better answer.

'You expect me to believe that?'

He swallowed. He could never lie to Zofia. 'They've given us until nine thirty tomorrow night, before . . .'

She looked thoughtful. 'Okay, well, I'm going to work.'

'What do you mean? We're *at* work.'

'If Victor can't watch out for Catriona, one of us has to do it.'

'They've seen the photos.' Kasper gestured at his PC. 'So, they know someone is watching their place.'

'If they think it's a homeless guy, they won't be expecting me.'

'Okay, I'll do it.' He stood up.

'No, they know you by sight.'

'They've seen you as well, at Jehona's flat. And they've got your passport photo.'

She laughed. 'Nobody will recognise me from that.'

'It's not a laughing matter.' How could she be so blasé about this?

'You're right, but I've thought of that.' She held up a carrier bag from one of the local beauty suppliers a few doors up and produced a black wig.

'I still don't think you should go on your own. Don't forget they've threatened you.'

'We've got until tomorrow night . . .'

'I'll come with you.'

'What, you're going to protect me?'

His bottom lip wobbled. 'At least I can call for help.'

'Sorry, I shouldn't have said that.' She squeezed his shoulder.

'No, you're right. This is all my fault. I'm useless—'

'Sorry, Kasper, I haven't got time for this.' She swept out into the hall.

'Be careful. Make sure you keep—'

The slamming of the door cut him off.

He grabbed his jacket and followed but only to the top of the stairs. *Get real.* He wasn't going to physically stop her, and as she said, she should be safe until tomorrow. He returned to his desk. All he had to do was find Victor and persuade him to hand over the gloves.

Tomaz watched in silence as Marko ended the call, disabled the voice distortion app and threw the phone onto the desk.

From across it, Milan watched his brother with a thoughtful expression. 'That tramp must have the gloves.'

'Yeah,' Marko said with a nasty grin, 'and we know why he can't get hold of him.'

'You think it's funny when the police find the gloves on the dead man?'

Marko reddened.

Milan turned his attention onto Tomaz. 'Did you find anything on him?'

'Just his phone, like you asked.' Tomaz gestured at the grubby ancient Nokia in bits on the desk.

'That useless thing. It can't even take photos.' Milan pushed the pieces towards Tomaz. 'You sure he didn't have another phone, a proper one?'

'Positive, Boss.' Although once he found the phone, he'd not carried out a thorough search. It was bloody dark, and the guy stank. Even with gloves on, he hadn't wanted to touch him.

'Maybe you got the wrong guy?'

Tomaz swallowed. 'He was the only one out there.'

'And he's the one been hanging around?'

Tomaz wasn't sure. They all looked the bloody same. 'I think so, Boss.'

Milan looked at his brother. 'What do you think?'

Marko frowned. 'I thought he had a dog.'

Milan fixed his gaze on Tomaz. 'Well? Did he have a dog?'

'Not with him, Boss.'

'Maybe he sends it to a kennel for the night.'

'I don't know—'

The slap on the desk made the pieces of the phone jump. 'Find the right fucking guy.'

'Right, Boss.' Tomaz stood and headed for the door.

'Take that crap with you.'

Tomaz returned and swept the pieces of the phone into his palm.

'That paper your lads found in that snoop's office.' Milan addressed his brother. 'It had the name Victor on it, and an address in Bristol?'

Marko's reply faded as Tomaz closed the door behind him.

CHAPTER 27

Zofia stormed out of the office, annoyed at herself for snapping at Kasper. His fragile self-esteem didn't need her clomping over it with her big size sixes. How the hell had they got here? Not only was she involved, however tenuously, in the murder of a terrified young woman, but two sets of gangsters – she had no doubt that's what Robertson was – had their eyes on them.

'Going somewhere, Miss Dabriski?'

Oh God, Grimes. That was all she needed. 'I was, Chief Inspector. Did you want to see me?' He'd brought his assistant. 'Sergeant Bowling, isn't it? Could you tell him my name is Dąbrowski? I appreciate some people struggle to learn.'

Bowling tried to hide her smile. 'Can you give us a few minutes of your time, Ms Dąbrowski?'

Zofia let them inside and followed. Kasper must have seen them on the entry camera and met them at the entrance to the office with a sickly smile.

'Mr Grimes, to what do we owe this pleasure?'

'Don't try to soft-soap me.' Grimes marched across the office and poked his head into the meeting room. 'Right, this will do. Both of you, in here.' He jerked a thumb at the door.

'Can we just do it here, whatever you're here for?' Zofia asked. 'I've got work to do.'

'We can do "it" back at the station if you want, miss. I'm here as a courtesy, professional to professional.' He looked between her and her brother. 'Which will it be, then?'

Zofia strode into the room, put the lights on and marched to the head of the table. 'Do you want to make a start, Chief Inspector?' She put her bag down and produced her tablet.

Grimes took the seat at the other end and Bowling sat to his left. Kasper joined his sister, opposite the sergeant.

'No refreshments, then?' Grimes said.

'What would—'

Zofia cut her brother off. 'We haven't got any milk.'

Grimes studied her in silence. His sergeant wore an amused expression, not hostile, but neutral. Next to Zofia, Kasper fidgeted, and she sensed him wanting to fill the silence, so gave him a warning glare.

'You recall my last visit?' Grimes said. 'It was only on Monday, so even you won't have forgotten. I warned you to keep out of our investigations.'

Kasper reacted. 'But we haven't—'

'Chief Inspector,' Zofia interrupted him again, 'can you tell us why you're here and what you want from us?'

Bowling leant across the reddening Grimes. 'We're investigating the murder of a young woman, Jehona Sorokin. A homeless man who's been seen hanging around Sackville Square dumped her body at Crumpsall hospital—'

'And I warned you,' Grimes butted in, 'to stay away.'

'What has a homeless man got to do with us?'

'The last time we came, my eagle-eyed sergeant saw him sneaking out of your office.'

The blood drained from Kasper's face and Zofia hoped the two officers hadn't noticed. 'You must have been mistaken, Sergeant. He might have been going to the chicken shop next door, or the lawyer. They deal with immigration law, and a lot of asylum seekers are homeless.'

'He's not a bloody asylum seeker,' Grimes assured her. 'I don't know why he came here, but I'm guessing he's working for you, and I bet it's off the books.' Grimes studied both of them with a satisfied smirk. 'He's a suspect in a murder investigation and if you withhold any information you may have about him, I'll take you both in.'

'Don't you think if he took the woman to hospital, he's unlikely to be the killer?'

Grimes jerked a thumb at Bowling. 'That's what she says.'

'It makes sense, Boss.' Bowling slid her phone towards Zofia. 'Here's the image of him passing Victoria Station the night he left the victim at the hospital.'

A blurry picture showed someone who might be Victor, but you couldn't mistake the silhouette of Oscar. Zofia's mind raced. 'You didn't mention he owned a dog. Yes, he came here. Victor someone, he looked a bit scruffy, but you can't always tell by appearances.'

'We think it's a standard Schnauzer. There won't be many on the streets.' Bowling took her phone back. 'What did he want?'

'His daughter's missing and he asked how much we'd charge to find her.' Did he even have a daughter? 'He's not been back. You get that often. We're a luxury service.' Her pulse raced. She couldn't recall ever lying to the police. She avoided looking at Kasper, but realised he was wound up tight. And she needed to warn Victor that the police could identify him because of Oscar.

'Yeah, luxury.' Grimes looked round at the cheap furniture and almost bare walls.

'Do you have any details for this Victor?' Bowling held a pen.

'Sorry, we didn't take his details. We don't in most cases, we get a lot of enquiries which go nowhere.'

Bowling slid her card across the table. 'If you remember anything . . .'

Zofia picked it up. 'Do you know much about the victim, where she lived and worked?'

'We think she worked at the casino in Sackville Square—'

'Thank you, Sergeant.' Grimes stood, pushing his chair back against the wall with a bang. 'We don't share intelligence with civilians, especially those we don't trust.'

Zofia let them out and returned to find Kasper still at the table. 'Why did you lie to them?' he said.

'What did you want me to say? "We've been spying on the Novaks and we know who killed Jehona but haven't told you"?'

'We should have told them about the threats and asked them for protection.'

'You said yourself you thought Grimes might be working for the Novaks. Now we're supposed to trust him?'

Kasper took a deep breath and covered his eyes. 'No, you're right. But if he finds out, we'll lose our licence.'

'That could be the least of our worries.' She shouldn't have said that, Kasper was already stressed. 'Look, I'll continue the surveillance if I can. You going to be alright?'

'Yeah. I'll see you in a bit.'

She picked up her wig and left. Kasper wasn't cut out for this. She wasn't either. When they'd started the agency, it had been fun, and she'd loved seeing Kasper do something he enjoyed. It had sure beaten working as a research chemist, especially being treated as a lackey by the older men, but having to lie to the police on top of the other stuff wasn't what she signed up for. Once they got through this, she'd have a serious think.

She reached the car. *Now, come on, Zofia, this too will pass.*

She turned onto Cheetham Hill Road, stopped at the first set of lights, and checked her mirror. Two cars behind her sat a large van with bull-bars on the front. She was sure she'd seen it parked up near the office. She'd passed it when she went to get the wig, rushing past a gaggle of young mothers pushing babies. The side door had been open and she'd seen it empty.

She drove on, keeping an eye on it. At the next junction, she indicated left, and the van did the same. When the lights changed, she drove straight on, as did the van, now directly behind her. A very wide tinted sun strip hid the occupants' faces, but three bulky men sat in the front.

Few cars moved on this normally busy road. How long would it take two of them to overpower her and throw her in the back before driving off? She doubted anyone would even realise what was happening. She realised she'd had a lucky escape earlier when walking past it. A surge of panic squeezed her insides.

She retrieved her phone. But how long before the police got to her? What would she say? There's a van following me? What were the chances they'd do anything? She should drive to the nearest police station. But so many had closed. Where was the nearest? What about a fire station? One of her friends had advised her to call the fire service if she was in trouble. At least they'd turn up.

Broughton fire station wasn't far. She'd go there. A bus lumbered towards her as she approached Broughton Street, a long line of cars behind it. Without indicating, she shot across the front of it, earning a long blast of its horn. Heart racing, she steered onto the side road and straightened, just missing a line of parked cars. She raced along, driving too fast for the road.

The van hadn't followed, and she relaxed. Up ahead, a removal lorry, its back doors open, blocked her way. Two men backed out, a length of carpet balanced on their shoulders. Without thinking, she took the next left. The roads round here followed a grid pattern. She'd take the next right and continue her way. As she approached the junction, a van pulled into the road.

She saw the bull-bars and slammed her brakes on. Parked cars lined both sides of the road, making it impossible to pass the van. She reversed, then backed into a gateway to turn round. As she pulled out, the van slewed to a stop in front of her. Two figures leapt out of the front and ran towards her.

Although terrified, she made sure she locked the doors and leant into the car horn, fumbling her phone with the other hand. The men flanked her car, both wearing masks. The one nearest produced a gun, signalling her to stop. She lifted her fist off the horn, let her phone slip out of her grip and raised her hands.

CHAPTER 28

I'd spent the rest of the morning on the move, Oscar accompanying me, and we avoided the city centre. At least he could be with me if we stayed away from Sackville Square. Once the rain stopped, my clothes dried out, but my body still felt like a block of ice. We shared the tuna sandwich for lunch, but Oscar turned his nose up at the orange.

What's going to happen to our new home?

'What do you mean?'

Kasper won't pay you to wander the streets.

'No, you're right.'

Oscar's reminder that I wasn't doing what Kasper paid me for went round my head. The thought of being arrested for murder should have trumped anything else, but I knew I hadn't done it and believed that, in the end, they wouldn't charge me, let alone convict me. My priority was still to get back on my feet and reclaim my family. Kasper's money secured my ticket to that destination.

I returned to Sackville Square to see if the police had left. We crossed Canal Street and the pale, brutalist bulk of the hotel behind the square loomed over us. I realised I couldn't continue my surveillance of the pink door. Groups of police still wandered the city streets around my patch. Oscar, keen to get to his crate, wanted to press on.

'Look, mate,' I pointed out, 'they're probably looking for you as well. After you bit that bloke . . .'

But he attacked you first.

'Yeah, I know. Life's unfair and then you die. Come on.'

We doubled back to the canal and made our way towards Piccadilly. Not only was I losing money from Kasper, but because I kept on the move, I wasn't earning anything to keep me going. I had a bit of cash left, but I'd need to buy clothes and bedding.

The best places around the gardens were already taken, so I wandered back down Mosley Street, following the tram tracks towards St Peter's Square. People also occupied each of the prime spots on the route. We paused in the square, taking in the sense of space and surrounded by buildings in a variety of architectural styles. It shouldn't have worked, but it did. A row of tents lined up alongside the hoarding around the town hall extension, a reminder, if anyone needed it, of how many others lived on the street in this city. By way of an obscene contrast, a chauffeur-driven limousine pulled up outside the magnificent hotel ahead of us, a room which would cost all the money I'd saved in six months.

The hooting of a passing tram dragged me out of my reverie. We pressed on down Oxford Street towards the railway station. Again, every good site was taken. I bought myself a takeaway coffee to keep warm and racked my brain thinking of where to try next. I could continue onwards, but although it became a busy thoroughfare, a high proportion of the pedestrians were students with little spare cash, and with so many relying on electronic payments, I suspected most wouldn't recognise a coin if they saw one.

The rain returned, and it didn't take long for my already damp clothes to become saturated. As I approached the railway bridge, I heard a familiar voice and followed the sound. Under an arch used to store the outdoor furniture from a local bar, Brother John held forth to a small audience.

'Victor, join us.' Brother John gave an expansive wave, inviting me to take a seat as though he were welcoming me into a luxurious salon rather than beneath a cold and damp railway arch. 'And your loyal hound.'

Oscar hadn't needed the invitation and busied himself getting reacquainted with Trixie, who sat under the table at Craig's feet.

I placed my coffee on a table and sat on a wooden chair, giving a silent greeting to Craig and Toff.

'We were just talking about the excitement at the shelter last night, Brother. We wondered what happened to you.'

Heat infused my cheeks as three pairs of eyes focussed on me. I didn't want to discuss finding the girl in case they, like the police, got the wrong idea.

'What happened to you?' Craig said.

I hesitated. 'I thought . . . I didn't want to get involved, so I legged it.'

'They were hunting for a killer.' Craig's glare kept me pinned to my seat.

'I don't blame you for slipping out, Brother,' John went on. 'They kept us up for hours, asking stupid questions.'

'What . . . What did they ask you?'

'As Craig said, they were looking for someone in connection with the murder of a young woman. Someone with a dog.' John stared at Oscar, still oblivious to us humans as he greeted Trixie.

'I didn't . . . Look, I never . . .'

'You look frozen solid. Haven't you got any dry clothes?'

I'd been shaking since I sat down, and not just from the cold. 'They're all over Sackville Square, the coppers. That's where my stuff is.'

'I rescued this. I told them it was mine.' Craig produced my backpack and passed it to me.

'Oh, thanks, mate.' I checked on my valuables, gave Oscar the pouch of food I'd left in there and took out my waterproof and spare jumper.

'Is that all you got?' John said.

'Yeah.'

'Toff, you've got some clothes which will fit our friend here. Why don't you go get them?'

Toff's eager expression changed. 'But you gave them to me.'

'I'll get you some more. Go on, lad.' Steel entered John's voice and the young Scouser didn't argue. He waited until the young man left. 'Now, what have you got yourself mixed up with?'

Craig and John studied me until I grew uncomfortable. How much should I tell these two, who I barely knew? Would they hand me in to the authorities in the hope of a reward? They knew I was involved in something dodgy, and most times, they'd have nothing to do with the authorities, but how would they respond to the death of a young woman?

I gathered myself and gave my explanation. 'I was on Hazelbottom Road going past a warehouse and I saw two men pull out wheelie bins . . .' Then I told them what I'd done. When I finished, they studied me. My mouth had dried, and I poured the last dribble of icy coffee down my throat and waited for John to respond.

'What were you doing on Hazelbottom Road?'

I didn't want to tell an outright lie, and I'd hoped the vague account of my reason for being there would suffice, but John's shrewd gaze told me he needed more. 'I'm doing a bit of work for a PI. Keeping an eye on a few people.'

John's eyes widened as he worked out how I'd got the money I'd paid into the bank. To his credit, he said nothing about it. 'Why can't they go to the police and explain what you were doing there?'

'They've had issues with the policeman in charge and now the gangsters involved have threatened them.'

Craig leant forward. 'Is it the Novaks?'

'How did you know?'

'Do you think we're out of our heads all the time and don't see what's going on?'

I recoiled. Although he'd saved me from a beating and helped me get into the hostel last night, he still presented an intimidating figure. 'Of course not, but I only know about them because I'm watching their place.'

'The one on Sackville Square?'

'Yeah.'

Before I said more, Toff arrived with a carrier bag, which he emptied onto the tabletop with a 'Help yourself.'

The worn but clean clothes looked my size, and I chose a pair of cords, a shirt, another jumper and a jacket. They smelt musty, but I couldn't complain. After putting them on, I transferred my belongings into the new pockets and folded my damp outfit. Once in dry clothes, I soon warmed up.

Once I'd sorted myself out, John leaned into me again. 'Does your friend still want you to watch the Novaks' place, Brother?'

'Yes, why?'

'You obviously can't do it while the police are after you.'

'Are you offering?'

'Maybe not alone, but the three of us could cover for you until about ten at night.' John gestured at the two men flanking him. 'What are we looking for?'

'He's interested in a young woman. Her family is trying to find her.' I took out my phone. Would they be tracking my phone? Although I suspected they might have Kasper's phone bugged, I didn't know enough about what they could do about tracking me. Would they even pick up a signal from under the arch? I'd risk it for a few moments.

The phone powered up and, locating the image of Catriona Robertson, I passed the phone to John.

'Who's she?'

'Just a missing young woman. Have you seen her?'

John shook his head and handed the phone to Craig, who studied it before sharing it with Toff. I took the phone off the young Scouser.

'Shall I send you the image, John?'

'Yes, please, although Craig won't need it. He could draw her now and get it 100 per cent right.'

John dictated his number, and I punched it in. 'Sorry, John, no signal.' I stepped out of the archway and moved away a few paces. The phone beeped, announcing the arrival of an email. I opened it, expecting an angry missive from Kasper.

> Give us the gloves or you'll regret it. You're not invisible Victor. We know where you live. You have one day before we take a trip to Bristol.

How the hell did they know I came from Bristol? Had I let it slip to someone or was it a lucky guess? They can't have known where my family lived. I looked around the gloomy alleyway. Were they tracking me right now?

Once my message to John arrived at his phone, I turned mine off and, taking my backpack and spare clothes, left the three companions. I walked towards Oxford Street, passing the stylish brick hotel which had once been an insurance company's headquarters. The uniformed porter standing inside the elegant arched gateway glanced sidelong at us, paying attention to Oscar, as if expecting him to bolt inside.

Now I'd recovered Oscar's lead, I got it out. 'Come on, mate, you'd better put this on.'

Would it be better if we stayed apart, so people don't associate us?

He had a point.

Did I tell you I found the woman you were searching for?

'What? No. When? Where?'

Keep your hair on.

'Well, when were you going to tell me?'

I'm telling you now. I saw her this morning.

'Where?'

I'll show you.

Sensing my impatience, he trotted, and I followed him into Whitworth Street, passing too near Sackville Square for my liking. We pressed on, skirting another magnificent building, a former fire station. Another legacy of the city's Victorian and Edwardian heyday. I couldn't help contrasting the ornate brick building with the utilitarian steel and concrete replacement on the northern outskirts of the city centre. We crossed Piccadilly and onto Ducie Street. Despite the cold, I grew warmer.

Oscar then led me along a canal towpath and after five hundred paces, we climbed steps back up to the road and crossed Great Ancoats Street before entering a grid of cobbled streets enclosed by converted mills and modern apartment blocks.

I'd heard from long-term residents that people once avoided these streets, even in the daytime. Now, trendy bars, restaurants and shops lined the pavements, and the fashionable set flocked here. Appetising aromas drifted from the eateries we passed. Oscar led me to a converted mill with a sign advertising a penthouse for sale at an obscene amount of money, and stopped.

I gathered my breath and looked around. I had a strong sense of déjà vu. I must have brought Oscar here on one of our walks. 'Where is she?'

She left her scent trail round this doorway.

'What do you mean, scent trail?'

She regularly goes into this building. She lives here.

'You've seen her go in?'

I don't need to. I can smell her.

'You mean someone wearing a similar perfume has gone past here?'

Give me strength. Imagine someone has sprayed 'Catriona lives here' in big red letters. That's what her scent trail tells me.

I suspected we'd wasted our time, but now I was here, I'd wait for a while, just in case. A coffee shop and convenience store sat on a corner opposite. The sense of familiarity strengthened. I'd definitely been here before and the owner had brought me a coffee while I sat outside. I set up shop under an overhang on the pavement. Almost immediately, a woman gave me a few coins. Once I'd stopped moving, it gave me time to think. The message I'd received had unsettled me and preyed on my mind. How had they got my email? And how did they know I was from Bristol? Were my family at risk? I needed to speak to Kasper.

Here she is.

Oscar's bark jerked me out of my reverie. I fumbled my glasses on and spotted a woman heading to the entrance. With a shock, I realised I'd seen *her* before. Here, going into that building. As I retrieved my phone, I saw I'd left it off. I pressed the power button and glanced up. She'd almost reached the door.

'Shit!'

Oscar leapt to his feet and ran at the woman, barking. She recoiled, pausing in the entrance. My phone chimed and I took a series of photos, hoping one would be in focus. Oscar checked I'd got my pictures. As he did, two men we'd not noticed ran past the woman. One went for Oscar, and the other came for me. I grabbed my backpack and ran, leaving my takings behind.

CHAPTER 29

The gunman standing alongside Zofia's door signalled her to unlock the car. As she did so, his companion came round and dragged her out. Using more force than necessary, he pushed her towards the van while the gunman kept the pistol pointed at her. Despite her panic, Zofia's mind stayed clear. Would her phone lead her brother to find her car? But then how would he find *her*?

They reached the side door of the van, and the gunman pocketed his pistol. He grabbed her other arm, and they threw her into the van before jumping in. The vehicle pulled away before they closed the side door, but it slammed shut as they slowed at the next junction, plunging them into darkness.

'On the floor, face down,' the one with the gun said.

As she lowered herself to the floor, a hand pushed her in the back and the van cornered. Her head bounced off the wheel arch and she landed on the carpet-covered steel floor. Lights flashed before her eyes and her hand came away wet from her forehead.

'Hands behind your back.'

She hesitated.

'Now.' The toe of a boot jabbed into her ribs.

'Ahhh!' She moved her arms.

A large hand pulled her wrists together and tied them with a zip tie, tightening it. She gasped again. The hand pulled her hair, lifting her head off the floor. A roll of polycarbonate tape screeched and one of them wound it round her mouth. The stink of damp underlay attacked her.

She ignored her growing headache and took deep breaths to slow her heartbeat. Had anyone witnessed her kidnap? She'd noticed nobody on the street. Her only hope was someone from one of the buildings had seen her. But with the van blocking those from across the road, she doubted it.

Would Kasper come to find her? Probably not until it got dark.

She'd dropped her phone in the car's footwell and kicked it under her seat. With any luck, nobody would see it before Kasper traced it, although with the doors open and the key in the ignition, she doubted the car would be there for long.

They'd given them until tomorrow night, so what had changed?

With a jolt, she realised they'd stopped. She held her breath and waited. The side door slid open, and the men jumped out. Neither had spoken since they'd tied her up. She turned on her side to see through the opening and squinted. She couldn't see much except for a breeze block wall. A roller-shutter lifted, and the van lurched forward before coming to rest. The engine died.

The two men appeared in the opening. One grabbed the collar of her jacket and dragged her out. She landed on concrete. Air left her lungs, and she lay gasping. One of them shoved a hood over her head. The odour of stale rice filled her nostrils. She'd landed on her hip and elbow, and both hurt like hell.

Before she could check her injuries, hands grabbed her and pulled her upright. She swayed, doubled over, trying to breathe. They pushed-led her for a few steps before one of them shoved her into a chair. Then they disappeared.

She sat, gathering her wits. Although her ribs and head hurt from the journey, and her elbow when she'd landed on the floor, she didn't think she'd broken anything. She hated not being able to see and tried to remove the hood, but with her hands tied, she couldn't even loosen it. Then she decided to leave it. The fact they'd worn masks, and now put a hood on her, meant they probably didn't intend to kill her.

She explored her prison. The chair she sat on had to be at a desk or table. She stood and walked a few paces, but after banging into pieces of furniture, she retraced her steps and sat.

After a long wait, during which she lost feeling in her hands, voices came closer. Steps approached and she tensed. A hand ripped the hood off. She closed her eyes.

'You can open 'em,' someone with a local accent said.

Three men stood facing her across a desk. All wore masks, characters from a superhero franchise. As she'd guessed, she sat at a desk and the room contained a few pieces of office furniture. They'd painted the walls white. She could still smell the paint. Rust-coloured carpet tiles covered the floor. The notion that the tiles were the same colour as dried blood hit her at the same moment as the thought that they might have painted the walls to hide bloodstains. Acid filled her mouth, but she swallowed it down. She mustn't be sick while her mouth remained taped.

One of the men produced her house keys. They must have grabbed her handbag. The man in the middle, wearing a Wolverine mask, picked them up.

'Home keys?' He swung the enamelled keyring of a stylised rustic cottage.

She stared at him, and he nodded at one of the others. He grabbed her chin, then ripped off the tape covering her mouth, taking some of her hair. Her skin burned, and she gasped before gulping in air.

The hand on her chin tightened. 'Home keys, yes?'

'Yes.' She closed her eyes.

'Alarm code? I've seen the box, so don't lie to me.'

'We don't use it.'

The punch snapped her head back, knocking her chin out of the other man's grip. Her vision faded and the metallic tang of blood filled her mouth.

'I said don't lie to me.'

Red drips collected on the desktop.

'Well?'

They didn't use it, but he wouldn't be satisfied without the number, so she gave it him.

'See, that wasn't so hard.' He pointed at her injuries. 'Get her cleaned up.'

Captain America left the room, returning with a green first aid kit. He used some cotton and wiped antiseptic on her forehead and cheek. The cotton took on the same colour as the carpet tiles. If he'd scarred her, she'd kill him.

He took out a plaster and stuck it on her forehead.

'Just leave it. That will do.'

'What about this one?' He prodded the wound on her cheek.

'Leave it.'

He closed the first aid kit before placing it on a filing cabinet behind him.

Wolverine produced a phone and said, 'Smile for Kasper,' then took a photo as she glared at him. He checked it, then said, 'Okay, guys let's—'

The shrill sound of a bell cut him off.

'Who's that?' he demanded of the others.

They shrugged.

'Go and check.'

Captain America charged out of the room and footsteps clanged on metal stairs.

'Jesus,' Wolverine said. 'Tell him to keep the noise down.'

The third figure, wearing a faded Spider-Man mask, followed his colleague out of the door. They returned after two minutes, gripped by an air of panic.

'Police,' Captain America said.

A surge of relief washed through Zofia.

'Shit! How many?'

'Just the one, the darkie woman detective.'

He must mean Bowling.

'Right, you, put this on her over there.' He threw the roll of tape at them. 'If the copper gets past me, you know what to do.' Wolverine produced a gun and left the room. The other two produced knives and came towards her.

CHAPTER 30

Thoughts of how to escape the threat from the Novaks swirled round Kasper's head as he sat at his desk. They'd spent ten days monitoring the headquarters of the Novak operation and had only seen Catriona once. They had to be keeping her somewhere. He'd traced the owner of the car she'd arrived in, but it belonged to Marko Novak, and he'd registered it at his home address. So it was likely a dead end.

He checked the notes Zofia had made from the information she'd found at Jehona's flat. Two addresses had cropped up. What if they kept Catriona at one of those? He checked them on the map. The nearest was the one where he'd left the camera. He had a few more in a drawer. He'd take them with him and get them to cover both premises. After last time, he'd have to make sure he did a better job of hiding them.

He locked up and set off for Vale Park Industrial Estate. Despite the Friday afternoon traffic, it only took five minutes. The lack of security cameras on the spur which led to the Novaks' building again struck him. The premises he'd used last time seemed empty, its car park deserted. They probably finished early on a Friday. He pulled in and parked his car round the back, hidden from the Novak building.

He took two cameras and walked to the front, where they would have a view of his target building. A large van with bull-bars pulled up to the front of the building and he stepped back behind the wall. When he peered round it, two men got out of the back of the van. That seemed strange. Why weren't they in the front? He snapped some pictures with his phone as they opened the roller-shutter and drove inside.

He'd finished securing the second camera to a tree with a view of the main entrance when a car pulled up outside the Novaks' place. A woman got out and studied the building. With a shock, he recognised Bowling, the policewoman who'd accompanied Grimes. Had the police traced the building the blue bin came from? She walked up to the front door and pressed the bell. Nobody responded. Why weren't they answering? He'd just seen three of them go inside.

His relief that the police had traced the building without the information he'd kept from them lasted until he realised the gangsters would assume he *had* spoken to the police and were certain to take their revenge on him *and* Zofia. He had to warn her. Her phone rang out as he watched the policewoman do a circuit of the building. *Come on, Zofia, answer.* She must have put it on silent while on surveillance.

Another vehicle arrived, a van, and he assumed it was the forensic team in support of Bowling, but no, he could just make out the logo: Great Bear Security. The van pulled up alongside Bowling and a bearded security guard got out. He looked like the one Victor described. He dialled Zofia again, with the same result. Bowling got back in her car and drove off. He watched with a mixture of disappointment and relief. They couldn't have connected the building to Jehona's death, otherwise they'd be here mob-handed.

The gangsters could still believe he'd grassed them up, though. Thoughts he didn't want crowded in. Then he rang Zofia again. He listened to the ringtone until the voicemail kicked in this time. 'Shit!'

He rushed to his car and set off for Sackville Square. Most traffic was leaving town, so he made good time and parked up near where he expected to find Zofia. Police remained in the square, still questioning people and, avoiding them, he completed a circuit. Where the hell was she? He rang again, no answer.

He needed to track her phone. She couldn't object now, but he could only do it from the office. He rushed back to the car and soon found himself sitting in the rush-hour traffic leaving the city.

By the time he reached the office, he'd convinced himself she'd been the victim of a variety of scenarios. He rushed to her desk and woke her desktop before punching in her password. He logged on to the app and entered the code for Zofia's phone. A map of the locality flashed up, so she hadn't gone far.

The red dot shone on a side street halfway from the office to Sackville Square. Why would she go down there? The area contained warehouses and cash-and-carries. He reached for his pad to note the address, but it wasn't where he usually left it. A quick search of the desk drawers confirmed it wasn't there. With a mild sense of disquiet, he used a scrap of paper. After locking the office, he made his way to Zofia's phone.

He found her car in the driveway to a cash-and-carry selling fancy dress. The shop looked like it had been closed down for a while, the padlock securing the gates rusty. He rang his sister. The distinctive tones of Amy Winehouse singing 'Rehab' came from her car. She never left her phone anywhere.

With a growing sense of unease, he reached the driver's window as the voicemail cut in. He peered into the car and saw the keys in it. He opened the door and found the phone under the seat. He retrieved it and locked the car.

What the hell should he do now?

CHAPTER 31

Once I'd shaken off my pursuer, I wandered back to where we'd left Brother John and the others. They'd be long gone, but I hoped Oscar would go there. Without a base, I felt untethered. Fortunately, he'd had the same idea and sat there, waiting.

'Well done,' I said, at last. He'd be insufferable, but he deserved the praise.

To my surprise, instead of crowing, or going on about me forgetting to turn my phone on, he came up and licked my hand. The rain had stopped, and despite shaking off my pursuer, I didn't feel comfortable staying here. 'Shall we go to St John's Gardens?'

He stepped alongside me as we went back along Oxford Street, passing between the Central Library and the hotel Hitler had supposedly wanted as his headquarters in the North. Still wary, I couldn't help checking over my shoulders.

Oscar gave me a disdainful glower. ***I've got it covered.***

'If you don't mind, *I'll* check if anyone's following me.'

You think you'd see someone before I hear or smell them?

'I'm not getting into "my senses are better than yours". You check and so will I. We'll see who detects them first.'

I can guarantee it will be me.

'Whatever.'

We arrived at St John's Gardens. Nobody sat on the benches surrounding the stone cross, so I took my waterproof off and sat on it on the nearest bench. I'd not checked the photos I'd taken of Catriona, and I did so now. I scrolled through them with mounting disappointment. Although most were too blurred to use, a couple were good enough for someone who knew her to recognise. At least we knew where she lived now. The contrast with the grim accommodation they'd allocated to Jehona, and the other women couldn't have been more dramatic.

Why were we looking for that woman?

'Her family wanted us to find her.'

What if she doesn't want them to find her?

'What do you mean?' I hadn't considered that.

It didn't look like she was being treated badly. Not like the other women. Wouldn't she just contact her family?

Oscar was right. They acted more like chauffeurs and bodyguards than minders keeping her in line. 'What if she is the same as the others, but one of the Novak brothers has taken a fancy to her and they're treating her better because of that?'

You really think that?

I dismissed Oscar's doubts and retrieved his brush and comb. Grooming him always relaxed me and even now it worked. By the time I finished, a steady drizzle fell. I clipped him on the lead, put my stuff in the backpack and, wearing my waterproof, set off. Lunch was a distant memory, and I was freezing, so I got a pie and chips. I'd left my takings behind, so I used some of Kasper's money.

Oscar studied me as I ate my chips.

'What?'

Don't I get fed?

'I gave you a sachet of dog food.'

Ages ago.

'An hour.'

I'm a dog. I've got no sense of time, as you keep telling me.

Unable to contradict him, I gave him a few chips, but he wasn't having any of my pie. We walked on, me lost in thought. Although I'd told John and his cohort about my predicament, I hadn't discussed the threatening message. Part of the reason was my fear they'd withdraw the offer to help me if they considered the job dangerous. Kasper was the only person I could discuss it with, and I didn't want to ring him. I also had the good news about seeing Catriona.

Mindful of his instruction not to go to his office, I considered where he lived. We'd seen signs for Old Trafford Cricket Ground when he'd taken me there, so I headed towards it. An hour later, I'd almost reached the cricket ground. In the early evening darkness, I cast around for landmarks I'd recognise.

Oscar sat on the pavement and studied me. ***You're lost again, aren't you?***

'I'm not lost.' I spotted a familiar billboard and pulled Oscar behind me. Twenty minutes later, following a series of direction changes, and accompanied by ever more vocal complaints from Oscar, I found myself outside Kasper's house. My legs hurt and the sole of my right shoe was now parting company with the upper. Worried about the reception I'd get, I hesitated, but after checking my surroundings, I approached his door and knocked. To my relief, steps shuffled inside, and the peephole darkened. Bolts drew, and a lock clicked.

Kasper snatched the door open, flooding the path with light. 'What the hell are you doing here?'

'You told me not to come to the office.'

'I expected you to phone me.' His bloodshot eyes searched behind me, then rested on Oscar. 'You've brought *him*.'

'Well spotted. More evidence of your detective skills.'

I expected him to slam the door in my face, but instead, he stepped aside.

'You'd better come in.' His creased tracksuit bottoms and hoodie suggested he'd been home for a while.

I walked past into the kitchen, and the aroma of toast hit me. An open laptop sat on the table and next to it, a plate with two slices of toast on it.

He pushed the plate at me. 'Help yourself. There's tea in the pot over there.'

I hung my backpack over a chair and sat at the table. Although I'd not long eaten, I'd learned to never refuse food and grabbed a slice. Oscar's rapt focus on the toast in my hand didn't need interpreting, and I gave it to him. I stuck the other slice in my mouth and grabbed a mug, pouring myself a drink.

Kasper stared at me, arms folded. 'Have you come to give me the gloves?'

'I told you, I need to give them to the police to clear me.'

Kasper didn't reply, but when I sat down, he swung the laptop round. An image of Zofia with her eyes and mouth burnt out filled the screen. Even though I knew it was only a photo, it hit me like a punch in the gut. He then showed me the two emails accompanying it.

I closed my eyes. 'What did Zofia say when she saw them?'

'What do you think she said?' He snatched the laptop back.

'Where is she?'

'They've got her.'

'What do you mean?'

He studied his hands. 'She went to Sackville Square—'

'You let her go on her own?'

He winced. 'Yeah, they gave us until tomorrow night.'

'And you believed them?'

He looked like he wanted to punch me, but took a deep breath instead. 'Anyway, she wasn't there. I tracked her phone and found it in her car about a mile from the office.'

'How can you be sure they've taken her?' Was someone tracking *my* phone? I'd switched it off after the message came through and hadn't dared put it on since.

'She'd never leave her phone.'

'Have you reported it?'

'You saw the email.'

This reminded me of *my* email, and I retrieved my phone. Before I could call up the message, Kasper reached for the backpack and grabbed a shoulder strap.

'What the hell you playing at?' I dropped my phone, caught the other strap and an unseemly tug-of-war ensued until he knocked my mug over.

Oscar jumped up and growled at him.

I released the backpack and leapt backwards as a stream of tea rushed towards me.

'Shit!' Kasper jumped to his feet and pulled the roll of kitchen towel out of its dispenser. Still holding my backpack in his right hand, he pulled several sheets of paper off and used them to form a dam to soak up the tea. 'Look what you've done.'

'*I've* done? You took my bag.'

Oscar looked from me to Kasper and back, and I signalled him to relax.

Kasper focussed on mopping up the tea and, taking my chance, I snatched my bag back. He glared at me.

I clasped the backpack to me, both arms across it. 'I don't know why you want this. The gloves aren't in here.'

'Oh yeah, you said that about my camera.'

'Here, have a look.' I opened the top zip and went to empty it onto the table.

'Okay, okay, I believe you.' He continued mopping.

I zipped the bag up and replaced it on the chair before helping him clean up. I took some paper from the roll and mopped up the puddle which had formed on the floor.

'Leave it,' he said. 'I'll do it. Get yourself another cup.'

I supposed it would have to do as an apology, and dumping the soggy towels in the bin, I rinsed my mug and emptied the teapot. Kasper finished tidying up, and I retook my seat.

'I get you're worried about Zofia,' I said, 'but you don't need to attack me.'

'I need those gloves. You saw the photo.'

'Yeah, but even if you gave them gloves, how will they know we've given them the right ones?'

'What do you mean?'

'They're a pair of bloodstained disposable gloves with teeth marks in them. How difficult would it be to fake a pair?'

'That's not a bad idea.'

'What do you mean?' I didn't like his sly look.

'Why don't we fake a pair and give them to them? Then when we have Zofia back, we hand the real ones to the police.'

He had a point, but I could see the flaw, and a terrifying idea wormed its way into my head. 'They'll have thought of that.'

'You think they'll hang on to Zofia until they've carried out forensic tests on the gloves?'

'I'm saying they won't let Zofia go even if we give them the gloves, *if* they suspect we might have substituted them. There's only one way to make sure they don't come to light.'

Kasper thought for a few moments and came to the same conclusion I had. 'They have to get rid of us, don't they?'

Unable to speak, I nodded.

The silence stretched until Kasper cleared his throat. 'Are you saying we do nothing and let them hurt Zofia?'

'Of course not. But they won't let her go—'

Kasper slapped the table. 'I will not do nothing. She's my sister and if they'd kidnapped me, she'd not be giving up on me.'

'I'm not saying give up.'

'So, what do we do?'

I expelled an exasperated breath. 'I don't know, but we can't let them have the gloves because then we'll have nothing and they'll still probably kill Zofia, and us.' The thought they may have already killed Zofia hit me, but I had to believe they hadn't.

All the fight left Kasper, and he sank down in the chair.

My mind churned. Dealing with psychopathic gangs of people-traffickers was a bit out of my experience. I returned to the email which had brought me here.

'Can I see the emails they sent you?'

'Why?'

'I want to check who sent it.'

'You think they sent it from their personal email, JohnPsycho@gmail.com?'

I stifled a retort, knowing we needed to stay on task. '*I* got one as well.' I took my phone out of my pocket and opened the email browser. 'You going to tell me who sent yours?' I dictated the email address.

'It's different. They've probably set up dozens if they're involved in scams. What does the message say?'

I told him. 'They're obviously bullshitting about knowing where I live, but how did they find out my name?'

Kasper gulped and grew paler.

'What? Did you let my name slip?'

'They must have seen the emails from you when they broke into my office.' He looked shifty.

'No point in worrying about it now. I need to keep off the streets, anyway. As you've probably guessed, it's not my real name.'

'No.' Kasper couldn't hold my gaze.

'What?'

'Sorry. I did some research on you. You're Peter Timothy, aren't you?'

Him saying my name sounded strange. 'Do you want a round of applause?'

'Not appropriate, Victor— Or do you prefer Peter?'

'Let's stick with Victor, shall we?'

'Okay. Look . . .' He fidgeted for a moment. 'I . . . I might have . . .'

'Spit it out, Kasper.'

'Okay.' He hesitated. 'I wrote your home address on a pad in my office.'

Ice slid down my spine. 'So?'

'Since the break-in, the pad's missing.'

The ice filled my insides. 'Why the hell didn't you tell me?'

'I didn't think. I . . . I hoped the pad—'

'You never think.' I wasn't listening to his pathetic excuse as I punched a speed dial I hadn't used for months. The phone rang out, and I ended the call. Although Carol had changed her mobile number after throwing me out, they'd kept the same landline number, and I knew Helen's by heart. It too rang out, going to voicemail. By the third time I rang it, panic seized me.

'I must warn my family.' I rang the house phone but again, nobody answered.

'Shall I phone the local police?'

'And tell them what?'

'That we think your family is at risk. I'm so sorry, Victor.'

'So am I. How are we going to get them to believe us? Tell them the men have already kidnapped your sister?'

'We can't do that.'

'I'm going to have to go down there.'

'Let me take you to the station—'

'I'm taking your car.'

He blinked at me. 'Can you drive?'

'I passed my test before you left school. Where are your keys?'

'You can't take it. I need it, in case I need to pick Zofia up.'

'Use hers. You said you found it abandoned in town. Get a cab and pick it up.'

He stared at me.

'You *owe* me, Kasper.' I jabbed a finger at him. 'If you hadn't written my name and address down . . .'

He avoided my gaze, guilt trumping his panic and fear.

'Please, Kasper. I just need to warn them and then come back.'

'Okay, I'll drive you. We'll need fuel.'

I tried both numbers while he got ready. No answer. I hoped I wasn't too late.

CHAPTER 32

Kasper drove through South Manchester and joined the M6. I rang the two numbers again. No replies from either. Panic had by now fully seized me. I had no doubt something had happened to my family.

'How long did you live in Bristol?' Kasper said.

I didn't reply straight away. 'Believe it or not, I'm not in the mood to make small talk.'

'Nor am I, but I'm going out of my head about my sister. You're thinking about your family. I thought it might help keep our minds clear to talk about something else.'

He might have had a point. 'Okay. I moved there to do my degree and stayed.'

'What degree did you do?'

'Didn't you find all this out when you snooped into my life?'

Kasper frowned at me. 'Maths. Wasn't it on your LinkedIn page?'

I nodded.

'And you've got two daughters.'

'That's not on my LinkedIn page.'

'It's on the 2021 Census. Peter and Carol Timothy.'

'There you are, then. You know everything about me.'

'Nowhere near everything.'

I looked at my handset. Was it too soon to ring again? Signs for Stoke appeared.

Kasper cleared his throat. 'How did you end up . . . you know, on the streets?'

The question I expected, but wasn't ready to answer. I stared at the stream of cars and lorries we passed on our left. Kasper didn't press me, accepting my reticence. The time to destination on the satnav showed two hours. I took it as an omen and made the calls. Panic made my breath short as I listened in vain.

'Where the hell are they?'

Kasper focussed on driving.

'My wife threw me out.' I jerked a thumb at Oscar, sleeping on the back seat. 'Oscar came with me. He'd been "mine" more than hers. We stayed with a mate for a couple of weeks. Someone offered me a flat in Manchester, cheap, but not great. I took it. Then they found out about Oscar.'

Oscar stirred at the repeated mention of his name. ***I wondered how long it would take you to blame me.***

I twisted in my seat. 'Get back to sleep.' I straightened. 'They chucked me out, but I didn't have enough money to get a new place, especially with a dog.'

Why don't you get me put down if I'm such a burden?

'Shut up.'

'What?' Kasper studied me with a puzzled frown.

'Talking to the dog.'

'Oh, right.' Kasper glanced back at Oscar. 'What about work? Didn't you have a job in Bristol?'

'They sacked me. Embezzlement, but I didn't do it.'

My denial sat heavy until Kasper said, 'I'm sure you didn't.'

I snorted. 'Everyone claims it's not their fault, don't they?'

'No, I didn't mean that. I do believe you.'

For some reason, it mattered that Kasper believed me. 'You'll have found out, from my LinkedIn profile, I worked as a data analyst for a private healthcare company. I ran a department of nine staff, and I found out one of them was syphoning money out of a fund we used to pay people who took part in clinical studies.

'It wasn't a huge amount and, apart from stealing from the company, she did a great job. I confronted her, and she admitted it. Her husband had abandoned her and their three children. She promised to stop, and we agreed on a plan to return the money. She couldn't afford to repay it any time soon, so . . . I started doing it.'

'So, what went wrong?'

'Before I paid it all back, someone else noticed.' The memory still made me sick. 'This person and I weren't friends, so he told my boss.'

Yeah, you know what they say, no good turn goes unpunished.

I ignored Oscar.

'But you must have explained what happened.'

He shrugged. 'I wasn't popular at work right then. Eight months earlier, we'd been the subject of a takeover bid. If it had gone through, we'd have each got thousands. I realised they'd based the bid price on a mistaken valuation. They'd assumed we owned the copyright to a process we used, but we licensed it. And when I pointed it out, the bidder withdrew their offer.'

'How much did you lose?'

'Me personally? Between eighty-seven and ninety-three grand after tax.'

Kasper whistled. 'And Carol knew about that?'

'Of course, I told her.'

'But what about the woman you helped? Didn't she say anything?'

'Yeah, she said she'd noticed *I'd* taken the money, but I'd threatened to blame her unless she shut up.'

'Bloody hell.'

'Yeah.' Even now, the memory ignited a fury. 'They gave me the choice of repaying the final bit and resigning, or they'd sack me and get the police involved.'

'Why didn't you call their bluff?'

'The number of times I wish I had. But I had a family to support, and I reckoned I'd have no problem getting a job. A rival company had already offered me one in Bath. Better money.'

'Why didn't you take it?'

'Once I left, the offer disappeared. Someone from my old company made a phone call.'

'Why did your missus chuck you out?'

'I didn't tell her straight away.' I drew in a deep breath, let it drain out of me. 'I spent three months pretending to go to work while I hunted for another job.' Kasper made a pained face. 'When I came home from another fruitless interview in Gloucester, she was waiting for me. Someone sent her a letter telling her what happened, but claiming I'd had an affair with the woman I'd tried to help.'

'Bloody hell. And she believed them?'

'She checked our savings account, saw the missing money . . .'

'Didn't you tell her your side?'

'Of course I did. We'd already been going through a rocky patch, and whoever sent the letter included photos of me and the young woman in a pub. I'd thought it safer to discuss her problem outside work. In one of them, she gave me a hug. It was when I offered to start repaying the money for her.'

'How much?'

'What's that got to do with it?'

'Well, if it was a few hundred, it would be easier to believe there was nothing untoward—'

'There *was* nothing going on. I told you.'

'So how much?'

I hesitated. 'Four and a half grand.'

Kasper whistled again. 'No wonder your missus suspected something.'

'You take the side of a woman you've never met over me?'

'No, I just meant, I can see why she'd be suspicious, not that she was right.'

An uneasy silence filled the car. The satnav showed an hour and a half to go. Time was crawling. I retrieved my phone and punched the redial button.

'Hello.'

The reply caught me by surprise. Was this Carol's new man? 'Can I speak to Carol?'

'Who shall I say is calling?'

'Her husband. Now, can you get her to the phone?'

Muffled voices and then Carol came on. 'Peter?'

'Where have you been?' Not my best response.

'None of your business.'

'I've been ringing for hours.'

She paused for a few moments. 'Why?'

'What do you mean, why? I wanted to make sure my daughters were okay. Aren't I allowed to?'

'But why now? You've been gone six months without contacting us, so why now?' Her voice rose.

'I want to speak to Helen.'

'You can't—'

'You can't stop me, Carol.'

'She's not here. Someone took her. The neighbours heard a row.'

The air left my lungs, and I struggled to reply. 'What's happened?'

'Why don't *you* tell me? You know, don't you? What have you done, you bastard?'

'I've done nothing.' I'd never heard Carol swear.

'Of course not. It's never your fault. You just happened to ring when my daughter gets kidnapped?'

'No. I . . . I . . .' My mouth dried.

'Bugger off, Peter.'

The line died, and I stared at the blank screen.

Kasper said, 'Something wrong?'

'Well spotted, Sherlock.' I gazed out of the windscreen. *They've taken Helen.* What the hell could I do? The notion of her ending up in a bin made me feel sick. If they touched her, I'd . . .

My phone rang, and I answered. 'Look, Carol—'

'Mr Timothy?' The man's broad Bristolian accent took me back.

'Who's that?'

'Avon and Somerset Police, Mr Timothy. It appears someone might have taken your daughter, and your wife thinks you might know something about it.'

I couldn't deny it, but what could I say? 'She's wrong.'

'Look, Peter— Can I call you Peter?'

I didn't speak.

'I can understand if you feel you're not getting access to your kids. To be honest, I'm in the same—'

'You think I've taken her?' I gave an ironic laugh. 'I wish.'

'So, you *do* know who has?'

What could I tell them? If the Novaks heard we'd gone to the police – and they would if they had a mole in the Manchester force – they'd make an example of Helen or Zofia. And I feared it would be my daughter.

'Tell Carol I'm sorry.' I ended the call and switched my phone off.

CHAPTER 33

'Do you want to press on to Bristol?'

Kasper's question caught me by surprise.

Did I? What would that achieve? The police suspected me of being behind Helen's kidnapping. Carol clearly believed it. I could picture myself stuck in a police cell, unable to help my daughter.

'Victor?'

'What?' I glared at him. 'No. Sorry. Let's go back.'

He pursed his lips and indicated to come off at the next junction.

'If you hadn't told them where my family lived, this wouldn't have happened.'

'I didn't tell them.'

'You might as well have.'

He slowed as we approached the roundabout. 'Look, we'll get nowhere bickering. Let's get back home. We can decide what to do once we're back.'

'Yeah, okay.'

We took the northbound carriageway and continued our journey in silence. My mind worried at the problem, but didn't come up with a solution. I retrieved my phone and opened the email from Helen's kidnappers.

I wrote a reply: Please let my daughter go. What do you want me to do?

My job before my fall involved solving complex conundrums, but my brain seemed to have become jelly. Every time I approached the problem, an image of Helen cruelly shoved in a blue bin would fill me with fear and panic. Despite knowing the route home, Kasper programmed the satnav, and it showed ninety minutes to go.

How was Emily coping? And my God, what about Helen? I tried not to think about her in the hands of those killers, but kept compulsively going back to it.

My phone pinged. An email. It had to be a reply.

'Aren't you going to see who it is?'

We both knew who it was. After staring at it for a few moments, I opened it with trembling fingers.

> *Give us the gloves and you get her back safe.*
> *And no pigs!!!*

'They want the gloves.' Would they release her? I had to believe they would.

'You going to hand them over?'

'I don't have a choice, do I?'

We drove in silence until Kasper said, 'Shall I ask one of my contacts to track Helen's phone?'

'Can you do that?' I feared the kidnappers would have taken it off her, but Helen might have been able to hide it.

We came off at the next services and Kasper made a call, wheedling with a guy. I let Oscar out for a walk and came back as Kasper finished his call having sorted something out. After grabbing sandwiches and caffeine-infused drinks, we set off, me driving. Kasper's phone rang, and my knuckles turned white on the steering wheel.

He listened, making little comment, then ended the call. 'The phone's not in Bristol. They last pinged it near Dursley around five. He'll ring us if he gets an update.'

That was almost six hours ago. 'They'd have been on the M5, taking her back with them to Manchester.' I pressed the accelerator. Although we were only doing eighty, the car juddered.

After half an hour, I couldn't wait any longer. 'Should we check if he's found anything?'

'He'll ring us as soon as he's got something. Let's go to my house and we can rest.'

We left the motorway and made our way towards Stretford. Kasper's phone rang. 'Yeah . . . Where? . . . Yeah, I know it, thanks.'

'He got something?'

'She's switched it on. It's in Crumpsall—'

'Near the hospital?'

'He's only got a rough location, within about a quarter mile, but it's near . . .'

'Near where?'

'It's near Vale Park.'

My insides twisted. Where they'd dumped Jehona's body. 'Put it in the satnav.'

'You sure we should go there?'

'I have to get near her, at least. Think, plan something, on the way.'

Despite my desperation to get there, I stuck to the speed limit. Getting pulled up would be disastrous. The miles passed glacially. With the fuel light flickering, we hit the Mancunian Way. Less than four miles to go.

Then, as we got closer, the miles to our destination went down too fast and before I was anywhere near ready, we'd got within the last mile. Two minutes. Sweat coated my hands, and I wanted to vomit. I opened the window a crack and icy air rushed in.

'Can you smell that?'

Kasper sniffed. 'Maybe someone's having a bonfire?'

'At one in the morning, in mid-February?' My sense of foreboding increased.

The map showed one more turn before we reached our destination. I slowed and indicated. Ahead of us, blue light flashed from the pavement. It appeared too low to be on a car and too faint. As we got close, the headlights illuminated it. A lamp hanging from a hydrant. Red hose snaked from two outlets heading down the road leading to our destination.

'Shit!' I unclipped my seatbelt.

We turned down the side road, and I screeched to a halt. A police car, blue light flashing, sat fifty metres down, blocking the road. Beyond it, a jumble of vehicles: several fire engines, but cars among them. I jumped out, ignoring Kasper's shout, and Oscar's bark.

With a shout of, 'Stay, boy!' I ran on unsteady legs.

My steps faltered as I got closer. The gates protecting the unit lay open, the padlocked chain lying on the ground. Two fire engines sat in the car park, one on huge jacks with telescopic arms reaching down to the ground. Two men climbed into the cage, studying the roof.

Firefighters from the other vehicle ripped the roller-shutter off the main entrance and smashed the door behind it open. A column of thick black smoke poured out of the top of the opening. A line of hose lay in bights near the opening. I needed to find Helen. I ran to the opening.

Two firefighters stopped me. 'Whoa, mate, you can't go in there.'

'My daughter. She's in there.'

They exchanged a look.

One of them said, 'If she is, we'll find her. Please leave it to us, sir.'

His companion spoke into a mic on his tunic. More people joined us, and the urgency already evident in their movements increased. Powerful arms led me away. The two who'd intercepted me removed their helmets and, with practised ease, started up their breathing apparatus before replacing their headgear, picking up the hose and testing it.

Before they could enter, a muffled explosion drove flames through the opening. The windows on the upper floors blew out, showering broken glass on those below. With a crash, part of the roof collapsed.

My legs gave way, and I slumped to the ground. 'HELEN!'

CHAPTER 34

After letting the firefighters lead me from the building, I'd watched it for several minutes. Flames leapt out of the hole in the roof and as the firefighters unsealed the openings, they released the mass of smoke and fire filling the building. Nobody could survive it. The thought of Helen trapped in there twisted my insides. And it was all my fault.

'Come on, mate, let's get you somewhere warm.'

A gentle hand rested on my shoulder. I let the firefighter lead me away and put me into the back of one of the fire engines. The faint odour of smoke lingered in the cab and, pushing a pair of shoes to one side, I sat on the bench seat. I couldn't see the fire, but I didn't need to. The scene played out in my head, vivid and in full colour.

The front door opened, and someone climbed into the front cab, making the vehicle rock. Then the firefighter who'd led me there spoke a series of stilted phrases which made little sense. Was he talking to me? Before I replied, a speaker crackled, and I listened. I deciphered the exchange, realising they'd not found anyone yet. The exchange ended, and he got out, then the rear door opened.

'Alright, mate. How you doing?' He didn't wait for an answer. 'I'll find us a brew in a sec, but is it alright if I make a few notes?' He waved a pad at me.

‘What for?’

‘I’ll have to fill out an incident report. You know what it’s like, as with every big organisation, the fire service runs on forms.’

‘Yeah, whatever.’

I answered his questions with my thoughts still on events in the building a few dozen paces away.

‘What makes you think your Helen’s in there?’

I needed to think about this one and not implicate myself in anything. ‘We tracked her phone to here.’

‘How did you manage that?’

I backed away from him: ‘Why do you need this for your fire report?’

‘Sorry, mate. I’m just curious.’

He seemed genuine, so I let it go. The radio summoned him, and he left to deal with it. My mind drifted back to the fire and Helen, so I didn’t focus on his message until I heard, ‘. . . detective is en route.’

The uniformed officers at the fire concentrated on keeping the rubberneckers away, so I hadn’t worried about avoiding them. But a detective would be a different matter. I craned my neck to peer at the building through the windscreen. The flames grew smaller, and even in the dark, the smoke took on a lighter shade of grey. The cab vibrated as the engine ticked over. As I sat there, the heat in the cab seeped into my flesh and my eyelids grew heavy.

The driver’s door opened, and I sat up. He spoke to someone, and a woman answered. I slid across the bench as the door opened. A tall, mixed-race woman wearing a dark jacket smiled at me. She introduced herself as DS Collette Bowling, and produced an ID which I didn’t need to examine. I recognised her from when I’d seen Grimes. I checked the handle to the door on the side opposite her, but she looked like she could leap across the cab and put me in a chokehold before I got the door half open.

I answered her questions, doing okay until she asked me Helen's age. Just then, her phone rang. I sat for a few moments as she turned away, part of me wanting to flee but another part thought, why bother? If my actions had led to Helen's death, why run? But the thought I might be wrong, and my daughter might still need me, made up my mind, and I eased open the door.

The blast of cold air dispelled any drowsiness left in me, and I slid to the ground before pushing the door shut. I jogged down the side of the fire engine and back towards the main road, the thought of Helen needing me giving me energy. Part of me wanted to wait nearby, to find out what was going on, but I couldn't risk hanging around.

I continued to the main road, keen to find Kasper and decide what to do next. The stench of smoke followed me. I saw his car just ahead, in a side street opposite. It sat near the junction with the main road, under a lamppost bathing it in yellow light.

He jerked awake when I tapped on the window. A patch of drool clung to the driver's window, and the glass had flattened the right side of his face. With a startled expression, he studied me before unlocking the car. I walked round and let myself in. On the back seat, Oscar stirred.

'What's happening?' Sleep blurred Kasper's speech. A faint voice burbled in the background.

'Is that the police radio?'

'What? Yeah, it is. So, what's happened?'

He meant with Helen, and I couldn't say. 'They're still putting the fire out, so . . .'

'I'm really sorry, Victor. If I could take back what I did . . .'

'Not your fault. It's those bastards who snatched her.' I still resented that he'd put my family at risk, but I reminded myself his sister was still missing, and he looked so contrite. I couldn't blame him.

'Why have you come back to the car?'

'The police, a detective, arrived and wanted to question me.'

He reached forward and increased the volume on the radio. '. . . crime scene technicians on their way, ETA oh three forty.'

I checked the clock. Ten minutes.

'They must have found something,' Kasper said.

I didn't need him to tell me, and I stared at the dashboard until it went out of focus. How the hell could I tell Carol and Emily about this?

'It might not be Helen.'

'Oh yeah, so who would it be? Zofia?'

He blanched. 'No, it couldn't be Zofia. I was here after she disappeared, and it was empty. But it might be another woman.'

'Yeah, you're right.' I hated myself for hoping it was someone I didn't know. Someone's daughter, sister, niece. Anyone, provided it wasn't my girl.

Then the radio exploded into life. 'Private ambulance required.'

'What does that mean?' I asked Kasper.

'Roger that,' said the dispatcher's dispassionate voice.

'Kasper?'

He cleared his throat. 'It means . . . It means they've found a body.'

CHAPTER 35

'What do you want to do?' Kasper waited for me to answer.

'Do? What can I do?'

A furry head burrowed between the seats and Oscar licked my hand. I leant into him and fondled his ear.

'I can take you round there.'

But I didn't have to be there. I could imagine it all. Helen's scorched remains coming out in a body bag and being thrown into the back of a black van.

'Let's go home.'

Kasper looked at me for a long moment before starting the car. Memories of my Helen played in my mind. I'd have to tell Carol *and* Em. How had I let it come to this? A surge of anger at Kasper made me want to grab the steering wheel and force him to crash the car. If he hadn't written my real name and address down, they'd have never touched my family. I'd come all the way here to spare them any association with my predicament, and now I'd pulled them all into something far worse. I'd ruined us all.

'You can stay as long as you need.'

Stay? Stay where? Oh. With them. The offer took me by surprise, and I realised he must be feeling guilty. But it wasn't his fault. I should direct my anger at those who took her. But what could I do to them in retaliation? I still had the gloves. Even if the person they could convict hadn't directly harmed Helen, whoever had, cared about him.

'I'm going to send the gloves to the police.'

'What about Zofia?'

'What about her?'

'They've still got her. I can't risk anything happening to her.'

In my anguish about Helen, I'd forgotten about his sister.

'Please.' His voice broke.

A mixture of anger and guilt washed over me. I wanted to punish those who hurt my girl, but what if Kasper was right and I ended up punishing his sister? She hadn't let the bad guys find out where my family lived. And it wasn't her who rang my phone, helping the security guys find it.

'If you hadn't . . .'

'If I hadn't what?'

I reminded myself Kasper hadn't hurt my daughter. 'I want to hit back at them. Make them suffer for what they did to Helen.'

'The police will find them.'

'They haven't so far. And I doubt the girl I found was the first one they've killed.'

Kasper drove on in silence. My thoughts returned to the scene of the fire and my imagination filled my mind with images of horror. I hoped my girl didn't suffer. They say the smoke kills most people. Would it be like falling asleep? I hoped so. *Stop torturing yourself.*

A faint voice came from the radio. Kasper still had it tuned to the police channel. I didn't want to hear the details and jabbed the off button. We arrived at his house a few minutes later. He parked opposite and sat studying the house for a few moments.

'What's up?'

'I didn't leave the lights on.'

'You sure?' I cast my mind back to when we left. Was it only twelve hours ago? I didn't remember seeing lights. 'What should we do?'

'I'm sick of this.' He got out, slammed the door behind him and marched to the house.

'Hold on, Kasper!' I let Oscar out, jogged after Kasper and grabbed his shoulder.

'What?'

'What if they've booby-trapped it?'

He pulled out of my grip. 'Don't be stupid.' He reached the door and put his key in the lock. After a long pause, he turned the key and pushed the door open.

I held my breath, but nothing happened. Inside, someone had switched on every light. Oscar paused at the threshold and made a noise I'd never heard him make.

'What is it, boy?'

He stood, his attention on the stairs.

Kasper made straight for the kitchen and I followed him, bumping into him as he halted.

I peered over his shoulder. Every drawer had been pulled out and dumped upside down on the floor along with the contents of the open cupboards. The aroma of spilled herbs mixed with the ripe smell of spoiling food coming from a melting pile in front of the fridge-freezer. Meltwater lay on the floor in shallow pools. On the door of the fridge, someone had written *welcome home* in red letters.

Oscar cowered between my legs, trembling.

'Is that blood?' I said.

Kasper picked his way across the floor to study the writing. 'Looks like it.'

'Whose?'

Kasper paled. He'd obviously had the same idea I'd had.

A sense of being observed made the skin on my neck tingle. Oscar's continued cowering added to my dread. I left Kasper and checked the front room. Oscar followed me and I paused outside the door, body tense. I pushed the door open and leapt in. Like the kitchen, the room had been turned over, but there was nobody waiting. My pulse slowed.

'Look!' Kasper stood in the doorway and pointed.

I followed his finger. The same person had written *suprise upstairs* on the television screen.

He glanced at the ceiling, and after a moment, mounted the stairs. I followed. Oscar stayed at the foot of the stairs and whimpered.

'You're creeping me out, boy.'

He lowered his body to the carpet.

Half sick with dread, I followed Kasper onto the landing where the light blazed. Four closed doors led off it, two on each side of the corridor. He paused outside the nearest one before turning the knob and pushing the door open. The lights illuminated a bedroom with a double bed and pale wood furniture on a cream carpet. The mattress lay on the floor, the bedding ripped off it. Clothes on and off hangers lay scattered around amongst upended drawers.

Kasper backed out and closed the door. The door opposite opened to a small room containing a desk, a low filing cabinet and an office chair. Papers lay on every surface like flat flakes of snow.

We approached the two doors towards the back. The next door he opened led to the bathroom I'd used on the first day I met Kasper. I'd remembered that day as something positive, the start of the opportunity to get back on my feet. It felt nothing like that now. Looking past Kasper, I saw nothing more terrible than the contents of the bathroom cabinet mingled with the dirty clothes from the linen basket in the bathtub.

Kasper jerked the light switch off and pulled the door shut. One room remained. Whatever surprise awaited us lay in there. His hand rested on the doorknob for ages, then he twisted and shoved the door. Blackness greeted us. He reached in and switched on the light.

'What the hell?'

Over his shoulder, I saw another mess, but also a small, fur-covered body on the wardrobe door, pinned to it with a knife. Blood leaked from it.

'Bastards.' Kasper stepped into the room.

The same author had used a finger to write *your next* in red on the door underneath.

CHAPTER 36

When Bowling had turned up outside her prison asking questions, Zofia had tried to control her trembling. Two men flanked her, the one in the Captain America mask holding the knife at her throat. The stink of stale sweat wafted off him, confirming his own nerves. She'd strained her ears, listening for Bowling. Would she try to gain access and, if so, what would happen?

The sound of a vehicle approaching made her guards tense and Spider-Man's Adam's apple bobbed as he swallowed. Police reinforcements? She studied her captors. Their body language suggested they weren't keen to carry out Wolverine's orders, but would Wolverine himself put a bullet in her?

She could just hear Bowling's voice and a deeper man's voice. It didn't sound like she was issuing orders. Then it went silent, and a car started. The man outside laughed. Zofia's two captors relaxed and removed the knife from her throat. The man in the Wolverine mask returned shaking his head, still carrying the gun.

'Your brother's not very bright, is he? We told him not to call the police.'

He signalled to the men flanking her. The one with the Spider-Man mask left the room while the other gripped her arm with one hand and held a knife at her throat. She tried to stop shaking. The other one returned, now wearing rubber gauntlets and holding two items: a glass bottle and a piece of cardboard. He un-stoppered the bottle and held it in front of her above the sheet of card. A chemical stench she recognised attacked her nostrils. Hydrochloric acid.

Wolverine pointed his camera at her. She closed her eyes, but opened them again, determined not to let Kasper see her fear. They took a short video as Spider-Man poured a few drops onto the card, causing it to disintegrate and release pungent fumes which made her cough. The thought of what the acid would do to her skin made her cringe, but then she imagined her brother watching the video, and her courage returned. With it, her fury at what her captors were putting them through. Then, placing the hood back on her head, they returned her to the other room.

Exhausted by her ordeal, she lay her head on the desk and slept.

Loud voices disturbed her. How long had she slept?

'Okay, we've been told to leave.' It sounded like Wolverine.

The door opened and footsteps approached. Two hands grabbed her and pulled her to her feet before propelling her across the space. Zofia sensed their passage through a doorway and then another, and then they stopped. The stench of stale exhaust fumes penetrated her mask. A vehicle door opened and then they lifted her, dumping her into the van but not closing the door.

'Shall I make a start upstairs?' It sounded like Captain America.

'Change of plan,' Wolverine shouted. 'Let's get out of here. Another crew will be here to clean—'

A loud banging interrupted him, and someone outside shouted a greeting.

'Here they are. Let's go.'

The door crashed shut, then a cacophony as more doors slammed, the engine started, and the deeper note as a larger engine came into the space. The van moved forward, then paused. Several voices spoke, excitement clear in their tone. One mentioned a surprise and after exchanging greetings, the van sped off, again buffeting Zofia every time it changed direction. She wedged herself into the side of the space, trying to stop the pummelling. They stopped far sooner than she expected, and the door opened.

None too gently, they dragged her out and dumped her on her feet. Fresh exhaust fumes attacked her nostrils. It sounded like they were indoors, but in a large space. A man led her across the floor until her ankle hit something hard and she cried out through the tape covering her mouth.

'She can't see, you idiot.'

The man leading her grunted, then seized her calf and lifted it before forcing it onto a step. 'Lift your feet.'

Piss off, you creep. If she ever got the chance to hurt these men, she would welcome it.

The echoey clang as they climbed the metal treads told her they were still in a large space. At the top, they led her through a door, then along a narrow corridor. The clumsy oaf leading her bounced her off the wall.

The floor felt softer beneath her feet. They must be on a carpet, and the smell of stale cooking told her they must be near a kitchen. They paused, and a door opened. Her captor thrust her through the opening. Metal clicked. It sounded like a flick knife. The oaf grabbed her hands, pulled her arms back and cold metal pressed against the inside of her wrists. Then, with a sawing motion, he cut the band securing her. He pushed her forward, slammed the door, and a lock clicked.

She stood until the sounds of the men faded, and silence reigned. Zofia flexed her wrists, and her hands tingled. She lifted the hood off, but the darkness remained. Her fingernails found the end of the tape across her mouth. She ripped it off, and, ignoring the pain, gulped in air.

The chemical, floral smell of air freshener struck her as incongruous. Where was she? She looked around, but couldn't penetrate the darkness. There had to be a light switch near the door. With her hands held out ahead of her, she made her way to where she thought it was. Her palm brushed against a wall, and she moved along it, then hit the doorframe. Next to it, the plastic box of a light switch.

Nothing happened when she flicked the toggle. 'Bugger!'

As her night-sight improved, she could make out objects in the room. Two dark shapes stood alongside the wall to the right of the doorway. She reached for them and touched a plastic handle.

A wheelie bin?

She lifted the lid, and the stench of bleach made her eyes water.

'Oh shit!'

CHAPTER 37

Kasper sat on the bed, eyes vacant and shoulders slumped. I wanted to join him, but one of us needed to take charge. For the first time since I'd hit the streets, a sense of purpose invigorated me. I inspected the object pinned to the wardrobe door. A stuffed toy. So why was it bleeding? The edge of a plastic pouch showed behind it.

'Bastards.' I left him and went downstairs.

Oscar saw me on the stairs and stood, wearing a worried expression but wagging his stumpy tail.

'You alright?' I stroked his head.

Are we going? I don't like it here.

'Not for a while. We're going to have to clear up.' He followed me while I checked both front and back doors. Neither appeared damaged, and the downstairs windows remained locked. How the hell had the intruders got in?

Of course, Zofia's keys. The alarm hadn't gone off. Had Kasper set it? I couldn't remember. I wandered into the hall and checked the panel. I saw no obvious signs of tampering. They must have got Zofia to tell them the code. With a new sick sensation overlaying the old, I returned to the kitchen.

The message on the fridge looked like whoever wrote it had worn gloves. It appeared to be blood, not paint. They must have brought it with them. I stared out of the kitchen window into the darkness and saw only my reflection. Why were they doing this? Whoever was behind this enjoyed terrorising people. And they had my daughter.

Were the culprits still out there? I suspected they'd gone. Had they known Kasper's whereabouts when they broke in? The idea they were monitoring our movements made me shiver, and I moved away from the window.

I found a bin liner under the sink and returned to the stairs.

Oscar whined when I mounted the first step.

'I won't be long.' I left him sitting at the bottom of the stairs.

In the back bedroom, I found Kasper in the same position. Beyond him, the bloodied teddy bear presented a macabre sight. Turning the bin bag inside-out and wrapping it round my hand, I approached it.

Kasper stirred himself. 'What you doing?'

'I'm getting rid of this. We can't leave it up there.'

He stared at it for a moment. 'I suppose not. But don't throw it away. It was Zofia's.'

'Is the knife yours?'

'Why?'

'If they brought it with them, it might have their fingerprints or offer some other kind of evidence.'

He examined it from the bed. 'It's from the knife block in the kitchen.'

I slipped the bag over the bear, wrapped my left hand in polythene and seized the handle of the knife. Whoever did this had banged the blade in, and it took a few waggles to loosen it enough to remove. The toy, and the clear polythene pouch behind it, fell into the bin liner. I let go of the knife, which landed on them, and tied up the bin liner.

'What you going to do with it?'

'Will you be calling the police?'

'What, and find they've done the same to my sister next time?'

I carried the liner to the door, deciding to leave the blood somewhere safe in case he changed his mind. Could they get forensic information from it? A label on the pouch, stained and unreadable, might give a clue to where it came from. Was it human or animal?

Downstairs, Oscar hadn't moved, but his attention focussed on the bin liner, and I lifted it high, out of his reach. He followed me into the kitchen, where I checked the knife block, noting a missing knife from a set with the same handle. Kasper was right. I picked up one of the empty freezer drawers off the floor and, making sure the bin liner wasn't leaking, I placed it inside the freezer and closed the door.

Oscar studied me with a disgusted expression.

'I'm preserving it in case it's needed as evidence.'

It wasn't the right time to tell Kasper what I'd done with the blood, and I didn't want him or Zofia to have a shock, so I found a pad and pencil in a drawer and out of habit wrote, '11 FEB BAG OF BLOOD'. I examined the note. *Idiot, as if he's going to get mixed up with any other bags of blood in there.* Not wanting to write another, I placed the note in the drawer and closed the freezer.

'What you doing?' Kasper stood in the doorway.

'You feeling better?'

He waited for *my* answer.

'Do you want me to wipe this message off?' I pointed to the reddish-brown letters on the door.

'I don't know. Fingerprints?' He looked lost.

'They wore gloves. Shall I photograph it and then remove it? Unless you're thinking of telling the police . . .'

'What would you do, Victor?' He staggered to the table and sat.

The unexpected appeal hit me like a punch and the pressure to make the right decision paralysed me. 'Shall we leave it for a bit? Decide later, after we've tidied up.'

'Yeah, good idea.' He spoke in a low monotone.

'Do you want to start upstairs, and I'll do this?' I waved a hand around the kitchen.

'Sure. Yeah.' He heaved himself to his feet and climbed the stairs.

I rescued some chilled meals, bagged all the frozen stuff and the spilled packets of food in bin liners and stacked them beside the back door. Not wanting to dwell on Helen's fate, I focussed on the mundane task of tidying the kitchen. By the time Kasper came back down, I'd finished the kitchen and was putting the final items back in the living room.

'I'm not sure how you display your books.' I pointed at the bookshelf.

'Don't worry, Zofia will—' He took a deep breath and his eyes glistened.

'Okay, I'll just put them back.' I bent and picked up the final few books.

Kasper sighed. 'I don't know about you, but I can't continue.'

'What? What about your sister?'

'No, I meant I need to get my head down. I'm exhausted.'

'So am I.' But I doubted I'd sleep.

He looked around the kitchen. 'I can't stay here.'

Which meant I couldn't stay, either. I'd got used to the idea of staying, but thinking about it, I was probably safer on the street. 'Have you got a sleeping bag?'

'What?' He stared at me, puzzled.

'If we're sleeping outside, you'll need to keep warm and dry.'

'I thought I might contact my cousin.'

'Oh, right.' I doubted his cousin would welcome me, *or* Oscar.

'I'll ring him.' He patted his pockets. 'I must have left my phone upstairs.'

Without a task, my mind drifted to the fire and Helen. Was I certain she'd died in it? I should contact the police, discover what they'd found there. But could I face it? I wanted to slump in a corner and roll into a ball. But I needed to find out, and do it without endangering Zofia.

I powered up my phone, found the email from the kidnappers and typed a reply: Why did you have to kill my daughter?

Oscar licked my hand. ***Are we going?***

'Don't worry, boy. Soon.'

I patted him. Why weren't they answering? I typed, Answer me, you bastards.

I stared at my message.

It buzzed. She's not dead but do what you're told and watch your mouth.

She's still alive?

Yes!!!! But don't piss us off now fuck off.

I stared at it, disbelieving.

'Victor?'

I jerked, dropping the phone on the table.

Kasper was standing in the doorway. 'Did you hear what I said?'

'She's alive, Kasper.' I jumped to my feet and hugged him.

'Who?'

'Helen, my Helen.'

'How do you know?'

I picked up my phone and showed it to him.

He read it. 'That's great news, Victor.'

His lack of enthusiasm annoyed me until I remembered his sister was still missing. 'What did you say to me? I didn't hear it.'

'My cousin can't put Oscar up. He lives in a flat and they're quite strict.'

His concern for me and Oscar surprised me. 'Why don't *you* stay? We'll be okay.'

'I also thought I might put my cousin at risk.' He pointed at the bloody message on the fridge.

'Good point.' We stared at each other for a long moment, then I asked, 'Do you want to get your sleeping bag?'

He nodded dully. 'Yeah. Yeah. I'll get it.'

'You'll need to put on some warmer clothes.'

He left the room, and I listened as his steps sounded on the stairs.

'You hear that, Oscar? Helen's okay.'

He wagged his tail and smiled at me.

To keep busy, I cleaned off the writing on the fridge and did the same on the living room mirror. Now suddenly hungry, I put the kettle on and hunted for bread. I remembered bagging a half-thawed loaf and found it near the top of one of the bin bags. I unsealed the bag, prised four slices off and put them in the toaster.

Kasper returned as it popped. He placed two rolled-up sleeping bags and a backpack on the floor inside the door and accepted my offer of tea and toast. I made some for Oscar and placed a plateful on the kitchen table. We sat, facing each other, and chewing.

Kasper spoke with his mouth full. 'I've been thinking. Why don't we stay at the office?'

'Haven't they already been there?'

He nodded.

'So, they know where it is.'

He swallowed. 'Yeah, but I'm probably safer there than I would be on the street.'

I could see his point. 'I've been thinking as well. Some of the guys I've met on the street are pretty switched on about what goes on in the city. I think we should co-opt them. They could—'

'Whoa. Hang on, I don't want any Tom, Dick or Harry knowing my business.'

'You hang on. These are people I trust.' Did I trust them? I supposed I did, as much as I could trust anyone these days. 'They've been watching Sackville Square for me until late evening.'

'They're doing what? What do you mean?'

'You want the place monitored, don't you? I can't do it from here.'

'How much did you tell them?'

'What's there to tell? You asked me to search for Catriona Robertson, and that's all you told me, so I did the same.' I still hadn't told him I'd found – or more accurately, Oscar had found – where she lived. I did now.

'When did you find out?'

'This afternoon.' I checked the time. 'Yesterday afternoon.'

'And you're telling me now?'

'Funnily enough, I've had other things on my mind.'

'Sorry, yes.' Kasper calmed. 'Did you get any photos?'

'Her bodyguards saw me and chased me.' I showed him the best one.

He examined it with a frown. 'It could be her, but I don't think we can use that.'

'Sorry.'

'Don't worry.' He returned the phone. 'What do you want to do about finding Helen?'

The reminder that although Helen wasn't dead, those monsters still held her, drained all my energy in a single stroke. 'I don't know.'

'Do you think they've taken her to where they're keeping Zofia?'

I'd not thought about it, but I needed to. My daughter needed me. 'That makes sense. You can guard two people as easily as one.'

'But where are they?'

'I'm pretty sure they've got them in Manchester.'

'That doesn't really help, does it?'

'It tells us where we should focus our search.' I didn't need his negativity. 'Have they sent you any more messages?'

He retrieved his phone. 'Shit, I've got a message from yesterday afternoon.' He opened it and what little colour remained in his face drained away.

'What is it?' I reached for his phone and took it from his trembling hands.

A photo of a battered Zofia, a cut on her forehead, a swollen cheek and blood crusted round her nostrils. I shared the short accompanying message with him.

Wot part of no fucking pigs dont you understand?

'What should I say to them?'

'We haven't spoken to the police.' Despair made his voice crack.

I punched in a reply. I haven't spoken to them.

Nothing happened for a long time, and we waited, not daring to breathe. Were they asleep or just not replying because they'd already disposed of Zofia? Then, the phone buzzed, making us both jump.

they just turned up on spec did they

Kasper wasn't in any state to reply, so I punched in a response. Maybe one of your people let something slip.

you think were fucking stupid

No, but I swear I've not spoken to the police. Please believe me. Would this convince them?

The phone announced the arrival of another message. No text, but a short video. Zofia with terror in her eyes. A hand in a gauntlet held a piece of cardboard in front of her face. Another poured a clear liquid onto it, and it disintegrated between the camera and Zofia's stricken features.

CHAPTER 38

Zofia slammed the lid on the bin and examined the gloomy room. A large dark shape sat in the centre of the space, and she shuffled towards it. A sofa with a pale mound on one end. Exhausted by what she'd gone through, she slumped into it. The mound contained a pillow and duvet. They smelled musty, but not too bad. She placed the pillow on one end of the sofa and lay down, pulling the duvet over herself. As she warmed up, her eyelids grew heavy until she slept.

Something woke her. A noise? She listened, but heard only her breathing. Faint daylight leaked through the windows, revealing the room. She sat up on the lumpy sofa and studied her surroundings. About five metres by six, the room had a false ceiling with some dislodged tiles. The wall on her right comprised windows with bars on the inside. Behind her, a whitewashed block wall. The other walls looked like stud partitions, and a solid door in the wall at right angles to the window provided the only way out of the room.

Apart from the large faux-leather sofa in the middle of the room, a series of metal cupboards and two filing cabinets lined the block wall. The duvet slid off her shoulder, and shivering, she pulled it back. In the cold, the pressure on her bladder grew intolerable. She got up and strode to the entrance.

'I need the loo.' She banged on the door, then listened. She shouted again and banged, but no response. Had they all gone home or were they just ignoring her?

By now, she'd become desperate. She glanced around the room. In the corner furthest from the door, she found a bucket with a lid. Under the lid, a roll of toilet paper. 'Oh, gross!'

Unable to hold on, she removed the roll, faced the door and pulled her jeans and panties down. Time slowed, and she concentrated on listening for anyone coming. Grateful to finish, she dressed and covered the lid.

Cold seeped into her and she wanted to hunker down under the duvet, but she forced herself to explore, not that there was much to see. The first three cabinets contained nothing but a few scraps of paper and torn envelopes. A roller-shutter closed off the fourth, but she couldn't lift it. Did it contain something she could use to escape? If she wanted to get away, she needed to do it before they came back.

She struggled with the shutter and searched for something to help her open it. A flat metal bar about fifty centimetres long lay in the bottom drawer of the nearest filing cabinet. She cut her finger on a sharp edge on the drawer as she retrieved it. She took the bar to the cabinet and slid it under the roller door. She levered the free end upwards. The bar bent, but the door lifted a centimetre. Enough to slide her fingers underneath.

She pushed both hands under it and pulled upwards. The roller resisted, then emitted a screech and lifted. She paused and listened. Nobody came. Maybe they *had* gone home. The roller stuck about halfway up. Frustrated, Zofia wrestled with it. With a creak, the side runners came free, and she fell backwards. The shutter unrolled, the end hitting the floor with a crash and clang of metal.

A sharp pain shot through her injured hip and ribs, and she sat, winded. If anyone remained in the building, they must have heard that. She waited, but after long minutes, nobody came. The shutter hung down like a torn curtain. She got up, and in a fit of frustration, she kicked it.

As it lifted, it exposed a shiny metal rod. Eighty centimetres long and three in diameter, it would make a good weapon. She picked it up. Solid and heavy, it gave her a sense of power. She slapped her left hand with it. Yes, this made a splendid weapon. She closed the filing cabinet, tidied the roller-shutter, then collected the metal bar and rod and took them to the sofa.

She got under the duvet and slid the two weapons under the bedding, ready to access if the opportunity to use them arose.

Despite listening intently, Zofia didn't hear anyone moving about. The light from the windows didn't brighten. She pushed the duvet away and shivered, but resisted the urge to snuggle under it. As she straightened, she pondered what to do with her weapons. She left the heavy metal rod under the bedding, then returned to tuck it behind a cushion in case they removed the duvet.

The bar, she would need. She took it to the furthest filing cabinet, which occupied the corner, its back against the block wall and its side along one of the stud-partition walls. She'd been thinking of how to escape and had devised a plan.

She pulled on a drawer handle to check inside, but it didn't move. This one *would* be locked, wouldn't it? Knowing her luck, it would be full of papers. She searched for a key but didn't find one.

Nothing for it but to move it, and grabbing the handles of the middle two drawers, she pulled. It resisted, then jerked forward a few centimetres on the carpet tiles. She took four goes to get it out of the space and she paused, warm and breathing hard. If she heard anyone coming, she'd have to just push it back part way and hope they didn't notice.

She listened at the door and, hearing nothing, returned to the corner and examined the section of wall she'd exposed. A narrow strip under the paint showed where they'd taped the join between two pieces of plasterboard. She used the edge of the metal bar to hack at the bottom of the strip and lifted the end. After a few attempts, she loosened a short strip, then, gripping the tape, pulled.

The dust released made her sneeze, but she'd exposed a section of joint fifty centimetres long. She worked the bar into the gap between the two sheets of plaster. The edges crumbled, and she exhaled in frustration before changing her attack. Ten minutes later, she'd exposed three nails. She peeled the heavy paper away, taking with it chunks of plaster and exposing the metal upright on one side.

More plaster came away and the pile she'd accumulated grew. It would prevent her from pushing the filing cabinet back, unless . . .

She opened the bottom drawer of the other filing cabinet and, using a piece of the paper she'd peeled off as a dustpan, moved the broken plaster into it. She worked for another twenty minutes until she'd exposed two uprights and removed a piece of plasterboard eighty centimetres high. Once she kicked through the plaster on the other side, the opening would be large enough for her to escape through.

A sound alerted her. A car door? She scrambled to her feet and scraped pieces of plaster off the carpet. After dumping them in the adjoining drawer, she shut it and pushed the filing cabinet she'd moved back towards the space.

It slid back a few centimetres but jerked to a stop. A sound had made her pause. Were those footsteps on the stairs? Shit, they were!

She straightened the cabinet. It stuck halfway out, but you couldn't see the opening she'd made. A bolt drew, and a key turned. Too late. She ran to the sofa, threw herself on it and dragged the duvet over her as the door opened.

Wolverine stepped into the room and stepped aside as Captain America walked in carrying a paper bag. Zofia, hot and her heart thumping, hoped she didn't look too stressed. She could feel the metal rod against her leg, but she didn't have a chance against two of them. She resisted looking at the filing cabinet.

Captain America walked up to her and lowered the bag on the carpet beside the sofa. 'Got your breakfast.'

She pretended not to notice the tattoo of a snake which appeared as his sleeve rolled up. 'Thanks. Can I have a wash and use the loo?'

Captain America glanced at Wolverine, who shook his head. 'There's a bucket there.' He gestured towards it and sniffed. 'It looks like you've found it. And don't piss on your hands and you won't need to wash them.'

Zofia's face grew hot, but she held back her angry retort. 'Do you know what the time is?'

'Yeah, I do. You got somewhere you need to be?' The two men sniggered.

She wanted to wipe the grins off their faces.

'Anyway,' Wolverine said, 'you won't be here much longer.'

'What do you mean?' Were they going to let her go?

He ignored her question and gestured to his companion. Captain America walked to the exit. His mask wasn't on straight, and the other end of the snake tattoo ran across the bottom of his neck. Was he the shaven-headed thug she'd seen? He had the build.

The men left, pulled the door closed, and the locks clicked. Zofia let out a breath, and sat up. A delicious aroma came from the bag. A bacon and cheese panini and a cup of tea. Both were still warm, so they must have got them from nearby. Conscious of her dirty hands, she held the sandwich using the bag it came in and took a bite.

She chewed two mouthfuls before taking a sip of the tea. Disgusting. They'd put sugar in it. She forced it down and ate some more.

A car started up, and she paused, listening. Then it drove away. They'd gone.

She finished the food and glugged the last of the tea. She wiped her lips and fingers with the paper napkin in the bottom of the bag, and placed all her rubbish in it. Before she carried on with her escape plan, she should check they'd gone. She listened, but didn't hear any movement, and made her way to the filing cabinet. She'd only pushed it back halfway, so removing it should be easier.

But it wasn't, and only after wrestling with it for far too long did it finally come out. She'd just got her breath back when a sound made her stop. Someone at the door. The lock clicked. She'd never get to the sofa in time and whoever came in must see the hole she'd made in the wall.

CHAPTER 39

The sound of Kasper moving about had woken me, and I opened my eyes. The windows at the rear of Kasper's office didn't have blinds and grey light leaked into the room.

'You awake?' Kasper's speech sounded slurred.

'I am now. What time is it?'

'Half seven. I'm making coffee. Do you want some?'

I'd slept for an hour, no wonder I felt rough. 'Go on, then.' I'd grown out of the habit of having coffee for breakfast.

Oscar sat under the window, pretending to be asleep. I slid out of the sleeping bag and rolled it up before going for a wash in the toilet washbasin. When I came back, a mug steamed on the desk nearest my sleeping bag.

'It was so uncomfortable I couldn't sleep.' Kasper rolled his shoulder. 'Even putting the cushions from the chairs in the waiting room on top of the mat didn't help.'

'It's a lot more comfortable than a sheet of cardboard.' I pointed to the other camping mat he'd brought from home.

'Yeah, your snoring didn't help.' He yawned again.

We sat in silence, enveloped in a fog of fear and recriminations, and sipped our coffees. I slurped mine, and Kasper cringed, so I made a point of slurping it again. Kasper finished his coffee and went for a wash.

Oscar got up and sauntered to me. ***Any food?***

'You'll be the first to know.'

He stretched, then trotted to the next desk and cocked his leg.

'OI. NO!'

He showed his tongue and lowered his leg. ***Just joking.***

'Hilarious. No need to ask if *you* slept well.'

I checked my phone. No messages, but what did I expect, one from the kidnappers saying they'd let Helen go? The fear they'd lied about her being alive, something which had disturbed my sleep, returned. With a sense of panic, I opened the browser and checked the local news sites. I found the story on the fire beneath a picture showing the burnt-out unit. The first few paragraphs gave a bare outline of the incident, but didn't mention casualties. I scrolled on and read the entire article.

No mention of them finding a body. So, maybe they hadn't lied. But it made sense if they had. Once they killed Helen, they had no hold over me.

Kasper returned and put his towel and wash bag on his desk. 'I'll get bacon butties from down the road.'

Get me one. Oscar sat up, wearing a hopeful expression.

'Can you get something for Oscar?'

'Yeah, same?' He looked at the dog as if expecting an answer.

'He'll eat anything.'

No, I won't. Definitely not broccoli or cabbage.

'Does *he* look like he eats broccoli?' I asked him.

'Sorry?' Kasper gave a puzzled frown.

'Nothing.' He must have thought I was cracking up.

He left, and I checked other news outlets. Two of the nationals had covered it, but neither mentioned a body. I'd finished reading all I could find about the incident when the front door opened. I froze until Kasper shouted a greeting. He charged into the room, accompanied by a mouth-watering aroma.

‘This one’s for you, Oscar, no brown sauce.’ He removed a barm from a paper bag and placed it on the bowl he’d put down. ‘I’ll plate these and get coffee.’

He disappeared into the kitchenette and returned with a plate and mug for me. The aroma of coffee mingled with that of cooked meat. I opened the bag and pulled out a white bap containing what seemed like half a pig.

‘I wasn’t sure what you wanted, so I put brown sauce on it.’ Kasper got his, sat at his desk and tucked in.

I took a bite and chewed. ‘This bacon tastes odd.’

‘Sorry, I should have said, it’s turkey. They have lots of Muslim and Jewish customers, so bacon’s a no-no.’

Neither of us spoke for a few minutes as we demolished our breakfast. My mind pondered the implications of Helen not being in the burnt-out building.

‘There’s no mention of a body in the reports about the fire.’

‘Uhuh.’ Kasper swallowed. ‘I read a few while waiting for these.’

‘I wondered if the police now knew the dead woman in the bin came from there. The people holding Zofia obviously thought you’d said something.’

‘You think the Novaks burned it down to destroy evidence before the police got a search warrant?’

‘It seems a bit of a coincidence otherwise.’ A thought occurred to me. ‘How would the Novaks discover the police were on to them?’

Kasper snorted. ‘There are rumours they’ve got police in their pockets, but quite a few people would know if Grimes applied for a search warrant. The leak could be anywhere.’

‘Could this Grimes be the leak? Is that why you don’t like him, because he’s dirty?’

Kasper drained his drink. ‘I don’t think so, but I saw his sergeant, Bowling, at the unit on Vale Park, *before* I knew Zofia had disappeared. *She* must have tracked the Novaks' people down. That's probably what panicked them into setting the place on fire.'

I continued scrolling through the news while Kasper took the dishes away. A familiar address jumped out at me.

> **Second dead homeless man found in Sackville Square**
>
> Police discovered another unidentified homeless man in Manchester city centre. Police said he appears to have been attacked sometime in the early hours of this morning. A spokesman described it as a frenzied attack which they're treating as murder.

I finished reading the rest of it until Kasper returned, and I showed it him.

He read it. 'What do you think?'

'When they killed the first homeless man, I thought the people who'd attacked me had come back and attacked another poor sod, but read the bit about all his stuff being stolen.'

'What about it?'

'Who steals from a homeless man? Unless they want to search through his stuff for something.'

A lightbulb seemed to go off in Kasper's head. 'You think the Novaks' men killed the poor bastard, believing it was you?'

'They must have thought they'd got me when they killed the first guy, then when they realised I was still alive . . .' Had my email asking about Helen led to the death of another homeless man?

'Why, if they've got your daughter?'

We already knew the answer. They intended to kill me and Kasper to make sure they had the right gloves. And that meant they had no intention of releasing Helen, or Zofia. I swallowed the acid in my throat.

'Victor?'

'We know they're not going to release them.'

'We can't be sure of that. Why kidnap Helen, then?'

'You told them I was refusing to give you the gloves. They obviously thought they needed more leverage over me.'

Kasper looked like I'd kicked him in the stomach. 'I'm so sorry, Victor.'

'It's not your fault.' Although part of me disagreed, we needed to work together.

'What should we do?'

'We must find out where they're keeping them.'

'And do what?'

I wasn't sure. But I couldn't do nothing. 'Try to free them.'

Kasper looked doubtful. 'How?'

'I don't know precisely, but do you have a better idea?' Then quickly the germ of a plan took root, but would it work?

Kasper sighed. 'Okay, but Zofia and I checked the land registry, and they don't own any properties except the houses where they live. We found a company that owns the flat Jehona lived in, KND Holdings, and we've checked all the buildings they own.'

'And?'

'None of them would work as a place to . . . The neighbours are too close.'

My thoughts raced as I considered possibilities. 'Did you check the ownership of the cars I photographed?'

'Of course. They're registered to offshore-based legal entities.'

'Not a surprise, but do those entities own properties?'

Kasper started up Zofia's computer and logged into it. 'You work at this one.' He opened her browser and clicked on a link on her bookmarks bar. 'This is a site we use, which does the same as the land registry database.' He logged in and left me to it.

Apart from the car which delivered and collected Catriona, each car I'd photographed belonged to a different company. We split the work and checked the databases.

After forty minutes, my enthusiasm had faded.

Kasper looked as despondent as I felt. 'They must be using different companies for the properties.'

We sat in silence for a few moments. The idea was growing, and it involved Craig and his knowledge of the Novaks. I messaged John.

Kasper let out a yelp. 'We know where at least one of their properties is. We were there a few hours ago.'

'Of course.' I punched in the address of the warehouse on Vale Park Industrial Estate.

I found the name of the company which owned the warehouse. A check of the land registry site showed they owned three other properties. 'Kasper.' My voice rose in excitement.

'What?' He stood behind me, looking over my shoulder.

I pointed at the addresses.

'They're not far,' he said. 'Do you want to print them off?'

A printer whirred into life, waking Oscar and making him bark. As Kasper hovered over the device, my phone rang.

'Hello, Brother. I've some good news.'

'Great. I could do with some.'

'Craig has seen the young woman you're looking for. Do you want to meet us?'

'Yes, where are you?' I wanted to put the idea to them.

'We're not far.' He gave me the address.

'What's happened?' Kasper stood holding three sheets of paper.

I told him.

'Did he say he's got a decent picture?'

'I'm sure he will have.'

'Yeah, okay. So why are we seeing him? We need to check these places out.'

'I need to see him about . . . something.' I wasn't sure Kasper would be enamoured with my idea. To my surprise, he didn't push for specifics.

'Okay. Where is he?'

'Fitzgeorge Street, at somewhere called Sandhills. I don't know where it is.'

'Don't worry, I know it. It's five minutes in the car but it's in a park, so we'll have to walk.'

I collected my coat and retrieved Oscar's lead. 'Come on, boy.'

'Are you bringing him?'

'You said it's in a park. He's not been for a walk yet.'

Kasper rolled his eyes and ushered me out.

Oscar gave him a glare as we passed him. ***Do you want me to use your carpet as my toilet?***

The drive took less than five minutes. We crossed a stream labelled the River Irk. The road followed the river until we reached a short, cobbled street on our left. Kasper took it, then pulled over. Ahead, below a railway line, a metal gate barred our way. Above it soared a brick arch, its sides lined with glazed tiles and a mural.

I led Oscar through a small side-gate and let him off the lead. He marked territory for real this time. Kasper stood by the car riveted by his phone.

'Come on, Kasper, stop staring at your phone. You're like a teenager. Anyone would think you don't want to go.'

'You seen this?' He thrust his phone at me.

An image of me, almost me, stared out. 'Where the hell did they get this?'

'Isn't it the one you used on LinkedIn? They've aged you and added a beard and long hair.'

I scrolled down the screen.

The above picture is an AI-generated image of Peter Timothy, who also goes by the name Victor. Underneath is a photo taken shortly before he disappeared from his home in Bristol. The police want to speak to him in connection with at least two murders.

CHAPTER 40

I stared at Kasper's phone and read the report again. 'Two murders?'

'Read on.'

> Police found his fingerprints on the murder weapon used in the killing of an unnamed homeless man in Sackville Square in the early hours of Saturday morning. Police aren't sure if he's involved in the earlier murder in the same area.

'They can't have found my prints. I didn't do it.'

The skin on my back itched, and I scanned our surroundings. We were alone, but the sensation of being observed didn't fade.

'Come on.' Kasper took his phone off me and strode past. 'We don't want to be late.'

I tried to order my thoughts and hurried to catch up. Oscar dawdled, inspecting every tree and shrub we passed. Birds gave shrill calls of alarm as he disturbed them.

'Come on, Oscar, we're meeting Trixie.'

He rushed past me and overtook Kasper.

The path climbed and two figures waited under the trees at the top. Oscar reached them, and a shrill bark replied to his greeting.

They made a fuss of Oscar, who focussed his attention on Trixie and her pink ribbon. The trees had trapped the smell of rotting leaves which lay on the grass and something more pungent. A black plastic bag full of dogshit hung from a branch.

'Thanks for coming, John, Craig. This is Kasper.'

'Hello, Kasper,' Craig said. 'We've got pictures of the woman we're searching for.' He pulled out his phone. 'She arrived at Sackville Square last night at twenty forty-three and left at twenty-two eleven.'

Kasper reached out for the phone. I crowded round to see the screen. The image showed a blurred figure getting out of the front passenger seat of a black SUV. Kasper scrolled through the images, but that was the best one.

To my amazement, Kasper didn't criticise Craig and handed the phone back. 'Thanks.'

'Shall I send it to you?'

'Sure.' He gave Craig his email address.

Although disappointed by the images, I wanted my friends to make a good impression on Kasper. 'Did you get the registration, Craig?'

'Of course.' Craig recited a number.

I checked it against the photo I'd taken of the car when I'd failed to get her picture. The same.

John coughed. 'We've got some bad news as well, Brother.'

'What?'

It was Craig who replied. 'You asked John about the Novaks. Their thugs are hassling homeless people. They're looking for someone of your description, with a dog.' He glanced at Oscar, who lay oblivious alongside Trixie on the grass. 'You should probably leave Manchester for a while.'

'I can't.'

'I strongly recommend it, Victor.' Brother John's tone brooked no argument, and yet I argued.

'They've kidnapped my daughter. Getting her back is all I care about.'

'Sorry, Brother. I didn't know.' His manner changed. 'What happened?'

I told them and showed the messages.

'What do you want us to do?'

'They've got her somewhere in Manchester. I need to find her—'

'They've got my sister as well,' Kasper said.

'Victor can't go to the police' – John pointed at me – 'but you can.'

'They've threatened to maim her with acid.'

I broke the silence which greeted this revelation. 'Craig, I know you were in the army. Do you think you could help us get them back?'

'Infantry,' John said. 'In fact, he was in the Special—'

Craig's glare stopped John, and he said, 'Do you want to give us five minutes?'

'Sure.' I led Kasper back down the hill. Once out of earshot, I voiced my fears. 'What would we do if they said no?'

'I'm more worried about them not being able to do it.'

'You heard John, Craig was Special Forces. Probably SAS.'

'How long ago? They don't look in the peak of health. We'll be up against young thugs who work out.'

'What do you want to do, give up?'

'No, I'm just saying.' He stood, watching them.

Kasper was right. I knew that physically, I was a shadow of the man I'd been only a year ago, and I didn't drink or do drugs. How long had those two been on the street?

Both John and Craig made calls, and it was nearer fifteen minutes before John called us back.

'Okay. We can help.' He gestured for Craig to take over.

'I've wanted to take the Novaks down for a long time. Although they import most of the girls who work for them, they've snatched some young women off the streets. We've been looking for some of them for a while.'

'And now they've got my daughter.' The thought they would coerce her into working for them after they'd finished with me made me feel sick.

'We'll help you get her back.' John patted me on my shoulder and signalled for Craig to continue.

'I've made a few calls and we've got several good people who'll help. The only problem is finding where they're holding them. They control a lot of property.'

'I went to some of them,' Kasper said, 'but they wouldn't be any good for keeping prisoners. Victor and I found four industrial units they control.'

I stepped in. 'I'm pretty sure they're keeping Helen in one of them. We're going to check them once we've left here. Once we know where they are, we can let you know.'

Craig studied us with what seemed to me increased respect and nodded.

The shortage of time preyed on my mind. 'How quickly can you get your people together?'

Craig rubbed his chin. 'Most of the guys I know are down south. I can get half a dozen good guys by tomorrow.'

'That will take too long. We've only got until tonight, nine thirty, before they kill or at least harm both my daughter and his sister.'

John's confidence evaporated, and he exchanged a look with Craig, who said, 'I'll have to make some more calls.'

I wanted to make a start. ‘Okay, you two sort out how we’re going to do it. Kasper and I will check the—’

‘It’s not a good idea for you to be seen in public,’ John said. ‘The Novaks have put a price of a thousand on you and I doubt many would turn down that sort of money.’

Including you two? I glanced around, suddenly feeling vulnerable.

CHAPTER 41

The door burst open, and Captain America appeared at the threshold holding a can of pop and a bag of crisps. He jerked to a stop and stared at the empty sofa. Zofia froze as he scanned the room with an air of panic. He did a double take when he saw her and if he'd not been wearing a mask, she was sure she'd have seen his jaw drop.

'What the fuck you been doing?' He dropped the can and crisps before charging at her.

Zofia, paralysed with fear, tensed, awaiting the impact. The crisp packet popped with a loud bang as he stepped on it. The sound distracted him, and Zofia ducked out of range. He shadowed her and she moved towards the windows. He advanced, and she retreated in a chilling parody of a dance. Out of the corner of her eye, she checked the open doorway. Then feinted to her left and as he followed, she raced towards the door and flew through the opening.

'Oi! You fucking bitch. Come back.'

A loud crash and cry of pain followed her and she jumped down the stairs, taking two steps at a time. At the bottom, she hesitated. Three doors confronted her, one on each side and a third ahead. Which way? A sound behind her. Captain America sagged at the top of the stairs, hanging on to the banister, his mask askew and blood running down his exposed chin.

She reached for the door in front and her pursuer yelled at her. The door didn't move. *Shit!* A sound came from her left and she darted towards the opposite door. It opened into a large, gloomy warehouse. Two cars sat in the centre of the space. The stench of exhaust fumes filled the air.

To her left, a roller-shutter blocked off a large opening. Against the rear wall sat a row of pallets stacked with boxes and plastic drums. In a gap between them, a green exit sign sat above a door. The sound of heavy treads on the metal steps galvanised her, and she ran to the exit sign. An acrid chemical stench came from the pallets, and warning signs covered the drums and boxes. Instead of a push bar, four bolts secured the door, one each at the top and bottom and two on the side opposite the hinges. She'd pulled three open when a voice yelled at her.

A man without a mask burst through the door she'd come in. Behind him, Captain America hobbled. She reached up and grabbed the top bolt as shoes slapped on the concrete floor. It stuck, and she jerked it. Then her lungs emptied as a shoulder charged into her lower back and propelled her into the doorway. Her skull smashed against the wood and her world exploded.

She woke, a shocking pain in her head and lying on her side on the floor. Where was she? She opened her eyes but could still see nothing. The musty smell told her they'd placed the bag over her head again. Unable to open her mouth, she realised they'd taped it up. She moved, and pain infused her ribs, head and even her legs. The bastards had given her a good kicking.

She tried to move her arms, but they'd tied them behind her back. Her left arm didn't even react. Had she broken it? Pins and needles attacked her shoulder as sensation returned. She tried to sit up, and after a struggle, realised they'd secured her legs. Unable to move, she snorted in frustration and lay there.

Her memory of the moments before she passed out returned. She'd seen both the one who'd attacked her *and* Captain America, who'd removed his mask. It was indeed the shaven-headed thug who'd confronted her at Jehona's flat.

They wouldn't let her go now. Tears poured down her cheeks.

CHAPTER 42

The clippers buzzed and my beard fell off my face in clumps. For the first time in months, I could make out the outline of my jaw. The barber John had brought me to helped homeless and struggling people. He'd led us to a back room with a single chair facing a mirror surrounded by a bank of lights. I studied John's reflection as the barber placed a new blade in the razor. John appeared serene, but thoughtful, and I wondered what was going through his mind.

I discovered, to my surprise, that I utterly trusted him to help me find my daughter. What did I really know about him, or about Craig? Such doubts struck me as luxuries neither I nor Kasper could afford. We were out of time, and backed deeply into the darkest of corners. Simply trusting my instincts about these men was easily my best, if not only, choice.

The touch of cold steel to my throat returned me to the present. Ten minutes later, my shorn appearance bore little resemblance to the picture the police put on the news and social media channels. My hollow-eyed face didn't even resemble the photo they'd used. The one taken before I disappeared from my family's lives. I remembered having it taken at the end of last February, less than a year ago, so I could renew my passport for a holiday in Crete.

I could just remember the sense of excitement, especially from the girls, when I booked the holiday. Then, in just a few weeks, everything went belly-up. I knew from Helen's messages that they'd not gone.

The sting on my cheeks and sharp odour of cheap aftershave ended my reverie. The events of the past week seemed to have reawoken memories I'd tried to avoid. The barber stood behind me, holding the hair-covered cape. John and I thanked him and left by a side door before making our way to Kasper's office. I considered the half hour we'd spent getting my haircut time wasted, but seeing my picture distributed on every social media site had persuaded me to take the time.

Kasper waited outside in his car and, saying goodbye to John, I got in.

Kasper appraised me and started the car. 'I wouldn't have recognised you, Victor. Short hair suits you.'

Oscar sniffed. ***You stink like a cheap whorehouse.***

'That's not very nice.'

You can say that again.

'What?' Kasper frowned.

'I'm talking to Oscar.'

You've got the money to cut your hair, but not enough to get mine trimmed.

'We've been through this.' I turned to Kasper. 'Where are we going?'

'Is that me or the dog you're talking to?'

'Which one of you is driving?'

He rolled his eyes. 'I checked the nearest place out. It's a cash-and-carry. I had a good look round. There's nowhere they could hide prisoners. The guy I spoke to says they've been renting it for six years.'

'Okay, so we got these two left.' I picked up the sheets I'd printed off and checked the address of the top one. Grimshaw Lane. It sounded like the sort of place to avoid.

As Kasper drove, I looked up the address on my phone. It came up with the details of an electrical wholesaler and I checked the website. It seemed legit and had hundreds of reviews. I feared we were wasting our precious time, but the satnav said we'd be there in two minutes. Kasper drove into a small, enclosed car park and I released my seatbelt.

'You sit tight. This is a long shot, but we should check while we're here.'

The other vehicles were all vans and pickups with bodywork covered in names and logos, or estate cars with ladder racks on top. I opened the main doors to be hit by warm air permeated by the smell of PVC. The inside comprised a large open space laid out with racks full of electrical items and several rooms at the back. Each of these, apart from the toilets, had windows into the main area.

I rejoined Kasper. 'Where's the next one?'

'That way, about a mile.' He started the car and reversed out of the space.

Neither of us voiced our concern that we'd reached the last of the addresses we'd located. I found it on my phone as the satnav announced our imminent arrival. The place was just off Oldham Road, and I suspected it would be too busy to be suitable. We found nowhere to park, so Kasper dropped me off. Light rain fell, matching my mood.

The place was being used as a garage, and I walked into a small yard full of cars. A dark SUV grabbed my attention. I'd seen it before, but where? An open roller-shutter framed a busy, well-lit workshop with cars in various states of repair. To the right of the gap, a wooden door opened. Two people came out, a man and a woman. I stopped as if punched in the gut. Catriona Robertson and Marko Novak.

They walked towards the car I'd noticed. Of course, I'd seen her get into it on Sackville Square. With shaking hands, I took out my phone and stared at the screen, hoping they wouldn't notice me taking pictures. I took several, hoping some would come out. The thought of ringing Kasper to follow them passed in a moment. Finding our loved ones was all that mattered, however fearsome Mr Robertson was.

Catriona got into the car, and I walked towards the opening, peered in and checked. Three people worked on various cars and the stench of engine oil filled my nostrils. An open door at the back of the unit led to the small backyard. Another dead end.

The SUV had gone, so I checked the photos. Result! At least two showed Catriona. I texted Kasper, Where r u?

I found him on the next side street. 'Anything?' he said as I got in.

'Yes and no. It's a no with regard to finding Helen and Zofia, but I saw Catriona with Marko.' They acted like a couple. What was that about?

'Seriously?'

I passed him the phone.

'Good work, but where does that leave us with finding our families?'

'I don't know, maybe John and Craig will have something.'

Kasper started the car and pulled away. Oscar pushed his head between the two seats, and I stroked his ears. A sense of despair descended on me as we returned to Kasper's office. We had less than eight hours to find Helen. Focussed on the hypnotic wipers, I jerked when we stopped and peered outside.

'Why have we stopped?'

Kasper pointed ahead. 'Zofia's car is just up there.' He passed me the keys.

'Okay, Oscar, let's go.' I got out and opened the back door.

Oscar checked the rain and stared at me. ***You're joking?***

'Come on.'

No chance.

Even Kasper sensed his reluctance. 'Don't worry, I'll take him.'

I closed the door and found Zofia's car in a gateway leading to a disused warehouse. I operated the remote, and the lights flashed. It appeared undamaged, and I got in. The faint aroma of Zofia's perfume lingered. I turned the key, and with a shudder, the engine caught. I flashed the lights, and Kasper drove off. The deep-seated cold of an abandoned car made me shiver, but I arrived at the office a few minutes later.

Kasper buzzed the front door, and I trudged up the stairs. He and Oscar had already made themselves comfortable.

Kasper said, 'Can you send me those photos? I'll forward them to our client.'

'Now?'

'What else are we going to be doing?'

I sent the images and texted John with the office address, telling him to join us. Maybe we could brainstorm something. I sat at Zofia's desktop. Had she found anything out about the places the Novaks owned? I'd watched him logging on to her machine and used her password.

I opened maps on her browser and checked her browsing history. She'd looked up Vale Park but also Dallimore Road down near the airport. I opened the map and studied it. Another industrial estate.

'Kasper, why did Zofia investigate an industrial estate in Wythenshawe?'

'Did she?' Kasper looked up from his screen, then realisation bloomed. 'Of course. The paper she found in Jehona's flat.'

I had no idea what he meant.

'When Jehona disappeared, Zofia went round—'

'You let her go on her own?' I remembered the two heavies we'd seen on our visit.

'She didn't tell me she was going.'

I could well believe it. 'So, what's this address?'

'Someone in the flat had hidden a piece of paper listing places they got taken to. One was Vale Park, and the other, Dallimore Road.'

'You got the full address?' I opened the land registry web page.

'She photographed the paper. It should be in her image library. Do you want to make a start? I'll finish this report to Robertson.'

'Can't that wait?'

'Well, just see if it needs two of us. Anyway, I've almost finished.'

I found it and punched in the address and the name of the owner came up, along with details of the other properties they owned. I read the results with a sense of excitement. 'It's going to need two of us to do this. There's a shedload of addresses.'

The doorbell rang, and Kasper gave me a panicked yelp.

'John and Craig are coming by.'

He relaxed and, checking the camera, buzzed them in. Oscar leapt to his feet and greeted the newcomers, disappointed when he realised Trixie wasn't with them. Kasper sorted out refreshments and we gathered around Zofia's desk.

Before I could start, John passed me his phone. 'You'd better read this, Brother.'

A picture of Helen stared out at me. Underneath, a headline read 'Missing teenager may be in Manchester'.

I read down, but the article offered no information, just a mix of conjecture and speculation. I handed John his phone, my insides churning.

'How have you got on with recruiting people to help?'

Craig shuffled his feet. 'I've got two people, ex-military. Both reliable. I'd trust them with my life.'

I tried to hide my disappointment. Just two more?

'That's six of us. A righteous force with God on our side.' John smiled. 'We have others willing to help, but they're like Toff, not the sort who can do much in a fight.'

'Will six be enough?' I asked Craig.

'Sure, plenty.' Craig's reassurance seemed too glib, but what choice did we have?

'Have you found them yet?' John asked.

'We've found a list of buildings the Novaks own through a shell company. We were just collating them.'

'Just let me finish this report for Robertson, and I'll help you.' Kasper returned his attention to his keyboard.

John and Craig looked at me with puzzled expressions.

'That's the man whose daughter-in-law we're searching for.' I still didn't know why Kasper seemed so eager to do it while we still had to find his sister.

'Right. What can we do?' John said.

'We've got the address of another building where they took that girl I found in the bin. The company which owns it owns a load of others. We need to get the details and eliminate them as somewhere they could be holding our family.'

'Craig's your man, a real whiz with computers.'

I studied the large shambling man with scepticism. 'I'll start up the spare machine and I'll see if Kasper has a laptop for you, John.'

He laughed. 'Not my forte, Brother. If you give me the office Wi-Fi code, I can check any premises on my phone.'

I started up the spare desktop, remembering the password from the other day. It had the same software as Zofia's machine, and I gave Craig the name and the list of their properties came up. 'You start at the bottom and work up. We want the full address. John, you check the occupier.'

Craig whistled. 'There must be sixty-three properties there.'

I gave John the Wi-Fi code, left them to it and returned to Zofia's desk. The list ran to sixty-three. Lucky guess? I'd finished three when Kasper stood. 'Right, that's Mr Robertson off our back.'

'Who is this Mr Robertson, Brother?'

'Um . . . he's a businessman from Aberdeen and they think the Novaks are coercing his daughter-in-law.'

'She didn't appear under duress,' Craig said.

Kasper nodded. 'I agree. But you don't know what hold they might have over her.'

Although I wanted to focus on Helen, it was something I'd wondered about.

Kasper's phone rang, and he checked the screen. 'Sorry, it's Mr Robertson.' He answered it and walked into the conference room, closing the door behind him.

By the time he came out, I'd checked another eight addresses. 'Everything okay?'

'Errm . . . yeah. How far have you got?'

I'd collated eleven addresses, but Craig and John had checked twenty.

'That's great.' I started to believe that we might succeed. 'Well done, you two.'

'All Craig's work.' John gestured at Craig, whose fingers flew over the keys.

Kasper raised his eyebrows. 'That's bloody quick, faster than Zofia, and she's trained.'

'Lots of ignored talent on the streets, Brother.'

With the three of us working on it, we ploughed through the work.

Craig finished first. The large black printer in the corner of the room woke up and chattered, spewing out sheets of paper. Kasper and I followed suit and printed off our work. John retrieved its output and placed them on Kasper's desk.

He prodded the stack. 'How are we going to check all these?'

The enormity of our task hit me. 'Shall we eliminate those outside Greater Manchester?'

'What if they're keeping them just over the border?' Kasper said.

'Let's put those which are borderline in a pile and come back to them.'

Five minutes later, we'd sorted them into three piles. The biggest, twenty-seven properties, represented those we needed to check.

'It's still a lot.' Kasper looked defeated already.

I used my irritation as a spur. 'You've been checking the occupiers, John. Any occupied by genuine businesses we recognise?'

'Some were occupied by branches of national chains.'

'We can discount those.'

That left us with twenty-one. Still too many. 'John, you had some more volunteers. Are they up to checking properties in the city centre?'

'Not just the centre.' Craig opened the map on his computer and studied the twenty-one sheets. 'We can check these nine.'

'Kasper, can you check some in your car and I can use Zofia's car to check on the others?' I passed the twelve sheets to Kasper. 'I don't know the area. Tell me which ones to do and I'll find them.'

'Okay. You take these, they're all on the northeast side of Manchester.'

John murmured into his phone in the far corner. I imagined him coordinating his troops. Craig returned to his desktop. 'Let me know when you've checked a premise so we can cross it off. I'll coordinate our operation, so we're ready to go once we've identified the correct address.'

Craig's menacing and brooding persona had morphed into an efficient commander, and you could see the soldier he'd once been. The change was so great that Kasper didn't object to leaving the two homeless men in charge of his offices.

I followed him to the exit and called Oscar. He raised his head from the corner where he lay under the radiator.

You don't need me, do you?

'We're looking for Helen.'

At the mention of her name, he joined me.

At the car, Kasper checked the time. 'We've got five hours to find them and get them out.'

Yeah, like I need reminding. My mind couldn't help dwelling on the fact that even if we found them in time, we were up against a well-organised and violent criminal gang.

CHAPTER 43

The Saturday-afternoon traffic meant the two miles to my first target took fifteen minutes. At least City weren't playing at home, otherwise I'd be stuck all day. The satnav led me to a building on a busy road with nowhere to park. I found a space on a side street and made my way to the building. My destination formed part of an old factory divided into smaller units. Other units flanked it and it opened onto a small car park on the main road.

The front of the unit presented one large opening, protected by a blue timber gate. I pressed the bell push by the wicket door in the gate and waited. Above, an arched window showed a light. Nobody came, so I kept my finger on the button. The ringing echoed until the door was snatched open.

A bearded man filled the opening. 'What?'

'Hi, I'm after work.'

'Manager's busy.' He pushed the door.

I blocked it with my hand. 'I'm desperate.' Why was he so keen to get rid of me?

The dark eyes studied me from below a prominent brow ridge. The man wore overalls open to the middle of a hirsute chest, and rank body odour wafted off him. He studied me for a few seconds before turning away.

'Carl!'

I gazed past him into a garage with the bonnets of two top-end cars showing. He moved to block my view.

Carl arrived. 'Yeah, what do you want?' Smaller than the doorstop, he looked less of a Neanderthal. The odour of Swarfega accompanied him, and he wiped his hands on a rag.

'I'm looking for work. I used to do bodywork.'

'Oh, yeah, where?'

'Down in Bristol.' I smiled. 'I've got my City and Guilds level three.'

'Oh yeah? Do you want to come in?' He stepped back. In his hand, he held a letter addressed to Aardvark Auto Bodies.

Bugger! What do I do now? I didn't have time to string him along.

'Good afternoon, sorry to disturb you,' said a voice I recognised. 'Who's in charge?'

Bowling, the policewoman. *Shit!* I was glad I hadn't yet turned toward the voice. But I did see Carl frown at my reaction.

'I am,' he said. 'Can I help you?'

'Police.' She held up an ID card.

'Cheers, Carl, I'll speak to you later.' I put on my broadest Bristolian accent and backed away, angling my face away from Bowling. I spun round and forced my shaking legs to walk, but once out of the yard, I ran back to the car, jumping in and starting it. With an apology to Zofia, I pulled out, leaving rubber on the tarmac. In the back, Oscar sat up and poked his head between the two front seats.

Have you found her?

'I found the policewoman.'

She's nice.

'You won't be saying that if she arrests me.'

You want to bet?

I drove away, checking my mirrors every few seconds, and after five minutes, pulled over to the side of the road and parked up, my hands trembling. My heart still raced. I didn't think she'd seen me, but what was she doing there? Had she been doing what I was – checking on who occupied the premises? Why else would she be there?

What are you doing?

'I'm trying to gather my thoughts.'

Aren't we in a hurry?

'Can you let me think?'

Oscar sniffed and returned to his seat.

I checked the next sheet. Places would close soon, and we'd run out of time. Something about the letter in Carl's hand snagged my memory. Council tax. Of course, the Novaks' company owned the building, but it was the occupier who paid the council tax.

I rang John. 'Who paid the council tax for the place on Dallimore Road?'

To his credit, he didn't ask why and shouted the question to Craig. Moments later, he told me. 'Ash and Caulk. They're posh accountants.'

'Can you check another place?' I gave him the Vale Park address. The name of the accountants struck a chord.

He came back with the same answer.

'Why would a firm of accountants want two warehouses?'

'Kasper's gone to the one at Dallimore Road. I'll ask him what he's found.'

'Before you go, can you ask Craig to see if Ash and Caulk pay anybody else's council tax?'

I waited, my mind worrying at why I recognised the accountant's name. Two bearded men walked past the car and Oscar barked, startling all three of us, then curled up on his seat again, ignoring the glare I sent his way. That was when it hit me: of course. Ash and Caulk. That was where Miles worked. My first, humiliating encounter with him flashed up in my memory, clear and sharp.

Someone had shouted 'Not round here, Miles' at him when he'd been attacking me. It must have been one of the bouncers warning him off for causing trouble too close to their headquarters. Did the bouncers – the Novaks' men – know Miles because his firm worked for them?

My phone rang. 'Kasper said the place was empty,' John said. 'He got over the fence and peered in through a back window.'

'Okay, how many of those places did Ash and Caulk pay for?'

'Eight. Our guys are checking three, you've got two and Kasper another three.'

'Okay, tell everyone to focus on those. I think the accountants are paying the council tax for the properties the Novaks occupy. Which are my two?'

I picked out the sheets with the two addresses. For the first time, I allowed myself to believe we might actually find Helen and Zofia. I entered the next address in the satnav. The instructions sent me towards the city centre. In the gathering dusk, I drove past the City ground and a fire station on my way. The rain had eased, and the wipers scraped across the dry windscreen until I stopped them.

Riverpark Road ran between industrial buildings and a cemetery. I found the unit I wanted and pulled over across the road and opposite the next property. It looked like a standard example with ground-floor industrial space and offices above. Steel shutters protected the lower openings and metal bars the windows above. Detached, and surrounded by a high, spike-topped fence, it put me in mind of the one where I'd found the dead woman – an uneasy association.

A metal sign on the fence announced that Great Bear Security protected these premises. Of course they did.

A large pickup sat in the yard at the side of the unit. I took a few photos with my phone, but I needed to get closer. 'Come on, Oscar, I'm letting you out for a wee.'

But I don't need one.

'I don't care.' I got out and opened the back door.

It's cold and wet and I really don't need a piss.

'Get out before I kick you out.'

I got him out of the car and crossed the road, stopping by the fence in front of the unit. The door slammed open, making my heart jump. Two men came out. Even in the gloom I recognised the shaven-headed thug I'd seen wheeling Jehona's body. A cut on his forehead leaked blood. My pulse racing, I watched them and listened. They walked towards the pickup and set to bickering.

'Well done for pissing Marko off.'

'It wasn't my fault.'

'How the fuck did you let a woman do that to you? She's a private snooper, not a trained killer.'

My breath caught. It had to be Zofia.

'I stood on the can of pop I took her and went flying.'

A short, harsh laugh. 'Teach you to be so soft.'

'Well, I taught her a lesson.'

I must have made a noise because they looked at me.

'What you doing?'

I recognised the speaker as the other one who'd pulled out the wheelie bins. A surge of fear and anger constricted my throat. The two men walked up to the fence, aggression surging off them. I could make the car before they got round the gate, but I mustn't do anything to make them suspicious and move Zofia.

I pointed at Oscar as my pulse hammered in my throat. 'My dog needed to pee.'

They looked at each other, seeming to relax, and the uninjured one said, 'What is he?'

'A standard Schnauzer.' My mouth dry, I could barely speak.

'Can he fight?'

Oscar went up to the fence and growled at them. ***Come here and I'll show you.***

They both laughed.

I joined them. 'Come on.' I grabbed Oscar's collar and led him to the car, my legs shaking.

Thanks for your support.

'If I'd said yes, they'd have produced a pit bull with a head bigger than your body.'

Hmm, just showing a bit of belief in me once in a while would be nice.

'Don't start.' I opened the back door. 'Get in.'

I've not had a piss yet.

'Just get in.' I slammed the door behind him and slumped in the driver's seat.

The urge to roar away, leaving half the tyres behind, gripped me, but I resisted. They'd drifted back to the vehicle but still watched me and, giving them a wave, I started the engine. My leg shook on the clutch, but I managed not to stall and pulled away.

One of them got in the pickup and the other returned to the front door. I kept my attention on the mirror, but a blast of a horn jerked my attention to the front. A van swerved away as I'd drifted across the white line. I yanked the car back into its lane.

Look where you're going.

'Thanks for the warning.'

If you want me to drive, let me sit in the front.

I focussed on driving. Ahead was a T-junction and I indicated right. When I next checked my mirror, I almost pissed myself. The pickup loomed in the rearview just two car lengths behind me.

The driver must have seen me almost hit the van. Panic prevented me from thinking. *What should I do?* I'd planned to head to Kasper's office, but I couldn't do that now. *Think, think, you idiot.* A few hundred metres further on, I passed under a bridge and turned off onto a road leading to a new housing estate. With a pounding heart, I watched the pickup in the mirror as it slowed, but then drove on past the end of the road. When I was sure they'd gone, I pulled over and stopped the car.

What you doing now?

'Didn't you see him following us? It was the bloke in the pickup.'

Do you want me to check behind or in front? I can't do both.

'One would be helpful.' After letting my breathing return to normal, I gathered my wits and made a call.

'Hello, Brother.'

'John, I've found her.' I told him what I'd discovered.

'Well done. I'll get Kasper to come back and Craig can get the troops ready. Are you coming back?'

'No! I'll stay here and keep watch.' With the pickup gone, I reckoned they'd probably left only one guard behind, the shaven-headed thug.

'Not a good idea, Vic. What do you think would happen if they came back and saw your car? They're already suspicious of you.'

My whole being wanted to go back and at least keep them under surveillance, but John was right. 'Okay. I'm on my way.' The sooner I got there, the sooner we'd be back to rescue Zofia and, I hoped, Helen. But how? I still had no idea.

CHAPTER 44

The rain had restarted and even at five thirty, the sky had darkened, reflecting my mood. I drove into the car park behind Kasper's office and stopped the car. He wasn't back yet, but arrived as I got out of the car, slewed to a stop, cut the engine and ran to me.

'John says you've found them.'

'Shall I go through it upstairs with you and the others all at one go?'

'Come on, then.' He rushed off.

I let Oscar out and we jogged to the entrance. Kasper waited at the bottom of the stairs with the door open. We ran up the stairs without speaking and burst into the main office. Both John and Craig were on their phones but ended the calls as we arrived.

Kasper turned on me. 'Okay, what's happened?'

'I've found Zofia.' I summarised what I'd heard.

'They've hurt her?'

'We need to focus on getting her out, Brother.'

'Have they?' His blue eyes focussed on me, a mixture of pain and anger in them.

'I'm sorry, that's all I know.' Had they hurt Helen? Was she even there, and if so, could we rescue her? I realised I needed to focus and used the adrenaline still flowing through my system to carry me through. 'What's happening with your mates, Craig?'

'They're coming here.'

John said, 'I've drawn a plan of the unit on Riverpark Road. Did you take any photos?'

I downloaded them onto Kasper's computer, and we all crowded round.

'While you do that, I'll check on the owner of the pickup.' Kasper strode to the nearest free desk and punched keys.

While I talked them through the photos, John produced the map he'd drawn on a sheet of paper. Alongside it, he laid an aerial photograph.

I tapped it. 'Is that the site?'

'Craig printed out a Google Earth image of the address when you phoned me.' He'd made some notes on his drawing, adding to them as I spoke.

Kasper let out a satisfied 'Got you,' and we all stopped.

'What you found, Brother?'

'The car's registered to Marko Novak, the younger one.' Kasper punched keys.

I remembered a comment the uninjured thug made about upsetting him. 'One of them mentioned him, but he was in another car when I saw him earlier this afternoon.'

'He must have changed vehicles. He's had plenty of time to do so.'

'Or one of his men is using his car.'

'So what?' Craig said. 'He's either there with his men, or he's left them to guard the prisoners. But in my mind, there's no question we've got the right place.'

I realised I'd been harbouring doubts, but Craig was right.

He returned his attention to Kasper's screen. 'Shall we have a look at the target?' We all crowded round.

Craig pointed at the screen. 'We need to get through the roller-shutter.'

'And the gates,' John said.

I hadn't thought of that and the recognition I didn't have a clue how we would rescue Helen and Zofia disheartened me.

'Don't worry, that's sorted,' Craig said. 'I've got a friend, Digger, to get us a JCB.'

'The guy who helps out at the shelter?' I'd wondered at his nickname. The fact he could drive an earth mover explained it.

'That's him.'

'Who's this bloke? Can we trust him?' Kasper said.

John nodded. 'Digger's a good man.'

'Okay, you've arranged our access,' Kasper said to Craig, 'but what happens once we're inside?'

John replied, 'Craig's got all that in hand.'

Craig went to the printer and returned with two sheets of paper. 'This is the layout of the inside as submitted to building control when they built the unit.'

We studied the plans, and Craig's phone buzzed. 'It's Digger.' He took the call. 'What you got for me?' Craig listened, wrote down an address on the plan and ended the call.

He told us what Digger had arranged and where we were meeting him.

Kasper provided an easel and whiteboard, and we taped John's drawing of the site on one side, my photo of the building below it, and the plans of the unit on the other. Despite my misgivings, I had to admit, it looked professional.

Just as I had arrived at that conclusion, the bell announced a visitor to Kasper's office, and everyone froze.

CHAPTER 45

The bell rang again, an impatient note.

'That will be the others,' John said quietly.

Kasper waited for Craig to identify them before buzzing the door open. Oscar stood, ears erect, and faced the entrance. Footsteps shook the stairs and the two men surged in through the doorway. They wore jeans and camouflage jackets – not smart, but better turned out than street dwellers. Craig rushed forward to greet them and the three of them blathered, their voices and bodies filling the space. The newcomers appeared fit and strong, and their bearing suggested their ex-military background.

'Welcome, Brothers.' John's voice boomed, and the others fell quiet. 'Thank you for coming. Kasper, Victor, these are Ned and Darren.' Everyone nodded greetings.

I tried to memorise the men's names. Both kept their brownish hair cropped, but Ned sported a moustache.

John continued. 'We're here to get Victor's thirteen-year-old daughter back and find Kasper's adult sister. And as a bonus, we get to give the Novaks a bloody nose.'

At the reminder of the task facing us, grim expressions replaced their smiles. It reminded me of the Duke of Wellington's words when inspecting his troops before the battle of Waterloo: *I don't know what effect these men will have upon the enemy, but, by God, they frighten me.* Maybe we would rescue Helen and Zofia.

John signalled to Craig, who took over. 'Right, listen up.' He stepped towards the easel and tapped John's map. 'This is our target. Zofia and Helen are in this building.'

It felt as though I should lead the operation – it involved my daughter, and I'd brought John and Craig into this – but that was just emotion. Craig clearly had the necessary expertise. He outlined his plan and allocated tasks to everyone, including me and Kasper. He sounded compelling, although I still worried I may have got it wrong, and Helen and/or Zofia weren't there. And even if they were, were we too late?

Craig finished his briefing. 'Any questions?'

'How do we gain access?' Ned said.

Craig outlined what he'd arranged with Digger. 'Any more questions?'

'Weapons?' Darren asked.

'Haven't you brought the bats?'

'I meant, what weapons do *they* have?'

For the first time, Craig became uncomfortable. 'It's possible they'll have firearms. But we'll have the element of surprise.'

Hearing this spoken aloud, that didn't seem like such a potent element. I hadn't entertained the thought that the Novaks' men might carry guns. I studied my fellow 'troops' for signs this might give them pause, but none of them seemed fazed. Even Kasper seemed sanguine, as if we were discussing a walking expedition.

'Any other questions?' Craig studied each of us in turn and, as if compelled, I shook my head.

Craig's phone rang and he listened. 'Thanks, Digger, we're on our way.'

'Everyone got this?' Craig pointed at the whiteboard, then removed the plans and wiped everything.

The realisation we were about to break the law hit me. I'd imagined myself a righteous crusader, fighting for the return of my daughter, but we were proposing to attack a group of men, and people would get hurt. Too late to pull out, and the police already wanted me. That presented a problem for another day. As I reached the front door, Oscar barked.

John stopped and studied Oscar. 'Are you bringing him?'

In the excitement of the briefing, I'd almost forgotten about him. 'Come on, boy.'

'Hang on,' Kasper said. 'We don't want a dog getting in the way when we're trying to rescue your daughter.'

'He'll help comfort her when we get her. She was his favourite.' I dared not think how traumatised she'd be when we found her.

I attached Oscar's lead, and we charged out of the door. A battered Land Rover Defender, its rear number plate obscured by mud, had joined our cars. The two ex-soldiers went to it and opened the back. Ned took out two bulging bin bags and Darren removed a sack and a carrier bag.

'We'll go in your cars.' The sack rattled as Darren moved.

'I'll take you and John.' I led them to Zofia's car and opened the boot.

Darren placed the sack and carrier bag in and slammed it as I let Oscar into the back. Darren joined him, and John took the front seat. Kasper took the other two, and we set off in convoy, me leading. We didn't want to use the satnav, so John directed me towards our destination. The Saturday-night rush hour had started, and we battled through stop-start traffic, torn between the dread of what faced us and the fear we'd be too late. My stomach roiled, and my breath caught in my throat. I focussed on driving, pushing my anxiety away.

'Next left, Victor!' John shouted.

I spun the wheel as we drew level with the junction. Kasper's car followed me, accompanied by squealing tyres and angry horns.

'You okay, Brother?'

'A bit more notice next time.'

I recognised the fire station I'd seen earlier and the cemetery on the other side. We were very close to our target, and my insides tightened.

'Left up there.' John gave me a few seconds to make the turn.

I pulled onto an unlit cobbled street. The headlights illuminated glimpses of scrapyards lining the lane. A light showed on our left. John directed me towards it, and we drove through a metal spike-topped gate in a similar fence. The distinctive shape of a JCB earth mover sat in the glow cast by my headlights. A figure next to it waved, and I stopped the car.

We all got out, and I recognised Digger from the soup kitchen. The odour of fuel and old engine oil permeated the atmosphere.

'Sorry to hear of your troubles, Victor,' Digger said. 'Will you be driving the transport?'

I looked around for Craig, but Kasper's car hadn't arrived. 'Erm . . . I think so.'

'In that case, I've got a surprise for you.' He handed me a set of car keys and gestured behind him at a van hidden in the gloom. 'It doesn't look like much but runs okay. Use that for transport so nobody spots the cars.'

'Thanks.' Something else I hadn't considered.

Kasper's car pulled up beside us. Craig got out and stepped away with Digger. Everyone else gathered at the back of Zofia's car. Darren removed the sack and distributed what looked like a baseball bat to each. Ned took out the carrier bag and gave everyone a ski mask and gloves. I took them and put them in my pocket, embarrassed I'd not even thought of it.

'Grab yourself a weapon, Victor.' John gestured to the sack.

I wasn't a fighter, but I had no choice now. Darren handed a stick to me, and I hefted it. Not a baseball bat, but solid and heavy. Although holding it reassured me, I suspected it would bring little comfort if facing someone with a gun. Panic gripped me as I studied my companions. *You mustn't let your daughter down.*

Craig finished talking to Digger and faced us. 'Right, listen up. Digger is going ahead and will take out the two gates. We're going in that.' He pointed to the van.

'You give me a three-minute start and then follow,' Digger said. 'We don't want a convoy, it will attract attention. You got any more of those?' He pointed at my club. 'Just in case.'

Darren produced another from his bag. Digger took it to the JCB, and we trooped over to the van. Closer inspection revealed it to be a minibus. Digger hadn't locked the doors, and the others piled in. The JCB engine burst into life and even in the gloom, a cloud of exhaust darkened the sky. The bulldozer set off with a roar, leaving a silence behind. I set the timer on my phone and looked around the darkened yard.

'I'm going to bring Oscar.'

'You can't bring the dog,' Ned said.

'I'm not leaving him here. He can guard the minibus.' Without waiting for a response, I went to collect him.

When I opened the car door, he examined the ground and eyed me as if I'd made an indecent proposal. 'Come on, we're getting Helen.'

His ears pricked up, and he stepped out, picking his way across the yard to the minibus. He wet the rear wheel and got in. I got in the driver's seat and adjusted it. I'd not driven a minibus for a while, and hoped I'd not forgotten how. But that wasn't my main worry.

I twisted the key, holding my breath as the engine turned over, then fired. My phone pinged and the atmosphere in the minibus thickened. Acid filled my mouth and my left leg shook as I engaged the clutch to change gear.

CHAPTER 46

Zofia lay on her side, tears of frustration seeping from her eyes. After falling onto her side three times, hitting the hard floor, she wanted to give up. She lay still, struggling to breathe through her nose. Exhausted and terrified, her mind drifted.

Someone opened the door. The shaven-headed thug walked in without his Captain America mask, but with a plaster on his cut. He appeared really pissed off. In his hand, he held a pistol. Zofia cringed. He walked up to her and loomed over her writhing body. With a sneer, he took aim and fired.

Zofia jerked awake, sweat pouring off her. She couldn't see, but the musty smell told her the bag was still on her head. Her captor's expression of contempt before he shot her in her dream made Zofia determined she'd at least be sitting up when they came to kill her. Gathering her strength one more time, she levered herself upright, but this time she overdid it. She fell the other way. Instead of hitting the floor, she bounced onto something soft.

After a few seconds, she realised what had happened. She'd fallen against the side of the sofa. She gave thanks and used it to get upright. Once she'd turned herself to position her back against the sofa, she checked all her limbs, relieved her left arm seemed to be okay. If she could free her hands, she'd be able to breathe properly.

But how to free herself? She'd left the metal rod she'd used to make a hole in the wall behind the filing cabinet, and anyway, it wasn't sharp enough. But the edges of the drawer she'd got it from were. Where was the cabinet? She pictured the room. If they hadn't moved the sofa, she needed to make her way to the back corner over her left shoulder.

She gathered her strength and, moving like a caterpillar, she headed off. After what seemed an age, her feet hit a wall. Furniture ranged in front of the whole of the back wall, so it had to be the side, the one she'd made a hole in. She moved parallel to it, hitting something within a few seconds. The sound it made told her she'd found the filing cabinet.

Triumphant at reaching it so fast, she turned her back to it. By leaning forward, she could raise her hands to reach the drawer handle, but it wouldn't move. She screamed with frustration, the sound muffled to a murmur by the tape. Then she remembered the end one was locked. She slid across to the unlocked one and fumbled the drawer open. With a struggle, she got to her knees and, with her back to the drawer, moved her hands along the edge until she found the burr which had cut her. It was awkward to reach it with her hands fastened, but by twisting her body, she could hold the cable tie against it.

It took a few attempts before she got into a good rhythm. The plastic grew hot on her wrist, then her hands parted. She pulled the bag off her head and ripped the tape off her mouth. She knelt, gasping and massaging her wrists. Darkness had fallen and she could barely make out the shapes in the room.

Although she'd freed her hands, how to free her legs? She couldn't fit her feet into the drawer and do what she'd done with her hands. She inspected her ankles. They'd used tape to fasten them. *Thank God!* She used her nails to find the end and then worried it loose.

A noise made her pause. Was someone coming? It didn't sound like steps, but something was happening downstairs. She pulled at the end of the tape and, gripping the piece she'd loosened, unwound it from her legs. Her first attempt to stand led to her falling against the filing cabinet, but by using it to support her, she got upright.

Another sound. This time she did hear someone on the stairs, in a hurry. She rushed to the sofa and reached it as the door burst open and light leaked in from the corridor. As in her nightmare, the unmasked, shaven-headed thug stood in the opening holding an automatic.

CHAPTER 47

Digger stamped on the accelerator and the JCB engine roared. The ungainly vehicle lumbered towards the gates of the unit where they were keeping Helen and Zofia. The pickup I'd seen earlier had returned, parked at the side of the building. My already pounding heart thundered in my chest. The gates parted with a crunch as it powered through with barely a pause. I rushed in behind it, but a huge hand grabbed my shoulder, pulling me back. One of the gates crashed to the ground in the spot I'd have occupied.

'Thanks, Craig. I—'

'No names! Now put your mask on.' Craig already wore his and carried a club in his other hand.

I rolled the ski mask over my head and followed. The JCB barrelled on towards the building and hit the roller-shutter, which provided a bit more resistance before giving way with a scream of tearing metal. The digger jerked forward, and the metal slats cascaded onto the roof of the cab and into the bucket. Light flooded out of the opening, blinding me.

The vehicle drove into the building, crunching into a parked car before stopping. A surge of terror almost paralysed me, but seeing the others run in through the opening gave me courage. Apart from the car the JCB smashed, another sat next to it. There had to be three men here, the younger Novak and two more. *At least.* Digger jumped down and checked the cars. Against the back wall sat a row of pallets stacked with boxes and drums. On my right, a doorway led to the rest of the building.

Craig had already charged through it, and the rest of our force followed him. Although I'd imagined them to be an intimidating squad when I'd seen them in Kasper's office, in the harsh light of this warehouse, the crew looked pitiful. Before my courage deserted me, I followed.

I ran into a corridor going left to right with a door ahead and a staircase on my left. Craig charged through the doorway in front, followed by John. Darren and Ned took the corridor. Kasper and I rushed upstairs, as Craig's plan demanded. Yells came from behind the door Craig had entered, and the sound of blows landing. I hoped they'd come from our team and ran on up the stairs.

A scream came from ahead. Helen or Zofia? They were still alive, but someone was hurting one of them. A surge of adrenalin pushed me past Kasper. As I reached the top step, a shot rang out. I froze, but realised it had come from downstairs.

'HELEN?'

'VICTOR?'

Zofia's cry came from behind a doorway two paces away. I charged in through the open door. A man held Zofia down on a scruffy sofa in the middle of a room. I raised my club, but saw he had a gun. I stopped. He grinned and pointed it at me.

I shouldn't have hesitated.

His gaze drifted past my shoulder, and I heard Kasper's breathing. To make up for my error and salvage something, I moved to my left to give him two targets. Zofia moved, but I couldn't tear my gaze from the gun. His grip on it tightened, and I knew he was about to shoot me.

Another shot rang out downstairs, distracting him for a moment. I threw my club and launched myself at him. He fired as I reached him. The explosion deafened me as I crunched into him. He was far bigger than me and I didn't expect to survive, but instead of battering me, he crumpled. Had I hit him that hard?

I scrambled to my feet and examined him. He lay inert on the floor. Blood flowed from a wound on his head. Zofia stood on the sofa, a metal rod in her hands, its end smeared with blood. She dropped it.

'Zofia.' Kasper ran to her, and they held each other.

I examined the darkened room, illuminated by the light from the landing. 'Zofia, have you seen Helen?'

'Helen?' Tears streaked her cheeks.

'My daughter, they've got her.'

'Sorry, no.'

She had to be in one of the other rooms.

I looked for my club but couldn't see it. The gun lay near the unconscious thug's hand, and snatching it up, I ran out of the room and turned left. Two more doors led off the corridor. I gripped the pistol. Was the safety off or on? I didn't even know what a safety was, but he'd shot at me so it had to be off.

I pushed the door open and charged in, pistol first, my action informed by the crime dramas I'd watched. The light from behind me illuminated some cupboards, and I realised it silhouetted me. But if the Novaks had more men here, they'd have come out by now. I found a light switch and harsh strip lights illuminated a none too clean kitchen.

I backed out, almost knocking into Kasper. 'Shouldn't we call an ambulance?' He gestured at the room containing the fallen thug.

'Sod him. I need to find Helen.' I charged to the next door and pushed it open, not bothering with the armed-police theatrics. Thick acoustic tiles covered the back of the door. I found the switch and crimson lights illuminated a bare room, six metres by four.

Acoustic tiles lined the walls and ceiling, and I guessed the floor which lay several centimetres above the corridor.

A recording studio? The stench of bleach assaulted my nostrils. If it was a recording studio, why no equipment? I stepped onto the laminate floor and looked around the windowless room. Behind the door, I found a tile with a dark, discoloured mark on it. It resembled a liquid splash. Blood. Had they killed Helen in here?

'VICTOR!' Kasper's shout broke my trance, and I left the room.

He stood with Zofia near the top of the stairs, and I ran up to her.

'Did you see anyone else here with you?' A mixture of adrenaline and fear made me tremble like an over-tightened guy rope.

'Just the men.' She pointed into the room where we'd found her. 'Him and two—'

I stepped into her. 'What about a young girl?'

Kasper inserted himself between us. 'She hasn't. You've already asked her.'

'No, sorry, Victor.' Her eyes filled, and she looked crestfallen. 'I'm so sorry.'

My belligerence deflated like air escaping from an airbed. A shout came from downstairs, reminding me of the battle below.

'Come on,' Kasper said. 'We can't be sure they had her, Victor. She's probably somewhere safe.' He put an arm across Zofia's shoulder and led her to the stairs.

I wanted to believe him, but they'd told me they had her and I knew she wasn't with her mother. But wherever she was, it wasn't up here. Heavy treads pounded on the stairs and, energised by fear, I stepped past Kasper and Zofia, gun raised.

Craig paused mid-stride and stared. 'Where did you get that?'

I lowered it to my side. 'I took it off one of the men.'

He held out a hand and stepped towards me. 'Give it to me.' He took it. 'Have you found everyone?'

'Just Zofia.'

'Victor searched the other rooms.' Kasper's voice wobbled. 'There's nobody else here.'

'Let's go. People will arrive soon.' Craig clattered down the stairs.

The rest of us followed. I brought up the rear. 'We heard shooting,' I called ahead to Craig. 'Is—'

'We'll talk later. Now we need to get out.'

Zofia trembled, so I took my jacket off and draped it over her shoulders. Ned waited at the bottom of the stairs. He carried a gun in one hand and his club in another.

'I need to get my club.' I ran back up the stairs. We'd got into this mess because I lost Kasper's phone. I didn't want Craig's friends to get in trouble because of evidence from the club.

'Just leave it!' Craig's shout followed me up the stairs, but I carried on.

I ran into the room. The thug had gone. At least Zofia hadn't killed him.

'You looking for this?'

I spun to face the shaven-headed thug. Blood ran down his face, almost blinding him in one eye, but the expression in the other left me in no doubt what he intended. He hefted my club and advanced into the doorway. With the light behind him, I could no longer see his features.

The doorway darkened behind him, and I glanced past him.

'Oh, yeah,' he said. 'I'm not falling—'

Kasper's club landed with a solid thunk, and the man collapsed like a falling tree. I took my club from his meaty hand. The metal rod Zofia had used lay on the sofa. It would have her fingerprints on it, so I picked it up and turned. My stomach tightened when I noticed the two blue bins alongside the wall.

Not daring to breathe, I set down my weapons and opened the lid of the first. The stench of bleach knocked me back. It was empty. I hesitated before opening the second but a shout from Kasper injected me with urgency. I opened the second, not daring to look. When I saw that container empty as well, I sobbed, coughing as the bleach hit my throat. I slammed the lid and followed Kasper down the stairs. The others had left, and I trailed him into the warehouse. As we rounded the JCB, I saw the others. They stood just outside the opening.

'What's up, Craig?' I stepped out with a sense of foreboding.

Craig ignored me. Beyond him, in the gap where the gates had been, sat a black SUV. Its passengers had fanned out on each side, facing us. Each carried a weapon far more deadly than the two automatics and blunt instruments we could muster between us.

CHAPTER 48

'Drop the guns,' one of the armed men facing us said.

I recognised him. Milan Novak. How had they got here so fast? Even if we'd triggered a silent alarm, we'd only been here six minutes.

'Don't make me repeat myself.' Milan didn't sound like a man used to being disobeyed.

Ned lowered his automatic and, after a moment, so did Craig.

'Lay them down and kick them this way.'

They both did as instructed, and Milan approached, stepping over the weapons on the concrete. 'Move to the side.' He jerked the barrel of the automatic pistol to the wall alongside the open gateway.

Zofia whimpered, and Kasper held her to him.

'Don't worry, everything will be okay,' I whispered to her. Inside, I thought anything but. Convinced Novak would kill us all.

'What have you done to my brother and our men?'

Nobody answered, so I spoke. 'One of them is unconscious upstairs. I caught him trying to kill my friend.'

'You're the fucking tramp, are you?' Milan gave a nasty sneer. 'Take your mask off so I can see you.'

Before I kill you, I finished for him. I removed my mask with a trembling hand.

'We've tied up the two we found downstairs.' John's intervention took Milan's attention off me. 'They're unharmed.'

'You.' Milan pointed at the nearest gunman. 'Check.'

He jogged past us into the opening.

Milan gestured at the pistols behind him. 'Did you bring those with you?'

What was the right answer? Again, nobody else volunteered. 'I took one off your man upstairs.'

'Did you now? You're full of surprises, aren't you? For a tramp.' He gestured at his remaining two men, and one came forward, collected the pistols and deposited them in the back of the SUV while the other kept his weapon trained on us.

'Where's my daughter?'

Was there someone else in the car? The dark tint made it impossible to tell.

I stepped forward. 'Is she in there?' I peered at it, trying to see.

'Stay where you are, Victor.' The automatic pistol in Milan's hand jerked, and I stepped back. 'Well, you see,' he went on, 'we didn't actually *have* your daughter.'

'What?'

'When you started bleating about her going missing, I thought, why not play along?' His face split into a nasty grin.

I don't think I'd ever hated anyone so much. A distant headlight swung towards us. Cars had been passing the end of the lane a hundred metres to our right since we arrived, but now, one of them had turned into the road. Was it coming here? The three other units on this turn-off looked deserted. The vehicle rolled up the lane and stopped halfway. In the gloom, I doubted they could see the guns.

'Get rid of them.' Milan addressed the man who'd picked up the pistols.

He set off toward the vehicle.

'Fuck me! Don't take the Uzi. Just tell them this is private property and to sling their hook.'

The man hesitated, then placed his weapon in the car with the two handguns and left.

Milan shook his head slowly. 'Just can't get the staff anymore, can we, Victor? Maybe I should give you or your mates a job.' He gave a look of regret. 'If only I didn't have to—'

His man had almost reached the newcomers when a volley of gunfire cut him down. I stared, uncomprehending. Flashes came from my left. Before I could check what they were, someone dragged me to the ground.

The sound of machine-gun fire and breaking glass filled the air. A man behind me shouted, 'They've killed—'

Then splinters of brick thudded into my back and hair as bullets pounded the wall above me. Where was Zofia? Kasper had already covered her with his body.

Suddenly, the shooting paused. Boots clattered on concrete.

'Stay down everyone and nobody gets hurt.'

Was that a Scottish accent? I caught a glimpse of three armed figures coming from the direction of the vehicle in the lane. One stayed outside, covering us, and two entered the building. Muffled shots came from inside and the two men came out.

'Remember,' said the man with the Scottish accent. 'Stay down.'

The boots retreated, doors slammed and an engine roared away. Craig got to his knees, cautiously straightening.

'Okay, it's over.'

I heard him as if through a blanket as my ears carried the echoes of the shots. Milan and his henchman lay in a tangled, bloody heap on each side of their vehicle. The one sent to get rid of the newcomers lay in the middle of the lane.

'Let's go, before anyone else arrives,' Craig said.

'What about the one who went inside?'

'No worries there.'

I checked the opening and saw his remains. It looked like he'd been running out when they shot him.

Kasper and I helped Zofia to her feet and guided her past Milan's vehicle towards our van. I stepped over a stream of blood leaking from Milan's wounds. The stench of blood and spilled entrails making me gag.

'There's a woman in there.' Zofia had paused at the car and stared through the open passenger door.

Something tumbled inside me. *Helen?* Had Novak been having fun at my expense? I stepped up beside Zofia and checked, but the figure was too big to be Helen. The woman had got the door open before she died, and the overhead light illuminated her pale face. Her mouth lay open in a silent scream. I stepped between Zofia and the body, and Kasper led her to the minibus.

Digger already sat behind the wheel with the engine running. I gladly got in the back. I trembled so much I didn't think I could drive. Oscar let out a whine and jumped over the seats to me, barking.

I embraced him. He broke free and looked at me, as if asking why I hadn't brought Helen with me.

'Sorry, boy, she wasn't there.'

The doors slammed, and the minibus moved away.

I still saw the dead woman, and I realised why I'd recognised her. She was the one we'd been searching for. Catriona Robertson. A sense of failure overwhelmed me, and tears streamed down my face.

Zofia's gentle hand grabbed my shoulder. 'You okay, Victor?'

I patted her hand. 'Yeah, sure, just a bit overwhelmed.'

We passed the dead gunman and reached the T-junction. Traffic had died down, and we pulled straight out. Blue lights appeared ahead.

'Take your masks off, everyone,' Craig said.

The police people-carrier shot past without slowing, and I looked back to see it heading for the scene of the shootout. We'd just made it out in time. But we were a long way from being free and clear. I only relaxed a bit when we arrived at the scrapyard.

We all got out. Darren collected the weapons, including Zofia's metal bar. Ned asked Kasper to open his boot and retrieved the two bin bags.

'Okay, everyone get changed.' Ned put the bags on the floor and removed two empty bags from the top of the first one. 'Put your outer clothes, ski mask and gloves in these.'

'What you going to do with them?' Kasper said.

'Burn them. They'll have forensic evidence on them.'

'This is my favourite jacket.'

Ned smiled. 'Shall I get it dry cleaned?'

'Come on, stop messing.' Craig brushed past, threw his jacket and shirt into the empty bag and helped himself to replacements. 'We're less than half a mile from the incident.'

This reminder, not that we needed it, spurred us on as much as the cold and we were soon ready to go. Digger drove the minibus behind a pile of crushed vehicles. He returned in a small hatchback and wound the window down.

I leant down and took his hand. 'Thanks, Digger. I don't know what we'd have done without you.'

'Bugger me. That's the best fun I've had in ages.' He glanced at Zofia. 'Apart from the shootings, obviously. See you at the shelter for dinner next week.'

The rest of us got into the two cars and headed back to Kasper's office. We took the same passengers: Zofia, going with her brother. Images of what we'd done, and thoughts of Helen, tumbled round in my head. Where was she? Had we left any sign of our presence? We'd worn gloves and dumped all our clothes, but was it enough? Would they blame us for the deaths? Who in hell had shot Novak and his thugs? Despite my turmoil, fear spiked every time a set of blue lights rushed towards us on their way to the incident.

I groaned when I realised Zofia would have left traces during her captivity.

'What's wrong, Brother?'

I glanced at John. 'I'm worried about DNA transfer.'

From behind, Darren spoke. 'Don't worry, all your gear will be incinerated before the end of the night.'

'I'm worried about Zofia. She'd been in there since yesterday. Her DNA will be all over the place.'

'Don't worry, Brother. We can come up with something to tell the police.'

Although we'd taken different routes, we reached Kasper's office together. Considering what she'd been through, Zofia seemed surprisingly sanguine. Ned and Darren transferred the sack and bags of clothes into their car and, accompanied by our sincere thanks, left. The rest of us trooped into his office behind Kasper, me bringing up the rear with Oscar.

We'd got Zofia back, but where was Helen?

CHAPTER 49

The smell of fried food enveloped us as we made our way upstairs. We slumped into chairs scattered around the office. I took the chance to examine Zofia. She looked pale and exhausted. A bruise covered her left cheek, and another highlighted the cut on her forehead.

'Is that a fried chicken shop downstairs?' Craig asked.

'Despite being here for six months, we've never eaten their food.' Kasper stood. 'Shall we give it a go?'

Ten minutes later, we sat round the desks with buckets of food and tins of pop in front of us. Despite not thinking I was hungry, I tucked in, and we ate in silence, although my thoughts tumbled over each other. Once we'd finished, we washed our hands and sat round a desk.

'What's happened to your daughter?' Zofia studied me with sympathy.

'From what Milan said, they never took her.'

'What made you think they did?'

'They discovered where my family lived.' I glanced at Kasper. 'When I found out, I rang the house and Helen's mobile, but couldn't get a reply. Kasper gave me a lift down, but I got through when we reached Gloucester. The police were there because Helen had disappeared following an altercation with two men.'

'The Novaks' men?'

'That's what I thought.' My throat thickened, and I swallowed.

Kasper took over. 'We traced her phone to Crumpsall, so Victor thought they'd taken her to Vale Park, but someone burnt it down.'

'Oh, God.' Zofia covered her mouth. 'That explains what I heard them say. I was there, but a policewoman arrived. I think it was Bowling—'

'Yes, I saw her,' Kasper said. 'And you were inside at the time? I didn't realise. They thought we'd gone to the police.'

'Yes, that's when I got this.' Her eyes filled, and she touched the bruise on her cheek.

I wanted to comfort her, but stayed in my seat.

She regained control of herself. 'Then they moved me and a "clean-up crew" took over.'

'Yeah, they certainly "cleaned up".' I recalled the blaze. 'Was there anybody else in the building with you?' I still didn't know if I could believe Novak.

'Sorry, I didn't see or hear anyone apart from my captors.' She looked thoughtful. 'Where's her phone now?'

'No idea. I've not rung it since we visited Vale Park.' I took my phone out and dialled Helen's number. It wasn't off and my hopes lifted. Why hadn't I done this before?

'Hello?' A youthful voice.

'Helen, it's me.'

The call ended.

I tried again, but the voicemail kicked in. 'They've switched it off.'

'I'll see if we can find it.' Kasper retrieved his phone and made a call.

'If she's in Manchester, I'm sure we can find her, Brother,' John said. 'We'll make some calls.' He and Craig retreated to the far end of the office, phones glued to their ears.

'I'll check the missing persons message boards.' Zofia moved to her desk and woke her computer.

I felt useless. I knew few people who could help me. And the idea of Helen alone on the streets made me feel sick. How could I help her? Oscar and I could try to track her down. Of course, Digger would know plenty of people, although he'd already done so much for us tonight. In my desperation, I rang him.

'Victor, how can I help you?' In the background, people laughed and cutlery clashed.

'It sounds like you're in a restaurant?'

'Some call it that, but we don't have many Michelin stars.'

'Are you at the community centre?'

'Been here all evening.'

'Of course you have. I'm looking for my daughter.'

'Still not found her? What can I do?'

'We think she's in Manchester. Can you put the word out? I'll send a picture.'

'Consider it done.'

'Cheers, mate. I can't thank you—'

'Yeah, whatever.' He ended the call.

I forwarded the picture of Helen to him and put the phone down. What would I do if we didn't find her? The Novaks might not have taken her, but they weren't the only predators out there.

Kasper ended his call. 'The phone's off, but it was last seen at the Trafford Centre.'

'We should forget the phone,' Zofia said. 'Whoever answered it must have stolen it.'

I had to agree. 'At least we know she came to Manchester. I can't imagine anyone going down to Bristol to nick Helen's phone.'

We looked at each other, our expressions asking, 'What now?' In the far corner of the room, Craig's voice rumbled, then John's phone emitted a shrill tone, and he answered it.

'Hello, Brother?'

He listened for a few moments.

'Thank you, Brother.' He ended the call. 'Toff's just seen her at the bus station.' His phone pinged, and he brought it to me.

The image of a cold and exhausted-looking Helen stared at me, a wary expression pinching her face.

Zofia stood. 'Come on, let's go.'

I grabbed my coat. 'Do you have a spare jacket for Helen, Zofia?'

'In there.' She pointed at one of the cupboards. 'I keep a few coats in case I have to change them as I follow people.'

'We'll get going.' John stood by the exit.

'Thank you, John, and you, Craig. I don't know how—'

'Stow it.' Craig's grin belied his tone, and he punched me on the shoulder.

'Anytime, Victor.' John shook my hand, and they left.

Zofia had rummaged inside the cupboard and produced a bulky red ski jacket. 'This do?'

The doorbell rang, and I jumped. 'John and Craig must have forgotten something.' Part of me feared it might be the police, or even the rest of the Novak gang.

Zofia moved first, and she checked the entry screen.

'There's nobody there.'

I headed to the door, and Kasper followed me down the stairs. At the bottom, under the letterbox, sat a small brown parcel. I bent down to pick it up.

'Be careful, it could be booby-trapped.'

I stared at it. On the outside, in block letters, it said, 'TO KZD FOR A JOB WELL DONE.' I knew those dimensions, and the weight was right. 'It will be money.'

I handed it to Kasper and returned to the office. Zofia, wearing a pale blue jacket, stared at the package. He handed it to her, and after reading the message, she ripped it open. Inside, five thousand in fifties.

'Robertson, I presume. What was he doing in Manchester?' She exchanged a look with her brother, and they suddenly understood something.

'Helen's waiting.' I also started to understand. Robertson's men had been our 'rescuers', but why kill his missing daughter-in-law along with the Novak brothers?

'Sorry, Victor.' She gave the bundle to Kasper, and he slipped it inside his jacket.

'Come on, Oscar, we're getting Helen.'

He lifted his head from his front paws. ***For real this time?***

'I'm not waiting for you.'

He skittered across the floor in his rush to catch up. After a brief argument, Kasper let his sister drive. Oscar and I sat in the back, me not daring to hope we'd found Helen. Oscar licked my hand, and I ruffled his ears. Zofia made good time in the early morning traffic. We were in the only private car in a sea of taxis taking revellers home or on to clubs.

It was all I could do not to urge her on. We arrived at Chorlton Street and Zofia pulled into a taxi rank. I grabbed the ski jacket and jumped out, stopping Oscar leaping out after me.

'Don't worry, I'll be back with her.' I ran towards the bus station and looked around, frantic for sight of my daughter.

'VICTOR!'

I recognised the Scouse accent and ran towards it.

'Where is she?'

'I don't know.' Toff seemed distraught. 'Two people were talking to her when I found her. Maybe they took her—'

'Didn't you try to stop her?'

'I didn't see her go. Sorry, I went out to get a signal to send John the picture.'

I noticed a driver checking the lights on one of the parked buses.

'Miss, did you see a young girl?' I turned to Toff. 'What was she wearing?'

'Jeans and a blue hoodie.'

I looked at the bus driver. 'She's my daughter and she's run away.'

My frantic expression must have convinced her as she pointed towards Sackville Square. 'She went that way with a couple.'

I left Toff behind as I ran along Bloom Street towards the square. Kasper shouted something as I ran past the car, but I ignored him. Claws scrabbled on concrete and Oscar appeared alongside me. I ran into the square. Three figures in the far corner approached a car parked outside the pink door, two adults and the smaller figure of my daughter. They'd reach the car long before I got there.

'HELEN!'

Oscar had already set off and halved the distance between us.

I shouted again.

Helen turned towards us. The woman with her grabbed her arm while the man opened the car door. Helen struggled, then stamped on the woman's foot. Oscar arrived and jumped at the man. The cacophony, Helen's cries and Oscar's barks attracted attention. I arrived at the same time as Zofia's car screeched to a halt beside me. The couple got into the car, which roared off. Oscar watched it, barking his defiance.

Helen ran into my arms. We held each other, sobbing and trying to speak but not making sense. Her thin body shook with cold and fear.

'Don't worry, you're safe now.' I stroked her back.

Zofia appeared, holding the red ski jacket, which I must have dropped. I took it from her.

'Put this on.' I slid it over Helen's shoulders.

Oscar, satisfied he'd seen off the threat, joined us and she bent down to hug him. 'Thank you, Oscar. You're so brave.'

Toff had caught up and stopped a few paces away and I thanked him.

'Shall we go?' Zofia said.

Oscar, looking pleased with himself, jumped in the back and Helen followed. I squeezed beside them onto the back seat and Helen leant against me. Had we been a minute later, I could have lost her forever. The knowledge made me feel sick. What would I have told Carol and Em?

'Did either of you get the reg of the car?'

'Done.' Kasper held up his phone. 'And I've sent a picture to Bowling.'

At least I could trust the policewoman, and held Helen tighter. Her trembling eased as she warmed up, and when we stopped, she was dozing. I peered out of the window, unsure where Zofia had driven to, and realised we'd arrived at her and Kasper's home. I woke Helen, and we got out.

'Is this your house, Dad?'

I fumbled for a reply, my face getting hot.

Zofia saved me. 'I brought you to our home, it's . . . it's closer.'

I mouthed, 'Thank you,' as she led the way down the path.

We gathered in the kitchen, and I was glad I'd cleared up before we left. We sat with hot drinks while the microwave heated a meal for Helen. Although desperate to discover what had happened to her, I waited until she'd eaten before bombarding her with questions.

'I was really fed up with Mum, like I told you last week. Then on Friday night, Em had something on at her dance club, so Mum took her there, and I was at home on my own. These two men came—'

'Gangsters?'

'What? No, Dad.' She rolled her eyes. 'Bailiffs. They said Mum hadn't paid for the TV, so they came to take it. I wouldn't let them, and we had a row. They left, and I burst into tears and came to find you.'

'Why didn't you ring me?' What had I been doing Friday afternoon? Just over a day ago, but might as well have been a fortnight.

'I . . . I knew you'd tell me to stay with Mum. I thought that if I came here, then you couldn't do anything about it. At least for a few days.' She reached down and stroked Oscar, who'd not left her side.

'How did you get here?' I had visions of her hitchhiking.

'I got the bus. That's why I went there tonight. I bought a return ticket.' She took a juddering breath, and I stroked her hand.

That was Helen all over, sensible even while running away from home. 'What happened to your phone?'

'I fell asleep on the bus, and someone took my backpack. I had all my stuff in it.'

'How did you get money for food? Where did you sleep?'

'I hid some money in my socks. It sounds gross, but it meant I had something. Some students told me about a twenty-four-hour burger place and the guy there let me hang out there for a few hours. The rest of the time, I wandered about. It wasn't so bad.'

'What happened at the bus station?'

'The woman spoke to me. She knew my name and said she'd take me to you, so I let them, but then they tried to get me to go in the car and it all at once felt wrong. I said no and fought with them . . . and then you came along, didn't you?' She stroked Oscar's head. 'And bit that nasty man.'

Oscar looked even more pleased with himself.

Zofia said, 'The missing person report said you might be in Manchester and mentioned your dad was up here.'

'At least we found you in time.' *But only just,* I reminded myself. 'Do you want to have a shower and sleep?'

'Can I speak to Mum?'

'Of course.' I felt ashamed I'd not once thought of contacting Carol or Emily to tell them we'd found Helen safe.

CHAPTER 50

It took several rings before Carol answered with a tired, 'Hello?'

'Carol, it's me—'

'What the hell do you want, you bastard?'

The greeting took me aback, but of course, Carol believed Helen had been kidnapped by people connected to me. 'I've got Helen.'

A short silence greeted my revelation. 'What do you mean? You did take—'

'No, we found her in Manchester.'

'Can I speak to her?'

I handed the phone to Helen. 'Mum!'

Helen dissolved into tears as she listened to her mother. A shriek from Emily carried over the handset and the sisters exchanged endearments. A sense of being left out filled me with a heavy sadness.

'I'll ask him.' Helen looked at me. 'Can I go home now?'

I'd not thought that far ahead and the realisation this wasn't a decision in my power embarrassed me.

'Of course we can take you.' Zofia gave me an encouraging smile.

'Yes, Mum, I'll see you soon.' Helen ended the call and took a tissue from the box Zofia held out.

'Right, I'll get the car ready.' Kasper stood.

Zofia placed a hand on his arm. 'I'll drive her. You're exhausted.'

She dismissed his objections, and he eventually gave in.

'I'll come with you.' I hoped bringing Helen back would give me some credit with Carol, and I desperately wanted to see Em.

We all stood and Oscar, who'd been at Helen's feet, jumped up. 'Can we take Oscar with us?' Helen stroked his head.

'Of course. Shall we go?' Zofia spoke to her brother: 'You stay here, and I'll see you later.'

'*I'm* coming with you. I don't want to let you out of my sight.'

Kasper brought up the rear, locking the house, and we made our way to Zofia's car. Helen and I sat in the back, Oscar on the seat beside us. Would Helen want to take him with her? Carol wasn't a fan, but she might relent because of Helen's ordeal. I'd miss the guy, despite his contempt for me.

'Do you want to keep Oscar, Helen?'

What makes you think I want to go back to Bristol?

'You're talking to me now, are you?'

Helen gave me a puzzled look. 'He's your dog, Dad. I love him, but you need him with you.'

My throat thickened and I swallowed.

Oscar nuzzled into Helen's lap. We fuelled up and Kasper bought a bag of drinks and snacks for the journey. I held Helen's hand, not sure what to say to her, but content to be with her. Any 'dad' questions I might have about her life seemed trite, and I no longer had the right to ask them. The fear she'd ask me about my life in return kept me silent.

Zofia studied me in the mirror. 'We should tell the police we've found Helen.'

They still wanted me in connection with two murders, something I'd been avoiding thinking about. 'Carol will tell the local force. That's who she reported it to. And what did you say to Bowling, Kasper?'

'I just told her the couple in the picture were picking up kids from the bus station. I didn't want to get Helen involved . . .'

Or us, I finished for him. None of us wanted to speak, so Zofia put on music, and bands I didn't recognise accompanied us on the rest of the journey.

Signs were pointing to Gloucester before Kasper spoke. 'What are we going to do with Robertson's money?'

I'd guessed Robertson and his men had killed the Novaks, but they'd also killed his daughter-in-law, who I suspected was their real target. And I'd helped them find her. I'd wait until we'd dropped Helen to ask. She didn't need to know.

Zofia answered. 'Can you give a thousand to Victor?'

'A thousand?'

'You think it should be two?'

Kasper sighed and pulled out a bundle of fifties held together by a paper band.

'You'd better give him some for his friends. Another thousand?'

Kasper said, 'They didn't want paying.'

'Did you ask them?'

I felt sorry for Kasper. I'd realised they had money problems. 'The help Craig and John gave us was beyond anything we could pay them, but I think five hundred would be a nice gesture.'

Kasper counted out the money and handed it to me. Mixed emotions surged through me. This brought me so much closer to my goal, but I saw it as blood money. I'd noticed Helen's scuffed shoes and too-small hoodie.

'Here.' I offered Helen five hundred.

'What's that for, Dad?'

'Birthday and Christmas, for both of you.'

The hug she gave me was worth ten times the amount. My vision blurred, and I turned to the side window, mourning the time I was missing with her.

◆ ◆ ◆

I must have dozed, as I jerked awake, and the car had stopped. A kaleidoscope of bloody corpses and gunshots clung to the edge of my mind. Helen squeezed my hand.

'We're here, Dad.' She turned her attention on Oscar. 'It was lovely to see you.' She ruffled his ears and kissed him on the nose.

I got out and paused on the pavement, studying my old home. Helen joined me and slammed the door. I put an arm across her shoulders, and we held each other for a dad-and-daughter moment. Helen stood on tiptoe and whispered in my ear.

'I can tell you've been ill, Dad. You don't have to hide it from me.'

My eyes filled, and I swallowed my denial. To tell her the truth would hurt more. 'I'm fine now. You don't need to worry.'

'Are you sure?'

'A hundred per cent.' I held her tighter.

Curtains twitched in the downstairs window and our front door swung open. A scream of delight accompanied Em as she rushed her sister. Helen slipped my arm and ran to meet her. Carol joined them, a joyful scrum of yelps and sobs. Oscar scratched on the car window and whined.

I know how you feel, mate.

The excitement died down and Carol transferred her attention to me. She must have noticed the change in me but hid her surprise well. 'Don't think because you brought her back, you're forgiven.'

'Mum, it's not his fault,' Helen said.

'How can you say that? After what he did to you—'

'He did nothing. It was all my fault.'

These words stopped Carol. In the silence, I smiled at Em. She hesitated a moment, then ran to me and gave me a tight hug. I buried my face in her hair, blinking away more tears.

'Dad, do Kasper and Zofia want to come in?' Helen ignored her mother's outraged expression.

Kasper and Zofia declined the invitation and, telling them I wouldn't be long, I followed my family into our former home. The familiar hallway looked tired. I'd promised to redecorate it, but then events had interfered.

Before I closed the door, a car horn tooted, and Zofia called me. The urgency of her shout dragged me outside. A police car rolled past, searching for a parking space.

'I have to go.'

'But you've done nothing wrong, Dad.'

She didn't know about the murders. And that's just how I wanted to keep it. 'Yes, but they'll keep us here for ages. I'll see you soon, love.' I held her and Em joined us.

Another shout and I rushed out, jumping into the back as Zofia pulled away. Two uniformed officers made their way from their parked car and glanced at us as we passed. I made a fuss of Oscar, making sure they saw him. Who suspects a man with a dog? It seemed to work as they continued onwards.

We'd still got to deal with the Manchester Police when I got back, but I'd worry about that tomorrow. For now, my family were safe, but I wondered when I'd see my daughters again.

CHAPTER 51

Still thinking about my lost family, I didn't hear Kasper until he prodded me.

'Did you hear me? We need to get our story straight about Zofia.'

'With the police, you mean?'

'They're bound to question her. Her DNA will be all over the room they kept her in.'

'Of course.' I turned to Zofia. 'What will you say?'

'I want to keep you two and the other guys out of the picture. What if I say the Novaks released me before the gunfight?'

'That's the best idea,' Kasper said. 'Then they won't link you to what happened. You hit the guy upstairs over the head with the iron bar, and we don't know how he is. If they released you before that happened, then they can't place that at your door.'

'We hit him as well, didn't we?' I wasn't going to let Kasper off.

The fact we had attacked the kidnappers, and I didn't know if Craig and the team downstairs had killed any of them, meant we'd be in deep trouble. I was sure I could talk my way out of the two murders I was suspected of, but not anything that happened when we attacked the warehouse. I'm not a good liar.

I took a deep breath. 'We should stick as close to the truth as possible. What if you say you heard shooting, Zofia, and someone came in and released you? Don't forget, we left after the shootings and stepped past the bodies. That way, if you've stepped in blood or other stuff, you can explain how it happened.'

'They'll want her to give a description of the men.'

'They kept a bag over my head most of the time. What if I say they left me there until they left?'

'That won't work,' I said. 'The police arrived moments after the shooting, so how did you get away?'

They considered this.

'Also, if you saw people shot, why didn't you go to the police?'

'Okay, what do you suggest, then?' an exasperated Kasper said.

I'd been considering this on the journey down to Bristol. 'What if you say that during the shooting and fighting, you had a bag over your head, so saw nothing?'

'Why didn't I take it off?'

'They'd tied your wrists, you've still got the marks. Then someone came into the room, and they took you with them. That explains how you got away.'

'Yeah, but then what?' Kasper said.

'They rang you to collect your sister and dropped her off.'

'What about traffic cameras? I'm sure we're on several on the way to Bristol.'

I'd forgotten about that. 'Okay, what if they left you somewhere for a few hours, then rang Kasper and he picked you up on the way back?'

'They'll check phone records.'

Signs showed us approaching Birmingham, about halfway. 'Okay, we come off here and find a phone box. I'll ring Kasper's mobile and then we can say they left you somewhere nearer home, like Northwich.'

Zofia smiled into the mirror. 'That could work, Victor.'

Kasper looked unhappy. 'We're pretty sure Robertson's men killed the Novaks, and they'd have gone back to Aberdeen. This is going to throw the police off the scent. If they think the killers went south . . .'

I wasn't sure it would make much difference. 'Do you want Robertson caught? If he's behind it, you could be dragged into this.'

'But his men killed those people.'

'Including his daughter-in-law. Why?'

Kasper swallowed. 'She attacked his son before she ran off. She battered him with a hammer and put him in a wheelchair.'

Zofia's mouth dropped open in horror. 'That means . . . you agreed to help find her so they could take revenge?'

'I didn't know all that until long after I'd agreed to find her. I . . . I tried to back out, but by then he'd paid us and made it clear pulling out wasn't an option.'

Events were falling into place. 'What about when Jehona was killed? You knew someone with a propensity for attacking people with hammers was near her. You could have pointed the police in her direction.'

'I'd heard a rumour a week ago, and that said she'd stabbed him. I asked a contact to investigate, and only found out about the hammer yesterday. And then Zofia disappeared.' Kasper threw up his hands.

Zofia looked at me. 'I'm sorry, Victor.'

'It wasn't your fault.' I stared at Kasper, waiting for his apology.

'Sorry. That's why I want them caught.'

'But if they are, they'll drop you in it.' And me.

'Victor's right, Kasper. They also saved our lives.'

Kasper's objections weakened, and we pulled off the motorway and did as I suggested. We refined the plan, and what each of us would say, as we continued the journey, taking a detour via

Northwich, making sure we triggered a speed camera on the way back to Manchester.

As we neared Manchester, Zofia said, 'Shall we drop you off at our place before we go to the police?'

'Why can't we go home and get some sleep?' Kasper said. 'You must be exhausted. Then we can go to the police?'

'How do we justify the delay?'

'But you saw nothing.'

'I'm with Zofia on this, Kasper.'

'Right, so it's two against one.' Zofia winked at me. 'So, our place first?'

Being at their place on my own for many hours wouldn't have felt right. 'Drop us in town.' At least it wasn't raining.

Zofia put up an argument until Kasper joined me and she agreed. She insisted on stopping at their office to get a sleeping bag and mat.

Zofia let us out on Princess Street. 'Are you sure you don't want to come to the police station with me and hand yourself in? They're still looking for you and it will be better if they don't catch you.'

'I know, but I'll do it in the morning at the police station in the Town Hall.' I couldn't handle an interrogation now.

'If you're sure.' She got out and gave me a hug, then said goodbye to Oscar before swapping seats with Kasper.

He held out his hand. 'Thanks for everything, Victor.'

Oscar and I watched them drive off.

He looked at me accusingly. ***We could be in a nice, warm house now.***

'I know. Come on, let's get some sleep. It will be light soon.' Once alone, I realised I had a thousand pounds on me. The sooner I gave half to John and Craig, the happier I'd be. In the meantime, I stuffed it in my socks, glad I wasn't walking far.

We arrived in Sackville Square and checked my stash. I hoped the police, having had a presence there for a few days, wouldn't return so soon. Someone had found my sleeping bag and spare clothes and scattered them next to the bins. I put them in a pile under shelter. They could wait until the morning. Oscar's crate wasn't too badly damaged and within a few minutes, we both fell into an exhausted sleep.

CHAPTER 52

The urge to run away almost overcame Zofia's resolve as they approached the North Manchester Division police headquarters. Although it was the early hours of Sunday morning, light spilled out of every window in the boxlike glass and pale concrete structure. They'd discussed whether to come here or go to their local station. The advantage of the latter was that Grimes didn't work there, but this was his case, and they'd have to speak to him sometime. At least if she spoke to him now, it would be over with, and she wasn't sure her nerve would hold out for a second interview.

Kasper opened the main door and let her go ahead. A buzz filled the place and people moved about with energetic purpose. She supposed even for this station, six or seven shootings in one day presented an exceptional workload. She let Kasper speak to the receptionist and took a seat in a soulless reception area. As she sat down, her energy seemed to leak away and the fact she'd not slept properly in she couldn't remember how long suddenly hit her.

Kasper sat next to her. 'You okay?'

'Not bad, but I'm exhausted.'

'I'm not surprised. I said we should have gone home first.'

'We're here now.' She didn't want this argument again.

'Dabriski, I should have known you'd be involved.' Grimes's voice cut through the hubbub.

'Chief Inspector, how delightful to see you.' Zofia spoke before Kasper could correct the policeman. She stood and offered her hand.

Bowling, at Grimes's shoulder, smiled and took it. 'Zofia, good to see you again. I understand you want to make a statement.'

'What about you?' Grimes prodded Kasper's foot with his shoe.

'I . . . Why do I need to?' Kasper reddened.

'Weren't you there?'

'Shall I give you my statement, Chief Inspector?' Zofia asked. 'Then you can decide if you need to speak to my brother. All he did was collect me once they released me.'

'Hmm. Don't go anywhere,' he said to Kasper, then turned on his heel and strode away.

Bowling gave Zofia an encouraging smile and fell in behind her as they followed Grimes into a surprisingly spacious interview room, where Grimes waved her towards a seat on one side of a rectangular table.

Bowling switched on a recording device. 'Ms Dąbrowski, we're here to take your statement with regard to your involvement in an incident at Riverpark Road on Saturday eleventh of February. You're not under caution, but if we suspect at any time that you have been involved in a crime, we will halt the interview and will continue to question you under caution. Is that clear?'

'Yes. Thank you.'

'Right,' Grimes began. 'First thing first: what were you doing at Riverpark Road?' He fixed her with his gaze.

Zofia had replayed the events and arranged them in the order which made sense to her. 'I left our office just after your last visit and noticed a van following me.' She described the vehicle. 'I turned off onto Broughton Street. I thought if I drove into the fire station on Bury New Road, I might be safe.'

'Good thinking.' Bowling smiled. 'But you didn't make it?'

'A lorry blocked the road, so I turned down Woolley Street, but the van came the other way. I tried to go back but two men with guns came at me, and I stopped the car.'

'Can you describe these men?'

'Big, not as fat as you.' She gestured at Grimes. 'More like bodybuilders.'

'I'll have you know this is relaxed muscle, young lady.'

Bowling rolled her eyes. 'What did they look like?'

'They wore superhero masks, but I saw one later. He had a shaved head and hard, dark eyes. He also had a snake tattoo crawling up his neck.'

The officers exchanged a look before the sergeant continued. 'Did you see any of the others?'

'Another one had longish blond hair, a broken nose and pale blue eyes close together. I didn't see the leader without his mask on, sorry.'

'Don't worry,' Bowling said. 'Can you tell us anything else?'

Zofia described how the men took her in the van to one place, then moved her several hours later. When she mentioned being hit, Bowling pointed at her cut.

'Yes,' Zofia said. 'One of them punched me there. And this' – Zofia touched her forehead, still tender – 'was when I hit my head on the wheel arch of the van.'

'Can we take a DNA sample? It will help us identify the van if we find it—'

Grimes leant forward. 'And we'll need to eliminate you from DNA we find at the scene of the shooting.' He studied Zofia. 'Did they say why they kidnapped you?'

'What do you mean?' This threw her. They hadn't thought enough about this. She had to avoid mentioning why they were watching the Novaks, and who for. Especially if it ever came out that Robertson's people were behind the shootings.

'These are serious gangsters,' he said. 'They're dangerous, as you found out, but they don't often get involved with civilians.'

She waited. When Grimes didn't elaborate, she said, 'I'm sorry, do you have a question?'

Grimes raised his eyebrows. 'Could they have believed you were involved with a rival gang?'

'Why would they think that?' Her pulse rate elevated.

'One from north of the border?'

She almost choked. 'We have no involvement with organised criminals.'

'So, we'll not find any calls from Glasgow to either of you.'

Relief made her cough. He must have been given a wrong steer by one of his informers.

Bowling passed her a plastic cup of water and she took it with a thankful smile.

Grimes scowled at his sergeant, then leant towards Zofia again. 'You expect me to believe they never mentioned why they held you?'

'They didn't discuss it with me.'

'Maybe they discussed it with your brother. We'll find out later.'

Kasper wasn't great at thinking on his feet and Grimes terrified him. She'd have to come up with a reason and suggest it to him before he got dragged in here. 'Kasper took some photos in Sackville Square—'

Grimes wagged a finger. 'I warned you to stay away.'

'It happened before you came to see us on Monday.' Had that been less than a week ago? It seemed like months. 'It showed Jehona, the woman you found dead, and the man with the snake tattoo. They probably didn't want him passing it on to you.'

Grimes stared at her for a long moment. 'Right,' he said, 'that will do for now. We will need to speak again, so don't go on any holidays.'

Zofia stood. She needed to prepare Kasper before they got him in there. Whatever he did, he mustn't mention Robertson.

CHAPTER 53

A dream of Oscar chasing sheep on a motorbike morphed into another nightmare, as his barking woke me. I sat up in my borrowed bedding and looked around in the grey morning light. A patrol car had stopped on the far corner of the square about fifty metres from the nook I slept in. The driver studied me. I rolled my sleeping bag down my legs and stood. The door to the patrol car opened. I stumbled a few steps before my legs worked.

I ran towards Portland Street. Ahead lay the small car park now earmarked for development. They'd blocked the entrance with concrete blocks but hadn't fenced it in yet. I skirted the barrier and ran across the empty space, its rutted surface making running difficult. Fortunately, since my recent attacks, I'd taken to sleeping with my shoes on. Oscar ran ahead of me, glancing back at me and our pursuers.

They're catching up.

I glanced back. *Bugger!* I'd expected them to chase me in the car, but two figures on foot followed. One, a young gazelle, had almost reached me.

Look out!

Too late, I saw the low barrier and launched myself. The top of the fence smashed into my shin, and I clattered to the ground, sprawling face-first on the pavement beyond. The officer slammed into my back and twisted my arm behind my back.

'Aaargh! There's no need for that.'

He ignored me and more hands grabbed me. Metal clicked and handcuffs snapped on my wrists. Oscar sat on the other side of the fence, shaking his head and studying me with a look of disappointment.

'I didn't see it until too late.'

At least nobody I know saw me with you.

He trotted off as, using what I felt was excessive force, they dragged me to my feet, read out a caution and marched me to their car. Oscar followed us from a safe distance, but scarpered when they shoved me into the back of the patrol car.

At the police station, they led me into the custody suite where they searched me and removed my belongings, including my phone, money and bank card. The sergeant counted the money twice, and I ignored his question about where I got it.

They led me to the interview room and made me wait outside. Within a matter of moments the policewoman Bowling came out, followed by Kasper, who looked like he'd gone ten rounds with a heavyweight champion. We acknowledged each other, and I took his place in the interview room. I waited, rubbing at my shin where I'd smashed it.

The wait felt an age, but I'd got accustomed to enduring long periods of nothingness. The door banged open and a figure I recognised lumbered into the opening. Grimes, the policeman who terrified Kasper. He stared at me for a long moment, his expression that of an irritated crocodile, then sat across from me. Where was Bowling? My unease increased.

He checked they'd read me my rights and set up the recorder. 'Peter Timothy sounds like a hairdresser, no wonder you changed it. Victor sounds much more . . . manly.'

I waited for him to ask a question.

'Are you sure you don't want a solicitor?'

I'd considered this and concluded I didn't. A lawyer would probably advise me to say nothing, but I wanted to tell my story. 'Yes, I'm sure.'

'I understand we found over a thousand pounds in your possession. Do you mind telling me how you came by it?'

'No, I don't mind. Someone gave it to me.'

'You expect me to believe someone gave you a grand?'

'Believe what you want. I've not broken any laws.'

'We'll see about that.' He opened a folder I hadn't noticed him carrying. 'I've got a report here about your daughter, Helen. According to our friends in Avon and Somerset Police, they received a report from your ex-wife—'

'Wife.'

'What?'

'She's not my ex.'

'Okay. Your *wife* reported that someone had kidnapped your daughter and suggested you knew something about it. Do you have anything to say about that?'

'You think I orchestrated it from my secret lair at the top of the Beetham Tower?'

'Smartarse, eh?' He gave a nasty grin, which increased his resemblance to a crocodile. 'Let's skip forward a few hours and you arrived at the scene of a serious fire, started by persons unknown, claiming your daughter was inside.'

'I thought she was.'

'Why?'

I'd considered this question and, as I now intended to give them my photos, had decided on the truth. 'I'd seen two men come out of the building with a woman's body in a bin. When my daughter disappeared, I feared they'd taken her and were holding her there.'

'So, you admit you dumped Jehona Sorokin outside North Manchester General?'

'There's nothing to admit. I hoped to save her.'

'If you'd called an ambulance, she might have survived.'

I'd considered that every day since, but wouldn't give him the satisfaction.

He fidgeted in his seat and a foul stench filled the room.

'What were you doing there?'

'Just wandering. Believe it or not, there's not much to do on the streets. I get bored.'

He checked I wasn't taking the piss. 'Why did you think the same people would snatch your daughter?'

I couldn't mention the gloves. Now that the culprits were dead, I saw no need to implicate myself in any crimes I may have committed. They'd certainly punish me for withholding evidence in a murder. 'Apart from me witnessing them dumping her body, they found out I'd taken pictures of them with the dead woman on Sackville Square. I'm there most days. They told me they'd harm my family if I didn't give them the pictures.'

'*You* took the photos, not Kasper Dąbrowski?'

'I knew Kasper had taken some photos there. I saw him with a camera and recovered it for him.'

'Did you now? Would you say he's a friend of yours?'

'Not a close friend.'

'Why did you take these photos?'

My pulse thumped. 'They just looked dodgy. I thought I might make some money if anything happened.'

'A payoff?'

'Or a reward. If I wanted a payoff, they wouldn't have gone after my daughter. They'd have either arranged to pay me, or met me and bumped me off.'

He considered my answer. 'Why didn't you come to us?'

I held his gaze. 'You expected me to come in while you suspected me of murder?'

He glanced at the report. 'What did you do?'

'I found out they didn't have Helen. She'd run away to Manchester, looking for me.' I imagine she'd have given her local police force a statement by now.

'She just ran away?'

'Haven't the police in Bristol interviewed her?'

'Yeah, okay.' He sounded disappointed. 'So, you hid vital evidence from a murder inquiry because your daughter ran away from home?'

'I spoke to them, and they said they had her. Or at least . . .' I replayed the telephone call.

'What?'

'They didn't actually say they had her. I assumed, and they let me believe it.'

'You jeopardised a murder investigation because you "assumed"?'

'I genuinely believed my daughter was in danger. What would you have done if she was yours?'

Grimes studied the papers in front of him and shuffled them. 'Let's look at some other incidents we want to speak to you about. First, the death of Bennie Quinn?'

'It was Bennie they killed? Shit! I hadn't realised it was him. Was he the first one they killed or the second?'

'I ask the questions.' Grimes scowled at me. 'What do you know about his murder?'

'I didn't even know he was dead until you just told me.' The thought my message to his killers had led to his death hit me anew.

'How well did you know the victim?'

The question interrupted my self-recrimination. 'I saw him around. He was a nice guy. Came down from Newcastle a few years ago to live with his grandson, but it didn't work out.'

'What happened? You fall out over a bottle of booze or something?'

'I told you, I don't know how he died or who killed him. I don't drink, and Bennie never fell out with anyone. What happened to him?'

Grimes considered his words. 'Someone battered him to death in Sackville Square in the early hours of Saturday the eleventh. We found your fingerprints on the murder weapon.'

'You can't have!' Were they trying to fit me up? For the first time, I feared I'd not get out of this unscathed.

'Oh yes we can.' He slid a photo across the table. 'Can you explain why your fingerprints are on this?'

Still reeling, I examined the picture of a short length of scaffolding. I recognised it and swallowed. 'It looks like a piece of tubing I kept to defend myself.'

'To defend yourself?'

'You may have heard, Chief Inspector, but living on the street is a risky proposition. Everyone I've met living rough has been attacked on more than one occasion. I've been attacked, and I used it to protect myself.'

A calculating expression crossed the policeman's features. 'So, Bennie attacked you, and you used it to defend yourself?'

I couldn't imagine Bennie attacking anyone, and I was sure he'd not been one of the men Craig had seen off.

'If you did, that's an absolute defence to the charge of murder.'

'Although I have used it to defend myself, I've never hit Mr Quinn.'

'In the dark, you might not have recognised him.'

'I knew Mr Quinn. Well enough to be sure he'd never attack me. Anyway, the man I hit ran off, and the attack happened in the early hours of Thursday. I left the pole in my bedding. Anyone could have taken it.'

'How convenient. Where were you Friday night and the early hours of Saturday?'

'What time?'

'After 10 p.m.'

'On the M6, on my way back from Bristol.'

'Oh yeah. Why?'

'The men who I thought kidnapped Helen made threats, and when I couldn't get hold of her, I tried to warn her.'

He frowned at this. 'I presume you didn't have your own car. Did you steal one?'

I ignored his obvious attempt to bait me. 'Someone gave me a lift.'

'Again, how convenient. And I bet they'll give you an alibi.'

'We fuelled up and I'm sure you've got access to the motorway cameras.' Although sympathetic to Helen's anger at the increasing surveillance we endured, I was glad of it on this occasion.

'I'll need their names.'

Kasper and I had discussed the need for me to give the police his details, so I did.

Grimes gave a nasty grin. 'Well, well, we've already questioned Mr Dąbrowski, and he didn't mention taking you to Bristol.'

I didn't know what to say, so, for once in my life, said nothing.

'Did you stay in Bristol on Friday night?'

He knew I hadn't. 'We didn't get to Bristol. I'd been ringing every few minutes and Carol, my wife, answered, telling me what had happened. So we came back.'

'Why did you go to Vale Park Industrial Estate?'

'I told you, I thought I'd find Helen there.'

'Why?'

I didn't know the legal position of tracing her phone. 'I told you that as well.'

'Tell me again.'

So, I did.

'What time did you leave?'

'What time was Bennie killed?'

Grimes slapped the table, making me jump. 'Just answer the question.'

'Not sure, but your sergeant must remember, she questioned me.'

'Where did you go?'

'I went to Kasper's house.'

'You stay there all night?'

'We stayed in his office. Someone had broken into his house and left threatening messages in blood.' At least I could show him the blood.

'Nasty.'

The door opened and Bowling appeared. 'Boss, a word?'

Grimes gave her a furious glare. 'This better be good.'

CHAPTER 54

Grimes barged back in, slamming the door against the wall. 'Right, you can go, but don't leave the city. We may need to talk to you again.' He gathered his papers and stormed off while I digested his words. So, they hadn't linked me to Riverpark Road.

I followed him out. Bowling stood outside, watching him march away.

'What did you say to him?' I asked her.

She checked the corridor and studied me. 'You didn't hear it from me, but we found security camera footage of the Novaks' men attacking the old man.'

The confirmation of my fears hit me. 'Shit! They mistook Bennie for me. He'd still be alive if I hadn't contacted them asking about Helen.'

'Don't blame yourself, it's all on them. I'll put whoever did it away, if they're still alive.'

I believed her.

'Oh, and I'm glad you found your daughter.'

'Thanks.'

'And the couple Kasper reported trying to abduct her. You don't have to worry about them, they're in custody.'

I couldn't hide my shock.

She winked. 'We won't need her testimony. We caught them red-handed. They'll be doing a long stretch. Goodbye, Victor.'

A uniformed constable approached and led me to the custody suite where they returned my property. I left the building before they changed their minds. My phone showed 3 per cent battery. I needed to find somewhere to charge it. I tried the restaurant where Craig took me for breakfast, but it didn't do Sunday mornings.

With a sense of emptiness, I wandered into town. My visit to Bristol and contact with my previous life had awakened a sense of loss I thought I'd got over. Now I'd finished the job with Kasper, I had nobody to please but myself. But first, I needed to give Zofia's money to John and Craig.

They weren't in their usual haunts, but I at last found them in Angel Meadow. They sat on one of the steel benches and Craig was busy attacking the arm in the bench's centre. Trixie, today wearing a green ribbon, sat at his feet. As I got closer, I made out Oscar, hiding at the far end of the bench.

'Brother, we wondered why your Oscar was all alone.'

'Hello, John, Craig. He ran off when the police picked me up.' I gave him a 'disappointed in you' look, which he returned with interest.

What was I supposed to do? Overpower the two coppers and unlock your cuffs?

'You could have run interference between me and the young one who caught me.'

You could have cleared that one tiny fence. Even Trixie could have jumped it.

I didn't want to get into an argument, so I ignored him.

The bench's metal arm gave way with a screech of metal and Craig stuffed it in a nearby bin. 'I hate all this harassment architecture.'

'What did the police want with you, Brother?' John looked concerned.

'They asked about Bennie Quinn.'

'A sad business.' John crossed himself.

'His killer used my metal pole.'

'The one in your bedding?' Craig said.

'It had my fingerprints on it.'

'But they still let you go?'

'They found footage of the Novaks' men attacking him.'

'That was lucky. No questions about Riverpark Road?'

'Never came up once.'

The two men exhaled a slow breath. Had we got away with it? Despite our care, we couldn't be certain we'd left no trace behind. At least one of the men in the building had died at our hands. The words of the Novaks' man when he ran out of the unit and before the gunmen shot him went round my head. He'd clearly said 'They've killed—' before they cut him down. Which of the men in the unit had he found dead?

I could have asked Craig, but he might have told me. At least if I didn't know, I could pretend it wasn't the one Zofia and Kasper bashed over the head.

I remembered why I'd come.

'John, Craig: Zofia and Kasper wanted to thank you for everything you did. We all—'

'Don't be silly.' Craig cut me off. 'I owe you for this one.' He stroked Trixie.

'You knew?' How the hell had he found out I'd rescued Trixie? Did she speak to him like Oscar did me? But Oscar never tells me anything I don't already know.

'My mate lives near the canal. He saw you out of his bedroom window, but by the time he strapped his legs on, you'd got out.'

'But you, John—'

'We're mates, Brother. That's what mates do.'

The words made me warm. Had it taken until I ended up homeless to feel I belonged to a tribe?

I looked around and produced the five hundred pounds. 'Here, it's not a lot for what you did.'

Craig folded his arms. 'No, thanks.'

'What about the other guys? I don't even know them.'

He exchanged a look with John. 'How much is there?'

'Five hundred.'

'Okay, Brother, we'll take a hundred each for the other guys.'

'What about Toff? He found Helen.'

They stared at me, arms folded.

'Please. I can't give it back to Zofia, she'll refuse it.'

John relented. 'We'll take it. I'll give a hundred to Toff.'

I thanked them again and walked away with my remaining five hundred, a reluctant Oscar at my side. Although tempted to buy myself a slap-up brunch, my visit to Bristol had sharpened my appetite to get back on my feet. I'd put it all in my savings account.

Oscar and I returned to Sackville Square, and I sorted through my clothing and bedding, binning any which I couldn't use. I wondered how Kasper had got on with Grimes. Had they called him back in and questioned him about driving me to Bristol on Friday night? What about Zofia and her link to Riverpark Road?

CHAPTER 55

The next morning, I woke Oscar and clipped his lead on.

Where are we going?

'I need to pay some money into my account.'

I thought you didn't have any money. Look at the state of my pelt.

'I'll give you a brush. This money's so we can have a proper home.'

His ears pricked up. ***We're getting a proper home? When?*** He wagged his stumpy tail.

'Once I save up some money. Come on, let's get this paid in and see about earning some more.'

His disappointment palpable, he followed me. We took the scenic route, taking in a bend of the River Irwell and Peel Park. Oscar perked up as I let him off the lead to explore strange scents and mark a new territory.

As so often since it happened, my mind returned to the night at Riverpark Road. Would the police ever trace the gunmen who'd taken out the Novaks, their men and Catriona? I had a good idea who they were. So did Kasper and Zofia. Would Robertson and his gunmen regard us as loose ends to be tidied up? I realised I *really* wanted nothing bad to happen to them. What could I do to help them?

How was Helen coping? She'd seemed fine, but you never knew. I'd resisted calling or even texting. She'd put nothing on her social media, and I didn't know how to interpret that. The sky darkened, matching my mood.

'Come on, Oscar, let's go.'

He studied me from the obelisk in the centre of the park, one leg raised as he watered the base. ***What's the rush?***

'It's going to rain.' Almost before I'd finished speaking, the first drops fell.

By the time we left the park, it had set in, and I arrived at the bank wet through. The new jacket I'd acquired didn't keep me dry and after tying Oscar up in a nearby bike shelter, I entered the branch and joined the short queue, shivering. Once I'd paid the money in, I'd go to a nearby church community centre I'd heard gave out clothes to those in need and check if they could give me something waterproof.

I reached the front of the queue and gave the young cashier my card. She studied the screen with a puzzled frown before pressing a buzzer.

An uneasy feeling stirred. 'Is everything okay?'

She didn't reply, but an older woman appeared at her shoulder, and they held a whispered conversation.

'Hello? Can you tell me what's going on?'

'Mr Timothy?' The older woman straightened, holding my card.

'Yes?'

'Can we talk in private?' She directed me to a small, glass-fronted box on the other side of the room.

I waited in it, hovering above a radiator pouring out heat.

'Sorry about that.' She closed the door and gestured at one of the three chairs around a small table.

'I'll stay here, if you don't mind.'

A look of alarm crossed her face.

I gestured at the radiator. 'I need to dry off.'

'Oh, right. I'm afraid I've got bad news for you. Your account has been closed and here's your card.'

She held it out, cut into quarters.

The blood drained from my head. 'What do you mean, closed? I had over five hundred pounds in there.'

'*Had* being the operative word. It's a joint account, isn't it?'

Realisation arrived like a kick in the nuts. 'Carol, the cow!'

'The joint account holder, Carol Timothy, went into your home branch on Saturday morning. She's emptied it.'

'She can't. It's my money.'

'Technically, it's both yours. I can see you've paid it all in here, but . . . Sorry.'

I took a few moments to compose myself. She was sympathetic, but I wanted to swear and break something. 'Can I open another account? Just in my name.'

'Of course. We need some ID, driving licence, passport or similar. Plus two proofs of address, utility bills . . .'

'But you already know me. I've got an account with you.'

'Not anymore. I'm really sorry.'

The objections I wanted to pour out died on my lips. All I'd do was humiliate myself and bring the attention of the police. I stumbled out into the rain with what was now my last five hundred pounds, realising that whatever happened, I'd never be part of Carol's life. I welcomed the rain, diluting my tears. Oscar waited patiently as I made my way to the bike shelter and untied his lead.

He nuzzled my hand. ***You okay?***

'Yeah, I will be. Come on, boy, let's get something hot inside us. There's a caff round the corner in the covered precinct.'

I left Oscar outside, being fussed over by three small children, and ordered tea and two hot pasties. I took one and the tea to a table by the window and the second one to Oscar.

'Don't wolf it down, it's hot.'

Do you think I'm stupid?

'No comment.'

He fell on it and I smiled at the inevitable ***Ow, that's hot***.

They let me charge my phone, and I'd eaten half the pasty when it buzzed. Helen. I opened the message, my hands trembling.

Morning, Dad. On my way to school. Just wanted to say I love you. I'm working Saturdays at the greengrocers in Cabot Circus indoor market. Love to Oscar xxx.

PS Mum said you've put several hundred pounds into a savings account for me and Em. You don't need to, but we both appreciate it. I'll put it towards my uni fees.

I read it three times. I could forgive Carol and if I got down to Bristol on a Saturday, I could meet Helen. Lifted by the thought, I finished my pasty and drained my tea.

The phone rang just as I unplugged it. Kasper, via an encrypted app.

'Victor, it's Kasper.'

'Morning.' I stepped outside, away from prying ears. 'How are you and Zofia?'

'Not bad, thanks. We spent most of yesterday being questioned by our old friend Grimes.'

'What did he say?'

'That you'd incriminated us in all sorts, but we stuck to the story we'd agreed upon and, in the end, he let us go. I assume you did the same.'

'Are you asking me?'

'No, no, sorry. Obviously, you did, otherwise . . .' He cleared his throat. 'Can you get over here by eleven?'

'Yeah, I'll see you later.'

Did they have some work for me? Without getting my hopes up, I made my way to Cheetham Hill.

CHAPTER 56

The smell of fried chicken assailed my nostrils as I followed Oscar up the stairs to Kasper's office. He and Zofia waited inside, she making a fuss over Oscar as he walked in. The bruise on her cheek was yellowing at the edges but she otherwise looked well, and her smile improved my mood.

'Have you seen this?' She pointed at her monitor.

I walked round, sat in her still-warm seat and read the news story on the screen.

> **Manchester police solve ten-year-old Northern Ireland mystery**
>
> Police in Manchester seem to have solved a ten-year-old triple murder in Antrim. One of the victims of the mass shooting on Riverpark Road has been identified as Cathryn Ryan, who disappeared ten years ago after she and her close friend Mary Kelly, both aged thirteen, killed two of their abusers. Northern Ireland Police had already closed the grisly, perplexing case after concluding that Mary had then stabbed and buried Cathryn in an unknown location before taking her own life.

> It now appears that it was in fact Cathryn who had killed Mary, before staging her own disappearance and reinventing herself as Catriona Rourke. Police believe she first went to Scotland before coming down to Manchester. GMP has asked anyone who recognises her to contact them on this number.

Below, in the kind of photo of her I'd struggled to get, was the adult Catriona. But dressed up and enjoying herself. They'd also reproduced the original report from ten years earlier, one I'd recently read when I researched hammer attacks.

> **Horror in Antrim**
>
> Police made a grim discovery when neighbours called them to the home of the manager of the Castle Children's Home in Antrim. On arriving at the premises, police found the front door unlocked. The presence of bloody hand and trainer prints on the walls and floor downstairs warned them of what they might find.
>
> More bloody marks on the stairs provided further warning. What they found in the main bedroom horrified even the hardened officers who'd dealt with terrorist atrocities during 'The Troubles'. On the bed, they found the bodies of the manager and her husband. Both had been battered to death while they slept. The vicious assault left blood sprayed over the walls and furniture.
>
> 'It was everywhere,' one witness said.

> Police believe the attackers used two hammers found on the scene. Authorities later identified the bloody fingerprints of two of the victims' charges on the weapons. Police believe thirteen-year-old Cathryn Ryan and Mary Kelly had carried out the attack. They left a note accusing the manager and her husband of sexual and physical abuse. An examination of a laptop found on the premises revealed horrific footage confirming their claims.
>
> A farmer found Mary Kelly's body two days later in a barn nearby. She'd apparently taken her own life. A note found on her body claimed she'd killed her friend because Cathryn had wanted them to surrender to the police. She'd buried the body where 'nobody would find it'. Although she had no remorse about killing her abusers, she couldn't live with the guilt of murdering Cathryn. Police found a substantial amount of Cathryn's blood on Mary's clothing and on a knife found near her body.
>
> A police spokesman said they would probably never find Cathryn's body, but they were satisfied she was dead.

Zofia shook her head. 'The poor girls.'

I agreed. They'd have been the same age as Helen. Then I remembered Robertson's son, and Jehona and what Catriona had done to her. Thinking back to the night I found her: I was certain Catriona had been the passenger in the car that left before they dumped the bins. Oscar was also sure she'd been there. And who else had she killed?

Zofia scrolled on to a photo of the girls' two victims of a decade ago. It showed a bulky man in a suit towering over a slight woman with a razored bob, narrow features and high cheekbones.

'That's something,' Zofia said. She enlarged the image. 'That looks like—'

'Jehona.' I finished for her.

'Yes.'

Did that explain why Catriona had killed her, because she reminded her of her tormentor? Not that it mattered in the least. Doppelgänger or no, there was no justification for what Catriona had done. And maybe we'd helped stop her from killing more women. It eased my conscience to believe we'd not facilitated the murder of an innocent.

I tapped the screen. 'The report doesn't mention her marriage to the younger Robertson.'

'Probably for the best,' Kasper said. 'With any luck, they'll never find out. They were looking at a Glasgow connection, which doesn't exist. We don't want the police looking at Robertson.'

Relieved that Kasper finally got it, we sat in silence for a few moments. At last, I asked, 'Was that what you wanted to see me about?' Although I welcomed finding out about Catriona, I couldn't help feeling disappointed.

'Not entirely. Come on.' Zofia brushed past me and locked her screen.

I noticed how she and Kasper were dressed. 'Why have you got your coats on?'

'We're going somewhere.' She led the way to the entrance.

We travelled in her car and Oscar and I sat in the back. Where could they be taking us? I'd hoped they'd have work for me. Were we going to visit a potential client? But why take me?

Finally, I just put it to them: 'Where are we going?'

'Not far.' She could barely contain her glee.

I tried to formulate a guess, but gave up. I'd find out soon enough.

Kasper half turned. 'Do you want to do some work for us?'

'What is it?'

'Why, you got a lot on?'

'I don't want to find people for gangsters to kill.'

Zofia glanced in the mirror. 'That's not fair, Victor.'

Wasn't it? That's what we'd done, however unwittingly. But what I said was, 'You're right, sorry. Are you going to tell me?'

'Yeah,' Kasper said. 'We're helping an insurance company investigate a suspected fraud. It's a big job. And we might need your mates, too, if they're available. Usual rates.'

I couldn't help grinning. 'Yeah, it sounds okay.'

So, maybe it *was* to meet the client. I'd better get my head together. We arrived at a scruffy block of flats just north of the city centre.

They got out and stood beside the car. I let Oscar out and joined them.

'Okay,' I said, 'what are we doing here?'

Zofia gestured at the tower block. 'The flats on the ground floor are reserved for people who've got pets.'

I studied the ground-floor windows. 'And?'

They looked at me expectantly.

Realisation dawned. 'For me?' I stroked Oscar's back. 'For us?'

'If you want it.'

For a moment, my throat wouldn't function. Then I managed to reply, 'What do you say, Oscar? Do you want to have a warm, dry bed every night?'

You're not teasing me again, are you?

'No, boy.'

He barked.

'Oscar says yes.' I hugged Zofia and then Kasper, who patted my shoulder stiffly and took a step back, reminding me I needed a shower. Something I'd now be able to accomplish in my new home.

'It needs a few bits,' Zofia said, 'but we got some of them.' She opened the boot to reveal a selection of homewares, bedding and kitchen utensils.

I reached for my money, but she stopped me. 'They're a housewarming present.'

'I can't take all this.'

'We'll see.'

They helped me take the stuff into the flat and left.

Oscar and I watched them from the main entrance. I bent and ruffled his ears. 'Come on, boy,' I said. 'Things are looking up.'

Acknowledgements

This is the bit where I can, in a small way, acknowledge those who've helped me on my journey to get this novel published.

First, a small apology to the citizens of Manchester. I've taken a few liberties with the geography of the city, in particular Sackville Square, which doesn't exist but maybe should, minus the sex club.

The support of my family and friends continues undimmed, and I want them to know I never take it for granted.

Members of my writing group, South Manchester Writers' Workshop, give me constructive advice on my writing, and suggested bringing in Oscar, who has added so much to the story.

My agent, Clare Coombes, from The Liverpool Literary Agency, who gave me valuable feedback on the finished manuscript. She continues to be a strong advocate for my work, even my more challenging manuscripts.

The team at Thomas & Mercer, starting with Kasim Mohammed, who picked up and championed the series and Maisie Lawrence, who took up the baton, never easy to do. The entire team have been super supportive.

David Downing, of Maxwellian Editorial Services, Inc., who made editing this novel as pleasurable as the last three. His continued wisdom and insightful feedback give me great confidence that my novel will be in the best possible shape.

Ian Critchley, who copyedited the manuscript, picking up my verbal tics and innumerable embarrassing errors, while suggesting further improvements.

Jill Sawyer, who did the proofread and eliminated those errors that always slip through and threaten to undermine all the work that has gone before.

Dominic Forbes, whose excellent cover makes the book stand out.

Thank you also to Nicole Wagner, Dan Griffin and their respective teams for all their help.

If your heart was in your mouth as Victor and Oscar raced to find the missing people in time, then don't miss their next case, HUNTED. When Victor's homeless friend Sawney is found dead at an abandoned school, Victor investigates despite police ruling it an overdose. Can he find the truth and stop anyone else from getting hurt?

Get it now, or read on for an exclusive extract. Please note this content is not final.

CHAPTER 1

I woke with a start and sat up. The cacophony that had woken me continued, and I gathered my wits. Shouts and banging came from outside the door of my flat. Memories of the Grenfell fire in London, which I'd watched with my family in Bristol, jerked me into action. I jumped out of bed, grabbed my phone and slipped my feet into trainers. A dog barked. Was that Oscar?

I put my glasses on, stepped outside my room and turned on the light, squinting. Oscar stood in the narrow corridor outside my bedroom.

'Was that you?' I asked him.

He studied me with disdain. ***Did it sound like me?***

Someone banged on my door and the thunderous barking started up again.

Oscar's expression changed to alarm as I reached for the lock. ***What are you doing?***

'It could be a fire.'

I released it and the door flew open, smacking me on the forehead and dislodging my glasses. As I fell back against the wall, a brown blur flashed past me. The stench of weed which permeated the corridor outside almost overwhelmed me. Oscar's bark of alarm came from the kitchen.

A large, angry figure stood in the open doorway and grabbed my arm as I went to Oscar's aid. 'Oi, I want a word.'

A deep growl punctuated Oscar's cries for help.

I threw the hand off. 'Your dog's attacking mine in there.'

'I'll attack you, mate.'

I punched three nines into my phone. Oscar stood on the counter while a large XL Bully type lunged up at him. Without thinking, I grabbed the lead trailing from the spiked collar round its neck and jerked on it. I might as well have tried to rein in a rhino.

The dog had its front paws on the work surface and its enormous jaws gaping. Oscar pushed himself against the back wall between the toaster and kettle.

I thrust the phone into my pocket and used both hands to grip the lead. My efforts didn't seem to even register with the huge, lunging beast as its rear claws scrabbled against the floor. Lacking an elephant gun, I could only go on jerking on the lead until a hand grabbed my sleeve and wrenched me back to the kitchen doorway.

'Leave my fucking dog alone!' The intruder – a large, shaven-headed individual with a bushy beard which made him look like he'd put his head on upside down – jabbed a finger into my chest. Muscular limbs stuck out of his shorts and a vest. Tattoos covered most of his exposed skin, including his face.

'Leave your dog alone?' I said. 'Get it out of my house!'

The intruder barked some sort of reply, but I lost it in the wave of dizziness that washed over me. A jabbing pain radiated from my forehead. I dabbed at it and my hand came away red.

A tinny voice said, 'Which service do you require?'

I freed my other arm and retrieved my phone. 'Police. A psycho with a dog is attacking me in my flat—'

'Who you calling a psycho?' The intruder looked even angrier.

The dog let out a growl and Oscar barked in panic.

'Please come quickly,' I yelled into my phone. 'We're at Strangeways View, flat one a.'

The intruder snatched at the phone, knocking it out of my hand. I swung my elbow and smacked him in the face with it.

The man reared back, clutching his nose. 'Oi, bastard!'

His wild-eyed beast wheeled on me, jaws agape. I had just enough time to grab a stool and swing it between us. He sunk his teeth into the crosspiece between two of the legs, which disintegrated. I retreated towards the corner, the remains of the stool in my hand.

'The hell's going on here?' a familiar voice demanded.

We all stopped, even the vicious dog, and looked at Zack Cermak, the building manager. An ex-military type, Cermak didn't believe in small talk or smiling.

'This psycho and his animal broke in and attacked me and my dog!'

'I didn't break in. You let me in.'

Oscar had recovered his confidence. ***He's right, you did. I told you not to.***

Before I could respond to Oscar, the intruder released his nose and pointed a bloody hand at me. 'This guy's dog is eating the food I put out for Tyson.'

Oscar gave an indignant bark. ***I wouldn't touch that muck.***

'He wouldn't touch that muck,' I echoed.

'Oh yeah, so who's eating it, the faeries?'

'Probably you,' I muttered.

He lunged at me and I lifted the remains of the stool between us. Seeing an opening, his dog charged. I brought the stool down and the animal ran into a leg, nose first. It yelped and stopped. When its owner hesitated, I shoved the stool into his chest, pushing him into the kitchen table. A bowl of sugar and the salt and pepper set Zofia had bought me crashed to the floor.

'Hey, stop this, now!' Cermak stepped into the cramped kitchen. 'You.' He pointed at the dog owner. 'Get out and take your dog.'

He pushed himself off the table and pointed at me. 'He hit my dog!'

'What's your dog doing in his flat?'

'I told you, he's stealing Tyson's—'

'I don't give a damn. Now get back to your place, while you've still got one.'

The man glared at him, then bent to pick up his dog's lead and headed past the manager for the front door, muttering to himself.

Oscar stepped towards the front edge of the worktop and barked after the retreating dog. ***Go on, you coward. I'd have had you!***

The dog turned back with a growl.

Oscar yelped and leapt back towards the toaster, knocking over a glass, which smashed on the floor.

'Come on, Tyson, let's leave these two losers.' His owner heaved on the lead, giving me a look which should have killed me.

I lowered the stool and followed them to the door, locking it behind them. Once I'd secured it, Oscar jumped to the floor and strutted. I found my miraculously undamaged glasses behind the door and put them on.

Left alone with me in the flat, the manager wagged a finger in my face. 'First, you shouldn't let your dog on the work surface. It's unhygienic.'

Oscar gave him an incredulous stare. ***Unhygienic? Have you* seen *the state of the rest of the building?***

I shushed Oscar and replied, 'I don't "let" him up there. That dog attacked him, and he had to get away.'

'Second,' he went on, 'you'll need to repair or replace that stool.' He examined it. 'And get that blood cleaned off it.'

'What? His dog did that, you saw—'

'I don't care. It's your responsibility. And if we have any more trouble from you, you'll be out on your ear.' He pointed at the broken glass. 'And replace that.'

Too stunned to speak, I stared at him with my mouth open. Kasper and Zofia, my employers, had bought all the glasses in here when they found me this place.

Sirens sounded in the distance, coming closer.

'What the hell's happening now?' he asked.

I picked up my phone from the floor. 'I called the police.'

'What the hell you do that for?'

'We were being attacked in our own home!'

'I warned you when you moved in. Don't cause any trouble. The other residents don't like having the pigs around. It unsettles them.'

'What was I supposed to do? Let them kill us?'

Oscar lifted his muzzle. ***I was handling that Tyson, no problem.***

'It looked like it.'

'You what?' The manager gave me a puzzled frown.

I was just lulling him into a false sense of security. If you hadn't interfered . . .

The pain from my cut head and Oscar's false bravado pushed me over the edge. 'You were terrified, you coward.'

'What you call me?' The manager looked ready to punch me.

'I was talking to the dog.'

'Yeah, right.' With a shake of his head, he left, turning at the front door. 'Any more trouble, and you're out.'

The slam echoed.

That went well.

'Shut up and go back to bed.'

Oscar started talking to me after we'd been on the streets for a few months. Part of me had hoped it would stop once we moved into the flat, but so far, he was more vocal than ever.

After washing the blood off my hand, I checked my forehead in the bathroom mirror. The blood had dried, and I wiped it off with damp toilet paper. A scab was already forming over the wound, which sat on a bump the size of a plum, but it didn't need stitches. I returned to the kitchen and replaced the items on the table. Luckily, they'd survived their fall. Then I swept the broken glass into the dustpan and put it in the recycling. The stool didn't seem too bad, provided I sat on it straight. I wiped the bloody handprint off with a sponge and put it back at the table.

Two thirty. I had four hours before I had to get up for work.

A thump on the door set my pulse hammering, and I stared at it.

'Police. Are you okay in there?'

Relief making me tremble, I opened the door, letting in a fresh dose of weed. Two uniformed officers, looking much too young to be out alone, studied me.

'You call us out?' said the smaller but marginally more fully grown of the two.

Cermak hovered behind them.

'A misunderstanding, officers,' I assured them. 'A neighbour's dog got excited and bit my stool there.' I pointed towards the kitchen.

The officer with the speaking role stared at the bump on my forehead. 'You want to press charges?'

'No, as I said, a misunderstanding.'

'Right,' he said, looking relieved. 'In future, don't ring us unless it's necessary.'

'I'll remember that. Thanks, officer.'

The arrival of the police had created a stir, and several people lingered in the corridor behind them and the manager. One of them muttered, 'Fucking grass,' as I shut the door on the lot of them and leant against it.

Great. Already unpopular with my neighbours because I'd stopped several of them taking advantage of a fellow resident with learning difficulties, now, I'd upset the resident psycho and the manager, and everyone considered me a snitch.

CHAPTER 2

Jodie lay in her stinking bedding, unable to sleep, despite her exhaustion. What the hell made her volunteer for this? A sound made her freeze, and she strained her ears. Then a crash as a door smashed. Shit! Someone was coming, and they weren't sneaking in.

'Toff, wake up.' Jodie shook his shoulder and grabbed her trainers.

Like others on the streets, a well-developed sense of survival meant Toff usually slept lightly, but the relative safety of his billet had made him careless. Still groggy from the effects of whatever he'd taken the night before, he struggled to get out of his sleeping bag even as shouts and screams came from the corridor outside.

Jodie finishing tying her laces and shook him again. 'Come on.'

He at last pushed his bedding off. 'Where are my trainers?'

Faint light leaked in through the windows lining two walls of the large ground-floor classroom they'd chosen to sleep in. She found his shoes and thrust them at him as he struggled to his feet. Before he'd finished putting them on, the door from the corridor crashed open. The shouts grew louder as those who'd been sleeping in the next room fought with intruders. Smoke drifted in, bringing with it a stench that made her eyes sting. She scooped up her backpack.

Torch beams cut through the haze and illuminated the struggling figures in the doorway. The intruders looked like giant bugs the size of men. Was she still under the influence of the weed they'd smoked last night? Then she recognised their gas masks for what they were.

Toff, mesmerised, couldn't drag his gaze away from them.

She pulled at his sleeve. 'Come on, let's get out of here.'

Her tug stirred him, and he followed her. Glad she'd explored before going to bed, she headed for the other door, in the far corner. It led to the stairs and a way out, but as she reached it, Toff crashed to the floor behind her with a cry of alarm. She turned to check on him.

A torch beam swinging across the room revealed Toff kneeling beside a prone figure. It was Sawney. As Toff tried to rouse him, the bulky, bug-faced figures came closer. Apart from torches, they carried clubs. Two at the rear held the leads of large dogs, whose snarling filled Jodie with terror.

'TOFF!' she shouted from the far corner. 'LEAVE HIM!'

One intruder lifted what looked like a fire extinguisher and aimed the nozzle at Toff, who ran as a stream of evil-smelling liquid hit the prone body he'd abandoned, splashing up on Toff's retreating back and legs. The stench appalled Jodie and intensified when he joined her. She pushed him through the door and plunged after him, slamming it shut.

To her left was the route out, but she could see the torches of more men coming towards them.

Toff had stumbled to a halt behind her. Without waiting for him, she ran right, towards the stairs, taking them two steps at a time. At the top, she paused, chest heaving and throat rasping. Toff was still on the half landing.

'COME ON!' she urged him.

Boots clattered on the steps below and torch beams cut the air. When Toff had almost reached the top of the stairs, she ran, nearly tripping on a fallen light fitting in the dark. Toff caught up with her, bringing the stench with him.

Ahead, a pale strip indicated a door, and she shoved her shoulder against it. Toff added his weight, and they tumbled through it into a large space marked by moonlight leaking in through big windows. Several figures huddled together in the far corner. Two bookshelves stood by the door they'd just entered through, and desks gathered around the walls, leaving a sleeping area clear.

'Let's barricade this door.' Jodie gestured at the bookcases.

Toff helped her slide the nearest one against the door. Galvanised by their actions, the others pushed desks towards them.

'Help me with this one.' She strode towards the other bookshelf.

Someone banged on the door. Toff jumped, then, as the door pushed open, he leapt against it, shoving with all his might. His slight frame, weakened by months on the street, was no match for whoever was pushing.

'THEY'RE IN HERE, LADS!' the man shouted.

The gap widened until an arm came through it, holding one of the fire extinguishers. A rotten stench wafted from it. Toff slid back, his body trembling with the effort. Although paralysed by fear, Jodie forced herself to move and barrelled into the bookshelf, slamming the door against the arm.

'AAARRGGGHHH!' The man dropped his extinguisher and withdrew his hand. 'YOU FUCKERS!'

Fighting back had exhilarated the terrified Jodie. Kicking the dropped cylinder under the pile of chairs, she slammed the door shut and, along with the others, shoved the second bookshelf into place, along with a profusion of desks. Made for small kids, the desks didn't have the bulk to form a solid barrier, but still they stacked them against the door. More shouts and swearing came from outside. Jodie realised the barricade wouldn't hold them up for long.

'Is there another way out?' She examined the people she and Toff had disturbed. None looked big enough to be much help.

Something heavy smashed against the door, shaking their flimsy barrier.

One of them pointed. 'Window!'

Jodie ran to the nearest window and peered outside. Though they were only one floor up, the drop looked higher than she expected, at least five metres, and onto concrete.

The barricade juddered.

There was nothing for it but for her to pick up a chair, smash the window, and set about using the legs to clear the jagged glass.

'LOOK!' Toff shouted.

The door behind them had opened twenty centimetres, and the pile of furniture teetered.

'Everyone out.' She pointed at the opening.

Nobody moved.

Toff ran to the window and turned back to them. 'I'll lower you.'

At his intervention, they formed a queue. The first, a young woman with greasy hair and tattoos, climbed onto the windowsill. He lowered her, grunting with the effort. Jodie went to the window and watched as she dropped the last three metres. When she turned back to the door, she saw a head and a torch poking through the gap. There was no way they'd all get out.

'Next.' Toff helped a middle-aged man with a limp onto the windowsill.

Jodie took off her backpack and reached into the bottom. The cold glass told her she'd found what she wanted. She'd wrapped the bottle in an old towel when she'd collected it from home, and now she tore a strip off it, unscrewed the top and stuffed one end into the clear liquid. She found her lighter in a side pocket and, hands shaking, lit the rag. A blue flame hovered above the fabric, illuminating the bottle.

'What's that?' Toff asked.

'Some vodka I was saving for an emergency.' Jodie grinned. 'I reckon this counts as one.'

She threw the bottle at the doorway as the figure in the opening shoved his torso through it. The bottle smashed on the floor near his feet, the liquid leapt across the tiles, and then – did absolutely nothing. Just as Jodie had accepted she'd failed, a ball of blue flame expanded and enveloped the man's lower body. He screamed and his colleagues dragged him out. The flames licked at their sorry barricade, then spread hungrily across the timber desktops.

Jodie ignored the man's screaming and helped Toff lower two others to the ground. A third, an older man with a shuffling gait, waved them away.

'Leave me. I'd break me legs if I fell that far.'

'Come on, Ziggy,' Toff cried. 'We can't leave you.'

He shook his head and shuffled away into the far corner, coughing. By now, smoke filled the top half of the room. With streaming eyes, Toff gestured to Jodie to go next.

'We can't leave him.'

'What do you suggest,' Toff demanded, 'we throw him out? Come on, you next.'

Jodie shook her head. 'No, you go.'

'Don't fucking argue.'

A crash stopped them. She threw herself to the floor and peered at the far end of the room. A hole had appeared in the wall, near the corner. A battering ram of some kind withdrew, then smashed through the plasterboard, enlarging the opening. Adrenaline flooded her system.

Toff grabbed her shoulder. 'Jodie. Go.'

As she straightened, a fit of coughing seized her. She pushed Toff, and he got the message. He jumped onto the windowsill and lowered himself before dropping out of sight. She controlled her coughing as the battering stopped and boots clattered on the tiled floor. She crouched down, took a breath and jumped onto the windowsill. A figure appeared out of the thick smoke. At the next window, a metre away.

He saw her and lunged. She kicked at him, dislodging the man's mask. He screwed his eyes shut and coughed so she kicked him again, but waving his hand blindly, the man blocked her foot. She snatched up a shard of glass at her feet and slashed at his gloved hand.

He recoiled. 'Fuck!'

She didn't have time to lower herself. She peered through streaming eyes and jumped, hoping she landed right.

CHAPTER 3

Kasper Dąbrowski lifted his mug and inhaled, hoping the aroma of coffee would mask the stink of fried food from the shop below his office as he powered up his computer. He opened his emails and scanned the list of new messages. Mostly junk, but one address drew his eye. He clicked on it and read the message. His good mood evaporated.

'What's up?' his sister asked from the next desk.

'Robertson.'

The one word was enough to make Zofia join him at his screen. 'Just delete it.'

'He'll realise I've read it.'

'You didn't send a read receipt?'

'Of course not. But he'll realise I've received it when it doesn't bounce back.'

'That's not to say we've received it. It could be in your spam folder.'

Robertson wasn't someone he wanted anything to do with, but nor was he someone he wanted to piss off. 'What do you think I should do?' As usual, he was passing on the decision to his big sister. If only he'd done it when Robertson first got in touch.

Zofia exhaled in exasperation. 'We can't undo what's happened. Why don't you find out what he wants? Start by telling him how busy we are so we can turn him down.'

He doubted that would work, but no other route presented itself. He used a secure VPN and encrypted app to call the number Robertson had emailed him. The ringtone echoed, and he prayed nobody would answer.

'Yes?' The educated Scottish accent told him he'd dialled the right number.

He checked anyway. 'Mr Robertson?'

Silence.

'It's Kasper Dąbrowski, how are—'

'Good morning, Kasper. I've a job for you—'

'We're very busy at the moment, Mr Robertson.'

'I want you to look into a property in Miles Platting. It's a disused school called Mill View Academy which is on a site we're interested in. Find out who's responsible for it and let me know.'

'That will be the Department for Education, won't it?'

Robertson's chuckle sent a chill down Kasper's spine. 'There will be an individual. I prefer the personal touch.'

Kasper swallowed. 'We're snowed under. I'm not sure we can fit it in. If you like, I can recommend someone who can do it sooner.'

'I don't like dealing with new people, Kasper. I know you and your sister. You won't let me down. Shall we say next Monday?' He paused a moment.

Kasper's mouth dried.

Robertson filled the silence. 'Verra good. Here's the address.'

He dictated it as Kasper searched for a notepad, stopping when he saw his sister scribbling on hers.

'Speak to you on Monday, Kasper. Ring me on this number.'

'Oh, Mr Robertson?'

He waited in silence.

'What about payment?'

'The usual. I'll send it this morning.'

Kasper only kept a crypto wallet for his dealings with Robertson, and every time he accessed it, he felt like a drug dealer or kidnapper.

They sat in silence for a moment.

'That went well.' Zofia ripped the top page off her notepad and dropped it on his desk.

'What would you have done?'

She sighed. 'I'd imagine the same as you.' She ripped out the next three pages to make sure she hadn't left an impression.

Mollified, Kasper used the VPN and dark mode to open the map app on his desktop and typed in the address. 'Why's he interested in an old school?'

'Don't you think it's best if we don't find out?'

She was right. 'I imagine he wants to put in an early bid if it's for sale.'

'Yeah, right.' She didn't sound convinced. 'But whatever he wants, he'd better keep us out of it.'

'Amen to that.' Kasper considered how to do achieve that. First step: they couldn't leave a footprint from any of the enquiries they made for this project.

'I realise you were trying to put him off, but we are very busy,' Zofia said. 'Shall we get one of Victor's friends on it?'

'We're trying to be discreet.'

'Considering they were present at the scene of a massacre and, unlike us, none of them got questioned by the police, I'd say they're one up on us as far as discretion goes.'

She had a point. 'Okay.' He checked the time. 'Victor's supposed to be in by now. I'll find out why he's late.' He rang him.

'Morning, Kasper. You saved me a call. I'm going to be late—'

'You're late already. We've got a full day planned. I need you here now.'

'Something's come up. Toff's in trouble.'

'Can't you deal with it after work?'

'I owe him.'

Kasper forced himself to take a breath. Victor did indeed owe the young Scouser. He'd helped them find Victor's teenaged daughter.

'Yeah,' Kasper said. 'Okay.'

'I shouldn't be too long. It's only Miles Platting.'

Kasper checked the address on the piece of paper. 'Where in Miles Platting?'

'An old school—'

Kasper recited the address Robertson had just given them.

'Yeah,' Victor said. 'How did you know?'

'What's the matter with Toff? What's happened?'

'I'm not sure. That's what I'm doing now, going to have a look. I'll do it in my own time, so don't worry about paying me.'

'I'm not, but report back what you find.' He ended the call.

'Did I get that right? Victor's going to the place Robertson's interested in?' Zofia frowned and chewed her lip.

'Yeah.'

'He didn't say what's happened?'

'No, but something has, and it wouldn't surprise me if it's going to cause us problems. Too unlikely it's a coincidence.' A horrible thought he'd been trying to suppress fought to the surface. 'Do you think Robertson's planning to move his operation into Manchester?'

'Why would he?'

'With the Novak boys off the scene, there's a power vacuum in the Manchester underworld.'

'I bloody hope not, but hasn't the dad, Alex, stepped up?'

With what they knew about Robertson, and he about them, the thought of having the man as a neighbour filled Kasper with terror. But even more worrying was the thought of Alex Novak wanting revenge for his sons' deaths.

About the Author

© 2021 Steve Pattyson Photography

D. E. Beckler writes fast-paced action thrillers populated with well-rounded characters. Born in Addis Ababa in 1960, Beckler spent his first eight years living on an agricultural college in rural Ethiopia where his love of reading developed. After dropping out of university he became a firefighter and served nineteen years before leaving to start his own business.

Beckler began writing in 2010 and uses his work experiences to add realism to his fiction. Beckler lives in Manchester, his adopted home since 1984. In his spare time, he tries to keep fit – an increasingly difficult undertaking – listens to music, socialises and feeds his voracious book habit.

Follow the Author on Amazon

If you enjoyed this book, follow D. E. Beckler on Amazon to be notified when the author releases a new book!
To do this, please follow these instructions:

Desktop:

1) Search for the author's name on Amazon or in the Amazon App.
2) Click on the author's name to arrive on their Amazon page.
3) Click the 'Follow' button.

Mobile and Tablet:

1) Search for the author's name on Amazon or in the Amazon App.
2) Click on one of the author's books.
3) Click on the author's name to arrive on their Amazon page.
4) Click the 'Follow' button.

Kindle eReader and Kindle App:

If you enjoyed this book on a Kindle eReader or in the Kindle App, you will find the author 'Follow' button after the last page.